PRAISE FOR

The Big Switch

"The Hugo Award winner continues to delight in exploring the world of 'what if?' as he tackles a formidable subject in the third entry in his World War II series . . . The author's fans should enjoy this further permutation of world history."
—*Library Journal*

"The third volume of Turtledove's latest alternate-historical reworking of WWII, the War That Came Early, is definitely the strongest yet . . . this latest Turtledove saga is not for the faint of heart or weak of stomach. It *is* for lovers of high-quality alternate history." —*Booklist*

"[*The Big Switch*] contains one of the biggest divergences from history in [any] of Turtledove's novels. The change makes me want to read the next book now! This is one of the best Turtledove books since *How Few Remain*."
—SFRevu

West and East

"The novel most fully shines when the characters are allowed to strive for their full potential: Czech sniper Vaclav Jezek adopts an antitank rifle as his favorite weapon; German pilot Hans-Ulrich Rudel ingeniously modifies his aircraft; Soviet soldier Chaim Weinberg becomes a Party propagandist; and the Goldman family tries to achieve a semblance of normal life in Nazi-ruled Münster. The war is always present, though, and there's plenty to satisfy fans of military strategy, tactics, and armaments."
—*Publishers Weekly*

"And so it whirls on, the suspense building inexorably, thanks to two of Turtledove's gifts, in particular. One is for portraying so much of the action from the viewpoint of the grunts, or even civilians, who know little of what the Great Ones are up to until the consequences are all over them. The other proceeds from the first and is for envisioning WWII unraveling like an endless ball of yarn in the paws of an intelligent kitten. Keep reading or miss something exceedingly fine."
—*Booklist* (starred review)

"Turtledove is in top form as he traverses familiar and beloved terrain, the war years of the 20th century. The author's fans and lovers of military fiction and alternative history should welcome this addition to the genre."
—*Library Journal*

"As entertainment, [*West and East*] is as good as an alternative fiction, or historical novel, you are going to read this or any other year. But take a few deep breaths as you devour it with glee and ask yourself if the course of events and the Triumph of Good, we usually so happily take for granted is as secure or predictable, as we think. Reading Mr. Turtledove will make you wonder."
—*The Washington Times*

Hitler's War

"Turtledove is always good, but this return to World War II, one of his favorite turfs, is genuinely brilliant."
—*Booklist*

"The author's mastery of the ever-widening ripples that small changes make in history is unchallenged, his storytelling always gripping, and his research impeccable."
—*Library Journal*

"One can rely on Turtledove. He writes well and with confidence. He develops strong plots. Delivers well considered storylines. Take the most recent entry, *Hitler's War*. The novel is predicated on a single question: what would have happened if Britain's Prime Minister Neville Chamberlain had refused to allow Hitler to annex the Sudetenland? Again, change one thing and, like a kaleidoscope, everything looks different. One piece falls another way and all things are altered. . . . [*Hitler's War*] is solid writing and classic Turtledove."

—*January Magazine*

"[Turtledove] brings the deprivations of war to life in this vision of a very different WWII. . . . American Peggy Druce, caught behind the lines, gets a firsthand look at the period military hardware and nationalistic mindsets that Turtledove so expertly describes."

—*Publishers Weekly*

"Not for the squeamish . . . *Hitler's War* would qualify as realistic war fiction except for the alt-history setting. No generals, strategists and such here, just regular people. . . . If you like 'real war' novels the book is for you."

—Fantasy Book Critic

BOOKS BY HARRY TURTLEDOVE

The Guns of the South

THE WORLDWAR SAGA
Worldwar: In the Balance
Worldwar: Tilting the Balance
Worldwar: Upsetting the Balance
Worldwar: Striking the Balance

Homeward Bound

THE VIDESSOS CYCLE
The Misplaced Legion
An Emperor for the Legion
The Legion of Videssos
Swords of the Legion

THE TALE OF KRISPOS
Krispos Rising
Krispos of Videssos
Krispos the Emperor

THE TIME OF TROUBLES SERIES
The Stolen Throne
Hammer and Anvil
The Thousand Cities
Videssos Besieged
A World of Difference
Departures
How Few Remain

THE GREAT WAR
The Great War: American Front
The Great War: Walk in Hell
The Great War: Breakthroughs

AMERICAN EMPIRE
American Empire: Blood and Iron
American Empire: The Center Cannot Hold
American Empire: The Victorious Opposition

SETTLING ACCOUNTS
Settling Accounts: Return Engagement
Settling Accounts: Drive to the East
Settling Accounts: The Grapple
Settling Accounts: In at the Death

Every Inch a King

The Man with the Iron Heart

THE WAR THAT CAME EARLY
The War that Came Early: Hitler's War
The War that Came Early: West and East
The War that Came Early: The Big Switch
The War that Came Early: Coup d'Etat

The Big Switch

THE WAR THAT CAME EARLY

The Big Switch

HARRY TURTLEDOVE

BALLANTINE BOOKS | NEW YORK

The Big Switch is a work of fiction. All incidents and dialogue, and all characters with the exception of some well-known historical and public figures, are products of the author's imagination and are not to be construed as real. Where real-life historical or public figures appear, the situations, incidents, and dialogues concerning those persons are entirely fictional and are not intended to depict actual events or to change the entirely fictional nature of the work. In all other respects, any resemblance to persons, living or dead, is entirely coincidental.

2012 Del Rey Books Trade Paperback Edition

Published in the United States by Del Rey Books,
an imprint of The Random House Publishing Group,
a division of Random House, Inc., New York.

DEL REY is a registered trademark and the Del Rey colophon
is a trademark of Random House, Inc.

Originally published in hardcover in the United States by Del Rey, an imprint of the Random House Publishing Group, a division of Random House, Inc., New York, in 2011.

This book contains an excerpt from the forthcoming book
The War That Came Early: Coup d'Etat by Harry Turtledove.
This excerpt has been set for this edition only and may not reflect
the final content of the forthcoming edition.

Library of Congress Cataloging-in-Publication Data

Turtledove, Harry.
The big switch : the war that came early / Harry Turtledove.
p. cm.
ISBN 978-0-345-49187-9—ISBN 978-0-345-52638-0 (ebk.)
1. World War, 1939–1945—Fiction. I. Title.
PS3570.U76B54 2011
813'.54—dc22 2011002642

Printed in the United States of America

www.delreybooks.com

9 8 7 6 5 4 3 2 1

The Big Switch

Chapter 1

Vaclav Jezek slogged up a dirt track in eastern France. Crusted snow crunched under the Czech corporal's boots. Like anyone from central Europe thinking of France, he'd always imagined Paris blazing with lights and beaches on the Riviera packed with girls in skimpy bathing suits. Freezing his ass off in the middle of a war had never been in the cards.

But here he was, freezing his ass off. This would have been a nasty winter by Czech standards. From everything he could pick up—he spoke only foul fragments of French—it was a bloody godawful winter by French standards. Which didn't do anybody stuck in it one damn bit of good.

And here he was, in the middle of a war. And it was his own fault, too. When the Nazis jumped on Czechoslovakia in October 1938, he'd fought till he couldn't fight any more. Then he'd gone over the Polish border and let himself be interned. And *then* he'd agreed to join the forces of the Czech government-in-exile still fighting the Germans from its base in Paris.

A good thing, too, he thought, lighting a Gitane without breaking stride. He didn't breathe out much more fog with the cigarette than he had without it. Poland and Hitler were on the same side these days, both fighting the Russians. If he'd stayed in that internment camp, he'd probably be a German POW now.

Of course, he might yet end up a German POW. It wasn't as if the Nazis had gone out of business. They were playing defense in the west for the time being, not pushing toward Paris with everything they had. That was something. Things looked a lot better now than they had when Vaclav got to Paris. He could still get killed or maimed or captured if his number came up.

As if to underscore the point, German artillery grumbled off to the east. Shells screamed through the air. Vaclav cocked his head to one side, gauging their flight. This lot wouldn't come down anywhere close to him, so he kept marching.

The rest of the Czechs in his outfit made the same automatic calculation and did the same thing. They wore a motley mixture of Czech and French khaki uniforms. Most of them kept their domed Czech helmets in place of the crested French model. Vaclav did—he was convinced the Czech pot was made from thicker steel. The German *Stahlhelm* was better yet, but wearing one of those wouldn't do, not if he wanted to keep on breathing, anyway.

Most of the Czechs carried French rifles. That made sense. French quartermasters didn't want to have to worry about somebody else's ammunition.

Jezek, by contrast, listed to the right as he marched. The piece slung on his shoulder was longer and heavier than an ordinary foot slogger's rifle. It was made for wrecking tanks and armored cars. The 13mm armor-piercing slugs it fired would punch through twenty-five millimeters of hardened steel. It kicked like a jackass, too, despite padded stock and muzzle brake, but everything came with a price.

It also made one hell of a sniping rifle. Those big bullets flew fast and flat. And when one hit a mere human being, it commonly killed. Vaclav had picked off Germans out to a kilometer and a half. And he'd picked off a German sniper specially sent out to get rid of him: a compliment he could have done without.

Those 105s in the distance rumbled again. Again, Jezek cocked his head to one side. This time, he didn't like what he heard. "Hit the dirt!" he yelled. He wasn't the only one. The cry went up in Czech and French.

Even in his greatcoat, even with wool long johns, doing a belly flop into the snow wasn't his idea of fun. And the goddamn antitank rifle thumped him when he landed. The stupid thing wasn't content with bruising his shoulder every time he fired it. Oh, no. It wanted to leave black-and-blue marks all over him.

But snow and bruises weren't so bad, not when you set them alongside of getting blasted into ground beef. Half a dozen shells came down not nearly far enough away from the Czech detachment. Fire at the heart of the burst, dirt and black smoke rising from it, fragments whining and screeching through the air . . . Vaclav had been through it more often than he cared to remember. It never got any easier.

Nobody was screaming his head off. That was good, to say nothing of lucky. They'd flattened out soon enough, and none of the shards of steel and brass decided to skim the ground and bite somebody regardless.

A couple of Czech soldiers started to get to their feet. "Stay down!" Sergeant Benjamin Halévy shouted from right behind Jezek. "They may not be done with us."

Sure as hell, another volley came in half a minute later. One Czech swore and hissed like a viper, but only one. Bright red blood steamed in the snow under his leg. It didn't look like a bad wound—but then, any wound you didn't get yourself wasn't so bad.

As the injured man bandaged around, Vaclav twisted around (trying his best to stay flat while he did it) and told the sergeant, "You may be a Jew, but at least you're a smart Jew."

"Fuck you, Jezek," Halévy answered evenly. "If I'm so smart, what am I doing here?" He was redheaded and freckle-faced. He was a French noncom, not a Czech. His folks had brought him from Prague to Paris when he was little. Equally fluent in Czech and French, he served as a liaison between the government-in-exile's troops and his host country's army.

Before the war started, Vaclav hadn't had much use for Jews. But, in Czechoslovakia and now here, he'd seen that you could count on them to fight the Nazis with everything they had. Anybody who'd do that was all right in his book. Plenty of Slovaks had thrown down their rifles and hugged the first German they saw. Slovakia was "independent" these days, though the next time Father Tiso did anything Germany didn't like would be the first.

Since Halévy *was* a smart Jew, Vaclav asked him, "What d'you think? Can we get up now, or will those shitheads try to be really cute and throw some more shit at us?"

"What did I do to deserve getting asked to think like a German all the time?" The sergeant seemed to aim the question more at God than at Vaclav Jezek. That was good: God might have an answer, and Vaclav sure didn't. After screwing up his features, Halévy went on, "I think maybe it's all right. Maybe."

"Yeah, me, too. C'mon. Let's try it." Vaclav scrambled to his feet. Snow clung to the front of his greatcoat. He didn't try to brush it off. If it made him harder for the poor, shivering bastards in snow-spotted *Feldgrau* to spot, so much the better. Halévy followed his lead. So did the rest of the Czechs. They moved with no great enthusiasm, but they moved.

Stretcher-bearers carried the wounded man back towards a dressing station. Some of the other guys eyed them enviously: they were out of danger, or at least in less of it, for a while.

The German guns growled again. Jezek tensed, but these shells headed somewhere else. He nodded to himself. The artillerymen had a prescribed firing pattern, and by God they'd stick to it. Of course they would. They were Germans, weren't they?

A stretch of snow-covered open ground several hundred meters wide lay ahead, with woods beyond. Vaclav eyed it sourly. He turned to Halévy. "What do you want to bet the Nazis have a machine-gun nest in amongst the trees?"

"I won't touch that," the Jew answered. "And there'll be two more farther back covering it, so when we take it out it won't do us much good." He seemed no happier than Vaclav, and with reason. "Be expensive even getting close enough *to* take it out."

Vaclav unslung the antitank rifle, which made his shoulder smile happily. "If we send a few guys forward to draw their fire, maybe I can do something about it at long range. Worth a try, anyhow."

"Suits," Halévy said at once. He told off half a squad of Czechs to serve as lures. They looked as miserable as Jezek would have in their boots. The rest of the men looked relieved. A well-sited MG-34 could have slaughtered half of them, maybe more.

Flopping down into the snow again, Vaclav steadied the monster on its bipod. He aimed where he would have put the gun if he were on the other side. Even with a telescopic sight, he couldn't see anything funny. But nothing could hide a machine-gun muzzle when it started spitting fire. And maybe—he hoped—he'd spot motion when the crew served the gun.

Like sacrificial pawns, the handful of Czechs started crossing the field. They hadn't gone far before the machine gun opened up on them. That was German arrogance. Letting them come farther might have drawn more after them. But the Nazis were saying, *Thus far and no farther. This is our ground.*

They could think so. Vaclav shifted the rifle a few millimeters—he'd guessed well. *Blam!* He winced even as he chambered a fresh round. Muzzle brake or not, padded stock or not, shooting that mother hurt every goddamn time. His right ear would never be the same again, either.

Blam! This time, the scope let him see a German reel away with his head nothing but a red ruin. Another one stepped up. They wouldn't have caused so much trouble if they weren't brave. *Blam!* He killed that one, too, and then another one a few seconds later. "Forward!" Halévy shouted. "Everybody forward!"

Forward the Czechs went. More Germans ran over to keep the machine gun firing. Vaclav methodically shot them. Before long, his side had a lodgement in the woods. The MG-34 fell silent. Maybe they'd captured it, or maybe the guys on the other side had pulled it back.

Either way, he could go forward himself now. Another few hundred meters reclaimed. Sooner or later, the rest of France. Later—how much later?—Czechoslovakia. It would take a while. Oh, yes. The antitank rifle seemed to weigh a tonne.

THEO HOSSBACH STOOD in front of the goal of what had to be the worst football pitch he'd ever seen. The Polish field was frozen and lumpy. The ball could have used more air, but nobody could find a valve that fit its air inlet. Nobody much cared, either. The German soldiers were back of the line for a while. The Ivans weren't shooting at them, so they were letting off some steam.

The match was panzer black against infantry *Feldgrau*. Theo was the radio operator in a Panzer II. His black coverall wasn't warm enough. His teammates heated themselves up running and falling and bumping into one another—and into the *Landsers* on the other side. A goalkeeper just stood there, waiting for something horrible to happen . . . and freezing while he waited. Theo didn't complain. He never did. Come to that, he rarely said anything at all. He lived as much of his life as he could inside his own head.

If he had been moved to complain, he would have bitched about the quality of the match in front of him. Both sides would have been booed off the pitch if they'd had the gall to try to charge admission to an exhibition like this. He wasn't the best 'keeper himself, but he liked to watch well-played football. This was more like a mob of little kids running and yelling and booting the ball any which way.

One of the guys in black missed a pass he should have been able to field blindfolded. A fellow in field-gray seized control of the ball. The mob thundered toward Theo. He tensed. A good defense would have stopped the attack before it got anywhere near him. Unfortunately, a good defense was nowhere to be found, not here.

He also tensed because there was liable to be an argument if one got past him. He hated arguments. And the makeshift goals were made for them. A couple of sticks pounded into the ground marked each one's edges; a string ran from the top of one stick to the top of the other at more or less the right height. No net to stop the ball. Did somebody score or not? There'd already been two or three shouting matches.

But he didn't have to worry, not this time. A tall man in black headed the ball away from danger before the incoming infantry could launch it at Theo. "Way to go, Adi!" one of the other panzer crewmen yelled. Theo couldn't have put it better himself.

Adalbert Stoss took the praise in stride—literally. He ran the ball down, took it on the side of his foot, and expertly steered it up the field.

Theo watched his back with proprietary admiration. Adi drove the panzer on which he himself ran the radio.

Smooth and precise as an English pro, Adi sent a pass to the right wing, then dashed into position in front of the other side's goal. For a wonder, the guy to whom he sent the pass didn't let it roll past the touchline. For a bigger wonder, he sent back a halfway decent centering pass. And Adi booted it past two defenders and the infantry's 'keeper.

"Goal!" the panzer men yelled, pumping their fists in the air. The soldiers in *Feldgrau* couldn't argue, not about that one.

Glumly, the infantrymen started from the halfway line. Before they'd done much, Adi Stoss swooped in and commandeered the ball. He charged up the pitch with it, sliding past *Landsers* as if they were nailed to the dirt. Only a wild, desperate lunge from the enemy 'keeper kept him from scoring again.

"No fair," a panting foot soldier—right now a footsore foot soldier—complained. "You fuckers snuck a ringer in on us."

"Like hell we did." The closest panzer man pointed back toward Theo. "He's in the same crew as our goalkeeper."

"*Scheisse,*" the *Landser* said. "You ought to take him out anyway. He's too damn good."

"I didn't know, that wasn't in the rules," the panzer man replied.

"Well, it ought to be," the foot soldier said, bending over and setting his hands on his knees so he could catch his breath. "Playing against him is like going up against a machine gun with water pistols." He looked up. "Christ, here he comes again." Shaking his head, he clumped off.

Theo had known Adi Stoss was uncommonly fast and strong, even among the extraordinarily fit men of the *Wehrmacht.* He'd never seen him play football before. He was even more impressed than he'd thought he might be. If Adi wasn't good enough to make his living in short pants, Theo couldn't imagine anybody who would be.

Thanks largely to his efforts, the panzer side beat the infantrymen, 7–4. Soldiers in black passed bottles of the distilled lightning the Poles brewed from potatoes to soldiers in field-gray. Theo was glad to get outside some of the vodka. He wasn't normally much of a drinking man, but in weather like this he figured he needed antifreeze as much as his panzer did.

Sergeant Hermann Witt, the commander of Adi and Theo's machine, had run up and down the rutted field. He put an arm around Adi's shoulder. "Man, I didn't know you could play like that," he said expansively—his other hand clutched a bottle.

"Fat lot of good it does me." Adi sounded surprisingly bitter.

"You just made those ground pounders look like a bunch of jerks," Witt said. "Nothing wrong with that. They think we're out of shape because we don't tramp like horses all day long. I guess you showed 'em different."

"I like to play. That's all there is to it." Adi shook himself free of the sergeant.

Witt turned to Theo. "What's eating him?"

"Beats me." Theo had an opinion, which he kept to himself. As far as he was concerned, opinions were like assholes: necessary, but not meant for display.

The panzer commander frowned, lit a cigarette, and coughed. "I didn't mean to piss him off—he was great. But the way he acts, I could have told him he stinks."

Theo only shrugged. The less he said, the less he'd have to be sorry for later. At least Witt was interested in keeping Adi happy. That was more than Heinz Naumann, the previous panzer commander, had been. There would have been trouble between the two of them if Naumann hadn't stopped a bullet. Theo didn't like trouble, which meant he could have picked a better time to be born.

An infantryman came up to him. "You're in the same crew as that maniac?" the fellow asked.

"That's right," Theo said. "What about it?"

"If he drives like he plays, you're screwed," the foot soldier said. He swiped his sleeve across his forehead. Despite the cold, sweat stained his tunic under the arms. "He'll send you right into the Russian panzers, and they'll blow you to hell and gone. He doesn't know how to go backwards."

"We're still here so far." Theo looked to the touchline. His greatcoat lay over there. As soon as this mouthy guy—Theo saw anyone who talked to him as a mouthy guy—went away, he could find it and put it on.

"Don't get me wrong. He plays good," the infantryman went on. After a moment, he added, "You weren't bad yourself, dammit. I thought a couple of the shots you stopped'd go in for sure."

"Thanks," Theo said in surprise. He didn't think he was anything out of the ordinary. You did your best to keep the ball from getting past you. Sometimes you did. Sometimes you couldn't. Even if you couldn't always, you tried not to look like too much of a buffoon out there.

"Well . . ." More slowly than he might have, the man in field-gray figured out Theo wasn't the world's hottest conversationalist. "See you. Try and stay in one piece," he said, and walked off.

It was good advice. Theo hoped he could follow it. He was relieved when he found his greatcoat. Nobody who'd lost his own had walked off with it. If he found himself missing his, he might have done that. You didn't screw your buddies when you were in the field. People you didn't know could damn well look out for themselves.

There it was: the essence of war. You stuck with your friends and gave it to the swine on the other side as hard as you could. Theo knew who his friends were—the guys who helped him stay alive. He had nothing in particular against Russians, any more than he'd had before against Frenchmen or Englishmen or Czechs. But if they were trying to kill his pals and him, he'd do his best to do them in first.

The greatcoat fought winter not quite to a draw. The *Wehrmacht* needed better cold-weather gear. Boots, for instance: the Russians' felt ones far outclassed anything Germany made. Well, there was more a ground pounder's worry than a panzer man's. Theo snorted. It wasn't as if he had no worries of his own.

OUT IN THE North Sea again. Lieutenant Julius Lemp felt the change in the U-30's motion right away. The Baltic was pretty calm. As soon as you passed out of the Kiel Canal, you got reminded what real seas were like. And a U-boat would roll in a bathtub.

A rating up on the conning tower with the skipper said, "Somebody down below's going to give it back—you wait and see."

"Not like it's never happened before," Lemp answered resignedly. Once something got into the bilge water, it was part of a U-boat's atmosphere for good. All the cleaning in the world couldn't get rid of a stink. Overflowing heads, spilled honey buckets, puke, stale food, the fug of men who didn't wash often enough, diesel fumes . . . Going below after the freshest of fresh air was always like a slap in the face from a filthy towel.

He went back to scanning horizon and sky with his Zeiss binoculars. Looking overhead was purely force of habit. Clouds scudded by not far above the gray-green sea. The RAF wasn't likely to put in an appearance. But nobody who wanted to live through the war believed in taking dumb chances.

"Skipper . . . ?" The rating let it hang there.

Lemp's antennae that warned of danger were at least as sensitive as the metal ones on the boat that caught radio waves. Something was on the sailor's mind, something he wasn't easy talking about. The way things were these days, Lemp could make a good guess about what it was, too. All the same, the only thing he could do was ask, "What's eating you, Ignaz?"

"Well . . ." Ignaz paused again. Then he seemed to find a way to say what he wanted: "It's mighty good to be at sea again, isn't it?"

"Now that you mention it," Lemp answered dryly, "yes."

Thus encouraged, Ignaz went on, "The only thing we've got to worry about out here is the goddamn enemy. That's a good thing, *nicht wahr*?"

"Oh, you'd best believe it is," Lemp said, and nothing more. Somebody on the U-boat was probably reporting every word even vaguely political from him to the *Sicherheitsdienst*. Probably every even vaguely political word from the whole crew. That was how things worked right now.

The U-30 had been in port when some of the generals and admirals tried to overthrow the *Führer*. There'd been gunfire at the naval base. Who was shooting at whom was something about which it was better not to enquire too closely. The *Führer* remained atop the *Reich*. Two or three dozen high-ranking officers no longer remained among the living. The show trials were right out of the Soviet Union. Many more lower-ranking men had been cashiered.

But that wasn't the worst of it. The worst was that everybody in the military had to watch what he said and to whom he said it. If you couldn't trust the comrades alongside whom you risked your life . . .

Then you couldn't, that was all, and you took the precautions you needed to take. Out here, as Ignaz had said, it was only the enemy who was dangerous. Back in port, you had to worry about your friends. And how were you supposed to fight a war like that?

Carefully, Lemp thought. He had to fight carefully any which way. He'd had the misfortune to sink an American liner. History would not have been kind to the U-boat skipper who dragged the USA into its second war against Germany. Neither would that man's superiors. Fortunately, it hadn't happened. The *Reich* denied everything at the top of its lungs. The Americans couldn't prove what they suspected. Lemp's superiors still didn't love him, but they hadn't beached him, which was the only thing that counted.

He wasn't likely to find an American liner in the North Sea. This was a war zone by anybody's standards. British and French troops still hung on against the Germans in northern Norway. The only thing that could supply them or get them out of there was the Royal Navy. U-boats and *Luftwaffe* aircraft were making the Tommies pay. That didn't mean they'd given up, though. They were both brave and professional, as Lemp had reason to know.

In weather like this, the *Luftwaffe* was no more likely to get planes off the ground than the RAF was. If anybody was going to keep enemy ships from slipping through, it was the U-boat force.

Down this far south, Lemp didn't really expect to spy the foe. But he and the ratings on the conning tower braved awful weather and spray that froze in midair and stung cheeks like birdshot to keep binoculars moving up and down and from side to side. For one thing, the crew needed the routine. For another, as Lemp had thought not long before, you never could tell.

No planes in the sky now, though: neither English nor German. No smoke smudges darkening the horizon, not even when waves lifted the U-30 to their crests and let the lookouts see farther than they could otherwise. After a two-hour stint, Lemp and the crew went below, to be replaced by fresh watchers. You didn't dare let concentration flag; the moment you weren't paying close attention was bound to be the one when you most needed it.

This early in the patrol, the boat's stench wasn't so bad as it would get later on. Lemp wrinkled his nose all the same. But the reek inside the iron tube was familiar and comforting, no matter how nasty. And the dim orange light in there also made him feel at home, even if his eyes needed a few seconds to adjust to the gloom.

"*Alles gut,* Peter?" he asked the helmsman.

"*Alles gut,* skipper," Peter answered. "Course 315, as you ordered. And the diesels are performing well—but you can hear that for yourself."

"*Ja,*" Lemp agreed. It wasn't just hearing, either; he could feel the engines' throb through the soles of his feet. As Peter said, everything sounded and felt the way it should have. When it didn't, you knew, even if you couldn't always tell how you knew.

"You want the conn, sir?" Peter made as if to step away from the wheel. Discipline on U-boats was of a different and looser kind from what it was in the *Kriegsmarine*'s surface ships. Most of the spit and polish went into the scuppers. No officer who was happy pulling the stiffening wire out of his cap missed it. Lemp sure didn't. The men could fight the boat. As long as they could do that, who gave a rat's ass if they clicked their heels and saluted all the time?

He shook his head. "No, you can keep it. I'm going to my cubbyhole and log the last two hours of—well, nothing." Some of the rituals did have to be fulfilled.

Peter chuckled. "All right. Sometimes nothing is the best you can hope for, isn't it? Damn sight better than a destroyer dropping ash cans on our head."

"Amen!" Lemp said fervently. If a depth charge went off too close, the sea would crumple a U-boat like a trash bin under a panzer's tracks. It would be over in a hurry if that ever happened—but probably not soon enough.

Only a curtain separated his bunk and desk and safe from the rest of the boat. Still, that gave him more room and more privacy than anyone else enjoyed. He spun the combination lock on the safe. When the door swung open, he took out the log book. A fountain pen sat in the desk drawer. Long habit meant he never left anything on a flat surface where it could—and would—roll away and get lost. He opened the log and began to write.

WALKING IN A winter wonderland. That was how Peggy Druce thought of Stockholm. It wasn't that she didn't know about winter. She'd grown up in a Philadelphia Main Line family, and married into another. She'd skied in Colorado, in Switzerland, and in Austria back in the days when there was an Austria. So it wasn't that she didn't understand what winter was all about.

But Philadelphia put up with winter. Ski resorts seemed intent on making money off it—which, when you looked at things from their point of view, was reasonable enough. Stockholm enjoyed winter.

Part of that, no doubt, was enjoying what you couldn't escape. Scandinavia lay a long way north. If not for the Gulf Stream, it would have been as uninhabitable as Labrador. (She remembered a pulp story about what might happen if the Gulf Stream went away. She couldn't recall who'd written it: only that he was a Jew. Now that she'd seen Hitler's Berlin, that took on new weight in her mind.) But the Swedes did it with style. And the way they kept houses comfortable and streets clear of snow put Philadelphia—and every other place she'd visited in winter—to shame.

Not only that, all the lights stayed on through the long, cold nights. After her time inside the Third *Reich,* that seemed something close to a miracle. It had in Copenhagen, too . . . till the Germans marched in. Now the Nazis' twilight swallowed up Denmark, too.

Yes, Stockholm was a wonderful, bright, civilized place. The only problem was, she didn't want to be here. She had plenty of money. She wouldn't have been able to come to Marianske Lazne in Czechoslovakia without it, or to maintain herself when the war stranded her on the wrong side of the Atlantic. But, just as all the king's horses and all the king's men couldn't put Humpty Dumpty together again, all her jack couldn't get her back to the good old US of A, or to the husband she hadn't seen for well over a year.

Norway remained a war zone. Because it did, there was no air traffic between Sweden and England—no sea traffic, either. She wished she could go to Moscow and head for Vladivostok by way of the Trans-Siberian Railway. Though it *was* the long way back to the States, it would have done the job. But, with the railroad cut and Vladivostok under Japanese siege, that didn't work, either.

And so she stayed where she was. Stockholm made a far more likable prison than Berlin had. The food was better, and she didn't wonder whether everyone she spoke to would report her to the *Gestapo.* All the same, she wasn't where she wanted to be.

She'd never been one to suffer in silence. If she was unhappy, she let people hear about it. The American embassy in Berlin had got to know her much better than the clerks and secretaries and diplomats ever wanted to. (And, one drunken night, she'd got to know one of the diplomats much better than she ever expected to. She did her damnedest not to remember that.)

Now she bent the personnel of the embassy in Stockholm to her will—or did her best. Again, the trouble was that, even when they wanted to do what she wanted (and they did, if for no more noble reason than to get her out of their hair), they couldn't.

"I can't call an airplane out of nowhere, Mrs. Druce," said the undersecretary in charge of dealing with distressed travelers. "I haven't got a liner, or even a freighter, up my sleeve, either."

"Yes, I understand that, Mr. Beard," Peggy answered. To her secret amusement, Jerome Beard sported a hairline mustache. "But if you could arrange something with the German and British authorities . . ."

He ran a hand over the top of his head, from front to back. Once upon a time, he might have used the gesture to smooth his hair. But where were the snows of yesteryear? He was on the far side of fifty—a few years older than Peggy. He had one of the baldest domes she'd ever seen, though, and it made him look older.

"Why don't you ask me something easy?" he said testily. "Walking across the Baltic, for instance?"

"It's frozen over for miles out to sea." Peggy, by contrast, sounded as bright and helpful as she could.

Beard's harried expression said he understood she was being difficult but sugarcoating it. "Pardon my French, Mrs. Druce, but hell will freeze over before they cooperate. Last time around, both sides were perfectly correct. They did everything they could to help displaced persons like you. Now?" He shook his head. His bare scalp gleamed under the overhead lamp. "No. I'm very sorry, but it's not just a war."

"You said that before," Peggy pointed out. She was bound and determined to be difficult, regardless of whether she sugarcoated it.

"Well, what if I did?" Beard ran his hand over his crown again. "It's true. You have no idea how much those two regimes despise each other."

"Oh, yes, I do. I was in Berlin, remember," Peggy said.

"All right, then." The undersecretary yielded the small point. He wasn't about to yield on the larger one. In fact, he poured more cold water over it: "And the same holds true for France and Germany. The French don't merely hate the Germans, either—they're scared to death of them. That makes joint efforts even more unlikely."

"What am I supposed to do, then?" Peggy demanded.

"How about thanking God you're in one of the few countries on this poor, sorry continent where there's plenty of food and no one is trying to kill anyone else?" Beard said. "You couldn't pick a better spot to wait out the war."

"I thought the same thing about Copenhagen. Then I watched German soldiers get out of their freighters and march on the palace," Peggy said bitterly. "No guarantee the same thing won't happen here."

"No guarantee, no." Beard paused to fill a pipe and light it. The mixture smelled like burning dirty socks. "Swedish blend," he explained, a note of apology in his voice. "All I can get these days. But to come back to your point . . . The Swedes will fight. They've made that very plain to Germany. Since the Germans have plenty of other pots on the fire, Sweden's safe enough for now. That's the ambassador's judgment, and the military attaché's, too."

"And maybe they're right, and maybe they're wrong," Peggy said. "All I want to do is go home. It's 1940, for crying out loud. I was going to be in Europe for a month in fall 1938."

"You picked the wrong month, and the wrong part of Europe," Beard said.

"Boy, did I ever!"

"There may still be a way," he said. "You would have to take some chances." He shook his head. "No—you would have to take a lot of chances."

"Tell me," Peggy answered. "If I don't have to put on a uniform and carry a gun, I'll do it. And I'd think about putting on a uniform, as long as it isn't a Nazi one."

"You can still travel to Poland. From Poland, you can get to Romania. From Romania, you can probably find a ship that will take you to Egypt. Once you get through the Suez Canal, you've left most of the war behind you," Beard said.

Italy and England were fighting a desultory war over Somaliland and Abyssinia, a campaign neither one of them could get very excited about. But that was the least of Peggy's worries. "Like the kids' magazines say, what's wrong with this picture?" she replied. "If I fly in to Warsaw, say, the Red Army's liable to be running the airport. And if it isn't, the *Luftwaffe* will be. Besides, isn't there fighting in the stretch of Poland that borders Romania?"

"There is," Beard acknowledged. "But you could skirt it by going from Poland to Slovakia and to Romania from there."

For all practical purposes, going into Slovakia was the same as going back to Nazi Germany. There was no guarantee the Russians wouldn't invade Father Tiso's almost-country, either. Come to that, there was no guarantee they wouldn't invade Romania. As the embassy undersecretary'd pointed out, there was a war on. There were no guarantees anywhere.

Peggy'd told him she was willing to take a lot of chances. Had she meant it? "Well," she said brightly, "can you help me with the arrangements?"

Chapter 2

Staff Sergeant Alistair Walsh wore a shepherd's sheepskin coat on top of his greatcoat. His thick wool mittens came from the Norwegian countryside, too. He'd cut a slit in the right one so he could fire his rifle. He'd wrapped a knitted scarf around his face. The only flesh he exposed was that from his eyes to the brim of his tin hat. He was cold anyhow.

English, French, and Norwegian soldiers still hung on to Namsos, on the coast of central Norway. Sooner or later, the Fritzes were going to throw them out. That seemed obvious to Walsh. His superiors hadn't figured it out yet. He'd been in the army since 1918. He walked with a bit of a limp from a German bullet that had got him more than half a lifetime earlier. He wasn't surprised that he had a clearer view of things than the blokes with the shoulder straps and peaked caps.

Smoke rose from the direction of the docks. The Germans had come bombing again. They did it blindly, from above the clouds: to fly down below them was to risk flying straight into the ground. But they'd got lucky, damn them.

All the same, sailors and locals and, no doubt, some dragooned soldiers labored like draft horses to unload whatever ships hadn't been hit.

Without the stuff the Royal Navy brought in, resistance here wouldn't last long. Even with it . . .

Walsh had plenty of clips for his submachine gun. He wasn't too hungry. The artillery, though, was severely rationed. The expeditionary force's handful of tanks still running were low, low, low on petrol. He could hardly remember the last time a Hurricane, or even a Gladiator, had got airborne.

The Germans didn't have those worries. They held Denmark. Their planes and U-boats and even their pissy little excuse for a surface navy dominated the Skagerrak, the strait between Denmark and Norway. And they occupied the south here. Whatever they needed, they could bring in and bring up to the front with nothing to worry about except occasional ambuscades from Norwegian ski troops.

Of course, the Germans had ski troops, too. *They would,* Walsh thought, less angrily than he might have. He'd fought Fritz in two wars now, and trained to fight him in the gap between them. He had a thorough professional respect for the sons of bitches in field-gray. That didn't keep him from shooting them whenever he found the chance. After all, they respected his side, too, but they'd plugged him all the same.

Some French *chasseurs alpins* had been part of the expeditionary force. Damned if they didn't ski with berets on their heads. Nervous Allied soldiers had shot a couple of them anyway. Anything unfamiliar was assumed to be dangerous. More often than not, it was. The rest of the time? Hard luck for the poor bugger who'd made somebody jumpy.

One of the men in Walsh's company came up to him and said, "'Ere, Sergeant, can I talk to you for a minute, quiet-like?" His broad Yorkshire contrasted with Walsh's buzzing Welsh accent.

"What's up, Jock?" Walsh asked. They'd been together a long time. Catching the worried look on the big man's face, he added, "Is something wrong with the cat?" They'd sneaked the little gray-and-white beast onto the troopship that carried them here, and somehow they'd kept it with them ever since. Plenty of hard-bitten troopers would have been heartbroken if a shell fragment found Pussy.

But Jock shook his head. "Nay, it's not the beastie." He looked this way and that. As with Sergeant Walsh, his eyes and forehead were the only skin he showed. Seeing no one close enough to Walsh's foxhole to overhear him, he dropped his voice to a near-whisper and said, "It hurts when I piss—hurts powerful bad."

"Oh, for Christ's sake!" Walsh exploded. "Who have you been fucking?"

Soldiers used the word all the time, in every possible form and most of the impossible ones. But hearing it used in its basic meaning made Jock blush—Walsh watched the skin above his eyes redden. Hesitantly, he answered, "There was this lady in one o' the villages we went through a few days back. She gave my mates an' me bread an' boiled pork—an' she must've given me summat else to remember her by, too."

Coming down venereal was serious business. Your pay got stopped. Your family might even get a wire from the War Ministry—which was, of course, the last thing on God's green earth you wanted. Even so, Walsh said, "You'd better take it to the medical officer."

"Sergeant!" Jock yelped—pure anguish.

"I mean it," Walsh said. "They've got new pills that can really cure you. You take 'em, you keep it in your trousers for a bit, and a few days later you're fine. That's better than letting the clap stew."

"Nah. It ain't." The Yorkshireman shook his head again. "Ah don't wahnt nobody t'ken of it." His accent thickened as he got more upset.

Walsh set a hand on his shoulder. "Look, things are going to the devil around here. Nobody's going to worry about paperwork at a time like this."

"The sawbones will." Jock spoke with dour certainty.

"Tell the miserable quack to fix you up, and tell him to talk to me before he goes and gets all regulation on you," Walsh said. "I'll take care of it—you see if I don't."

"All right." Jock still sounded miserable, and well he might. He didn't seem so proud now of jumping on that friendly Norwegian lady, though doubtless he had been at the time.

An artillery barrage livened things up after Jock mooched off. Sure as hell, the Germans had plenty of ammunition, even if the expeditionary force didn't. In weather like this, shells didn't tear up the landscape the way they did in a more civilized climate. Snowdrifts muffled bursts. And even a 105 made a crater only a little bigger than a washtub when the ground was frozen hard.

After the barrage let up, the Fritzes came forward on foot. Machine guns and accurate rifle fire soon persuaded them that they hadn't blasted their foes to kingdom come. They pulled back, leaving a few bloody bodies on the snow between the two sides' lines. By the same token, wounded Tommies and *poilus* and squareheads went back toward Namsos for treatment, as Jock had before them.

Walsh hoped he could deliver on his promise to the Yorkshireman. Doctors were nominally officers. They didn't have to listen to a career noncom, though the ones with any sense commonly did.

Captain Beverly Murdoch seemed typical of the breed. Though overworked and indifferently shaved, his accent and the way he looked at Walsh declared him a member of the upper classes. *Chaps like him, it's no wonder a bloke like Trotsky gets a hearing,* Walsh thought irreverently.

"I am given to understand you wish this man treated for his social disease in an informal fashion." Murdoch's tone said that ought to be a hanging matter on the off chance it wasn't.

"Yes, sir." Walsh kept his response as simple as he could.

"Why?" The word sounded colder than the Norwegian winter enfolding them.

"He's a good soldier, sir. I've known him a long time. He took what he could get, but plenty of others would've done the same. I might myself, if the lady was pretty. So might you." Walsh hoped the quack wasn't a fairy. That would queer his pitch. "And the way things are right now, we need all the men we can find, and we need them with the best morale they can get. Since you have your pills—"

"I'd do better using them on wounded men than on those who diseased themselves," Murdoch broke in.

"Sir, he's wounded in war, too, in a manner of speaking. He never would have met that woman if we hadn't been posted to Norway," Walsh said.

"No, he would have got his dose from some French twist instead." Murdoch sent him an unfriendly look. "And I suppose you'll find ways to make my life miserable if I don't play along."

"How can I do that, sir? I'm only a staff sergeant." Walsh might have been innocence personified.

He might have been, but the doctor knew he wasn't. "People like you have their ways," he said sourly. "Half the time, I think officers run the army on the sufferance of sergeants."

Walsh thought the same thing, but more often than half the time. All the same, he said, "I'm afraid I don't know what you mean, sir."

"Yes, likely tell." Murdoch made a disgusted gesture. "All right. Have your way, dammit. He'll get the bloody sulfanilamide, and I'll write it up as a skin infection."

"Much obliged to you, sir." Walsh knew he might have to pay the sawbones back one day, but he'd worry about that when the time came. He *had* got his way, and Jock wasn't in a jam on account of it. Except for the Norwegian winter and the advancing Nazis, everything was fine.

HANS-ULRICH RUDEL had thought he'd flown his Ju-87 under primitive conditions in France. And so he had: with its heavy, fixed undercarriage, the Stuka was made for taking off and landing on dirt airstrips. All the same, he'd been flying in France, and France was a civilized country. Poland, now . . .

The pilot came from Silesia. He knew about Poles: knew what Germans in that part of the *Reich* knew about them, anyhow. They were lazy, shiftless, drunken, sneaky, not to be trusted behind your back. Nothing he saw in this village east of Warsaw made him want to change his mind. If anything, the Poles here were even worse because they hadn't been leavened by Germans the way they had in Silesia. They were well on their way to being Russians, and how could you say anything worse about a folk?

With no Germans in these parts till the *Wehrmacht* came to pull the Poles' chestnuts out of the fire, the only leavening they got was from Jews. A Jew named Fink ran the local pharmacy. Another one named Grinszpan was the village bookkeeper. Yet another named Cohen pulled teeth. A Pole owned the newspaper in Bialystok, the nearest real city, but his editor was a Jew named Blum. And on and on.

Rudel thought the Jews in the *Reich* had got what was coming to them after the *Führer* took over. He knew for a fact that Poles liked Jews even less than Germans did. But he and his comrades were forbidden from giving Jews what-for here. The Poles hadn't cleared them out of their own armed forces, even if they didn't like them. And, no matter how the Poles felt, Jews still had legal equality in Poland.

"Orders are orders," said Colonel Steinbrenner, the wing commander. "All we have to do is follow them."

"They're crazy orders," Hans-Ulrich complained. "The Poles are on our side, but the way they act, they might as well be Bolsheviks. Plenty of Jew officers in the Red Army."

Steinbrenner shook his head. He preferred a German-issue tent to a house in the village, which would probably be full of vermin. Hans-Ulrich felt the same way. The colonel said, "No, Lieutenant, the Poles are not on our side."

"Sir?" Hans-Ulrich repeated in surprise.

"The Poles are not on our side," Steinbrenner repeated. "If they sent troops to France to fight alongside our men there, those troops would be on our side. In Poland, we're on their side. They asked us in to help against the Russians. We have to play by their rules here, not by ours."

"No matter how stupid those rules are," Rudel said.

"No matter," the wing commander agreed. "The only reason the Poles don't hate us worse than the Ivans is, the Ivans hit them first. We can't afford to give them an excuse to turn on us."

That did make military sense. Even so, Hans-Ulrich said, "They ought to be grateful we're giving them a hand. Without us, the Russians would be in Warsaw by now, and how would the Poles like that?"

"Not much. They'd probably fall to pieces—and then we'd have the Red Army on our border," Steinbrenner said. "That would be just what we need, wouldn't it? With us up to our eyebrows in the west, they could give us one straight up the ass. They'd do it, too. In a heartbeat, they would."

Rudel didn't argue with him. When you were a first lieutenant, arguing with a colonel was a losing proposition. Besides, here Steinbrenner was pretty plainly right. "I guess so, sir," Hans-Ulrich said. "And everybody could see we were going to take a whack at the Bolsheviks sooner or later."

"That's what the *Führer*'s always wanted to do, all right," Steinbrenner said.

"But he's always wanted to pay the Jews back for betraying the *Vaterland* at the end of the last war, too."

"One thing at a time—when you can, anyhow," Colonel Steinbrenner said. "That's only good strategy. First we win the war. Then we take care of anything else that needs doing. You can count on the General Staff to have the sense to see as much."

Most of the high-ranking officers who'd tried to overthrow Hitler at Christmastime the year before served on the General Staff. Hans-Ulrich Rudel was not the most politic of men, but even he could see that pointing out as much to his superior would win him no points. Besides, he knew Steinbrenner was loyal. The wing commander had replaced another officer in France: one suspected of insufficient enthusiasm for the National Socialist cause. Where was the other fellow now? Dachau? Belsen? A hole in the ground? Better not to wonder about such things.

When the weather cleared enough to let him fly, Rudel felt nothing but relief. In the air, he didn't have to think about Jews or politics or the price of being mistrusted by the government. He had to look for Red Army panzers. That was it. When he found them, he had to dive on them and shoot them up. His Ju-87 carried a 37mm cannon under each wing. The extra weight and drag made the Stuka even more of a lumbering pig in the air than it would have been otherwise. If Red Air Force fighters jumped him, he'd go into some Russian pilot's trophy case. Till that evil day came, if it ever did, he was very bad news.

"Everything clear behind us, Albert?" he asked through the brass speaking tube.

"If it weren't, I'd be screaming my head off." Sergeant Albert Dieselhorst was rear gunner and radioman. He and Rudel sat back-to-back, separated by an armored bulkhead. If anyone had a better understanding than Hans-Ulrich of how limited the Stuka was in the air, Dieselhorst was the man.

The Ivans were masters of camouflage. Whitewash and concealment under trees or white cloth could make it hard to spot a panzer on the ground at a hundred meters, let alone from several thousand up in the air. But not even the Russians could hide the long shadows panzers cast on the snow. "There they are!" Hans-Ulrich yipped excitedly.

"Go get 'em, Lieutenant," Dieselhorst said. It was all news to him. Like Epimetheus in the Greek myth, he could see only where he'd already been.

Hans-Ulrich heeled the Ju-87 into a dive. He hung suspended against his harness for a moment. Then building acceleration shoved him back into his seat. It would be trying to tear the rear gunner from his and throw him out of the plane over his machine gun.

Down on the ground, the panzers swelled from specks to toys to real, deadly whitewashed machines. He dove from behind. When he struck, he fired a round from each gun at the engine compartment. The steel on the decking there was thin, and pierced to let heat escape. He hauled back on the stick as hard as he could to pull the Stuka out of the dive.

"Nailed him!" Sergeant Dieselhorst yelled through the tube. "He's on fire!"

"Good." Hans-Ulrich climbed as steeply as he could. He picked another camouflaged panzer and dove on it. Two more rounds. Another burning machine, or so the rear gunner assured him. Some of the crewmen on the other panzers popped out of hatches to blaze away at the Ju-87 with pistols and submachine guns, but Rudel wouldn't lose any sleep over that. Small-arms fire *could* bring down an airplane, but it didn't happen every day, or every month, either.

He blasted three more Russian panzers. The rest started up and skedaddled for the nearest trees. Then Dieselhorst said, "I'm getting reports of planes in the neighborhood."

"All right. We'll go home." Hans-Ulrich had heard the reports in his earphones, too. He hadn't wanted to do anything about that. Sometimes discretion *was* the better part of valor, though. He could gas up again and hit the Ivans on a stretch of front where they didn't have any air cover.

A flak shell burst under the Stuka, staggering it in the sky. No, the Russians didn't want him around anymore. He gave the plane more throttle. If they'd got set up a little sooner, they might have knocked him down. Not now.

"Just another morning at the office," Sergeant Dieselhorst said.

"*Aber natürlich.*" Hans-Ulrich laughed. Why not? Just another day at the office, sure—and they'd lived through it.

SERGEANT HIDEKI FUJITA had thought winter in the Siberian forests was about as bad as anything could be. It was worse than winter on the border with Mongolia, which made it pretty appalling. But winter in front of Vladivostok turned out to be worse yet. It was as cold as the rest of Siberia, with the same wet, heavy snowfall. But it was out in the open—nowhere to hide from the relentlessly probing Russian artillery.

The Red Army was always ass-deep in guns. Russian artillerymen had harried the Japanese on the frontier between Manchukuo and Mongolia. They'd fused their shells to burst as soon as they touched the treetops in the woods, showering Japanese forces astride the Trans-Siberian Railway with deadly fragments. And, here in front of their Far Eastern port, they tried to murder anything that moved.

They came much too close to succeeding. Kilometer upon kilometer of barbed wire and entrenchments ringed Vladivostok. The Soviet Union had always known it might have to fight for the place one day. If Japan was going to take it, her soldiers would have to winkle out the Red Army men one foxhole at a time.

More than a generation earlier, the fight for Port Arthur had gone the same way. Some of the men commanding at Vladivostok would have been junior officers in the earlier fight. Fujita hoped they'd learned something in the intervening years. By everything he could see, it didn't seem likely.

He mostly huddled in a dugout scraped from the forward wall of a trench. Digging was anything but easy. The ground was frozen hard as stone. It wouldn't collapse under shellfire, which was something. Not enough, not as far as Fujita was concerned.

Japanese and Russian cannon dueled with one another. Machine guns made sticking your head up over the parapet tantamount to committing *seppuku.* Runners who brought rice and other food up from the field kitchens risked their life with every trip. Even when they made it through, meals were commonly cold by the time they reached the front-line soldiers.

Rumors flew thick and fast as bullets. Some people said the Russian commander was about to surrender, the way the nobleman in charge of Port Arthur had in 1905. Fujita didn't believe that one. He'd spent too long fighting the Russians to doubt they were in earnest. They might bungle things—they weren't always skillful soldiers. But, no matter what they'd been like in 1905, no one who fought them now could think they'd quit so easily.

Other rumors claimed the Japanese would soon charge the works in front of them again. Fujita had to hope those weren't true. Too many frozen corpses still sprawled suspended in the wire ahead. Along with solidifying the ground, the cold meant dead bodies didn't stink. Having said those two things, you exhausted its virtues.

Fujita wanted the generals to come up with something brilliant, or at least clever. If they tried something like that, he was less likely to get killed or maimed than if they just pounded away. They didn't seem to worry about that. As far as generals were concerned, soldiers were only munitions of war, expendable as machine-gun bullets or 105mm shells.

Far off in the distance, Vladivostok itself burned. Black columns of smoke rose into the sky all day long. Japanese bombers pounded the city night and day. When, as occasionally happened, the wind blew from the south instead of the north, the half-spicy, half-choking smell of smoke filled Fujita's nostrils.

Russian fighters rarely came up to challenge the Japanese planes. The Reds hadn't had many fighters when Fujita got here, and they had fewer now. Fighters were short-range planes; the Soviet Union couldn't bring in more very easily.

Russian bombers, by contrast, flew over fairly often, for the most part at night. Fujita had no idea where they came from. Some landing strip up in Siberia? The northern, Soviet half of the island Japan called Karafuto and the Russians Sakhalin? No doubt it mattered to his superiors, who had to decide what to do about the air raids. To Fujita, they were only one more annoyance. Machine-gun bullets and the deadly artillery were worse.

And worse still was knowing his regiment was only an officer's whim from being thrown into the fire of a frontal attack. Many went forward. Few came back—even fewer unmaimed.

Shinjiro Hayashi, a superior private in Fujita's section, had been a student when conscription nabbed him. He still had a calculating turn of mind. "If we use up a regiment to take a stretch of ground two hundred meters wide and fifty meters deep, how many will we use to advance twenty kilometers on a front at least fifty kilometers around?" he asked.

When Fujita was in school, he'd hated problems like that. He tried to work this one, but didn't like the answer he got. "I don't know if there are that many regiments in Japan," he said.

"I don't, either, Sergeant-*san*," Hayashi answered somberly.

And what was Fujita supposed to do with that? A sergeant punished defeatism wherever he found it. And a sergeant had the right—the duty—to beat the snot out of his underlings when they didn't live up to his expectations, or sometimes whenever he felt like it. But the only thing the senior private had done was ask a simple question. They went back to Mongolia together, too.

Instead of belting Hayashi, then, Fujita said, "If you open your big yap any wider, you'll fall right in."

Hayashi got the message. "I'll be careful, Sergeant-*san*," he promised.

"You'd better," Fujita growled, but he didn't sound angry enough to frighten a nine-year-old, let alone a combat veteran.

Then they got something to be frightened about: an order to attack the Red Army positions in front of them. Fujita was a combat veteran, all right, and he was scared green. He spent half an hour sharpening his bayonet. He didn't think that would keep him alive, but it gave him something to do so he wouldn't have to worry—too much—about what lay ahead.

No artillery preparation. That, the officers said, would warn the Russians. And so it would, but it would also kill a lot of them, and flatten some of the wire in front of their trenches. What could you do? Live—if they'd let you.

He couldn't even tell his men the Red Army soldiers would have loot worth taking. In Mongolia, Russian gear and rations seemed luxurious to the Japanese. Not here. The Russians around Vladivostok had been under siege for months. Even by Japanese standards, they didn't have much.

The only covering fire the attackers got came from machine guns. Ever since the fight at Port Arthur, the Japanese had handled those aggressively. If the gunners shot a few of their own men in the back . . . Well, to everyone but the luckless victims, that was only a cost of doing business.

Mouth dry, Fujita ran forward, hunched over as low as he could go. The Russian Maxim guns needed only a few seconds to snarl to life. Bullets coming toward him, bullets snapping past him from behind . . . He'd been places he liked more. Less? Maybe not.

He tripped over something and fell full length in the snow. Two bullets, one coming and the other going, slammed together about where he'd just been. They fell beside him, sending up a small plume of steam. He hardly noticed, and had no idea how lucky he was.

He got up again and stumbled on. Not all the Japanese soldiers who'd gone down would get up again. If you lost a regiment taking a stretch of ground not very wide and even less deep . . . He called down elaborate curses on Shinjiro Hayashi's learned head.

Some soldiers had wire cutters. Some of them stayed unwounded long enough to get up to the vicious stuff and cut it. More Japanese soldiers, Fujita among them, pushed through the gaps and rushed the Russian trenches. A Red Army man popped up like a marmot. He aimed his rifle at the sergeant. Fujita fired first. He missed, but he made the Russian duck. With a cry of "*Banzai!*" Fujita leaped into the trench after him.

The Russian shot at him from almost point-blank range. He missed anyhow. Fujita lunged with the bayonet while the Russian was working the bolt. The point went home. The white man screamed and dropped the rifle. Fujita stuck him again and again, till he finally fell over. Even then, he kept thrashing on the cold hard ground until the sergeant shot him in the head. People could be awfully hard to kill.

Little by little, paying a price, the Japanese cleared the Russians from three or four rows of trenches. No, not much left in the dead men's pockets, though Fujita did get some Russian cigarettes—a little tobacco at the end of a long paper holder. He lit one. The smoke was harsh as sandpaper, but he didn't care.

Senior Private Hayashi sidled up to him and spoke in a low voice: "If clearing a space two hundred meters by fifty meters costs most of a regiment . . ."

"Oh, shut up," Fujita exclaimed. He tried to blow a smoke ring.

SPAIN WAS MISERABLY hot in summer and miserably cold in winter. Coming as he did from New York City, Chaim Weinberg had reckoned himself a connoisseur of both extremes. He had to admit, though, that Spain went further in both directions than his home town.

Spain seemed to go all-out in everything. American politics matched one side of the center against the other, and endlessly played the game of compromise solution. Communists like Chaim couldn't get a serious hearing there. And so he'd come to Spain with the Abraham Lincoln Brigade, to do what he could for the left-wing Republic against Marshal Sanjurjo's Fascists, who held more than half of it.

He'd sweltered. He'd frozen, the way he was freezing now. He'd argued in English, in Yiddish that often did duty for German, and in bad Spanish. The Republic ran on argument no less than on gasoline and high explosives. He'd learned to drink wine from a leather sack and to roll his own smokes. He'd killed. He'd been wounded. He'd got laid. If you were an excitable young man who hadn't done most of those things before (sweltering, freezing, and arguing came naturally), Spain could look a lot like paradise.

But if this was paradise, it needed rebuilding. Sanjurjo's men, and the Italian and German mercenaries who fought on their side, had done their best to knock Madrid flat. Their best was good, but not good enough. Buildings had chunks bitten out of them. Hardly any windows were glazed. Craters in streets and sidewalks made getting anywhere in town an adventure.

Chaim didn't care. The Madrileños carried on as if the war were a million miles away: as well as they could when going hungry or huddling in a cellar while bombs rained down didn't distract them. If the wine reminded him of vinegar or piss, if the cigarettes tasted of hay or horseshit or other street scrapings, well, so what? You could still get drunk. Whatever else went into the cigarettes, they had enough tobacco so you didn't think you'd quit.

And the people . . . Everybody called everyone else *tu.* The formal *Usted* hadn't been banned in the Republic, but anyone who used it might get sent off for reeducation. Women acted like men, in the shops, in the streets, and in bed. Yes, Chaim had got laid. If you couldn't get laid in the Spanish Republic, you weren't half trying.

Prisoners from the other side who were brought into Madrid had to think they'd landed on Mars. Where the Republic jumped on class and sex distinctions with both feet, under the Fascist regime they got enforced more strongly than ever. Enforcing the ruling class's dominance was what Fascism was all about.

Almost by accident, Chaim had got the job of reindoctrinating those prisoners. His Spanish still wasn't the best, but it did the job—and if he was fluent in any part of the language, it was Marxist-Leninist jargon. Besides, Spaniards were absurdly respectful of foreigners. The Fascists even respected Italians, for crying out loud! Prisoners assumed an American had to be a political sophisticate. Chaim knew better, but didn't let on that he did.

The POW camp was in a park near the center of Madrid. When enemy planes came over at night, they dropped their bombs more or less at random. They bombed their own people, too. Sometimes they blasted the camp's barbed-wire perimeter. That led to escapes: POWs on the loose in Madrid weren't much shabbier than anybody else, and looked, acted, and sounded like any other Spaniards. It also led to casualties.

Chaim still wasn't sure whether Joaquin Delgadillo, a man he'd captured himself, was the one or the other. Delgadillo wasn't in the camp any more. Chaim knew that. But whether the Spaniard had got away after a bombing run or been blasted into unrecognizable scraps of meat, the guards had no idea. They only shrugged. "One or the other," they chorused.

"But which?" Chaim demanded. "Differences are important."

"One or the other," the guards said again. They didn't get it. Maybe they needed to listen to his harangues, too.

Someone on this side of the wire listened intently to what he told the captured Fascists. The authorities wanted to make sure he preached only good, pure, true Communist doctrine. Heaven—the heaven he didn't believe in—help him if he showed himself out of step with what Moscow decreed to be so . . . or, worse, if he showed he'd fallen into the Trotskyist heresy. There were times when the old Inquisition had nothing on the Republic, though Chaim didn't think of it like that.

He didn't not least because his minder was one of the best-looking women he'd ever set eyes on. La Martellita—her *nom de guerre* meant *the little hammer*—filled out overalls in a way their designer never intended. Midnight hair. Snapping eyes, coral lips, a piquant nose . . . He was in love, or at least in lust.

La Martellita looked at him as if she'd just found half of him in her apple. If she didn't like what he said, she might be able to have him shot. He didn't care. If anything, the aura of danger that fit her as tightly as those overalls only made him hotter.

He didn't even know her real name. She wouldn't tell him, and he hadn't found anybody else who knew. One of these days, he would. And then, casually, in just the right spot, he'd call her by it. And then what? Chances were she'd tell him to fuck off. Even rejection, coming from her, seemed sweet.

Which was a good thing, because rejection and criticism were all he got from her. He did try to be more careful with the doctrine he preached to the prisoners. He didn't want to die at the hands of his own side. He didn't *want* to die at all. He aspired to be shot at the age of 103 by an outraged husband. He'd come to Spain to fight the enemies of Marxism-Leninism, not its friends.

When he said as much to La Martellita, she curled her kissable upper lip. "Then you shouldn't deviate from the Party line," she said, as if she were a bishop complaining about a priest's sermon.

Chaim was no priest. He didn't have to stay celibate. He didn't want to, either. La Martellita was also free. Unlike a lot of her Spanish sisters, she wasn't easy, though, not with him.

"Why don't you go play with yourself?" she said when she couldn't be in any doubt of his interest. Spanish women could also be very blunt.

"You'd be more fun," he answered honestly.

"Not with you, I wouldn't," she said. "You'd make any woman wish she were with somebody else." She stalked away. Maybe she didn't realize how her hips swung. More likely, she was doing it with malice aforethought.

Oh, yeah? he wanted to shout back, like a stupid kid. *Says you!* Every once in a while, he'd learned, keeping his big mouth shut came in handy. This looked like one of those times.

Maybe the way to her heart lay in the straight Party line. But Chaim, while a good Communist, was also an American to the tips of his stubby fingers. He enjoyed tinkering with ideas the way a lot of his countrymen enjoyed tinkering with motors. He tore them down and rebuilt them and did his damnedest to get them working better than ever. If they weren't always the same afterwards, so what? They were new and improved—two magic words in the States.

Not in Spain. (Not in the USSR, either: something Chaim preferred to forget. He knew about the gulags—knew they existed, anyhow, and held dissidents. He also preferred to forget that.) Here, a parrot did better than a tinkerer. Chaim had never been a parrot, and didn't want to start.

But he did want to jump on La Martellita's elegantly cushioned bones. "Weinberg wants a cracker!" he screeched in English. It wouldn't have made sense to the guards even in their own language.

Chapter 3

The dreaded call didn't always come with a knock on the door in the middle of the night. Lieutenant Anastas Mouradian was eating blintzes and drinking his breakfast tea when a hard-faced noncom carrying a submachine gun strode up to him in the officers' mess and barked, "Comrade Lieutenant, Colonel Borisov requires your presence. Immediately!"

Across the table from Mouradian, his pilot looked horrified. Sergei Yaroslavsky had warned him again and again that he was too sarcastic, too skeptical, for his own good. Maybe Sergei'd been right all along.

Nothing showed on the Armenian's swarthy face now. *Never let them know you're worried,* Mouradian thought. And a whole fat lot of good that would do him if they'd already built a case with his name on it. If the powers that be wanted to give him a plot of earth two meters long, a meter wide, and two meters deep, they damn well would, and that was all there was to it.

He got to his feet. "I serve the Soviet Union!" he said in his throatily accented Russian, hoping it wasn't for the last time.

Russians from Siberia talked about the whisper of stars: weather so cold that, when you exhaled, the moisture in your breath audibly froze. They claimed it never got that cold on this side of the Urals. Mouradian couldn't have said one way or the other. He'd never heard the so-called whisper of stars, but maybe the Siberians were lying about it.

Even without it, the weather seemed plenty cold enough. He was glad for his flying suit of leather and fur, and for the thick felt *valenki* that kept his feet from freezing. The Russians were good at fighting winter—and they needed to be. He often wondered why so many men from the south, where the weather was mostly decent, came up here to make their careers. When it got this cold, he wondered why he'd ever wanted to leave Armenia himself.

But the answer was simple. Armenia and the rest of the Caucasus were only a little pond. If you wanted to see how good you were in the ocean, you came north and measured yourself against the swarms of Russians. It had worked out pretty well for Georgian-born Joseph Dzugashvili, who commonly went by the Russian handle of Stalin these days.

Of course, things that worked out well for Stalin had a way of working not so well for other people. Mouradian glanced over at the sergeant with the machine pistol. The son of a bitch looked depressingly alert. Were a couple of NKVD men waiting for Mouradian along with Colonel Borisov? Would they ship him off to Kolyma or some other garden spot so he could find out about the whisper of stars for himself?

He'd know soon. Here was the wing commander's tent. The sergeant gestured with his weapon, telling Mouradian to go in. Sighing out fog but no stars, the copilot and bomb-aimer obeyed.

No NKVD men. Only Colonel Borisov, sitting behind a card table that held some papers and a tumbler full of clear liquid. Despite a brazier next to the table, water would have frozen in a hurry. But, knowing Borisov's habits, Mouradian would have been astonished had the glass held water.

Saluting, the Armenian said, "Reporting as ordered, Comrade Colonel."

"Yes." Borisov looked and sounded bleary. Had he started drinking this early in the morning? Or had he been at it all night, so it wasn't early for him? He stared at Mouradian out of pale eyes narrowed by a Tatar fold at the inner corners. "Are you capable of piloting an SB-2?"

"*Da,* Comrade Colonel," Mouradian answered. A copilot needed to be able to fly his plane. If anything happened to the pilot—a 20mm cannon shell from a Messerschmitt, say—bringing the bomber home would be up to him. Colonel Borisov should have known that. Chances were he did . . . when he was sober.

He took a slug from that tumbler and breathed antifreeze fumes into Mouradian's face. "Good," he said. "Very good, in fact." He reached for a pencil—and missed. Not a bit put out, he tried again. This time, he captured it. He made a check mark on one of the papers. "Get your things. We'll put you in a *panje* wagon and haul you off to the nearest railhead."

"I serve the Soviet Union!" Mouradian said, and then, "Comrade Colonel, where am I going? What will I be doing when I get there?" It still might be Kolyma, despite the blather about whether he could fly the plane. Some Russians were sheeplike enough to report to the gulag even without guards to make sure they got there. If Borisov thought Mouradian grew that kind of wool, he would soon discover that men from the Caucasus weren't so naive.

"You will report to Far Eastern Aviation. They're screaming for pilots there," Borisov told him. "I don't *know* what you'll be doing, but fuck your mother if it's not likely to be dropping rocks on the little yellow monkeys' heads."

So it would be Siberia, then. But he'd go there as a free man, a soldier, not as a disgraced prisoner. Mouradian suddenly felt ten degrees warmer, even if Colonel Borisov's tent remained cold as a hailstone. "I serve the Soviet Union!" he said yet again, this time gladly. "Ah, you have written orders for me?" Without them, he'd never get aboard the local train, let alone the Trans-Siberian Railway.

Borisov blinked owlishly. "Oh, sure. They're here somewhere." He fumbled through papers, then thrust one at Mouradian. "Here."

Mouradian eyed it. "Sir, this is a scheme for winning at dice."

"What? Give it back to me!" The wing commander snatched it out of his hand. He did some more shuffling. "This is the one you need."

The other one, no doubt, was the one Borisov needed himself.

Mouradian carefully examined the new document. Sure enough, it showed that Borisov was duly providing the pilot he'd been ordered to furnish. However . . . "Will you please put my name on it?"

"Oh, all right." By the way Borisov sighed, Anastas was asking for the sun, the moon, *and* the stars. The colonel scribbled. Mouradian checked again. It would do. Borisov had remembered who he was.

He went out to collect his things. The submachine-gun-toting sergeant still accompanied him. Sergei was in the tent waiting for him. "What are they doing to you?" the pilot asked, alarm in his voice.

"Siberia," Mouradian answered as he threw this, that, and the other thing into a duffel bag.

"*Bozhemoi!*" Yaroslavsky said. "I tried to tell you—"

"No, not the camps." Anastas' joke had worked almost too well. "Far Eastern Aviation. They'll make me a pilot so the Japanese can shoot me down."

"Oh." Yaroslavsky kissed him on both cheeks and gave him a hug. "Well, stay as safe as you can, you crazy bastard. I hope I see you after the war."

"That would be good. Or maybe we won't have to wait so long. Who knows? Who knows anything nowadays?" Mouradian slung the duffel over his shoulder and went out into the cold again.

The stone-faced noncom drove the *panje* wagon, too. With its boat-like body and big wheels, the wagon could get through winter snow and spring and autumn mud that stymied fancier transport.

For a wonder, the Germans hadn't hit the railway station. The young lieutenant who'd taken over for the civilian stationmaster gave Mouradian a seat in a second-class compartment. Mouradian shrugged. He could have got a hard bench instead. "You'll go out at twenty-three minutes past nine," the lieutenant told him.

He was impressed at the precision. The train actually rattled out of the station a little past noon. That left Mouradian and the other officers in the compartment resigned but hardly surprised. Only a fool or a German would expect a schedule and reality to have much to do with each other.

They shared bread and sausages and cigarettes and vodka. They told dirty jokes. Most of them were going on leave. They sent Mouradian pitying glances when they found out he wasn't. "Siberia!" one of them said. "That's a devil of a long way from here. From everywhere, in fact."

"I serve the Soviet Union," Mouradian said one more time. Here, the stock phrase meant *I'm stuck with it.*

"Don't we all, pal? Don't we all?" said a Red Army lieutenant who seemed to have more booze than he knew what to do with. So he shared with everyone else in the compartment. It was *samogan*—moonshine—but it was good *samogan,* as good as some of the legitimate (which is to say, taxed) firewater Mouradian had drunk. The army man was genially tipsy, too. He kept coming out with one funny, outrageous crack after another.

The rest of the passengers laughed like loons. Pretty soon, they were making their own outrageous cracks . . . all of them but Stas. Maybe the Red Army man was what he seemed to be: a fellow with plenty of hooch and a quick tongue. Then again, maybe his proper arm-of-service color was NKVD blue. Maybe he was looking to build some cases.

He wouldn't build one against Anastas Mouradian. Despite what Sergei said, Mouradian didn't run his mouth all the time, or in the company of people he feared were provocateurs. And vodka didn't make him lose his caution. Some Soviet citizens ended up in the gulag for talking too much while they were drunk. But the USSR had even more drunks than camp inmates. Plastered or not, most drunks knew how to keep their big mouths shut. And if that wasn't a judgment on the Soviet system, Mouradian didn't know what would be.

BACK WHEN HE was conscripted, Luc Harcourt had never imagined he would be proud of the two brown hash marks on his sleeve that proclaimed him a corporal. All he'd wanted to do was put in his time and get the hell out. He was a normal draftee, in other words.

Things looked different when you got into a war. The nasty boys in field-gray were doing their damnedest to overrun your country—and, not too incidentally, to murder you. What seemed a waste of time when he could have been working and chasing girls in the peacetime civilian world was suddenly a rather more important business.

He was proud of commanding a machine gun, too, and that his subordinates thought he was doing a good job of it. Joinville was a small, swarthy, excitable Gascon. They called Villehardouin Tiny. In fact, he was enormous: big and strong and blond and fair. He hardly said anything, at least in French—he was much more at home in Breton. Joinville had learned some of it, and Luc was starting to pick it up. It made a good language to swear in.

Joinville carried the Hotchkiss machine gun. Tiny Villehardouin toted the tripod, which weighed a couple of kilos more. Other soldiers—just who could vary—lugged crates full of the aluminum strips of bullets that fed the Hotchkiss gun. Luc, as befitted his exalted rank, carried nothing . . . except when they couldn't dragoon any privates into hauling whatever needed hauling. Then Luc took care of it. He'd been a private not so long before. He didn't have much dignity to stand on. That was one of the reasons the other men who served the machine gun thought he made a pretty fair leader.

So did Sergeant Demange, who'd given him the slot after the poor fellow who had it became a casualty. Demange's approval was worth having, especially if he was set over you. He was a professional noncom. He'd fought in the last war, and been wounded. A Gitane always hung from one corner of his mouth. It didn't keep him from being fluently profane. The milk of human kindness ran thin and curdled in him; he was the most cynical man Luc had ever met.

"You can really handle that motherfucker," he told Luc after a skirmish in which the Hotchkiss helped send the Germans off unhappy. "You see? You're not quite the stupid, gutless asshole you were when you got sucked into the army."

"Thanks a bunch, Sergeant," Luc said, in lieu of *Why don't you suck this?* He'd come far enough in his military career that he could sass Demange every now and again. He had to pick his spots, though, or he'd end up in the hospital, and not on account of the *Boches.*

"Any time, kid." Demange grinned, showing teeth all those smokes had stained a nasty yellow-brown—if they weren't that shade to begin with. He had to know what Luc was thinking. Mere thinking couldn't land you in trouble . . . unless Demange felt like putting you there.

Artillery rumbled, off to the east. Whatever the Nazis were after, it was nothing close by. Nobody Luc knew would get hurt when those shells came down. Sometimes that seemed to be the only thing that mattered. When you were in the middle of it, war could get very tribal.

"We should have pushed them back farther," Luc said discontentedly.

"No shit!" Demange exclaimed, the cigarette jerking up and down. "We should've given 'em the bum's rush, is what we should've done."

"How come we haven't?" Luc wondered.

Demange rolled his eyes, which were always tracked with red. It made him look angry, which he was—or, if he wasn't, he could have taken his act on stage. "How come? I'll fucking tell you how come. On account of the Germans scare half our generals shitless, and a big chunk of the other half want to hop into bed with 'em so we can all fight the cocksucking Bolsheviks together."

"That'd screw things up, wouldn't it?"

"Oh, just a little!" Demange spat out the butt, which was so short the coal almost singed his lips. He immediately took out the pack again. After he got a fresh one going, he grudgingly held out the pack to Luc.

"Thanks." Luc took a smoke, then bent over and leaned close for a light. He was several centimeters taller than Demange, who intimidated the hell out of him even so. And no doubt the veteran noncom knew what he was talking about here. Every squad in the French army had a Communist or two in it. No matter what the right-wing generals—almost a redundancy—thought, the Reds wouldn't be thrilled about fighting alongside the Nazis and against the fount of Marxism-Leninism.

Luc was no Communist. He didn't want to fight alongside the Germans, either. They'd come too close to killing him too many times. They'd killed friends, and wounded others. He respected their skill; he didn't think you could go up against Germans without quickly coming to respect it. All the same, as far as he was concerned, they made better enemies than allies.

Of course, a devil of a lot of generals felt that way about Russians. Sergeant Demange was right—they'd sooner go after the USSR than Germany. That, to Luc's mind, was carrying things too far.

The wind wailed down off the North Sea. Snow swirled in it. It had been snowing in a halfhearted way all morning long. Now anything more than a few meters away vanished behind that thick white cloak. Luc shivered in his greatcoat. The wind didn't seem to know it was there.

"*Merde alors!*" he shouted over that wailing. "How are we supposed to fight a war in such filthy weather? The *Boches* could bring up an armored division, but we'd never know it till the tanks started killing us."

"It's a cunt of a winter, all right," Sergeant Demange shouted back. "To hell with me if I remember a worse one, and I go back a fuck of a lot further'n you do. But you know what else?"

"What?" Luc asked.

"Goddamn Nazis're just as screwed up as we are. Two, three, five kilometers from here, some poor cocksucking *Boche* is sitting there shivering and scared to death our tanks are right outside his trench, getting ready to squash him into a blancmange. And he hates his generals and his politicians every fucking bit as much as we hate ours."

"Oh, yeah?" Luc said, deeply skeptical. "Why would he? His generals halfway know what they're doing. More than you can say about ours."

"Why? I'll tell you why." And Demange proceeded to: "Because his generals tried to get Hitler but screwed it up, that's why. Now nobody on the other side trusts anybody else. And when Nazis start not trusting each other, people end up dead." He twisted his skinny, ratlike face into an exaggerated look of regret. "Breaks my heart, y'know?"

"I'll bet," Luc answered, which squeezed a wry chuckle out of the sergeant.

Demange lit another Gitane. He could have been in a hurricane, with winds of 250 kilometers an hour and rain coming down like Noah's flood, and he still would have got his cigarette going. Cigarettes, after all, were *important.* "I've wasted enough time on you," he said. "Now I'll go waste it with some other sorry son of a bitch."

"Love you, too, Sergeant," Luc said. Laughing—and, of course, smoking—Demange ambled away. If the cold bothered him, he gave no sign.

"What was he going on about?" Joinville asked in his nasal accent after the sergeant was gone. He distrusted sergeants on general principles, as most privates did. Being a Gascon, he perhaps distrusted them more than most. He also hated the weather more than most. Before Luc could answer, the swarthy southerner added, “Whole German army’s liable to be waiting out there.”

Luc repeated what Demange had said about the *Boches*’ fearing the French army the same way.

“He said that?” Joinville asked. Luc nodded. Joinville grunted. “Well, he’s a prick, but I guess he’s not such a dumb prick.” By the way he eyed Luc, the same applied to him. Joinville might think Luc made a good commander for the machine gun, but he didn’t like authority of any sort. He made funny noises for Tiny, translating the talk into what passed for Breton. Villehardouin nodded to show he got it. They all crouched and waited for whatever happened next. Luc wished to God winter would finally give it up. Neither God nor winter seemed to be listening.

CORPORAL ARNO BAATZ had his knickers in a twist. Awful Arno often got his knickers in a twist, but for once he wasn’t pissing and moaning about Willi Dernen. Willi approved of that. He could handle the *poilus* who were trying to punch his ticket for him. But, as somebody famous must have said at one time or another, God deliver him from his so-called friends.

Awful Arno pointed southwest, toward the closest French foxholes. “For heaven’s sake, men, be careful as long as this damned blizzard lasts,” he said. “The frog-eaters could sneak a whole army corps past our pickets in weather like this.”

He went on like that every time a blizzard tried to bury the German positions in northeastern France under untold meters of snow. In this truly godawful winter, he said it and said it and said it some more. Willi was sick and tired of listening to him. (Of course, Willi had been sick and tired of listening to Awful Arno long before this winter rolled around, but that was another story.)

A soldier named Klaus Metzger said, “Hey, Corporal, don’t you figure the Frenchies are as worried about us as we are about them?” Exactly the same thought had gone through Willi’s mind, but he knew enough to keep his mouth shut. He didn't feel like drawing Baatz's fire today—life was too short. Metzger was a new replacement, and still naive about the ways of noncoms. Well, he'd find out.

And he did. Awful Arno swelled up like a puff adder about to strike. Willi didn't think puff adders turned that unhealthy shade of purplish red, though. "Don't you tell me what to figure! *I* tell *you* what to figure!" Baatz yelled. "Have you got that?"

"Sure, sure," Metzger said with a placating little wave.

It failed to placate. Awful Arno went plum-colored: not a hue a human being was meant to have. He screamed the question again, right in Metzger's face: "*Have you got that?*"

Memories of apoplectic drill sergeants in basic training must have come back to the luckless private. He stiffened to a rigor mortis–like attention. The heels of his boots crashed together. "*Jawohl, Herr Unteroffizier!*" he said. "*Zu befehl, Herr Unteroffizier!*"

Baatz went right on screaming at him. Baatz screamed at people for the fun of it. Willi didn't think screaming at people was much fun, but he'd known plenty of noncoms who did. Awful Arno had the disease worse than most.

And he had the rank that gave him the right to be a pain in the ass. After he finally made Klaus Metzger eat enough crow to keep himself happy, he stomped off to inflict himself on soldiers farther down the trench.

Metzger stared after him. "Wow! That was fun," the new fish said. "Is he always so bad?"

Willi shook his head. "Nah. Sometimes he's worse."

Awful Arno whirled. Willi'd forgotten he had rabbit ears. "What was that, Dernen?" he shouted.

"Nothing, Corporal." Willi was ready to lie to save his own skin, or just to save himself grief.

"*Ja, ja.* Tell me another one." But Baatz must have picked up tone rather than words, because he left it there. Willi celebrated by lighting a Gitane from a pack he'd taken off a captured Frenchman.

"Can I have one of those?" Metzger asked.

"Sure. Steady your nerves now that he's done fucking you over." Willi gave him the smoke, and a light.

Metzger's cheeks hollowed as he inhaled. Then he coughed. He eyed the Gitane with sudden wary respect. "What the hell do the Frenchies put in there? Tastes like I'm smoking barbed wire."

"That's real tobacco, kiddo, is what that is," Willi answered. "We mix ours with God knows what to stretch it further. You taste the straight goods again, you're not used to it any more. You forget how strong it can be."

"Strong? I hope to shit! One of these things could win the Olympic weightlifting medal if they ever hold the Games again," Metzger said.

"Not this year," Willi said. "We're playing a different game now."

The other *Landser* nodded. "Isn't that the sad and sorry truth?"

A mortar round came down a few meters in front of the trench. Willi hated mortars as much as anything in this different game. You could hear ordinary artillery coming, often soon enough to have a good chance to duck. If the shell didn't land right on top of you, you were probably fine. But only a faint whistle betrayed a mortar bomb before it burst. And ducking after it burst was what the Tommies called tough shit.

Metzger stared when Willi threw himself flat. He didn't know what to listen for yet. Come to that, Willi wasn't consciously aware of why he hit the dirt. He only knew he needed to. The bang and the snarl and screech of fragments slicing by overhead filled in the wherefores.

A moment later, Klaus Metzger stretched out beside him. "You all right?" Willi asked. Metzger wasn't screaming, but wounds didn't always hurt right away.

"*Ja*," the other soldier answered. "Took me by surprise. How'd you know it was coming?"

Willi shrugged horizontally. "There's a little noise. You'll get the hang of it pretty quick—especially if they keep this shit up."

More French mortar bombs were falling on or near the German entrenchments. Down the trench, from the direction in which Corporal Baatz had gone, someone started squalling like a stuck shoat. Was it Awful Arno? Too much to hope for, Willi supposed.

"Be ready when they stop," he shouted in between explosions. "That's when the froggies'll hit us on foot if they're going to."

"Right," Metzger said. "With all this goddamn snow, they'll be on top of us before we know they're here."

"More fun when a girl gets on top of you before you know she's there," Willi agreed. Klaus made a face at him. Willi went on, "Why d'you think they'd pick now to try it? I just hope like hell our machine gunners aren't off playing skat or something."

"You're a funny fellow, aren't you? Funny like the cholera, I mean," Metzger said.

"That's me," Willi said, not without pride.

The mortar bombs quit dropping. Even before officers' whistles shrilled, urging the men to their posts, Willi was up on a firing step, a round chambered and a fresh clip in his Mauser. Klaus Metzger stood beside him. Both men peered out into the snowstorm.

Was that motion there, or only Willi's anxious imagination? He didn't want to wait around and discover he'd made a mistake by getting killed. Nothing up ahead belonged to his own side—he was sure of that. Shoot first and ask questions later, then, just like a Western from America.

Klaus fired a split second after he did. Did the other *Landser* think he saw something, too. Or was he simply following Willi's lead? One of their bullets—they never did know which—was rewarded with a scream of anguish. The French soldiers sneaking up under cover of the blizzard opened fire then. Willi shot back, working the Mauser's bolt as fast as he could.

Other men along the line also banged away. The *poilus* weren't close enough to throw grenades into the trenches. Another minute or two of sneaking and they would have been. Willi slapped a new magazine onto his rifle.

Then the Germans' MG-34s opened up. The froggies cried out in despair. Machine guns put so many rounds in the air, they didn't have to be either lucky or good to hit you. They just had to keep firing, keep traversing so their bullets didn't all follow the same path, and sooner or later a man out in the open would stop one. Usually sooner.

The French attack petered out. Willi didn't know how many casualties the men in the crested helmets and khaki took. The swirling snow kept him from seeing most of them and let the *poilus* bring them back in their withdrawal. He didn't think this was a cheap little affair, though.

He turned to Klaus Metzger, who'd stayed steady as a veteran through it all. "You did good," Willi said, and clapped him on the back. "Here. Take a knock of this." He offered his canteen, which held some highly unofficial applejack.

"Whew!" Klaus said after drinking. "That's got teeth, but it sure hits the spot." They grinned at each other. Willi hoped he'd just made a friend.

SERGEI YAROSLAVSKY WONDERED what to make of his new copilot and bomb-aimer. Vladimir Federov looked more like a sergeant—or a private first class—than a second lieutenant. He was short and squat and powerful, with a broad face, high cheekbones, and gray-blue eyes that showed nothing. He cropped his sandy hair close to the dome of his skull.

As an infantryman, he obviously would have been first-rate. As a flyer . . . Sergei wasn't so sure. Anastas Mouradian talked too damn much. Stas *thought* too damn much. By all appearances, that wouldn't be Federov's problem. But Mouradian was outstanding in the cockpit. Sergei feared *that* wouldn't be Federov's problem, either.

A safe question first: "What's your father's name, Comrade Lieutenant?"

"Mikhail, Comrade Pilot." By his accent, Federov came from somewhere near Moscow. Not from in the city, or Sergei didn't think so, but also not from somewhere in the backwoods.

"All right, Vladimir Mikhailovich. I'm Sergei Valentinovich." Maybe Vladimir would turn to Volodya, as Anastas had become Stas. Or maybe not. Yaroslavsky shrugged to himself. Time would tell.

"And our bomb-dropper is . . . ?" Federov asked.

"Ivan Kuchkov. He's a sergeant, a very strong man, and nothing scares him," Sergei answered. "Of course, he has his quirks, but who doesn't?"

"Nobody, I'm sure," Federov agreed politely. "What are some of his?"

"Why don't you see for yourself? You'll meet him soon." Sergei didn't want to say that the bomb-aimer made the burly Federov svelte by comparison. He also didn't want to say Sergeant Kuchkov was one of the hairiest men he'd ever seen, not just on his head but all over his body. People called Kuchkov the Chimp, but not where he could hear them do it: he had a habit of throwing men who used the nickname through windows, doors, walls. . . .

And Sergei didn't want to say that Ivan conversed almost entirely in *mat,* the Russian sublanguage of ingenious obscenity. Sergei didn't even think the bomb-dropper had been a *zek* before the draft got him. If ever a man was made for *mat,* Ivan Kuchkov was that man.

Since he didn't want to say any of those things, he asked, "How did you become a flyer?"

"Oh, the usual way," Federov replied. "I was in *Osoaviakhim* when I was a kid, and I did well enough that they kept me at it after I got called up."

Yaroslavsky nodded. His own story wasn't much different. Nominally, *Osoaviakhim* was the national organization that trained civilian pilots. The skills a civilian pilot needed, of course, were the same as the ones flying a fighter or bomber required. No one ever said that out loud, which made it no less true. The Germans had used the same dodge to slide around the Treaty of Versailles' ban on military aviation.

As Sergei had unpleasant reason to know, *Luftwaffe* pilots and bombardiers were mostly excellent. As he also had unpleasant reason to know, his own country's standards were rather lower.

"How's the plane?" Vladimir Federov asked. "This'll be the first time I've been in an SB-2."

That news disappointed Sergei without surprising him. Experienced copilots like Mouradian were getting planes of their own. Inexperienced men were getting experience instead. *And what do I get?* Yaroslavsky wondered. He silently answered his own question: *I get to be a nursemaid, that's what.*

Aloud, he said, "When we supported the Spanish Republic, people called the SB-2 the fighting bomber—it was faster in the air than any of the fighters the Fascists were using."

"Yes, I've heard that," Federov answered.

"Well, forget it," Sergei said bluntly. "It was true when we were going up against biplanes. It sure as hell isn't true any more. German Messerschmitts are like sharks against mackerel. Even the Polish PZLs will outfly us and outshoot us. What we do when fighters are around is, we run. Otherwise, it's *dos vidanya, Rodina.*"

" 'So long, Motherland,' " Federov echoed. "So when do we get bombers that *can* hold their own against enemy fighters?"

"Probably never," Sergei replied, which made his new copilot give him a long, slow blink. He explained: "Bombers bomb. Fighters shoot bombers down. Sounds obvious, doesn't it? But it's not just obvious. It's true. Bombers carry more weight, they're less maneuverable, and they have fewer guns pointing forward. We do our best to hold off fighters, but we can't play their game. We play our own game instead."

Lieutenant Federov blinked again, the same way. It was an odd, stagy expression. Sergei wondered what lay behind it. Was Federov an NKVD man building a case against him because he had the gall to point out a plain truth? Too late to worry about it now.

"Come on," Sergei said. "You want to see the plane? I'll show you."

The SB-2 sat in a revetment. A white sheet hid it from prying eyes—and from Nazi reconnaissance aircraft. In the shadow cast by the sheet, a mechanic worked on the starboard engine. He sketched a salute for Sergei and gave Vladimir Federov a curious look: word that Mouradian had been transferred hadn't got to everybody.

Ivan Kuchkov was sitting in the pilot's seat when Sergei led Federov into the cockpit. The two men who didn't know each other stared. "Who are you?" Federov asked, at the same time as Kuchkov belligerently demanded, "Who the fuck are you?"

"That should be 'Who the fuck are you, sir?' " Sergei said, and made the introductions. The Chimp looked at Federov as if to say Red Air Force standards were lower than he'd thought. The new copilot looked at Kuchkov as if to say he hadn't expected to see one like this outside of a zoo. As meetings went, it wasn't a success. Sergei could see that right off the bat.

Federov didn't say anything much. Kuchkov muttered profanely under his breath, but not far enough under it. Sergei, and no doubt the new officer as well, learned that he thought Federov looked like a jerk and talked like a jerkoff. In point of fact, the Chimp expressed himself more frankly.

He expressed himself so frankly that Sergei leaned close to him. "Come on, Ivan," he said quietly. "You can't talk about a new crewmate like that."

"Why the fuck not?" Ivan returned, still not bothering to hold his voice down. "We're supposed to fly with that whistleass peckerhead? My dick we are! He'll screw us over some kind of way—you wait and see."

"How can you tell?" Sergei asked, clinically curious.

"*Bozhemoi!* Just look at the motherfucker. Fuck me in the mouth if he's not on the lam for something or other."

Sergei didn't think Vladimir Federov looked like a robber one jump in front of the law. To him, the new crewman seemed more like a would-be tough guy than the genuine article. Trying to explain that to Ivan would be pointless. It would also be hopeless, because the Chimp was no more inclined to listen than a veritable anthropoid would have been.

Disastrous introduction or not, they flew their first mission together three days later. They—and their squadron of SB-2s—bombed the train station in Bialystok to keep the Fascists from moving men and matériel through it. Federov seemed able to handle the instruments and calculations a bomb-aimer had to use. Sergei wasn't sure the plane's bombs hit the station, but they came as close as anyone else's.

After the SB-2 came back to the airstrip, though, Ivan Kuchkov said, "See? I told you he was a useless cocksucker." Sergei sighed. Weren't the Nazis enough trouble? Plainly, Ivan didn't think so.

Chapter 4

Sarah Goldman and her mother and father stood in a long line outside the Münster *Rathaus.* Everybody in the line—graybeards, younger adults, children, babies—was Jewish. Everyone except the babies (exempt by the tender mercy of the National Socialist German Workers' Party) wore on his or her clothes a prominently displayed six-pointed yellow star with *Jude* imprinted on it in big, black, Hebraic-style letters.

The Nazis had figured out a brand-new way to make life miserable for Jewish residents in Germany. (Jews were no longer citizens of the Third *Reich.*) They all had to get new identity cards. And on each of those cards would be a new first name branding its possessor as a Jew—as if everything else the *Reich* had done were somehow inadequate.

From now on, her father, Samuel Goldman, would legally become Moses Samuel Goldman. All Jewish men in Germany would have Moses grafted on in front of whatever their first name happened to be. All Jewish women would have a new first name affixed in front of their own, too. For them, it was . . . Sarah.

"No fair," Sarah said as the queue slowly advanced. "They shouldn't need to bother with me. My card's already fine. I could have stayed home and twiddled my thumbs instead of coming with you and—"

"Twiddling your thumbs here," Father finished for her. "Even if you've already got the name the government aims to give you, it's just as well you came along. The new card will probably be different from the old one some other way, too. The people who run things will be able to see who's, God forbid, using an old ID card, and all the people who are will catch it."

He'd spent many years in the classroom and lecture hall, passing on his knowledge of ancient Greece and especially Rome. Like an actor, he could put anything he wanted into his voice. A stranger walking by would be sure he approved of all the moves the government made. So would an informer. Sarah knew better. So did her mother. Neither Sarah nor Hanna Goldman said anything, though. Why stir up more trouble? Didn't Jews in Germany already have plenty?

Although a bright sun shone down from a blue sky, it was still bitterly cold. Sarah couldn't remember a winter that had dug its claws in deeper or clung to Germany, to all of Europe, harder. Neither could Father, who'd spent three winters in the trenches during the last war. That he was a wounded, decorated veteran made things a little easier for the Goldmans than they were for most German Jews. Not much, but a little. When you weren't in such good shape, you took what you could get.

Naturally, the Jews went into the city hall by a side entrance. If that line had snaked up the stairs to the main doorway, Jews might have—gasp!—inconvenienced Aryans. In the Third *Reich,* what could be worse? Nothing either Sarah or Nazi officials could think of.

Portraits of Hitler, Göring, Goebbels, and other Nazi *Bonzen* hung on the walls of the hallway along which the Jews had to go. Maybe it was Sarah's imagination, but the photographs seemed to be glowering at the Chosen People. Maybe it was her imagination, but she didn't think so.

When she whispered her thought to Father, he snorted softly and whispered back: "Chosen People, nothing. We're the Singled-Out People, is what we are."

"Yes!" Sarah exclaimed. The phrase fit much too well. God had singled out the Jews all those years ago, and now the Nazis were doing it instead. Didn't that mean the Nazis had assumed the mantle of divinity? If you asked them, they would tell you yes.

Along with the National Socialists' icons hung portraits of the local Party leaders, men nobody outside of Münster would recognize. They looked just as peevish as the Nazi big shots who ordered much of Europe around from Berlin. Maybe they were less ambitious, maybe only less lucky. Some of them seemed quite ready to start telling Czechs and Danes and Dutchmen what to do.

Down the hallway swept a strange apparition: the Bishop of Münster, in full ecclesiastical regalia: a uniform far older and, to Sarah's eyes, far more impressive than the quasi-military garb that so delighted the Nazis. He stopped and asked one of the Jews, "What are you poor, unhappy people doing here?"

The man explained. Even speaking politely to a Jew could land someone in trouble. But Clemens August von Galen was already in trouble with the authorities for having the nerve to complain about the way they tried to rein in the Catholic Church in Germany. If they wanted to toss him into a concentration camp, they didn't need to blame him for being friendly to Jews.

He rolled his eyes now at the answer he got. "This is a disgrace," he said, not bothering to lower his voice. "They aren't content with harassing you every other way they can think of? Now they have to rob you of your names, too?"

No one was brave enough to reply to him after that. Nazi functionaries clumped up and down the corridor in their shiny jackboots. Anything a Jew said would be noted and held against him.

"Disgraceful," the Bishop of Münster said again. Robes swirling around him, he strode away. Sarah was far from the only Jew who stared admiringly after him. You couldn't get in trouble for just looking. She didn't think you could, anyhow.

Her father leaned close and whispered in her ear: "If a few hundred important people had spoken up like that when things were starting out, none of this *Schweinerei* would have happened. None of it *could* have happened."

"But they didn't," Sarah answered.

"I know," said Samuel Goldman—former professor of ancient history and classics, now a road-gang laborer. No wonder he sounded bleak. Things *were* bleak for the Jews of Münster, as they were for Jews all over Germany.

Typewriters clattered up ahead as clerks made out the new identity cards. In due course, the Goldmans reached the front of the line. They duly surrendered their old cards. The new blanks, Sarah saw, had JEW printed on them in much bigger letters than the old ones had used.

"For all official purposes, you are now Moses Samuel Goldman," their clerk said as he handed Father his new card.

"I understand," Father answered. That was safe enough. He didn't have to tell the clerk whether he agreed or approved. But he couldn't very well fail to understand.

Mother got hers next. "For all official purposes, you are now Sarah Hanna Goldman," the clerk droned.

She also said, "I understand."

Then it was Sarah's turn. The clerk started to type, but hesitated. He got up from behind the desk and went over to talk with an older man a couple of desks away. Sarah couldn't hear what they said. Her clerk shrugged and came back. He typed again, this time with assurance: someone had told him what to do, and he was doing it.

Handing Sarah her new card, he intoned, "For all official purposes, you are now Sarah Sarah Goldman."

"What? That's silly!" she blurted.

"That is what regulations require in your circumstances. I have verified it with *Herr* Memminger, my supervisor." The clerk nodded toward the older man. He sounded as confident as a Catholic who'd just consulted with Bishop von Galen on a subtle theological point.

"It's still silly," Sarah said.

"If you feel strongly enough about the matter, you may make a formal complaint to the Office for Jewish Affairs in Berlin," the clerk said with no irony Sarah could hear.

She gulped. "Never mind," she said quickly. The last thing—the very last thing—she wanted was to draw the notice of the Office for Jewish Affairs. No matter how bad things were, they could always get worse.

"Very well," the clerk said. "Goldmans, is everything on your cards now correct? At this time, there is no fee for adjusting them. If you find an error later and return to have it changed, the law requires a ten-Reichsmark charge."

Did the law require the same thing for Aryans? It might. Governments were greedy whenever they found the chance. Sarah checked the card. Except for being ridiculous, it was accurate. So were her parents'. They all got out of there as fast as they could. Sarah, Sarah . . . When they were smaller, her brother would have turned it into a mocking chant. Even the Office for Jewish Affairs didn't know what had happened to Saul. Sarah did, but she would never, ever tell.

PETE McGILL WAS full of what a philosopher might have called existential despair. Pete was no philosopher. He was a hard-faced, raspy-voiced Marine corporal, one of the relatively small garrison charged with protecting the American consulate in Shanghai. Back in the days when the Marines, like similar forces from the European powers, protected their country's interests against Chinese mobs, the arrangement had been reasonable enough. (The Chinese didn't think so, but the next time any of the powers worried about what the Chinese thought would be the first.)

Things were different now, though. Like Peking (where Pete had served before coming closer to the coast, to a city where evacuation by sea was possible), Shanghai lay under Japanese occupation. The Japs had divisions' worth of infantry near the two big cities. The Western powers' companies of troops stayed on only because Japan didn't feel like cleaning them out. Existing on Japanese sufferance rubbed Pete—and the rest of the leathernecks—the wrong way.

But that was only an insult, an accident of geopolitics. It was plenty to piss Pete off. Existential despair, though? No way in hell. What drove him there was falling head over heels for a White Russian taxi dancer named Vera. She was a blonde. She was built. She was, in his admittedly biased opinion, drop-dead gorgeous. She screwed like there was no tomorrow. She was even smart. And, in spite of that last, she gave every appearance of having fallen head over heels for Pete.

It was the kind of romance officers went out of their way to warn you against. Blah, blah, blah till they were as blue in the face as a USMC dress uniform. A lot of the time, of course, a guy fell for a girl simply because he was horny. Or a girl looked at a guy and saw a meal ticket, a sugar daddy, maybe even somebody who could get her to the States.

Vera wasn't like that—Pete was sure of it. Oh, he'd bought her presents. But so what? In China, even a Marine corporal's miserable pay stretched as if rubberized. And he had looked into what it would take for her to go back to America with him. That was because he loved her and wanted to stay with her forever, though, not because she'd pushed him into it. He was as sure of that as he was of his own name.

By what the Marine lieutenant with whom he'd spoken told him, he had two chances of getting Vera across the Pacific: slim and none. And that was what really left him floundering in the slough of despond.

Being sloppy drunk sure didn't help. He sat in a bar not far from the consulate, one of a long procession of whiskey-and-sodas in front of him. The dive was called the Globe and Anchor. As its name implied, it catered to Marines. On the barstool next to him sat another leatherneck, a bruiser named Herman Szulc. He was a Polack with a Slavic spelling for his German name, which was pronounced *Schultz.*

Pete poured out his tale of woe. It wasn't as if Szulc hadn't heard it before. He had. But whiskey and loneliness made Pete talk—and talk and talk and talk. "I'll never get her back to New York City," he mourned, that being where he was born and raised and did such sketchy growing up as he'd done before the Corps got its hands on him. "Never!"

"Not if you play by the rules, anyway, sounds like." Szulc paid no more attention to the rules than he had to. If he weren't doing time in the Marines, he probably would be serving it in the state pen.

Pete was much more inclined to stay on the up-and-up. He had been, anyhow, till Vera discombobulated all his warning circuits. "How do you get somebody from China to New York if you don't play straight?" he asked. Before Herman could answer, he drained his latest whiskey-and-soda and waved to the bartender for yet another refill.

"Coming right up, chief!" the barman said in excellent English. If he watered his drinks more as his customers got drunker, well, hey, it was a tough old world and he had a family to support. He also wanted to hear how to get from Shanghai to New York City—or anywhere else in the USA—without losing sleep over all the tiresome formalities of immigration.

"You gotta know who to pay off," Szulc explained.

"Hey, this is China, man. Now tell me something I didn't know," Pete said. He supposed every country ran on cash and was lubed by the smooth slipperiness of greased palms. Chinamen were a lot more blatant about it than Americans, though. If you didn't fork over here, you could forget about anything you wanted. But if you played ball the Chinese way, you rapidly discovered all things were possible.

"Yeah, it's China. But you won't just be paying off Chinks," Szulc said. "You gotta find out which immigration people will look the other way when a gal without the right paperwork gets on a ship. Your girlfriend's white, anyway. If you'd fallen for one of those slanty-eyed broads, you'd be shit outa luck. Nobody'd put himself out on a limb for you then."

"Tell me about it," McGill said. America wanted a square deal for Chinamen in China. But God forbid if any Chinamen—or slanty-eyed broads, as Szulc put it—or Japs wanted to sully the US of A. We sure didn't want any more of them there. We didn't like the ones we already had.

That wasn't a problem with Vera, though. She was white enough to satisfy—hell, to thrill—a cross-burner in a sheet. *So I caught a break for a change,* Pete thought. *Hot damn! That makes one.*

"Do you know who the right guys to pay off are?" he asked.

"Couple of 'em," Herman Szulc answered smugly. "An English colonel who drinks too fuckin' much and this little old wizened-up Portugee who can maybe slide her out through Macao. You know what they say about that place—you can sneak anybody and anything through there, long as you know who to keep happy."

"How much will it cost me?" Pete said. "I ain't rich or nothing, you know."

"Like I am," Szulc said, rolling his eyes. He named a figure. Pete flinched. The guy behind the bar, who was listening avidly, too, didn't. How many silver Mex dollars did he have socked away? That many and then some.

Pete did more than flinch. He said, "I'm not gonna rob a bank for you, Herman."

"How much loot does your lady-love have?" Szulc returned.

"I'm not gonna take from her, neither," Pete said. If Vera paid her own way to the States, how long would she remember a Marine who helped her make connections? No matter how head over heels Pete was, he wasn't—quite—blind.

"Okay, okay. Don't get your tits in a wringer," Herman said. "I—"

"Wait a sec." There were other ways in which Pete wasn't blind, too. "How much would it be if you didn't glom on to a big cut from the fee?"

The other Marine looked affronted. "Look, ace, I ain't in this for my health. You don't want to keep me sweet, you can goddamn well go find these other guys for yourself."

An English colonel. An old, skinny, wrinkled Portuguese—assuming Szulc wasn't lying about the details, which wasn't what you'd call a lead-pipe cinch. "I didn't say don't take anything," Pete replied, backtracking a little. "But you screw the guys you may have to go to war with, will you trust 'em at your back?" Shrewdly, he added, "I bet I'm not the only one who wants to know shit like this."

"I already figured a discount into what I told you," Szulc whined.

"Swell. Now figure another one. I can go down to the waterfront, too," Pete said.

Herman Szulc snorted. "You try it, you'll end up wearing cement overshoes. You're a nice guy, Pete. You know what the Shanghai waterfront does with nice guys? Trust me, you don't want to find out."

"I can take care of myself." Pete believed it.

Szulc, by contrast, giggled. So did the bartender, though right away he tried to pretend he hadn't. His reaction did more to persuade Pete he was talking nonsense than Szulc's did. And Herman came down—some. They drank and haggled, haggled and drank. The guy behind the bar soaked in every word.

THEO HOSSBACH GATHERED with the rest of the panzer crewmen in his company to hear the word come down from on high. It came down through Captain Werner Schellenberg, the company CO. He read from a piece of paper that he must have got from regimental HQ: "To ensure continued loyalty amidst the pressures of our ruthless war against Bolshevism and international Jewry, we are going to introduce National Socialist Leadership Officers into the command structure. They will give the troops support in creating and maintaining a proper National Socialist worldview, and will see to it that all orders issued by the regular officer corps are in complete accord with National Socialist doctrines and ways of thought. This change in the command structure is to be implemented immediately." He looked out at the men he led. "Questions?"

Several hands shot into the air. Had Theo been a man who asked out loud the questions that formed in his head, his would have been one of them. Since he wasn't, he kept his hand down. So did Adalbert Stoss, though his expression was eloquent.

Captain Schellenberg pointed to one of the men. "Go ahead, Rudi."

"Sir, how are these National Socialist Waddayacallems different from the Ivans' political commissars?"

That would also have been the first question Theo asked. By the way the rest of the panzer crewmen nodded, it was uppermost in their minds, too. Everyone eyed the company commander. What would he say? What *could* he say?

"I'll tell you how they're different, boys. They're ours, that's how," Schellenberg answered.

That was blunt enough and then some. But it raised as many questions as it answered—probably more. "What do we need 'em for?" Rudi demanded, which was certainly one of those questions. "Are people in Berlin saying we've gotta read *Mein Kampf* before we plan an ambush? Soldiering doesn't work that way."

There was an understatement. Theo had looked at *Mein Kampf.* He admired Hitler for making Germany a respected nation once more. Looking at the *Führer's* book did nothing to increase his admiration. It struck him as rubbish—energetic, passionate, sometimes clever rubbish, but rubbish all the same.

Schellenberg chose his words with obvious care: "We need men who are loyal to the state and loyal to the government. If this is how we get them, I'm for it. Don't forget, we had generals trying to overthrow the government in the middle of a war. How can we win when something like that happens?"

Maybe the government shouldn't have started the war in the first place, Theo thought. But Schellenberg had a point. Nothing good would happen to the *Reich* if the government were toppled at a time like this. The war effort would surely have gone straight down the WC.

Then again, nothing good would happen to Germany if she lost the war Hitler had started, either.

"Other questions?" Captain Schellenberg asked. . . . "What is it, Bruno?"

"Sir, are these Leadership Officers"—Bruno spoke the name with obvious distaste—"going to squeal on us if we say anything they don't happen to like? *You* know how soldiers go on. If we can't blow off steam every once in a while, life's hardly worth living."

Several other men nodded, Theo and Adi and Hermann Witt among them. Bruno had it right. Soldiers *would* call their superiors and their civilian leaders a pack of idiots. Sensible officers paid no attention to most of that kind of talk. But what were the odds a National Socialist Leadership Officer would turn out to be sensible? Long, mighty long. The clumsy title seemed made to draw fanatics, people who know everything there was to know about Nazi doctrine but not a goddamn thing about panzers or rations or anything else that really mattered.

"They're not here to be rats," Schellenberg said firmly. "Honest to God, they're not. The government wants the *Wehrmacht* to follow its lead, that's all. So when we do have one of these fellows assigned to us, give him a chance, all right?"

Nobody said no, not out loud. Nobody in Theo's crew complained where he could hear it. Were he a more outgoing sort, he might well have complained himself. But keeping his mouth shut was his natural style.

He wasn't at all sure about Sergeant Witt's politics. The panzer commander did his job. He did it well: he was smart and brave. But, if he hated Hitler and everything the Nazis stood for, he had the sense not to shout it from the turret on the Panzer II. By the same token, if he pawed the ground and whinnied every time he heard the *Horst Wessel Lied,* he didn't advertise that, either.

Theo thought Adi Stoss had reason not to want a National Socialist Leadership Officer anywhere within a hundred kilometers of him. Then again, Adi also had reason not to discuss his reasons with anybody else.

Unless, of course, Theo was all wet. The radioman chuckled, very softly, to himself. *Me, all wet?* he thought. *Impossible! Couldn't happen! I'm much too shrewd to make dumb mistakes.*

The Leadership Officer got to the company after a nasty skirmish with some Soviet officer. Bruno went back to an aid station swathed in bandages. Scuttlebutt was, he might not keep his arm. Neither of his crewmates was even that lucky. The panzer men weren't in the mood to welcome Lieutenant Horst Ostrowski with open arms.

He didn't look like a wild-eyed fanatic. He wore an Iron Cross Second Class and a wound badge—he hadn't been commanding a desk in Dresden or something before he got this assignment. He talked about the need to beat the Russians so Central Asia didn't grab a foothold in Central Europe.

Everything he said seemed harmless enough. All the same, Theo wished he *were* back at that desk in Dresden, or whatever his previous assignment had been. Again, the radioman didn't think he was anywhere close to the only guy with the same wish.

BACK IN THE TRENCHES in front of Madrid, Chaim Weinberg didn't know whether to laugh or to cry. He did know he ought to be pissed off, and he was. He had a good notion of who'd screwed him, and he hadn't even got kissed. That pissed him off, too. La Martellita had a blowjob mouth if ever there was one—to look at, anyway. He'd never got to feel it on John Henry. Not against his lips, either, for that matter. She couldn't stand him, so she'd put him back where he started.

Only a handful of old sweats from the States were left in the Abe Lincolns. Spaniards filled out the ranks, as they did in all the International Brigades these days. The surviving Americans thought his return was the funniest thing that had happened lately.

"Watsamatter wit' you, boychik?" said another New Yorker, a Jew who went by the name of Izzy. "You had it soft in Madrid. How'd you manage to screw it up this time?"

Chaim didn't like that *this time,* not even slightly. "Talent," he said, and tried to let it go at that.

No such luck. Izzy was a born agitator. He was a New York Jew in the Abraham Lincoln Brigade—of course he was a born agitator. "What did you go and do?" he asked, eyeing Chaim shrewdly. "Get somebody important mad at you? Can't get away with that, boychik, not even in the classless society you can't."

"Oh, fuck off," Chaim answered. Izzy laughed like a loon. Chaim almost hauled off and belted him. He would have, if that hadn't been the same as admitting the other guy was right.

Izzy wasn't the only veteran who thought he was the most comical—and the dumbest—thing on two legs. He couldn't fight all of them, not if he wanted to live to do anything else. He didn't know what all he wanted to do later on, but one thing seemed glaringly obvious. He wanted to get an apology from La Martellita. If he couldn't get an apology, a blowjob would do just as well. Maybe better.

First he had to live long enough to collect one or the other (even both, if he got really lucky). He hadn't got sent to the trenches just because La Martellita put in a bad word somewhere. He hoped like hell he hadn't, anyhow. The Republic was trying to push the Nationalists away from the capital. Whenever the Republic tried something that took hard fighting, in went the International Brigades. That had been true ever since the Internationals got to Spain.

And, though Spaniards filled out the Brigades' ranks these days, it remained true even now. The Americans and Englishmen and Poles and Germans and Italians and Hungarians and God knew what all else who remained gave the International Brigades experience and *esprit de corps* no purely Spanish outfit could match. The foreign volunteers had and passed on experience the Spaniards couldn't match, too. Germans who hated Adolf Hitler's guts owned just as much professional expertise as the ones who fought in the *Legion Kondor.*

Naturally, Marshal Sanjurjo's men understood all that as well as the Republicans. Naturally, the Nationalists kept their own élite troops opposite the Internationals' positions. Naturally, any advance against those Fascist soldiers was a lot tougher than it would have been against the usual odds and sods who filled out the ranks on both sides.

You outflanked a bunch of odds and sods, they either ran away or surrendered. Raw troops were as sensitive about their flanks as so many ticklish virgins. You outflanked a bunch of men who knew what they were doing and really meant it, and they hunkered down, dug their foxholes deeper, turned their machine gun your way if they had one, and defied you to winkle them out. Doing it wasn't much fun.

"*¡Chinga tu madre!*" one of Sanjurjo's finest shouted back when a man from the Abe Lincolns yelled that he should give up. A sharp burst of fire followed the obscenity: this gang of Nationalists did have a machine gun.

Some of the bullets snapped by overhead much too close for comfort. "Boy, I wish I was takin' hot dogs outa boilin' water back at Coney Island," Izzy said.

"Yeah, well, nobody held a gun to your head and made you get on a boat," Chaim answered. "Now that I think about it, me, neither."

"*¿Qué dices?*" asked one of the Spaniards who plumped out the Abe Lincolns. Chaim thought he went by Paco, but wasn't quite sure. He'd never set eyes on the guy till he came back to the trenches.

"What's he say?" Izzy asked. He'd been in Spain as long as Chaim. He could cuss some in Spanish, but that was about it.

"He said, 'What did you say?' " Chaim answered. He did some more explaining, in both English and Spanish. Then he added, "I wish we had a mortar handy. That'd make those fuckers *and* their machine gun say uncle."

"*¿Qué dices?*" Paco asked again. Chaim repeated himself in the Spaniard's language. Then he had to explain the explanation to Izzy.

Paco spoke excitedly: "But we do have one!" He hurried away, staying low—he was learning.

"Where's he going?" Izzy said. "Is he running off, the little son of a—?"

"No, no," Chaim broke in. "He said we do have a mortar. Since when?"

"I dunno." Izzy shrugged. "I don't remember if the French Communist Party sent it to us or we captured it off the Nationalists."

If the Communist Party of the United States stashed a mortar and some bombs at its headquarters in New York City, J. Edgar Hoover and his G-men would land on it in hobnailed boots, close it down, and send the leading American Reds to jail for about a million years. Things were different in Europe. Political parties of the left and the right took themselves a lot more seriously over here. Chaim, who also took politics seriously (if he didn't, what was he doing in Spain?), leaned that way himself.

Paco not only knew the Abe Lincolns had a stovepipe, he knew where the critter was hiding. Maybe ten minutes later, mortar rounds started stalking the Nationalist diehards. The first one landed so far short, it was scarier than the enemy machine gun. But succeeding bombs walked toward and then came down on the battered foxholes Sanjurjo's men were holding.

All the same, the machine gun opened up when the Abe Lincolns moved forward. The mortar crew must have been watching, perhaps through field glasses. More bombs landed on the Nationalists. Now the nasty little piece of field artillery had the range. The new shells didn't scare the piss out of the guys they were supposed to help.

"Come on!" Chaim scrambled out of his own trench and ran toward the enemy line. "Follow me!"

The rest of the men in the assault party *did* follow him. He would have ended up slightly dead (or, sad to say, more than slightly) if they hadn't. The mortar hadn't put all the Nationalists out of action. Bombardments never did, however much you wished they would. A couple of men popped up with rifles. Shots from the oncoming Abe Lincolns made them fire wildly, though. And when one of Sanjurjo's finest tried to point the machine gun at the charging Republicans, Chaim shot him in the face. He fell back with a wild, despairing scream. It had to be the best—or the luckiest—shot from the hip Chaim had ever made.

"*¡Viva la Republica!*" Chaim yelled as he jumped after the would-be machine gunner.

"*¡Chinga la Republica!*" a stubborn Nationalist shouted back, raising a Lebel—a French rifle that had been outdated at the start of the last war—to his shoulder.

Chaim shot him, too. The old-fashioned rifle fell from his hands. It went off when it hit the ground, but the bullet buried itself in the dirt. Other Abe Lincolns were cleaning out the rest of the men who'd held them up.

A couple of Nationalists did try to surrender then. The Abe Lincolns disposed of them in a hurry. The new Spaniards who filled out the force were quicker to shoot than the remaining Americans. This wasn't about fighting Fascism to them. This was about getting rid of people who'd probably done horrible things to their loved ones. Chaim didn't know why they called a war inside one country a civil war. It was anything but.

None of the Americans said anything about the shootings to their Spanish comrades. It wasn't as if Sanjurjo's men didn't do the same thing. The machine gun also turned out to be surplus from the last war: a water-cooled German Maxim. Once in position, it was as good as any more modern weapon. Getting it there, however, was less than half the fun. It was more portable than an anvil, but only slightly. And the mount from which it fired was massive enough to let somebody preach a sermon on it.

Chaim said as much to Izzy, and got the groan he deserved. When he tried to translate the joke for one of the Spaniards, he discovered it worked in his language but not in theirs.

There were other things to worry about. Going on with the advance, for instance. He hadn't had any particular rank when this attack started. He still didn't, come to that. But both Americans and Spaniards seemed to expect him to tell them what to do next. He'd given an order before. It had worked. Not so surprising, then, that they expected more of the same.

He wanted to be a de facto officer the way he wanted a second head. His new order consisted of, "Well, let's go, goddammit."

They went. They drove everything before them. The Nationalists fled all the way to Valladolid, eighty miles west of Madrid. Marshal Sanjurjo was so dismayed, he hopped in a plane and flew back to Portugal. The Fascist cause in Spain collapsed. In Rome, Mussolini ground his teeth in fury. In Berlin, so did Hitler. Because of Chaim's brilliant command, the progressive powers won the war.

Well . . . no. It wasn't like that. Easier to dream of La Martellita going down on him than to look for so much from one grudged order. But the Abe Lincolns did capture that machine gun and go on to gain several hundred more meters of ground. Somebody must have put in a good word for Chaim, because a Republican major general (who wore overalls like a factory worker—and like La Martellita, though he didn't fill them out so well) came up to the new front line, shook his hand, and kissed him on both cheeks.

The major general had been eating garlic. "You did some political indoctrination in the city, *sí*?" he asked. Chaim admitted it. "Why did you leave that post?" the officer inquired. Chaim only shrugged. Taking that for modesty, the general said, "Would you like to go back?" Chaim nodded, hoping he didn't seem too eager. La Martellita would be furious. Aww—wasn't that too bad?

Chapter 5

The airport outside Stockholm. A tall, blond Swedish foreign-ministry official stamping her passport. "I don't believe this," Peggy Druce said dazedly. "It can't be true."

"If you like, Madame, I will pinch you." The official spoke almost perfect English. If he had a slight singsong Scandinavian accent, so did plenty of people from Minneapolis.

"But . . . But . . ." Only a few days before, Peggy had been thinking about Warsaw as a stepping stone to Hungary and, eventually, to Romania or Greece. Even though one of their staff members had suggested it, everybody at the American embassy was sure she was nuts for wanting to try it. That didn't mean the people there weren't helping her. Maybe they didn't care if she got blown up. Maybe they were glad to send her on her way even if the odds of that were pretty good. She didn't endear herself to everyone, not if people stood in the way of what she wanted. More than a few Nazis would have agreed with the embassy personnel about that.

Now, though, a big, beautiful Swissair DC-3 sat on the runway outside the terminal. It was going to fly from Stockholm to London, and she had a seat on it. The foreign-ministry official's gaze clouded, ever so slightly. "Now that Denmark and southern Norway are no longer considered a war zone, air traffic by neutrals has resumed," the man said, no expression in his voice or on his face.

Now that the Germans have sat on the Danes and Norwegians and driven the English and French way the hell up into the frozen north. That was what he meant. How did he feel about it? Swedes, Norwegians, and Danes might as well have been brothers. This fellow probably wasn't happy about being the only brother left free and independent. Then again, Sweden did a lot of business with Germany. Quite a few Swedes admired Hitler—one of Peggy's more alarming discoveries in what otherwise seemed a civilized country. So she didn't ask the official what he thought of the foreign situation. He could think whatever he damn well pleased. She was getting out of here. . . .

Wasn't she? He handed back her passport. Nervously, she asked, "Is there anything else?"

"No, Madame. May you have a safe and pleasant journey." He opened the door that led out from the terminal. Freezing air rushed in. Would winter *never* give up? He continued, "You are still very early, but you may board the airplane if you wish."

"Yippee!" Peggy said, and charged toward the American-built airliner. There was an expression the fluent diplomat likely hadn't heard before. Or did they show cowboy movies here? The mere idea was plenty to set Peggy giggling.

Speaking of accents, she could barely follow the Swiss steward's German when he asked for her ticket and passport. Seeing that he was talking to an American, though, he switched to pretty good English: "Yes, everything seems to be in order. You may be seated. We will take off in about an hour."

"You bet I'll be seated, Charlie!" Peggy said. The steward blinked. She didn't care. The DC-3 had two seats on one side of the aisle and one on the other. Peggy discovered hers was on the single side. She didn't care.

More passengers boarded, speaking several different languages. She recognized English, Swedish, French, and the Swiss dialect of German.

And two young Oriental men took the pair of seats across from her and jabbered at each other. Japanese? Chinese? Something else altogether? There she had no idea. When the steward tried German on them, they answered readily enough.

The steward closed the door and dogged it tight. The twin engines rumbled to life. The DC-3's cabin was soundproofed, but they were noisy even so. They got noisier, too, as the airliner sped down the runway and took off. Clunking noises from under the fuselage were the landing gear retracting. The wheels didn't stay down through the whole flight. A DC-3 was *modern.*

Flying through clouds was bumpy. It also made looking out the window a waste of time. She had a copy of *Gone with the Wind* a secretary at the embassy had given her. She'd read it back in the States, of course, but it was fine for a flight—nice and thick. They'd made a movie of it while she was stuck in Europe! That, she wanted to see. Would anybody still be running it by the time she got home?

Bump, bump . . . *bump.* She was glad she wasn't afraid of flying. She was also glad she had a strong stomach. If you got seasick, you could also get airsick, especially when the plane bounced all over the sky like this. Somebody noisily lost whatever he'd eaten before takeoff. He must have used the bag, because the stink wasn't bad.

Food on the plane proved as good as what Peggy'd had on dining cars in trains. Drinks flowed freely. If you needed not to think about flying, or about the war, they would lubricate your brain.

And then, out of nowhere, the lean shark shape of a Messerschmitt fighter all but filled Peggy's window. "*Mon Dieu!*" a French speaker said. "*Merde alors!*" another added. The 109 could have hacked the airliner out of the sky with the greatest of ease. Instead, the fighter pilot waved, waggled his wings, and zoomed away.

"This is the captain speaking." A voice came out of the DC-3's intercom, first in German, then in French, and finally in English. "The plane was confirming that we are who we claim to be. We may, I am told, expect the same reception as we near Great Britain."

Sure enough, a Hurricane came out and looked them over. It seemed less deadly than the Messerschmitt, though by all accounts it was a match for the German fighter—one of the few planes that were.

As the 109's pilot had before, the Englishman in the cockpit waved when he was satisfied and flew off.

That snow-dappled brown and green ahead—that was England. Tears filled Peggy's eyes. She'd made it! Well, almost. She still had to cross the Atlantic without getting torpedoed. If you were going to worry about every little thing . . .

More clunks from below said the wheels were going down again. The plane descended toward London. Peggy looked for bomb craters. The Nazis had boasted about blasting the British capital back to the stone age. One more lie from Goebbels, because she saw little damage.

And then she was down. The DC-3 came in with hardly a bounce. She felt like yelling *Yippee!* again, but she didn't. No point to making all the other people on the plane sure she was a lunatic. If she was, she could claim she was out of her mind with joy. At last—at sweet last!—she'd got to a place from which she could go straight to the States. She didn't care if she booked the fastest liner or some wallowing scow. She'd still get there.

Barring U-boats, of course. The Nazis still claimed England had sunk the *Athenia* to enrage America and drag her into the war. Maybe they believed that in Germany. Peggy didn't think it was good for anything but making flowers grow.

But the odds were still with her. Most ships traveling between England and the USA got where they were going. She really did figure hers would, too. She had every intention of taking the chance.

Stuffing *Gone with the Wind* into her purse, she stood up and headed back toward the door at the left rear of the cabin. Down a few steps after that, and then her own personal feet touched English soil. That, too, seemed just about good enough for a *Yippee!* Again, though, she refrained. Herb would have admired her restraint.

Herb! My God! She'd have to get used to having a husband around again. And she was going to have to keep her big mouth shut forever about a drunken night in Berlin. She'd guessed Constantine Jenkins was a fairy. Wrong! So wrong!

After she got her suitcase, she had to clear customs. The inspector frowned at all the stamps that bore the German eagle and swastika. "You've had a busy time of it, what?" he said.

"Buddy, you don't know the half of it!" Peggy exclaimed.

Something in her voice brought a thin smile out on his face—the only kind he had, she suspected. "I daresay I ought to give you to the matrons for a strip search and slit the lining of your bag here," he remarked. "I ought to, but I shan't." He plied his rubber stamp with might and main. "Welcome to the United Kingdom, Mrs. Druce. Welcome to freedom."

"Freedom!" Peggy echoed dreamily. "I remember that—I think." The customs inspector laughed, for all the world as if she were joking.

NOW THAT ALISTAIR Walsh had got to know him, Dr. Murdoch turned out to be a good source of information. "They're going to extract us," he told Walsh one freezing night—as if Namsos came equipped with any other kind. "Sounds like dentistry, eh?"

Walsh's shiver had nothing to do with the weather. He remembered—painfully remembered—wisdom teeth with which he'd parted company. Army dentists had never heard of the Geneva Convention. Turn them loose on the Fritzes and they'd likely win the war in a fortnight.

"Have you got another fag on you?" the staff sergeant asked. That was the other thing Murdoch was good for: the man was a tobacco magnet. In a place like this, where everything was always in short supply, that made him someone to reckon with. Sure enough, he handed Walsh a packet. Walsh took one—what he'd asked for—and gave it back. He didn't want the sawbones to think he was greedy. After a long, reverent drag, he asked, "Extracted? How?"

"Ships," Murdoch answered. "Get in under cover of darkness, be well away by the time the Germans realize we've flown the coop. That's the plan, at any rate—so they tell me."

What they told him was usually the straight goods. "What happens next?" Walsh wondered out loud. He answered his own question: "The *Luftwaffe* starts looking for our bloody ships, that's what. I don't suppose we've got air cover laid on?" He answered himself again: "Too much to hope for. Too far off for fighters to reach."

"I haven't heard anything about air cover," Beverly Murdoch admitted.

"When they find us, then, we're sitting ducks," Walsh said.

"Would you sooner be taken prisoner?"

"No-o-o," Walsh said slowly. "I'd also sooner not drown, though, if it's all the same to you. And I'd sooner not be blown to smithereens."

"What the deuce are you doing in the Army, then?"

That was another good question, no doubt about it. Walsh gave a rueful shrug. "I was in in 1918. Didn't seem to be much work on the civilian side when the last war ended, so I stayed in. They won't turn loose of me now till I do get blown up, or till I'm too old to soldier any more."

"The more fool you," Murdoch said, and Walsh was in a poor position to tell him he was wrong.

Thanks to the doctor's warning, he had a couple of extra days to ready his men for the planned withdrawal to the harbor. Everything had to seem as normal as possible, so the Germans wouldn't pursue with all their strength. That would be what the withdrawal needed, wouldn't it? Machine guns and maybe tanks banging away as Tommies and *poilus* and Norwegians tried to board ship? Walsh had been thinking what juicy targets they'd make on the water. They'd be even juicier if they got caught like that.

And a few men—volunteers all, and mostly Norwegians—*would* stay behind, to man Allied machine guns and try to create the impression that everybody was still in the lines. Walsh admired them without wanting to be one of their number. He aimed to go on fighting the war till the enemy was licked. Mooching around behind barbed wire, eating slop and hoping for Red Cross packages, held no appeal. The Norwegians had a chance of getting away and blending in with the scenery. He didn't.

On the appointed night, he made his way back toward the docks. Engineers often put up white tapes to guide men and machines in the darkness without showing a light. Here, they'd used black ones to stand out against the snow. It was a nice touch. He wondered where they'd got them.

High above the clouds, airplane engines thuttered. Bombs started raining down far behind the German lines. That was another nice touch. Fighters couldn't make it here from Blighty, but bombers could.

And if the RAF pounded the Fritzes, it would make them think the expeditionary force was staying, not going. Walsh hoped like blazes it would, anyhow.

Through the shattered wreckage of Namsos town, a woman's voice called out, "Good luck, friends! *Bonne chance, amis!*" The locals still appreciated what the soldiers from abroad had been doing. That counted for something.

"This way! Step lively! This way!" The authoritative voice could only belong to an MP. Sure enough, the fellow guided traffic with disks on sticks that reminded Walsh of the ones tank crews without radios used to communicate.

He shambled up a gangplank. Only when he was up on deck did he realize he'd boarded another destroyer. It could get in and out faster than a merchantman. It couldn't carry nearly so many men, though.

Or could it? If they packed people on like sardines going into a tin, maybe it could. They didn't even have olive oil to grease the works. They did have swearing petty officers. "Keep clear lanes, God damn you!" one of that unpleasant breed shouted. "If the sailors can't get to the guns, what're your bloody necks worth?"

That was an interesting question. But the fellows loading the destroyer and the ones trying to keep the ship battleworthy worked at cross purposes. Walsh sympathized with both groups. Everyone was trying to do his own job as well as he could. If everyone succeeded, they might get away yet.

Stranger things had happened. Walsh supposed they must have.

Someone whose watch had survived said they left port at half past two. They'd have several hours of darkness to get well out to sea. Nights were still long, though beginning to shorten. They'd be a small needle in a big haystack. It could work. It really could.

Walsh kept telling himself as much, right up to the point where he fell asleep. He was mostly standing up, with his head and arms resting against something metallic. Even through his greatcoat sleeves, he could feel the cold. He didn't care. He thought he could have slept upside down.

Someone trod on his toe. Someone else planted an elbow in his ribs. Each indignity half roused him, but no more. Even this was better than life in the trenches. And if that wasn't a judgment on the war he'd been fighting . . . He snored on.

He came back to himself with the sky beginning to go gray in the east. Some good Samaritan was shoving his way through the tight-packed soldiers with an enormous pot of tea in each fist. Walsh still had his mess kit. He held out the tin cup, and was rewarded with a weak, lukewarm brew with no milk and not enough sugar. It tasted wonderful.

As day came on, the soldiers looked apprehensively back toward the corrugated coastline from which they'd just fled. The destroyer was going flat out, kicking up an enormous bow wave. But one of the mournful lessons of this war was that ships couldn't outrun airplanes.

Lots of ocean. Only us here, Walsh thought. The other ships taking the expeditionary force back from Namsos had scattered. The Nazis would have to find them one by one. Walsh thought that made for good tactics. He wished to God he were more certain.

Sailors looked back toward Norway, too. Some of them had field glasses. One who did shouted out a warning. Walsh wondered why he bothered. The antiaircraft guns were already manned. The escaping soldiers couldn't go anywhere, because their mates already filled the places where they might have gone.

Walsh's mouth went dry when he recognized the sharkish fuselage with the inverted gull wings. *A Stuka. We would get a bloody Stuka,* he thought bitterly. He'd seen what they could do. He didn't want them trying to do it to him . . . again.

"Only the one bugger," Dr. Murdoch said beside him. That *was* something. The Germans must have scattered their planes across the ocean, searching for ships. Of course, the sods up there would have a wireless set. . . .

The Stuka climbed, then dove. Walsh watched in fearful fascination—what else could he do? All the antiaircraft guns on the destroyer went off at once, with a noise like the end of the world. The pilot took his plane down through the shell bursts as if they weren't there. Fritz or not, he had balls. The bomb fell free. The dive-bomber pulled up almost as sharply as it had plunged.

Blam! The bomb burst—about fifty yards astern of the destroyer.

The ship jerked as if she'd taken a left to the belly, but kept steaming. Here and there, men peppered—or men ripped to shreds—by fragments shrieked.

"I didn't see any more bombs under his wings. Perhaps they sacrificed payload for range," Murdoch said. Walsh hadn't noticed. The Stuka *didn't* seem to be coming back for another pass. It droned east, toward Norway, instead.

"We may live to see Blighty again," Walsh said. A moment before, he wouldn't have given tuppence for his chances. Hope—and exhaustion—made for a happier drunk than even champagne. He threw back his head and laughed.

ANASTAS MOURADIAN had got used to the way Russians did things in Europe. *Got resigned to the way they did things* might have put it better. You had to get used to it, get resigned to it, or you'd go mad. There were far more Russians than any other group in the USSR, especially when you added in the Ukrainians and Byelorussians, who weren't very different from Great Russians. (Great Russians insisted they were only variations on a theme. Ukrainians and Byelorussians disagreed, but usually just among themselves.)

Used to Russian ways or not, Stas didn't think it was an accident that so many Armenians and Georgians and Jews had risen so high in the Soviet hierarchy. Russians were stubborn. They were brave. They followed orders even better than Germans. From all he'd seen, though, few of them would ever set the world on fire with their brains.

Now here he was in eastern Siberia. It was like finding himself in a satiric movie. All the most Russian traits that annoyed him in Europe were exaggerated here.

Everything was slipshod. Even in Europe, aircraft maintenance hadn't been what he wished it would be. The Russian attitude was *Oh, what the hell—it'll probably fly.* Most of the time, it did. But not all the planes that didn't come back ran into German fighters. Some never should have tried to get off the ground to begin with.

If it was bad in Europe, it was worse out here. Spare parts were in chronically short supply—no surprise, not with the factories thousands of kilometers away. Most of the best mechanics were thousands of kilometers away, too, facing the Germans and Poles. The ones stuck in Siberia did what they could with what they had . . . when they were sober, anyhow.

They weren't sober often enough to suit Mouradian. If you weren't a Russian, you almost always thought Russians drank like fish. Stas had grown up with wine. He'd learned to handle vodka. If you were going to deal with Russians, that was self-defense. When Russian officers (to say nothing of Russian enlisted men) weren't up to anything else, they'd drink, often till they fell over.

He'd seen as much in Europe. Drunkenness was worse here, too. For one thing, drunks were liable to get posted to Siberia so they wouldn't cause difficulties anywhere that mattered. For another, there was even less to do in Siberia than in European Russia. That was doubly true through the long, dark, cold winters. The more you stayed drunk, the less you brooded on how boring everything else was.

And, as Stas had heard from more Russians than he cared to remember, alcohol was antifreeze. He'd heard it so often, he'd said it himself. That didn't keep plenty of Russian drunks from freezing to death.

Drunks, of course, also didn't make the best mechanics. The first glimpse Mouradian got of the SB-2s that flew against the Japanese besieging Vladivostok made him blurt, "This must be your junkyard."

Captain Boris Novikov looked pained. "No, no, no. These are the runners. You'll get one of them. You want to see the junkyard, come with me."

He exhaled fog and vodka fumes. He wasn't immune to the Russian national voice. He didn't wobble as he walked, though. Like a lot of his countrymen, he could hold his liquor. Was that national virtue or vice? Mouradian had pondered the question for a long time. Nothing he could do about it now.

He followed Novikov down a path that had probably started as a deer track. It wound through snow-draped pines that looked as if they belonged in a Christmas scene—only Christmastime was months gone. Stas was glad he had a good pair of *valenki.* The felt boots would keep his feet from freezing even in weather like this. He hoped.

"Don't worry," Novikov said brightly. "We haven't seen a tiger in weeks."

"I'm so glad," Mouradian answered. He was unarmed. Novikov had a pistol. Whether he could draw it if he did see a tiger, and whether it would do any good if he could, were questions the Armenian preferred not to contemplate.

His response made Novikov laugh. Stas wasn't sure why. They'd come more than half a kilometer. If a tiger did bound out and charge them, no one would hear them shriek. The beast could enjoy a leisurely luncheon.

Suddenly, the path opened out into a clearing. Captain Novikov waved a mittened hand. "Now this, Mouradian, *this* is the fucking junkyard."

And it was, too. Wrecked planes, bits and pieces of wrecked planes . . . Stas saw SB-2s, monoplane and biplane Polikarpov fighters, and other aircraft he had trouble naming. Some of the junk was new. Some was ancient and rusty. Some . . . If that wasn't a French fighter left over from the last war, Mouradian didn't know what it would be.

"When we need parts, we just come out here and take them," Novikov said. "It's a hell of a lot faster than ordering them from some bigger base that'll probably just go and pull them out of *its* junkyard, if it bothers answering us at all."

"But . . ." Stas tried to put his objections into words: "Quality won't be very high, will it?"

"It's a part," Novikov said patiently. "The fucking airplane will fly better with it than without it, right?"

"That's the idea, yes," Mouradian answered, which wasn't exactly agreement.

If Novikov noticed, he gave no sign. "Well, there you are, then."

"Yes, Comrade Captain. Here I am." That wasn't exactly agreement, either.

They went back to the main base. Groundcrew men were bombing up the SB-2s Mouradian had taken for junk. He met his new copilot and bomb-aimer. Second Lieutenant Nikolai Chernenko was new, all right—he couldn't have been more than nineteen. They shook hands.

"I'm sure you'll teach me a lot, Comrade Pilot. Here's to us!" Chernenko pulled out a flask. He talked with a Ukrainian accent Mouradian found hard to follow.

"To us!" Mouradian sipped vodka. Handing back the flask, he said, "Let's not drink too much before we go."

"What else is there to do?" Chernenko asked, honest curiosity in his voice. Stas had no good answer for him.

The fellow who actually dropped the bombs—and who fired the machine gun in the SB-2's dorsal turret—was a sergeant named Innokenty Suslov. He reminded Stas of Ivan Kuchkov: he was foul-mouthed and burly. He wasn't so ugly and hairy as the Chimp, but those were just details.

When the engines started up, they sounded better than Stas expected. Maybe Novikov ran a tighter ship than Mouradian thought. Or maybe it was fool luck. He had his opinion, which might or might not be worth anything.

Up into the air the SB-2 went. The formation the bombers flew was ragged, but most Russian formations were. Keeping right in place for the sake of keeping right in place was a German affectation. So the Red Air Force felt, anyhow.

Flying over Siberia's vast forests showed the sweep of Russia almost as well as getting here on the Trans-Siberian Railway. If not for the compass, Mouradian would have had no idea of his bearing. Everything down below looked the same in all directions.

But only one direction included Japanese fighter planes. The flight leader shouted a warning that dinned in Stas' earphones. Then he saw the fighters himself: monoplanes with fixed landing gear and wide wings. They were almost ridiculously maneuverable.

But they were supposed to be just as lightly built. And, for once, Intelligence knew what it was talking about. Pursuing another bomber, a Japanese fighter flew right in front of Stas' plane. He hardly had to aim before firing the forward machine guns. Pieces flew from the Japanese fighter. It seemed to break up in midair, then plummeted in flames toward the snow-covered trees far, far below.

"Good shot!" Chernenko whooped. And it was. Mouradian had just killed a man. He'd worry about it later. For now . . . For now, he would try to kill as many more men as he could with the SB-2's bombs. That was different. He didn't have to watch them. Or maybe it just felt different.

The SB-2 felt different after the bombs fell from it: lighter, friskier, eager to get away. Stas was also eager to get away. He gunned the bomber back toward the base hacked from the Siberian wilderness. It wasn't much—he'd already seen that. But going back to it beat the devil out of meeting the ground with a terrible, final thump like that poor goddamn Japanese fighter pilot.

SHOPPING TIME FOR JEWS in Germany was late afternoon: after the Aryans had got everything worth getting. With the war a year and a half old, Sarah Goldman found she minded that less than she had before the shooting started. She'd felt really deprived then. Nowadays, there was so little for everyone that even leavings weren't much worse than top of the line.

When you had to make do with old turnips and wilted cabbage and potatoes with black spots while other people ate veal and mutton, you felt it. When everybody stewed up turnips and cabbage and potatoes, so what if yours weren't quite so fine to start with as those of the Germans across the street? Sarah missed fresh milk, but so did the rest of the *Reich.* The only people who got any were small children and pregnant women.

One phrase seemed to be on everyone's lips: "To hell with the Russians." As soon as the fight in the east started, things on the home front got worse. It was as if the government had shaken itself and at last realized the war wouldn't be quickly won. And if it wouldn't, everything had to stretch as far as it would go.

People the age of Sarah's parents didn't just curse the Russians. They also said, "It was like this the last time, too." Sarah had heard about the terrible Turnip Winter of 1917 as long as she'd been alive. Now she heard the one finally passing mentioned in the same breath.

As proof the winter was finally passing, rain poured down from a dirty-wool sky in place of snow. Sarah's umbrella leaked. She had no rubber overshoes. No one did, not any more; the state had collected them to reuse for the precious war effort. If she didn't come home with pneumonia, it wouldn't be for lack of effort.

If she didn't come home with bread, pneumonia might not matter. She and her parents were liable to starve before disease could carry them off. That thought wasn't the only one to make her smile as she walked into the Bruck bakery.

Isidor Bruck, the baker's son, was her boyfriend. For a professor's daughter, that kind of boyfriend was a long step down—or would have been, before things went sour for German Jews. Now no one sneered if you found little bits of happiness wherever you could.

And having someone in Isidor's line of work had advantages it wouldn't have before rationing began to bite. The first time he gave Sarah an unofficial extra loaf, she felt guilty about taking it. But her stomach, and the thought of her parents' stomachs, had a logic of their own. Take the bread she did, and she never said a word afterwards except *Thank you.* Too bad Isidor couldn't get away with it more often; the Nazis closely monitored the flour the Jewish bakers used.

When Sarah walked in this afternoon, she was disappointed not to see Isidor behind the counter. His father stood there instead. David Bruck wasn't so plump as he had been before times got hard. He didn't look so happy as he had back in what Sarah increasingly thought of as the good old days, either.

He did manage a smile of sorts for her. "How are you today?" he asked.

"*I'm* fine." Sarah asked the question that could have so many horrible answers: "But how's Isidor?"

David Bruck didn't take offense at not being asked how he was himself. Sarah realized she should have done that the way people usually realize such things: just too late. The baker waved her words aside when she started to stammer out the polite question. "Isidor's fine," he answered. "But they've got him on a labor gang—repairing bomb damage."

"Oh, like my father," Sarah said. David Bruck nodded. She went on, "I thought they weren't supposed to take people who make food."

"Supposed to? Supposed to, they're not," Bruck said. "When they come in here with papers and with guns, though, are we going to tell them no? If they'd said I had to go out there, too, I would have gone." He wouldn't have been much use at shifting rubble. That wouldn't have stopped the Nazis. They laughed when they put Jews to work at things that were far from their proper trades.

"Tell him I was here, will you? Tell him . . . Tell him I'm thinking about him," Sarah said.

"I'll do that," Isidor's father promised. He cocked his head to one side. "And did you come in for bread, too? Or did you walk all that way in the rain just to tell me you're thinking about Isidor?"

"Bread might be nice." Sarah wasn't about to show him he could embarrass her. When you did that with a grown-up, you lost the game right there. And he'd spend the next six weeks doing everything he could to make you turn red again.

The baker raised a bushy eyebrow. "Well, all right. You have something to carry it in so it won't turn to mush by the time you get home?"

"I sure do." Sarah reached into her handbag and took out a much-folded, permanently creased piece of dusty, field-gray canvas.

David Bruck laughed out loud. "A shelter half! I had one of those in the trenches, too. So your old man kept his, did he? Yeah, that'll do the job, all right. It's waterproof—more or less."

"Mother found it at the back of the closet," Sarah answered. "She said the same thing—and that she wished she could wash it."

"Cooties are bound to be dead by now. Eggs, too, I'd think."

Sarah started to squeal in disgust. She caught herself in the nick of time—that was just what the baker was waiting for. Unfolding the oddly shaped piece of material—two of them, fastened together, would make a small tent—she said, "Put the bread in here, please."

"I'll do that," he said, and he did. It was war bread, black as coffee, but it wouldn't taste too bad. The older generation did agree it was better than what they'd endured in the last war . . . for the time being, anyhow. This was only the second winter of the fight, not the fourth. Bruck went on, "Now I need your ration book. Nothing's official till it gets put down there."

"Oh, yes. I know." Sarah handed it to him. He did what he had to do. When she got it back, she saw he hadn't deducted nearly enough points for the amount of bread he'd given her. "Wait. This isn't—" she began.

"You hush," he told her. "Some things may not be official, but they happen anyway."

His son did things like that for her, but his son had motives he didn't—or Sarah hoped he didn't. The way things were, she wouldn't say no. She told him what she'd told Isidor: "Thank you very much."

"You're welcome. And keep your eyes open. I'm not kidding. A lot of the time, going around the rules does you more good than going through them."

Her brother was in the *Wehrmacht.* That broke every rule the *Reich* had. Sarah still didn't know how Saul had managed it. Had he killed someone for his papers? That struck her as most likely. He was already on the run for smashing a labor gang boss's head after the bastard beat him.

Sarah said not a word about that. It was her secret, hers and her mother's and father's. Telling anybody else, anybody at all, put Saul in desperate danger. Come to that, it put all the Goldmans in that same danger. If the *Gestapo* found out what her big brother was doing, everyone would pay a price for it. The blackshirts would think all the Goldmans had known about it ever since he got away.

And they wouldn't be so far wrong, either. So many things they didn't need to learn. So many things nobody needed to learn. Sarah hadn't said anything about Saul to Isidor. She didn't say anything about him now, or even hint that she knew more about evading the rules than she let on.

All she did was look as wide-eyed and innocent as she could and say, "I'll have to remember that," as if it had never occurred to her before.

"See that you do," David Bruck said. "You might turn up some galoshes that way, or at least shoe leather so your feet don't soak."

"I'll be all right," Sarah said. It hadn't stopped raining while she got the bread. With the leaky umbrella, her feet wouldn't be the only wet parts of her. As she left the bakery, she raised it anyhow. It was—a little—better than nothing.

Chapter 6

Most German officers and enlisted men stationed in Poland went into the towns there to drink and to get their ashes hauled. So far, Hans-Ulrich Rudel had resisted temptation. He didn't drink anything they sold in a Polish tavern. Women . . . Going to an officers' brothel was always a way to let off steam, as it had been in the Low Countries and France. Up till now, he'd stayed away here.

"It's not bad," another pilot from his squadron told him. "Yeah, you feel like you're back around 1910, but it's not bad. A lot of Poles speak German. When you can't find one who does, there's always some Jew who'll translate for you. Yiddish sounds awful, but the Hebes follow regular *Deutsch,* too."

"Millions of them here!" Hans-Ulrich exclaimed. "I mean, millions! How can we put them in their place inside the *Reich* and ally with them here?" By the way he said it, he might have been talking about a sexual perversion. Fair enough: that was how he felt about it.

His comrade, a captain named Ernst Lau, was a couple of years older and far more worldly-wise. "How? Diplomacy, that's how. Every Ivan a

Polish Jew kills is one we don't have to worry about ourselves. And every Jew a Russian shoots . . . Well, there's a bullet that doesn't hit one of us."

"But it's crazy," Rudel said. "How can we trust them, with so many Jews in Moscow running things for the Russians?"

"Here's how. Listen, now," Lau said. "If somebody invades you, he's the enemy. Doesn't matter if he's got the same religion. He's still the enemy, 'cause he's trying to kill your wife and take your house away from you. Anybody who helps you throw him out is the good guy in the movie. That's the way it looks to me, anyhow."

It didn't look that way to Hans-Ulrich. He would have bet it didn't look that way to the *Führer,* either. He also would have bet Hitler had hardly more use for Poles than for Jews. The way things were these days, for Captain Lau to say anything else could be seen as disloyalty to the *Reich.* Rudel had no trouble seeing it that way—none at all. He was sure the SS and the SD wouldn't, either.

Then again, Lau was a brave flyer. Hans-Ulrich had seen as much, and would have been convinced of it even without the Iron Cross First Class on the other pilot's left breast pocket. Reporting him would cost Germany a man who could do the Russians—or any other enemy of the *Reich*—a lot of harm.

More than a few men fought bravely for the *Vaterland* while disliking the National Socialists who led the country. The paradox perplexed Hans-Ulrich, but he'd seen it before. Which came first, the country's needs or the Party's? Most of the time, Rudel would have said they were one and the same. Most of the time, but not always. Not here, for instance.

He wouldn't report Ernst Lau. Back in France, before this fight with the Russians heated up, he might have. But Germany was plainly going to need every man she could get her hands on. After the Ivans learned their lesson . . . That would be the time for Lau to learn his.

Rudel had thought they would fly more as the weather began to warm up at last. Instead, they found themselves stuck on the ground—literally. Poland's unpaved airstrips (smoothed-over lines in fields, basically) turned into swamps as the snow that had lain on them for months melted and soaked in. The same thing happened in France, but it wasn't so bad there, and there were more strips with concrete runways to help the combatants get around it. Hans-Ulrich gathered this was bad even by Polish standards, which was saying something—something unpleasant.

Panzers stuck in the mud, too. Germany had perfected the art of striking like lightning. It overwhelmed Czechoslovakia. It drove the Low Countries into quick surrender. It almost—what a painful word!—extinguished France. It did take the Channel ports and partly sever France's lifeline to England: a better showing than the Kaiser's army made a generation earlier.

And, here in Poland facing the Russians, it stopped with a wet squelch. When tracked vehicles got stuck, when horses and infantrymen went into muck up to their bellies, neither side could move fast. As often as not, neither side could move at all.

No wonder the pilots and groundcrew men who drank drank a lot, then. And no wonder the handful who didn't, like Hans-Ulrich, looked for something, anything, else to do. He finally decided to go into Bialystok with Lau and some of the other officers. Even looking around seemed appealing. He didn't have to carouse. He didn't intend to, either, even if they tried to inveigle him into it. Odds were they would, too. It wasn't as if he hadn't seen that before.

They rode into town in a wagon driven by a Polish farmer. It had a boatlike body and big wheels, and handled the slop better than anything the Germans had brought with them. "We ought to make these ourselves," Lau remarked. "If the mud's this bad here, it'll only be worse when we get into Russia."

"How *could* it be worse?" Hans-Ulrich asked.

"I don't know," Lau answered. "But I'll tell you something else, too—I don't want to find out." When Hans-Ulrich looked at it from that perspective, he decided he didn't want to, either.

Bialystok was as bad as he'd thought it would be, or else worse. It was a Polish provincial town. It was a Polish provincial town that had been part of the Russian Empire before Poland revived like the mummy in the American movie, which meant it had always been cut off from German *Kultur,* even the diluted version that seeped into Austrian Poland. And it was a Polish provincial town packed full of Jews.

Long black coats, some trimmed with fox fur. Broad-brimmed black hats. Sidelocks. Bushy beards. Women in wigs and scarves and dresses that swept the sidewalks—when there were sidewalks. Gabble in Polish, which Hans-Ulrich didn't understand, and in Yiddish, which he didn't want to understand. He felt as if two hundred years had fallen off the calendar.

Some of the shops had signs in Yiddish. The strange characters might as well have been Chinese, for all the sense they made to him.

The Jews eyed the jackbooted Germans in *Luftwaffe* gray-blue as warily as the Germans looked at them. It wasn't only past confronting present—*past confronting future,* Hans-Ulrich thought. The Jews knew what the National Socialist government of Germany thought of them. Even a Polish provincial town had its newspaper (yes, edited by a Jew) and its radio sets. The Jews knew, all right.

But Stalin's greed had put Poland and Germany on the same side. And so, no matter what they might be thinking, some of the Jews in their long coats nodded to the *Luftwaffe* officers. Along with his comrades, Hans-Ulrich found himself nodding back.

A big blond Pole—he looked like a big blond bear—ran the tavern the Germans picked. Rudel couldn't tell what the barmaid who came over to their table was. She was pretty—he could tell that. She understood German well enough, too. "Mineral water," he told her when she glanced his way.

She nodded. "With what?"

"Just mineral water, please."

She raised an eyebrow. He nodded back at her to show he meant it. Helpfully, Ernst Lau explained, "He gets his long trousers pretty soon, sweetheart,,but he doesn't have 'em yet."

She raised that eyebrow again. What color were her eyes? Not quite brown, not quite green. Hazel wasn't exactly right, either, but it came closer than any other word Hans-Ulrich could find. "He can drink what he wants," she said, her voice cool. Did Yiddish flavor her German, or only Polish? Once more, Hans-Ulrich had trouble being sure. On thirty seconds' acquaintance, he got the feeling he'd always have trouble being sure about her.

When she brought back the mineral water, she took the top off the bottle where he could watch her do it. The barman hadn't spiked it, she was saying without words. "Thanks," he told her, both for the bottle and for the courtesy. Then he asked, "What's your name?" The worst thing she could do was walk away without answering.

For a second, he thought she'd do just that. But, after the momentary hesitation, she said, "Sofia."

"Sofia what?"

"How did you know?" she said, and did walk off. What was he supposed to do with that? *Try to find out more,* he told himself, wondering if he could. He'd found one thing, anyhow: a fresh, good reason to come back to Bialystok. He wouldn't have bet on that when he climbed into the wagon.

"MOSCOW SPEAKING," the radio declared. Sergei Yaroslavsky didn't think he was likely to be listening to any other station. For one thing, he recognized the announcer's voice. For another, this was a Soviet radio set, and picked up only the frequencies of which the government approved.

The samovar in the corner of the Red Air Force officers' wardroom bubbled softly to itself. More officers drank vodka than tea, though. Sergei hadn't known Poland shared the *rasputitsa*—the mud time—with Russia. But the squadron's SB-2s weren't going anywhere for a while. Neither was anything else for a few hundred kilometers in any direction you chose.

"Happy day," somebody said. "What's gone wrong since this morning?"

In a different—perhaps not such a very different—tone of voice, a question like that might have earned the bigmouth who came out with it a trip to the gulag. It also might have done that if the pilots and copilots hadn't started drinking. You made allowances for somebody who got plastered, especially when you were on the way to getting plastered yourself.

"Valiant Red Army forces continue to press attacks against the subhuman Fascist German beasts and their Polish stooges. Considerable territory has been gained," the newsreader declared. If you'd never heard of the *rasputitsa*, you might believe that. Or if the considerable territory was to be considered in meters and not kilometers, it might even prove technically true. The war in Poland had really and truly bogged down.

But when they gave the fellow on the radio the lying copy, what was he supposed to do? Tell the truth instead, assuming he knew what it was? They'd shoot him. They'd do horrible things to him first, and worse things to his loved ones, no doubt where he could listen to them scream. He went along, the same way everybody else did.

"A Committee of Polish National Liberation was announced today in Pinsk," the man with the smooth voice continued. "Its role will expand as the workers and peasants of the peace-loving Soviet Union free their Polish brethren from the oppression they have suffered at the hands of the Smigly-Ridz cabal."

Smigly-Ridz was turning out to be Hitler's puppet, though odds were he would deny that if anyone called him on it. And the Poles on the Committee of National Liberation were Stalin's puppets. Sergei wondered if he would have seen things so clearly without the vodka sparkling through him.

"Yet another Japanese attack on the outworks of Vladivostok was repelled with loss yesterday," the newsreader said. "Red Air Force bombers punished the aggressors."

Sergei raised his tumbler. "Here's to Stas!" he said. The other flyers drank with him.

"In daring strikes, Soviet bombers also brought the fighting home to Tsitsihar and Harbin," the man continued. "The Japanese lackeys of the so-called state of Manchukuo had the gall to protest, but General Secretary Stalin and Foreign Commissar Litvinov rejected their foolish babbling out of hand."

"Good for Stalin!" growled Colonel Borisov, the squadron commander. The vodka made his nose red as a strawberry. It also made him sound even more sure of himself than he would have otherwise.

Heads bobbed up and down all along the table, Sergei's among them. He wasn't currying favor—he thought Borisov was right. *So-called state of Manchukuo* was right! The Manchukuans were just as much puppets of the Japanese . . . as those Poles in Pinsk were of Stalin. What went around came around, sure enough.

"In western Europe, France and England both claim gains against the Nazi hyenas," the announcer said. "German radio denies the claims. Dr. Goebbels, of course, is the prince of liars, but the degenerate capitalists of western Europe are not far behind. Be it noted that neither France nor England has properly suppressed its native Fascist movement. Significant factions within both countries favor abandoning the fight against the Hitlerites and banding together with them for a crusade against the stronghold of the proletariat on the march."

"Bring on the French swine! Bring on the Englishmen, too! We beat them after the last capitalist war, and we'll smash 'em again! See if we don't!" Yes, Borisov had taken a lot of vodka on board.

Vladimir Federov politely called him on it: "But, Comrade Colonel! Imagine the Nazis with no enemy in their rear. If they throw everything they have at us . . ." He let his voice trail away.

"We'll fucking smash 'em, I tell you!" Colonel Borisov thundered.

Federov wanted to argue more. Sergei could see as much. His gesture urged his copilot to take it easy. If Borisov remembered this after he sobered up, or if somebody reminded him of it, Federov would not be happy.

Anastas Mouradian would have shown what he thought with a lift of a few millimeters from one black, bushy eyebrow. Everyone but Borisov would have noticed, and nobody would have been able to prove a thing. Southerners had that subtlety. Federov, plainly, didn't.

The newsreader talked about overfulfillment of steel-production norms. He praised the Stakhanovite shock workers of Magnitogorsk, and added, "No German bombing plane will ever be able to reach them and disrupt their labors!"

He was bound to be right about that. How many factory towns beyond the Urals belched smoke into the sky around the clock as they made all the things the Soviet Union needed? Hundreds, maybe thousands. They would have been villages before the Revolution, if they were there at all. Distance kept them safe from Nazi bombardiers.

Germany couldn't hide like that. Soviet aircraft had already delivered stinging blows to East Prussia, and had even raided Berlin a few times. The great powers of the West were supposed to be mighty in the air. Why weren't they pounding Hitler's manufacturing centers harder? Didn't it prove how halfhearted they were in their war against the Fascists?

When the announcer started going on about wheat and barley production, Sergei stopped listening. Yes, the people of the USSR had to eat. Try as the fellow on the radio would, he couldn't make figures detailing the number of hectares to be planted anything but deadly dull.

"Collectivization continues to advance," he said proudly. "The very idea of personal property will soon fade away."

Sergei owned nothing. His flying suit, his rations, his billet, his bomber . . . all from the state. The vodka? He wasn't sure where the vodka came from. He'd downed enough of it so he didn't care, either. As long as he could get his hands on some whenever he felt the urge, nothing else mattered.

Once the newsreader got into the production reports and the economic news, you could talk over him without fear of being seen as uninterested in the life-and-death struggle on behalf of the workers and peasants—and without everybody frantically shushing you for opening your big trap. One of the pilots said, "Well, we've got a few weeks till things dry out. What happens then?"

"It should be the same kind of war it was last year," Colonel Borisov said. "And the Devil take England and France."

He was the squadron commander. Because he was, Sergei said only, "Here's hoping you're right, Comrade Colonel." The USSR was a classless society in law. In law, yes. But you'd still get the shitty end of the stick if you pissed off the fellow entitled to tell you what to do. Drunk or sober, Sergei knew that.

And, if he'd spoken his mind, he would have pissed Borisov off. Hitler hated the Soviet Union the way Stalin hated Germany. If the *Wehrmacht* had to stand on the defensive in the West so it could hit harder here, he feared it would do exactly that. If it did, could the USSR withstand the blow?

He had to hope so. Everyone who served the Soviet Union had to hope so. If not, it would be a rugged spring and a worse summer. The USSR was finally over the horrors of the Revolution. Even the purges . . . Well, they hadn't stopped, but they'd slowed down. Sergei thought they had, at any rate. Did the country really need a big, hard foreign war right now?

Need one or not, the USSR was liable to get one. No doubt history and diplomacy justified Stalin's demand for that little chunk of northeastern Poland last year. But the price for it might prove higher than anyone in his right mind would want to pay.

BACK IN THE DAYS before the draft sucked Vaclav Jezek into the Czechoslovak army, when he'd thought about France he'd pictured Paris and the Riviera—the parts you saw when you went on holiday. Imagining pretty girls wearing not enough clothes bronzing on the beach under the hot Mediterranean sun . . . Hell, it made you want to pack your bags and buy a train ticket right away.

Reality, at the moment, was rather different, as reality had a way of being. The harsh landscape of northeastern France was as much a monument to industrial man as the worst parts of Czechoslovakia, and that was saying a mouthful. It was as cold as it would have been back there, too.

Towns were jammed too close together. Piles of coal and slag heaps towered tall as church steeples and factory smokestacks. The dirt looked gray. Even though the war had shut down most of the factories, the air still held a chemical tang that made you want to cough. The foulness must have soaked into the soil.

And, to make things more enjoyable yet, the Germans seemed to plant a machine gun or a mortar on top of every hillock, natural or manmade. They had spotters in the steeples. For all Vaclav knew, they had them in the smokestacks, too. They had lots of artillery, and the gunners were very alert. They'd had time to dig in, in other words, and they weren't planning to go anywhere.

A mortar crew in *Feldgrau* up on top of a long hillock of rubble must have imagined they were lords of all they surveyed. Which only proved their imagination was as wild as Vaclav's had been when he thought about the Riviera. He'd sneaked through a sad, scabby-looking wood till he sprawled no more than a kilometer from the Nazis and their pet stovepipe.

"Can you hit them?" Benjamin Halévy asked quietly.

"With this baby? Sure." Vaclav patted the antitank rifle. "Question is, is it worth it? Once the first guy goes down, they'll take cover. And they can shoot back over the top of that thing. I can't hit them once they move."

"When they slide back to the other side, they can't see what's going on over here, right?" The Jew answered his own question: "Right. Not without an observer, they can't. And you can plug an observer. So, yeah, make 'em move."

"You're the sergeant." Vaclav steadied his piece of light artillery in the fork between a tree trunk and a stout branch. He had a good notion of the range. Next to no windage . . . He took a deep, steadying breath, then pressed the trigger.

As always, the report was hellacious. So was the kick. But one of those distant German figures spun and fell over. Vaclav had another round chambered in only a few seconds. The Fritzes were good, though. They flattened out and dragged the mortar off to where Vaclav couldn't see it.

"Now we find our foxhole," he said, and scurried back to suit action to word.

Halévy scooted along with him. "Their first few shots from the first position won't be real accurate. But . . ."

"Yeah. But," Jezek agreed. He put his butt, and the rest of him, inside the foxhole. Halévy's was only a few meters away. When you knew you'd get shelled, you didn't want to stay above ground, not when you didn't have to.

Yes, those Germans were good. The Czech and the French Jew with Czech Jewish parents had barely dug in when mortar bombs started whispering down into the woods. The flat, harsh cracks as they went off and the whining shriek of fragments slashing through the air made Vaclav wish Czechoslovakia had never heard of conscription. *Wish for the moon while you're at it,* he thought, and tried to fold himself even smaller.

Not all the shrieks in among the trees came from the bombs bursting there. Some were torn from the throats of the Czechs and Frenchmen the bombs wounded. "You all right?" Vaclav called.

"Depends on how you look at things," Halévy answered. "They haven't wounded me. But I'm not drinking champagne and smoking a fat cigar and feeling up the barmaid, either."

Jezek snorted. "Barmaids!" It wasn't as if he hadn't tried slipping his hand under their skirts now and then. It wasn't even that he hadn't succeeded, and gone on from there, a few times. But he couldn't think about them when he was getting shelled. He wondered why not. Even when they cussed you out for groping them, they were a hell of a lot more fun than what was really going on.

"Heads up!" Halévy said urgently. "You pissed the Fritzes off good."

Vaclav came up from his foxhole and discovered what the Jew meant. A couple of armored cars with German crosses painted on them were edging out from around the back of the slag pile the mortar had topped. Soldiers in coal-scuttle helmets loped along with them. His lips skinned back from his teeth in a savage grin. His antitank rifle wouldn't always do for tanks. But armored cars weren't armored against more than small-arms fire. He could make some poor damned German draftees thinking about the feel of a barmaid's stockinged thigh under their fingers even more unhappy than they were already.

He could, and he did. He knew where the driver sat in an armored car. After he sent two rounds into the first machine, it swung hard left and tried to drive up the manmade hill. The other armored car kept coming. Its toy cannon and machine gun sent death snarling through the woods, hunting him. Ducking back into the foxhole seemed the better part of valor.

He couldn't stay down there, though, not unless he wanted the *Landsers* moving with the armored cars to get in among the trees and pull him out with a bayonet like Frenchmen spearing *escargots* from their shells with skinny little forks. Life wasn't much fun when your choices lay between bad and worse.

Worse was, well, worse. He popped up again, glumly certain the assholes in that second armored car were just waiting to see him. And they were. Machine-gun rounds cracked past, a meter or two above his head. But he got off a couple of shots of his own before taking cover once more.

Benjamin Halévy's whoop told him they'd done some good. Cautiously, he peered out to see for himself. The other armored car had gone nose-down in a shell hole. If that didn't say he'd punched the driver's ticket, he didn't know what would. He chambered another round. Going after infantrymen with an antitank rifle was a lot like murder, but not enough to stop him.

But he didn't have to. Some of the Allied soldiers who'd come into the woods had a mortar of their own with them. The bombs started dropping among the sorry bastards in *Feldgrau.* Some of the Germans dove for the craters that pocked the landscape. Others beat it back toward the cover of the artificial hillock.

A couple of Fritzes did neither. One lay ominously still, right out in the open. The other writhed like an earthworm after a marching boot came down. Thin in the distance, his screams sounded just like the ones that would come from a wounded Czech or Frenchmen. Torment was a universal brotherhood.

Halévy's rifle barked: once, twice. The German stopped thrashing and yelling. He lay as quiet as his comrade a few meters off. Vaclav glanced over to Halévy's foxhole. The Jew looked faintly embarrassed. "I didn't want to listen to that racket any more," he said.

"Sure. I know what you mean," Vaclav answered. Sometimes the only favor you could do a man was kill him. Vaclav hoped even a Fritz would be kind enough to take care of that for him if he ever caught a nasty one.

Not yet, thank God! Benjamin Halévy was eyeing the hill made from industrial rubble. "How the devil are we supposed to clear the Germans off of that?"

Vaclav replied without hesitation: "Have to flank 'em out of it. They could slaughter a regiment that tried to go straight over."

"Too right they could," Halévy agreed mournfully. "But do you know how many positions just like this one there are all over this part of France?"

"Too fucking many. I've already seen too fucking many," Jezek said.

"Now that you mention it, so have I," Halévy said. "And at every goddamn one of them, the foot sloggers stuck in front of it are going, 'Have to flank it out.' But a lot of the time there's no room to go around the flank of one without bumping into another one head on."

"And so?" Vaclav said. "Infantrymen aren't dumb. They want to go on living just like anybody else."

"Uh-huh." The Jew nodded. "But the generals want to throw the Nazis out of France. And you know what that means."

"It means a lot of us end up dead whether we like it or not," Vaclav said.

"Yup. I'm afraid that's just what it means." Halévy nodded one more time.

CAREFULLY, JULIUS LEMP brought the U-30 into the harbor at Namsos. Except for a few diehard Norwegians up in the still-frozen far north—not enough men to matter—Norway lay in German hands. U-boats could put in and depart from any Norwegian port. That made it much harder for the Royal Navy to defend against them. It tore the North Sea wide open, and gave the submarines a running start on getting out into the Atlantic.

Well, up to a point, anyhow. Namsos wasn't worth much yet, not so far as the *Kriegsmarine* was concerned. English engineers had done their best to wreck whatever the new occupants might find useful, and to booby-trap whatever they couldn't wreck. As was usually true in cases like this, English engineers' best was all too good.

German engineers and labor gangs—some from the *Reich*'s *Organization Todt,* others made up of drafted local men—prowled the harbor, trying to set things right. Lemp supposed they would manage sooner or later. Given the battered state of everything he could see, he would have bet on later.

A man in naval officer's uniform waved to him from a half-burned pier. "You didn't see any mines in the fjord, did you?" the fellow called.

"Jesus Christ!" Lemp yelled back from the conning tower. "Haven't you cleared them yet?"

"Well, we think so," the other man answered.

That did not fill his heart with confidence. In fact, it made him clap a hand to his forehead. "*Heilige Scheisse!*" he said. "Why did you let me come in here if you weren't sure?"

"You made it, didn't you?" the officer on the pier said soothingly. "The marked channel was all right."

"Sure—and it was about a meter wider than my boat," Lemp said.

"What more do you need?" the other fellow said, proving he hadn't done any shiphandling lately. Lemp wanted to inquire about his mother, but didn't think the man on the pier would take it in the proper spirit.

He didn't care to quarrel with the ignorant fellow, anyhow. He could get food and water and fuel and ammunition for his guns here. Pretty soon, no doubt, the *Reich* would start shipping torpedoes up to the Norwegian ports, too. If the boats didn't have to go back to the *Vaterland,* they could stay at sea longer and travel farther—and they could hit the enemy harder.

If only France had gone belly-up like Norway! The French coast lay a lot farther west and south than Norway did. Lemp imagined U-boats staging out of Brest and St. Nazaire and Bordeaux. How long would England have lasted had that happened? The *Reich* almost starved the British Isles into submission in 1917. With that kind of advantage working for it, making England knuckle under would have been easy this time around.

Would have been, yes. Things hadn't worked out exactly the way the *Führer* had in mind. That was why there'd been machine-gun fire in Kiel when the U-30 came in at the end of last year. That was why so many high-ranking Army and Navy officers (only a few from the *Luftwaffe,* which had belonged to Göring from the start) were either dead or in places designed to make them wish they were.

And it was why, even in the notoriously easygoing U-boat service, people had to watch what they said these days. Every boat had a man or two aboard who would blab to the authorities ashore. Even a joke told the wrong way could get a good seaman hauled off between a couple of hatchet-faced *Sicherheitsdienst* officials. Men who were hauled off like that didn't come back again.

For now, Lemp refused to dwell on such things. What was the point, when he couldn't do anything about them? If he complained to his superiors, he'd find out for himself what the inside of a concentration camp was like. You might not care for everything the people running the country did, but it was still the *Vaterland.* You had to serve it as best you could.

Once the U-30 had tied up at the pier, Lemp asked one of the men who'd made the boat fast, "Do the Tommies ever pay you a call? Not very far from England to here—a lot closer than from England to Germany."

"Yes, sir," the rating agreed. "They've come over a few times. But the nights are getting short even faster than they are back home—we're a long way north, you know. We've got good flak, and we've got fighter cover. One thing that's plain as the nose on my face"—he grinned, being the owner of a pretty impressive honker—"is that the bombers can't fight fighters and can't run, either."

"That's not what people thought before the war started," Lemp said.

"I know." The rating lowered his voice a little: "If it weren't so, though, we would've knocked England flat by now, eh?"

"Wouldn't be surprised," Lemp said, also quietly. They smiled at each other and went about their business. A man could feel he was bucking the system just by speaking a few plain truths.

A man could also feel good about getting back to *terra firma.* Supper was chicken stew with fresh vegetables. The crew of the U-30 had been living off sausage and beans and sauerkraut long enough to get sick of them. They kept body and soul together, which was as far as praise would reach. The beer that went with supper was mighty welcome, too.

So were the showers in the barracks. Saltwater soap didn't get a man clean. Gerhart Beilharz toweled himself off with a blissful grin on his face. "I don't have to smell myself for a while, let alone everybody else," the *Schnorkel* expert said in delight.

"Harder for you to knock your brains out, too," Lemp replied. Beilharz was two meters tall, *not* the ideal height for a submariner.

One of the ratings added, "Now I can go to sleep without Heinz sticking his shoe in my ear—and Jens can curl up without my shoe in his."

"Now I can sleep without curling up," Beilharz said. As an officer, he got more sleeping room than ordinary sailors, but not enough for a man his size. Even Lemp's cabin—only a curtain shut it off from the rest of the boat—was tiny and cramped. Everything on a U-boat was cramped.

But none of the men got as much sleep as they all craved, because the RAF did come over that night. Air-raid sirens started screaming about the same time as the antiaircraft guns began to thunder. Between them, they made music to wake the dead. Lemp and the rest of the men from the U-30 staggered toward the zigzag trenches as bombs whistling down added one more horrible note to the symphony.

It was cold out there. Did Namsos *ever* warm up? Shivering, Lemp had trouble believing it. Next to him stood Beilharz, also shivering, in his white cotton undershirt and long johns. Lemp pointed at him. "Look!" he said dramatically. "A polar bear!"

"Oh, shut up . . . sir," Beilharz said.

Crump! Crump! Crump! The bombs went off one after another, not really close but not far enough away, either. Night bombing on both sides was more a matter of luck than of skill. Bad luck for Germany, and some of those bombs would hit the harbor. Bad luck for the U-30's crew, and some of them would hit right here.

Where were the fighters that dockside rating had bragged about? Night might not last long at this season up here, but it was nighttime now. How was a fighter supposed to find a bomber when he couldn't see it till he was on the point of running into it? The flak was firing by ear-sight, too: no searchlights working yet to pin bombers in their beams.

After half an hour or so, the engine drone overhead eased toward quiet. The antiaircraft guns banged away for another ten minutes. If falling shrapnel fractured somebody's skull—or smashed it—well, it was a tough old war for everybody, wasn't it?

"I wonder if I can go back to sleep," Gerhart Beilharz said as the sailors trooped into the barracks again. The yawn that followed declared he wasn't too worried about it.

Neither was Lemp. Some infantrymen were supposed to be able to sleep through air raids. He couldn't do that, but he wasn't so far away, either. He hurried to his cot.

Chapter 7

Life went on in spite of everything. Weeds began to grow in the Japanese trenches outside of Vladivostok. Sergeant Hideki Fujita admired the little bits of green amidst dun and dirty white. And, when one of the weeds sprouted little red flowers, he was as happy as if he'd raised it himself.

That meant the men in his section admired the flowers with him. If they were otherwise inclined, the certain knowledge that he would give scoffers a clout in the head kept them from showing it.

"Now I hope the Russians don't shell the poor thing," he said, and while he spoke he really was worried about it.

"Don't fret, Sergeant-*san,*" Senior Private Hayashi said. "A week from now, a million of these things will pop up all over everywhere. We'll get so sick of them, we'll start to hate them."

"I am not going to hate my plant," Fujita declared. Hayashi, wise in the ways of noncoms, nodded and shut his mouth.

Except for the plant with the little red flowers, not much seemed to change around the besieged Russian city. Fifty meters here, a hundred meters there, the Japanese lines tightened. Maybe the Red Army men defending the place were scrawnier than they had been when Fujita got there. They still fought as hard as ever, though.

When Fujita wasn't talking about his precious plant, he would talk about that. "Russians are funny people," he said wisely, puffing a cigarette. "As long as a Russian has a rifle or a bayonet or an entrenching tool in his hands, he's as dangerous as one of us would be. Maybe more so, because he's sneakier."

"*Hai,*" breathed the soldiers gathered around him. After all, he was speaking plain truth. Besides, he outranked them. They weren't going to argue. There were less painful ways to commit *seppuku,* if a man was so inclined.

He warmed to his theme: "But when a Russian's had enough, he just throws down his rifle and throws up his hands and smiles at you like a dog. He expects you to pet him and feed him and take care of his messes from then on out."

"*Hai,*" the soldiers chorused again—they'd all been in the trenches long enough to see the same thing for themselves.

"Disgraceful," somebody added. The men nodded. By Japanese standards, surrender was disgraceful. Facing the choice between surrender and death, a Japanese soldier was trained to choose death every time. He had no honor left if he decided to live. Even worse, he smeared his whole family with his shame. If he gave up, gave in, none of his relatives would be able to hold up their heads ever again.

And, because a man base enough to surrender had no honor left, you could do whatever you pleased with him after he fell into your hands. Russians and other Westerners were said to treat prisoners of war kindly. To Fujita and his comrades, that was incomprehensible softness, even madness.

To most of them, anyhow. Educated Senior Private Hayashi said, "My father fought against the Russians at Port Arthur." He waited for his own nods, and got them. Not many men in those muddy trenches didn't have older relatives who'd gone through the Russo-Japanese War. He continued, "He told me orders then were to go easy on prisoners, to treat enemy wounded the same way we treated our own, and not even to be too hard on soldiers who gave up when they weren't wounded."

Fujita started to tell him he was full of crap. Before he could, though, another soldier said, "Yeah, I remember hearing the same thing from my old man. Pretty crazy stuff, ain't it?"

Maybe it really was true, then. No one other than Fujita seemed inclined to contradict Hayashi. Instead of sticking out his own neck, he said, "Well, we aren't dumb enough to keep on with that kind of nonsense nowadays."

"Oh, no, Sergeant," Hayashi said quickly. Fujita hid a smile behind the rituals of lighting another smoke. Hayashi's education had made him smart enough to know where his next bowl of rice was coming from, anyhow. Fujita might not know so many *kanji* or be able to read and write Chinese, but he had the rank. A subordinate who annoyed him would pay and pay. His power might be petty, but for those in its grasp it was real as rain.

Behind the lines, Japanese guns thundered. Before long, Russian artillery answered. Wherever Fujita had faced the Red Army, he'd seen that it had cannon falling out of its asshole. More guns, guns with longer range . . . It was enough, more than enough, to make the poor sorry bastards who had to face those guns jealous.

Something a few kilometers behind Fujita's position blew up with a rending crash. All the soldiers shook their heads in sorrow. "*Eee!*" Fujita said, blowing out a stream of smoke. "There's some ammunition we won't get to use against the round-eyed barbarians."

He wanted to turn around and stand up in the trench to take a look at the cloud of smoke rising from that blast. He wanted to, but he didn't. That would be asking for a bullet in the back of the head from a Russian sniper. Peering through telescopic sights, waiting for a Japanese soldier to make a mistake and show himself, those round, pale eyes would be pitiless.

Despite that hit, the Russian guns fell silent again sooner than he'd expected. When he said as much, Senior Private Hayashi answered, "They've been doing that the past few days, haven't they?"

He made it a question so he wouldn't seem to contradict Fujita. And, making it a question, he made Fujita think back on it. Slowly, the sergeant nodded. "You know, maybe they have. I wonder what it means."

"Maybe they're running low on shells," a soldier said hopefully.

"If they are, we've got them," another man said.

"Not till they run out of machine-gun bullets, too," the first soldier retorted. Fujita nodded again. He'd heard stories about the Russo-Japanese War, too. Machine guns were the slate-wipers even back then. They melted regiments into companies and companies into squads. From everything he could see, the Red Army used more of them now than it had in the old days.

"Sooner or later, we'll beat them down," Hayashi said. "Whether it's soon enough to do us any good . . ."

He didn't go on, or have to. Foot soldiers were expendable. Everybody knew it, including them. If Fujita's regimental commander needed to take a height in front of him, he'd keep throwing men at it till he did. Why not? He could get reinforcements. Where would the Red Army find them?

The next day, the Russians raided off to the left of Fujita's position. They were after ground or prisoners to interrogate. They also made off with the Japanese unit's rice rations, which were about to be served. The Japanese troops got more a couple of hours later. The Russians got full bellies for a change.

More raids like that followed. Some of them succeeded in grabbing the booty. Others only cost the Red Army casualties. The Japanese began using field kitchens to bait traps. It worked as well with the Russians as it would have with any other wild beasts.

Because of such things, Fujita wasn't astonished when white flags started flying in the Russian trenches. He got a glimpse of grim-faced Soviet officers coming through the Japanese lines to confer with his superiors.

It wasn't peace, not yet. But it wasn't war. You could stand up and show yourself, and the Russians wouldn't shoot at you. Some of them came into the Japanese lines to beg. They weren't starving yet, but they were skinny. A lot of them had very fine boots. Fujita acquired a buttery-soft pair for a couple of mess kits of rice.

A Red Army man who spoke a few words of Japanese said. "Nobody come help we. Why go on fight?"

Because giving up makes you a thing, not a person, Fujita thought. But he wanted the Russian's belt, so he didn't say what was in his mind. He went on dickering with the fellow, for all the world as if he'd personally grown the rice he was offering. He got the price he wanted. The Russian couldn't say no, not if he aimed to get any food at all. Hunger was a terrible thing.

So was defeat. After three days of talks, the Red Army officers surrendered Vladivostok and the surrounding territory. They'd reached the same conclusion as the soldier with the belt: no one was coming to help them. Fujita wondered how many Russians were giving up and what the Japanese authorities would do with them all. He shrugged. It wasn't his worry.

ONE OF THE BRIGHT lads in Willi Dernen's company had managed to hook a radio to a car battery and make noise come out of it. The noise, at the moment, was a German newsman. "Radio Tokyo announced today that Vladivostok has at last passed under Japanese control, ending the second long siege in twentieth-century conflicts between the two countries. Having lost to Japan in the east, Russia will now surely also lose to the *Reich* in the west."

"How do they figure that?" a soldier said. "Now Stalin's only got us to worry about. *He* isn't in a big two-front war any more, 'cause he's already lost just about all of what he can lose way the hell over there."

A considerable silence followed. No one seemed sure what to say about the comment. The *Landser* had a point, which only made matters worse. At last, Willi took a shot at it: "Why don't you open your mouth a little wider, Anton? Then I can stick a land mine in there, and you'll blow your own head off next time you talk." *If you haven't done it already,* he added, but only to himself.

"Huh? What do you mean?" Maybe Anton was God's innocent, because he sounded as if he had not a clue.

Willi wasn't about to spell it out for him. Then again, he didn't have to. Corporal Arno Baatz took care of things with his usual style: "He means you sound disloyal, that's what. And you goddamn well do. If they say we'll whip the lousy Russians, we'll whip 'em, and that's flat."

"Oh, yeah?" Anton wasn't in Awful Arno's section, and had more leeway sassing him than Willi would have. "Has anybody told the lousy Russians about that?"

The Germans huddled in what had been some middle-class Frenchman's parlor. The power was out; otherwise, the bright boy wouldn't have needed his magic trick with the battery. Willi could watch Corporal Baatz turn red anyhow. "The *Führer* knows what's what!" he shouted. "We'll tell the Russians when we march through Moscow!"

"Moscow? Have you got any idea how far from Poland that is?" Anton said.

"I've got an idea that someone doesn't care a pfennig for Germany's leadership," Awful Arno said in a deadly voice. "And I've got a good idea of what happens to people like that, too."

"Only if some stoolie rats them out," somebody behind Baatz said. It should have been Anton, but maybe he really didn't know what happened to those people. If he didn't, he *was* one of God's innocents.

Awful Arno whirled as if his ass were on ball bearings. "Who said that?" he yelled. He wasn't red now; he was purple. "I'll smash your face in!"

No one told him a thing. That made him angrier than ever. Now that he'd twisted in a new direction, he gave other people the chance to talk behind his back. And someone was quick to take advantage of it: "Shut up and let us listen to the music, Baatz."

It was good music. Barnabas von Géczy was supposed to be Hitler's favorite band leader. Listening to *Komm mit nach Madeira,* Willi wished he were on a subtropical beach with a girl, not stuck in a lousy French village with a bunch of smelly soldiers. *A bunch of other smelly soldiers,* he amended—he was none too clean himself. If the almost-engineer would rig up some hot water, now . . . Too much to hope for.

Corporal Baatz heaved himself to his feet and stormed out of the battered house. "He's going to blab to the officers," someone predicted gloomily.

"As long as he doesn't blab to the SS," Willi said. He scowled at Anton. "You and your big yap."

"Me? What did I do? I was only looking at the military possibilities," the other soldier said.

"That's what you thought," Willi said. "Don't ask questions, man. Keep your trap shut and do your job. After the war's over, we'll straighten out whatever's gone wrong."

Anton eyed him. "Aren't you the guy who . . . ?" He paused, not sure how to go on.

"The guy who what?" Willi growled, though he didn't have to be a bright boy himself to know.

"The guy whose buddy ran off," Anton said.

"I don't know what happened to Wolfgang. I wish I did." Willi wasn't lying. He'd warned Wolfgang Storch to run off because the SS was about to grab him. And run Wolfgang had—toward the French lines. Willi hoped he was sitting in a POW camp somewhere in southwestern France. He would be . . . if the *poilus* hadn't plugged him instead. No way to know, not for Willi. Guys who tried to give up did get plugged sometimes, no matter what the Geneva Convention ordained.

"You clowns should put a cork in it, too," another *Landser* said. "Or take it outside, anyway."

Willi wanted to listen to the music, so he shut up. Anton left in a huff. Some people didn't even know when they were getting themselves in trouble.

When the song ended, somebody sighed and said, "That's not bad, but it isn't jazz, either."

All the other German soldiers in the battered parlor edged away from the music critic. In his own way, the fellow—Willi thought his name was Rolf—was as naïve as poor dumb Anton. The way things worked in the *Reich* these days, your taste in records was a political choice. National Socialist doctrine branded jazz as degenerate music, nigger music. If you liked it, maybe you were a degenerate or a nigger-lover yourself. The *Gestapo* would be happy to find out.

As a matter of fact, Willi was fond of jazz, too. But he liked his own skin even better. He wouldn't tell anybody he didn't trust about anything that might be dangerous. If you wanted to get along, you had to think about such things. Or, better, you had to tend to them so automatically, you didn't need to think about them.

He sat there, listening and smoking, for another hour. After a repeat of the news, an opera tenor started blasting out an aria. He got up and left then. The *Führer* loved Wagner. It put Willi in mind of cats being choked to an overwrought musical accompaniment.

For the time being, the Germans had the village pretty much to themselves. Only a few French families had stayed behind when the *Wehrmacht* rolled through. The rest packed up whatever they could and ran. Now they were stuck somewhere on the wrong side of the line . . . if they hadn't got bombed or machine-gunned from the air while they were on the road.

Off to the west, French 75s barked: a very distinctive sound. The shells didn't come down on the village, for which Willi thanked the God in Whom he had more and more trouble believing. It wasn't as if plenty hadn't already landed here. One of these days before too long, the Germans would fall back some more. *Poilus* in khaki would take the place of *Landsers* in field-gray. And German 105s would kill a few French soldiers, mutilate a few more, and knock down some houses that had stayed lucky so far.

And *then,* maybe, the people who'd run for their lives would come back to see what was left of the things around which they'd built their civilian existence. And they would cry and wail and swear at the Germans and shake their fists . . . and somebody would yank on a booby-trap left behind for the *poilus* and blow off her hand. Then the crying and wailing and cursing would start all over again, louder than ever.

"War is shit," Willi muttered, sincerely if with no great originality. He started to cross the main street, the only one in town you couldn't piss across. Then he stopped. The main drag ran east and west, straight enough to let somebody out there look a long way down it. If the froggies had posted a sniper, he'd be looking this way through a rifle-mounted telescope. Willi had done a little sniping, enough to start to get the feel for it.

He didn't know the French had put a guy with a rifle out there. No far-off rifleman had punched Anton's ticket for him. No sniper had got rid of Awful Arno, either. *Too bad,* Willi thought.

Rolf came out, too, a minute or so behind Willi. No surprise: if you liked jazz, dark deeds on the Rhine wouldn't be your cup of tea. Rolf crossed the street without hesitation. "You might want to watch—" Willi began.

He couldn't even finish the sentence before Rolf fell over, shot through the head. The distant report arrived after the bullet. Rolf didn't even twitch. He just lay there, bleeding. He must have died before he hit the ground. Willi shuddered. It could have been him. Oh so easily, it could have been him.

GOING WITH PETE McGILL had done wonders for Vera's English. The White Russian girl hadn't known much before they hooked up with each other. Now she was pretty fluent. Half the time, she even remembered not to roll her r's. Pete was proud of her—it showed how smart she was. She was a good deal smarter than he was, but that hadn't occurred to the Marine yet.

If Vera was really smart, her being smarter than Pete never would occur to him. Worrying about whether the girl you love loves you back or is calculating the best way to use you to get what she wants is not likely to make an affair last.

At the moment, Pete wasn't worrying about anything. He'd just got what *he* wanted, and his heart was still beating like a drum. Shanghai had any number of places where a man and a woman could walk in together, sign the guest book as *Mr.* and *Mrs.*, and be asked no questions. This was one of them. The room was small, but the mattress was fairly new and the sheets were clean. He wouldn't have fussed if they weren't, but Vera might have. *Women are picky,* he thought.

He rolled half away from her and turned on the lamp on the nightstand. With a little startled squeak, she made as if to cover herself. "Don't do that, babe," he said. "I love to look at you."

When he did, his manhood stirred again. Before long, they'd start another round. In the meantime, a different urge seized him. He rummaged in the trousers of his civilian slacks (till midnight tomorrow, he didn't have to look like a leatherneck) till he found his Luckies.

As he tapped one against the nightstand, he held out the pack to Vera. "Want one?"

"Sure," she said. The word came out just like that—perfect. She might have been born in the States. She took a cigarette, tapped it down on her nightstand, and waited for a light. Pete had to dig out his matches. If he'd been thinking, he would have grabbed them with the butts. If he'd been thinking, he would have been someone else altogether.

He lit a match. His cheeks hollowed as he applied the flame to the tip of the cigarette. Smoke filled his mouth, then his lungs. He dropped the match in the glass ashtray next to the lamp.

Vera leaned close for a light from the hot red coal at the end of his Lucky. As she too sucked in smoke, he cupped her breast with his free hand. She made a little noise that might have been a purr or a laugh. Once she had the cigarette going, she said, "You!"

She didn't say *Men!* That would have reminded Pete there'd been others—and how many others?—before him. She was more than smart enough to steer clear of that kind of tactical error.

She did say, "I like your American tobacco."

The way she said it made Pete feel he'd grown the weed, harvested it, and cured it himself. "Yeah, it's good, isn't it?" he said. He'd smoked Chinese tobacco every now and then. It was like inhaling a blowtorch flame. Any smokes were better than none, but still. . . .

After she'd leaned across him to grind out her cigarette (the room had only the one ashtray, and was lucky to have that), and after he'd taken more friendly liberties with her person while she did it, she asked, "How much longer will the Marines stay in Shanghai?"

"I've got no idea," he said, and he might have been proud of having no idea. As a matter of fact, he was. Like any well-trained hunting dog, he went where he was told and did what he was told. He didn't need to worry about that kind of thing for himself, and so he didn't. The question did provoke a little more response in him, though: "How come?"

"Because the Japanese can run over you any time they please. Because I do not want anything bad to happen to you," Vera said.

Pete grunted. Ever since the Japs overran Peking, he'd known that was true. More often than not, a Marine's pride kept him from admitting it, even to himself. "They mess with us, they've got a war on their hands. A war with the USA. They got to know we'd kick their behinds around the block so darn fast, it'd make their heads swim." That he censored the automatic Marine curses showed she wasn't just a joy girl for him—he really cared.

"They bombed the *Panay.* There was no war," Vera said.

"They apologized afterwards. That's why," Pete answered uneasily. "'Sides, they're busy fighting a war with the Russians. They wouldn't want to tangle with two big countries at once. Japs are crazy, sure, but they aren't that kind of crazy."

"They have what they want from Russia. They have Vladivostok." Vera's English was a lot better, yeah, but the way she pronounced the town's named showed what her native language was. "Now Russia has a hard time fighting them." She spoke with as much assurance as a general.

Pete was good and sure he would never want to suck on a general's bare tits, though. "What can I do about it?" he said. "I'm nothing but a two-striper. Nobody's gonna pay attention to me."

"Talk to your officers. Let them know your concern." *Let them know my concern,* Vera meant. Pete vaguely sensed that, but only vaguely. She went on, "Some of what you tell them will go into what they tell the people over them, the people back in America."

How could she be so sure of that? How much experience of the way the military mind worked did she have? When the question came to him like that, Pete shied away from it. It was almost as if his Corps buddies were razzing him about her. Hell, he didn't need them. He was doing it to himself, right there inside his own head.

What was going through his mind must have shown on his face. Vera suddenly looked impish. "When you turned on the light, I thought it was because you wanted to watch," she said. "Here. I give you something to watch."

And she did. Did she ever! She couldn't have been more distracting if she'd caught fire. She needed experience with men to know how to do what she was doing, too, but Pete didn't care. While she was doing it, he didn't care about anything.

After she got done doing it, he wanted to roll over and sleep for a week. Instead, he smoked another cigarette. Then he did something along those lines for her, too. That went a long way toward proving his love. He never would have done anything like it for anyone he didn't really want to please. If it also proved Vera washed more often and more carefully than other women he'd known—well, he didn't consciously notice.

He did notice she gave every sign of being pleased when he did it: one more encouragement for him to do it again. "How am I supposed to go dance tomorrow?" she said. "My legs are all unstringed."

He thought that was supposed to be *unstrung*, but he wasn't sure enough to tell her so. Correcting a girl who'd just paid you a compliment like that wasn't the smartest thing you could do, either. Pete might not have been the highest card in the deck, but he could see that. Squeezing the breath out of her seemed a better idea. It was more fun, too.

He wished she didn't have to go on working as a taxi dancer. He gave her what he could, but he didn't have enough to put her up the way she'd want to be put up if she quit. A Marine corporal was rich by Shanghai standards, but not rich enough to support a mistress. You needed an officer's pay for that.

Besides, he didn't want a mistress. He wanted a wife. That thrilled his superiors, too. It was one more reason they wouldn't listen to him if he came to them with stories of what the Japs were liable to do. Since he didn't see how he could explain that to Vera, he didn't try.

As they were walking back to the dance hall above which she lived, she waved at the European-style buildings all around. "All this? Pretty soon—poof!" She snapped her fingers. "What do you say? Rented time?"

"Borrowed." Pete only shrugged. "Nothing I can do about it, babe. I don't know if anybody can do anything about it."

"The Japs can," Vera said. "That is the point."

She wouldn't let it alone. If Pete hadn't been head over heels, that would have bothered him. It bothered him a little anyhow, but he overlooked being bothered. Yes, he was in love, all right.

THEY'D DONE SOMETHING unspeakable to Sergeant Demange. Luc Harcourt laughed and laughed. "A lieutenant? At your age? When you've been cussing out officers since before you had to shave? What is the world coming to?"

"Ah, fuck off," Demange said. His eternal cigarette quivered in fury. "I didn't ask 'em to do it. God knows I didn't want 'em to do it. But you can't tell the assholes no—they don't listen to you."

"Yes, sir, Lieutenant, sir," Luc said, and gave Demange the fanciest salute he'd torn off since training-ground days.

"It won't change anything," Demange insisted. "I've been running this fucking platoon full of cocksuckers anyway."

"Hey, but now that you're a lieutenant they'll figure you can run a company, or maybe a battalion," Luc answered. "Everybody knows how screwed up our high command is. They just went and proved it, that's all."

Demange said something about his mother that violated at least eight of the Ten Commandments. Then he added, "The real proof that those shitheads have lost it will be when they make you a sergeant."

"Now that you can't do it, somebody's got to disgrace the rank," Luc said reasonably. Demange's reply took care of the last two Commandments.

Luc wasn't eager to become a sergeant. If he kept avoiding bullets, though, he would before too long. Slots opened up as people's luck ran out. You didn't always need to meet a bullet. Somebody in another company in the regiment had tripped over a length of barbed wire he hadn't seen and broken an ankle. He'd be out of action for weeks, the lucky *salaud.*

Woods rose up ahead. Beyond them lay the village of Serzy-et-Prin. Beyond that, a good way beyond it, lay Reims, which was a real city. The *Boches* held Reims. They held Serzy-et-Prin, too. And there were bound to be bastards in coal-scuttle helmets in among the trees.

Demange pointed east, toward the woods. "Goddamn leaves *would* have to start sprouting just when they could hide some Fritzes." His scorn was so seamlessly perfect, it covered all of mankind and had room for Mother Nature as well. When Luc said as much, Demange spat. "That clapped-out old whore? All she's ever given me are lice."

"Like you're the only one." Just thinking about them made Luc want to scratch. He nodded toward the trees himself. "You going to order us in? Joinville and Villehardouin are ready to lug the Hotchkiss."

"Don't blame it on me," Demange said. "When the generals decide it's time to go, we'll go. Till then, I'll sit on my ass as long as I can."

He spat out the last Gitane's tiny butt and lit up the next. "How about one for me?" Luc asked.

Demange looked shocked. "What? You think officers waste tobacco on enlisted men? Fuck off, *cochon*!"

"Fuck off yourself . . . sir," Luc said. The new lieutenant gave him a cigarette. They smoked together, eyeing the woods they'd have to clear out sooner or later. Like Demange, Luc hoped it would be later. Luc pointed toward the new grass sprouting in the cratered field in front of the trees. "You've got to know the Fritzes have had time to lay mines there."

"As sure as your sister's got crabs," Demange agreed. "All part of the overhead."

"Oh, boy." Luc took his canteen off his belt. It was full of *pinard.* He drank some, then passed the rough red wine to Demange. The veteran's Adam's apple bobbed as he took a good swallow. Just for the moment, with nobody shooting at them and no order to advance, life didn't seem so bad.

The order to advance came the next day. Luc would have been more upset had he been more surprised. "Well, if we've got to catch the shaft, there are worse places to do it—I suppose," Joinville said. Villehardouin came out with something in Breton that Luc didn't understand at all. As Luc had told Demange, they were ready. So was the gun: he checked it himself. By now, he could do everything with a Hotchkiss gun but build one.

And so were the Germans. Whether a deserter warned them or they figured it out for themselves, they shelled the French positions on and off through the night. Luc huddled in a shallow foxhole, trying to doze. He didn't get much sleep, but the hole was deeper toward dawn than it had been at sundown.

"Come on, you sorry, silly *cons,*" Lieutenant Demange called when the eastern sky began to go gray. "Time to earn our *sous.*" He made more as a lieutenant than he had as a sergeant, but you didn't make a career of the Army to get rich.

"You heard the man," Luc told his machine-gun crew. They stumbled forward. There still wasn't enough light to see much. You'd never spot the mine that waited for you. You'd never spot wire, either, though Luc looked for some almost hopefully. A broken ankle didn't seem half bad.

Then, all of a sudden, he could see just fine. German parachute flares lit up the field brighter than noontime. French soldiers cried out in horror. "Down!" Demange screamed. "Get down. They're gonna give it to us."

Give it to them the *Boches* did. Their artillery opened up one more time. Now it was deadly accurate, thanks no doubt to forward observers watching the *poilus* scramble and dive for cover. For good measure, German machine guns at the edge of the woods raked the field. Traces might have been lines of blood drawn in the air.

When people started shooting at you, you flattened out. Demange had that right. Luc did his best to imitate a frog squashed by a tank. But he couldn't just lie there and pile dirt in front of himself with his entrenching tool. Commanding a machine gun meant he had to shoot back. If the Hotchkiss could knock out the German machine gunners, he and his buddies would have a much better chance of seeing the sun go down this afternoon.

Joinville and Villehardouin had hit the dirt, too. They were already putting the machine gun on its tripod. Luc crawled over to them, not getting a centimeter higher off the ground than he had to. "Fuck the fuckers!" Villehardouin said: the clearest thing Luc had heard from him in days.

He got down behind the Hotchkiss and squeezed the trigger. The gun roared through a strip of ammo. He probably wouldn't have any hearing left by the time he got out of the Army, but he didn't care.

Joinville fed fresh strips into the machine gun. One of the ammunition carriers was down, wounded or dead. Villehardouin crawled back to recover the crate. Luc fired, first at one MG-34, then at another. How many of the monsters did those Nazi *cochons* have? The other thing was, they all seemed to be shooting at him, and with better and better accuracy as sunrise neared.

"What I wouldn't give for a couple-three tanks right now," Joinville said. Luc nodded, not that that did either one of them any good. The brass didn't seem to have laid on any armor for this little dance. The Fritzes didn't have any in the neighborhood, so why should *la belle France* waste hers?

Why? To keep us from getting murdered, Luc thought. But that wasn't the biggest worry in the brass's minds, now or ever. The old men with all the gold braid and leaves on their kepis measured things out on their maps and went from there. Casualties? Just part of the overhead, as Demange said.

What Demange said now was, "Back! Get back! We can't break in there in a million years! Machine gun, give us covering fire!"

"Thanks a bunch, *Lieutenant*," Luc said under his breath. But it was the right order, even if it might make him a casualty. He tapped the gun with the heel of his hand, again and again, traversing it so it sprayed the whole front of the woods with fire and made lots of *Boches* keep their heads down. The more Germans who ducked, the more of his own buddies who'd get back to their holes. How he and the rest of the Hotchkiss crew would get back was an . . . interesting question.

To his surprise, it got an answer. The French artillery, which should have shelled the woods before the infantry moved out, chose that moment to wake up. Under cover of the badly timed barrage, the machine gunners made it back to what passed for safety in these parts. Luc drained his *pinard* to celebrate. He figured he'd earned it.

Chapter 8

Sergeant Hideki Fujita had been talking about prisoners of war not long before. Now here they were, thousands of them, maybe tens of thousands, crowded into barbed-wire corrals with Japanese machine-gun positions outside the wire to make sure they didn't get any bright ideas about breaking out.

The Russians looked . . . well, they would have had to perk up to look miserable. They'd been disarmed and hastily plundered after they surrendered, but they weren't plucked clean yet. Who could guess what goodies they hid under their dun-colored greatcoats? Those coats, and the hair—black, brown, yellow, once in a while startling red—sprouting in clumps on their faces, robbed them of their human outlines.

"Monkeys," Fujita said as he strolled around the camp. "That's what they look like. A bunch of monkeys." He mimed scratching himself under the armpits.

Senior Private Hayashi smiled and nodded. If a sergeant made a joke, a senior private thought it was funny. "Have you seen the ones that go in the hot springs in the middle of winter? The Russians are so hairy, that's just what they remind me of." He made his own joke: "And they're in hot water, too."

"*Hai.* They sure are," Fujita said. No matter what had happened during the last war between Russia and Japan, he couldn't see his own countrymen wasting much food or care on prisoners of war, especially when there were so many of them.

He was soon proved right—even righter than he'd expected. The regimental commander, Colonel Watanabe, gathered his men together so he could harangue them: "Soldiers of Japan, we have got to deal with this Russian pestilence!"

Along with plenty of other men, Fujita nodded. Hearing the colonel like this was safe enough. Usually, if his eye fell on you, it was because you'd screwed up. He'd make you sorry, which was one of the things colonels were for.

"Our regiment has been chosen for a high honor!" Watanabe went on. Fujita had a good idea what that meant. It meant that, whatever came out of the colonel's mouth next, they were stuck with it. Sure enough, Watanabe went on, "We have the privilege of removing many of the Russians from proximity to Vladivostok. That way, they can no longer endanger the city, which has become an integral part of the Japanese Empire."

A murmur of "*Hai*" ran through the men. Again, Sergeant Fujita joined it, though he wasn't quite sure what Watanabe was talking about. And then, suddenly, he was. They were going to guard the Russians while the prisoners went wherever Japanese officials had decided they should go.

Colonel Watanabe looked out at his men. "You must be severe. These prisoners have no honor left. Since they've surrendered, how could they? Some of them will realize this. Others will not care, and will act like the wild beasts they are. If they try to get away, you will dispose of them the way you would get rid of any other vermin. Do you understand me?"

"*Hai,*" the Japanese soldiers chorused once more. This time, Sergeant Fujita spoke firmly. He heard no hesitation from any of his comrades, either. It wasn't as if Watanabe had told them anything they didn't already know.

The colonel nodded to the regiment. "Good," he said. "I knew you would hear me in the spirit of *bushido.* Do you have questions?" He pointed to a captain from another company. "Yes?"

"Please excuse me, Colonel-*san,* but what arrangements will be made for getting the prisoners food and water on the march?"

"They are *prisoners,*" Watanabe said, as if to an idiot. "They will get what *bushido* says they deserve. Is that clear enough?"

"Oh, yes, sir," the captain said quickly. It was clear to Fujita, too. *Bushido*—the way of the warrior—said letting yourself get captured was the ultimate disgrace. A prisoner deserved nothing. Better he should have died.

As if reading his mind, Colonel Watanabe raised a hand in warning. "I have been told it is important that some of the captives reach the destination to which we are ordered to take them. They must not all fall along the way. So there will be food. There will be water." He shrugged. "Not what everyone would want, perhaps, but it can't be helped."

After the colonel dismissed the regiment, Fujita went to watch the prisoners some more. He nodded to himself. Monkeys. That was just what they looked like, all right.

"I'm sorry, Sergeant-*san,* but you must not go too close to the wire." The private who spoke to Fujita sounded nervous, and no wonder. Fujita outranked him. Persuading a superior to do what another superior had told you needed doing was liable to get you in trouble.

Not this time, though. "I'll be careful," the sergeant said. "I've never seen so many Westerners close up, that's all."

"Oh, no! Neither have I!" The private showed his teeth in a broad, relieved grin. "I never knew they were so ugly. Did you?"

"No. They look like they were taken out of the oven too soon. And all that hair! They might as well be Ainu, *neh*?"

"I don't know, Sergeant-*san.* I've never seen an Ainu—I'm from Shikoku myself." The private named the southernmost of the four main islands; the Ainu lived on Hokkaido, the most northerly. "All I know is what people say."

What people said was also all Fujita knew about the Ainu. He wasn't about to admit that to a no-account guard. He looked at the Russians. They stared back at him. Just as some of them had yellow or red hair instead of black, some had eyes of blue or green instead of brown. Were they really human?

They were humanly miserable. They stretched out their hands to him, palms up, like begging monkeys. Some of them knew a few Japanese words: "Food, please?" "Rice?" "Meat?" "Bread, sir?" "You have cigarettes?"

"You can ignore them," the private said. "Just about everybody does."

"Just about?" Even the qualification surprised Fujita.

"Some people are soft," the private answered. "You know—the kind who feed stray dogs in the street."

"Dogs are only animals. They do what they do because that's what they do," Fujita said harshly. "These Russians, they're a different kind of dog. They chose to surrender. They could have done the honorable thing instead."

"I would have," the guard said. Fujita believed him. Any Japanese would have. If you killed yourself, everything was over. Your kin would be sad, but they would be proud. The enemy couldn't humiliate you or torment you, and your spirit would find a refuge at the Yasukuni Shrine along with all the others who'd died well. What more could you want?

They got the prisoners moving three days later. Before they opened the gates to the enormous enclosure, a Japanese officer who spoke Russian talked to the captives with a microphone and PA system.

"I wonder what he's saying," Senior Private Hayashi remarked.

"You don't know Russian?" Fujita asked.

"Sorry, Sergeant-*san.* Chinese, and I was starting to learn German, but I hadn't taken much before I went into the Army."

"Well, you don't really need to know the language to work out what's what here," Fujita said. "It's got to be something like 'Behave yourselves and we won't kill you—yet.' What else would you say?"

"That should do it, all right," Hayashi agreed.

After the gates swung wide, the Russians shambled out. They even smelled different from Japanese: harsher, stronger, ranker. Waves of that distinctive stench rose from them as they moved. Their officers and sergeants shouted at them. Obedient as so many cattle, they formed neat ranks.

A Japanese lieutenant at the head of the parade gestured with his sword. Following the wordless order, the Russians trudged off toward the northwest: toward what had been the border between the Soviet Union and Manchukuo. Now all this came under the Emperor's purview.

Fujita couldn't have been happier. No matter how much marching this new duty entailed, nobody would be shooting at him. He didn't think the Red Air Force would try to bomb him, either. They'd blow up more of their own countrymen if they did. Any duty that involved only a small risk of getting killed looked mighty good to him.

PRETTY SOON, THE *rasputitsa* would be over. Already, Poland wasn't quite such a muddy place as it had been when things were at their worst. Hans-Ulrich Rudel could see that, before long, the ground would let panzers move and airplanes take off and land. When that happened, the front was liable to shift far and fast.

As long as it headed east—and he confidently expected it would—he approved of that. Why had they ordered him here, if not to push the front? And yet . . . And yet . . . He wouldn't be happy leaving Bialystok behind.

Even Sergeant Dieselhorst teased him about his reasons: "Ha! That's what you get for falling for a Jewish barmaid."

"She's only half Jewish," Rudel answered with fussy precision.

"*Führer* wouldn't care," Dieselhorst said, which was as accurate as the Pythagorean Theorem. As a good National Socialist, Hans-Ulrich knew that perfectly well. And Dieselhorst went right on sassing him: "Besides, even if you go mooning after her like a poisoned pup—"

"I do not!" Hans-Ulrich broke in.

"Hell you don't." Again, Sergeant Dieselhorst deflated him with the truth. "Like I say, even if you go mooning after her, she hasn't given you a tumble, has she?"

"I don't have to put up with this—this *Quatsch,*" Rudel said with such dignity as he could muster. Dieselhorst's laughter pursued him like antiaircraft fire.

He did have it bad. When his rear gunner wasn't teasing him, he knew that for himself. Which didn't stop him from going into Bialystok to find out if Sofia *would* give herself to him this time around.

"You again!" she said in mock surprise when he walked into the tavern. A couple of Germans who'd been regulars there longer than he had chuckled. He ignored them; they were foot soldiers, not flyers, so their opinions didn't matter to him.

Sofia's did. He sat down at a table, so she'd have to come over. If he'd perched on a stool at the bar, the bored-looking man behind it would have taken care of him. That was the last thing he wanted.

"Two bottles of vodka, right?" she said in Yiddish. She knew—she couldn't very well not know—he steered clear of booze.

"Tea, please," Hans-Ulrich said tightly. Ordering milk in a dive like this only made people laugh at you . . . more than they did anyhow. Besides, he'd found that milk you bought in Poland had at least a fifty-fifty chance of being sour.

"Tea." Sofia rolled her eyes, but she didn't laugh, not out loud. She came back a few minutes later with a glass—Poles drank tea Russian-style—and a pot that had probably come to Bialystok from England when Queen Victoria still sat on the throne disapproving of things. Hans-Ulrich, who disapproved of a good many things himself, felt more than a little sympathy for the late Queen.

But he didn't disapprove of Sofia. On the contrary. As she poured the tea, he slipped an arm around her waist. She made as if to pour some in his lap. He let go, the feel of her still warm on his fingers.

She set the teapot on the table. "What is it with you, anyway?" she demanded.

"What do you think it is? You drive me crazy."

"You *must* be crazy." She followed his German well enough, but the word she used, *meshuggeh,* was one he'd had to figure out from context. She pointed to the *Luftwaffe* eagle on his chest—the eagle holding a swastika in its claws. "You're wearing that, and you think I'd want anything to do with you? Maybe you don't drink, but I bet you smoke an opium pipe."

"I'm here—Germans are here—to defend Poland against the Reds," Rudel said. "Is that so bad? Does it make me so awful?"

"That's not so bad," Sofia said. She pointed to the swastika-carrying eagle again. "*That* makes you awful."

"Would you rather see Russian commissars buying drinks here?"

"Or not buying drinks." This time, she pointed to the teapot. "So you can quit *hokking* me a *chynik* about that." One more Yiddish phrase he'd picked up—literally, banging on a teapot, but stretched to mean making a fuss in general. "The Russians wouldn't come down on us because we were Jews. They'd just come down on us because we were here."

"Is that better?" Hans-Ulrich asked. Only afterwards did he think to add, "We aren't coming down on you. We're being correct." That was the best face he could put on it.

"It's better," Sofia answered. "In the last war, you people came here, too, and there were Jews in the Kaiser's army. Where are they now?"

"They . . . don't support the *Führer.*" Again, that was the best he could do.

"Can you blame them?" Sofia said.

"I don't care about such things," he said, which was a good long stretch from the truth. "All I care about is you." He came closer to veracity there, at least for the moment.

Sofia spelled it out in words of one syllable: "All you want to do is lay me."

"That's not *all* I want to do. I mean—" Hans-Ulrich broke off in confusion.

"What else? Do I want to find out?" she said. Before he could answer—and probably dig himself in deeper—she stalked off to tend to the ground pounders and locals at some of the other tables.

But she came back. She kept coming back. Hans-Ulrich thought she had to have *some* interest in him. If she didn't, she'd take his order, take his money, and ignore him the rest of the time. Or she really would pour hot tea on his crotch. He knew he was dense about such things, but that would get the message across.

"More tea?" she asked.

"Sure."

"All right. If you won't get in trouble because you had a *Mischling* bring you your teapot." She knew the word the Party used to describe half- and quarter-Jews. Away she went.

Hans-Ulrich felt the question as if a round of flak had burst under his Ju-87. Even if Germans couldn't treat Polish Jews the way they treated Jews back in the *Reich,* they weren't supposed to go out of their way to be friendly. He didn't just want to be friendly, either. He wanted to . . . But, as he'd told her, that wasn't the only thing he wanted, which complicated things further.

Before this latest failed coup against the *Führer,* he wouldn't have worried about it so much. Everything was tighter now, though. People who'd done fine in the field had disappeared because the security organs didn't think they were politically reliable. Rudel had always approved of that. Now he discovered the English poet's bell tolling for him.

"Here you go." Sofia plunked another teapot, steam rising from the spout, on the table.

"Thanks. You asked if I'd get in trouble for liking you." That wasn't exactly what she'd asked, but it was what she'd meant. "As far as I'm concerned, you're worth taking the chance on."

"Maybe you're brave. More likely, you're just stupid," Sofia said, which was a shrewd guess on both ends.

"What's so stupid about liking you?" Hans-Ulrich said plaintively.

That plaintiveness finally reached her. She'd started to turn away, but she swung back with a sharp gesture. "Wait a minute," she said, suspicious and wary as a cat. "When you say you like me, you don't just mean you want to go to bed with me. You mean you really like me." She might have been accusing him of some horrible perversion. For all he knew, she was.

He nodded anyway. His heart hadn't thumped like this when he was diving on panzers with his experimental guns to win the *Ritterkreuz.* The French might have killed him, but they wouldn't have left him alive and embarrassed. "That's right," he said.

"You *are* stupid," she said. Then she bent down and gave him a kiss that would have melted all the wax in his mustache if only he'd worn one. The German infantrymen whooped. Before he could grab her and pull her down onto his lap, she skipped back with a dancer's grace. "Be careful what you wish for. You're liable to get it."

And wasn't that the truth? All through the mud time, he'd wanted the chance to hit back at the Russians. Now he'd got it. The front *would* roll east. And when and how would he get back to Bialystok to see Sofia again?

THERE WAS A JOKE they told even in the God-fighting Soviet Union. It had to do with the atheist's funeral. There he lay, all dressed up with no place to go. It wasn't a very good joke, but when did that ever stop people?

Anastas Mouradian felt like that atheist in his coffin. He'd crossed the whole vast breadth of the USSR. He'd flown a couple of missions against the Japanese besieging Vladivostok. And now the city had surrendered. The war against Japan wasn't over, but the little yellow men had what they wanted. Now it was up to the Red Army and Air Force to take it back . . . if they could.

If Japan were the Soviet Union's only enemy, Stalin likely would have massed an army and an air fleet up around Khabarovsk for a drive down the line of the Trans-Siberian Railway toward Vladivostok. How was he supposed to do that, though, when the war with the Hitlerites was about to heat up ten thousand kilometers to the west?

"They'll send us back when the balloon goes up!" Nikolai Chernenko seemed excited at the prospect.

Whether he was or not, Stas wasn't. "That'll be halfway around the world for me, just to get back where I started."

His copilot didn't want to listen to him—no surprise, not when Chernenko was as young as he was. "Are the Germans better in the air than the Japs?" the kid asked.

Germans intimidated Russians in a way the Japanese couldn't come close to matching. Mouradian felt some of that himself. "They're very good," he said. "You can't get foolish or sloppy against them, or you'll end up dead before you've got any notion why."

"What do you mean?" Chernenko might have flown combat missions, but he was still a virgin in some important ways.

That thought told Mouradian how to go on. "Remember what it was like the first time you kissed a girl?"

"I sure do!" The enthusiasm heating the younger man's voice said he hadn't made the discovery very long ago—maybe the night before he left his parents' apartment or his collective farm to report to the Soviet military.

Was I ever that young? Stas wondered. In some important ways, he doubted it. Southerners took for granted things that shocked most Russians. But that was neither here nor there. Gently, the Armenian said, "Fine. Could anybody have explained what kissing a girl was like before you went and did it?"

Chernenko emphatically shook his head. "I don't think so!"

"*Khorosho.* For what it's worth to you, I don't think so, either. Well, fighting the Germans is kind of like that, only you can't try to take their bra off afterwards. You'll find out, if that's what the people with the rank want you to do. Then this will make more sense to you, if you happen to remember it."

The youngster frowned, with luck in wisdom. His spotty face dead serious, he asked, "Why do German fighter pilots wear brassieres? Does it help them against G forces or something?"

"Oh, Kolya, Kolya, Kolya." Mouradian gave up. They might both use Russian, but they didn't speak the same language. One of these days, raw Second Lieutenant Chernenko might turn into First Lieutenant or even Captain Chernenko. He'd grow up. It happened fast when people were shooting at each other. When that day came, he and Mouradian might be able to talk outside the line of duty and make sense to each other. Stranger things had happened. They must have, even if Stas couldn't think of any right this minute.

Meanwhile, even if Vladivostok had fallen, the war against Japan sputtered on. In Stalin's place, Mouradian would have patched up a peace with Japan so he could square off against Hitler undistracted. Maybe he was working on that. Maybe Foreign Commissar Litvinov was in Tokyo right now, making a face-saving deal.

But if he was, Radio Moscow wasn't saying anything about it. Radio Moscow had said as little as it could about losing Vladivostok. All it said was that the garrison commander had yielded the city against orders. If soldiers and civilians were starving, if there was no hope of rescue—and Mouradian knew all too well there wasn't—what could the general do but give up? That was how it looked to him. Radio Moscow saw things differently. And you didn't argue with what Radio Moscow said, except perhaps within the privacy of your own mind. Even then, you had to be careful lest your face betray you.

SB-2s flying out of the base near Khabarovsk bombed towns in northern Manchukuo. They flew across the Tartar Strait and bombed Karafuto. That was what the Japanese called the southern half of Sakhalin Island, which they'd taken in the aftermath of the Russo-Japanese War. The bombers also flew patrols over the Tartar Strait and down into the Sea of Japan. Orders on those missions were to attack and sink any warships they spotted.

German Stukas were ugly, ungainly planes. But Mouradian had been on the receiving end of their dives, and knew how accurately they could place their bombs. SB-2s weren't made for work like that. Stas was willing to try, but a long way from optimistic about the results.

Come to that, he was a long way from optimistic about finding warships, much less hitting them. This was the first time he'd ever seen the ocean, any ocean. It was as illimitably vast as the Russian steppe he'd traveled to get to Siberia. How were you supposed to find anything as small as a ship in all that wave-chopped gray-green sea? Clouds inconsiderately drifting across it didn't help, either.

Damned if they didn't, though. Nikolai Chernenko whooped like a savage. "There!" he said, pointing a dramatic forefinger. "A fucking battleship!"

Stas didn't know if it was a battleship or only a destroyer. He was no connoisseur of warships. But he knew damn well a warship it was. It bristled with guns and turrets, and its hull arrogantly knifed through the water. In these parts, it could only be Japanese.

"We'll go in low," he declared. The SB-2 was no Stuka, but maybe it could impersonate one in the cinema.

Chernenko frowned. "We have no orders to do that, Comrade Pilot."

He was a Russian, all right. And he was a New Soviet Man. Anything without orders was right up there with doubting Marxism-Leninism in the USSR's catalogue of heresies. But Mouradian answered, "We have no orders *not* to do it. And it gives us the best chance for a hit."

He watched his copilot and bomb-aimer chew. If he had to, he vowed to make the attack run himself, his way. But Chernenko's face cleared. Stas had shown himself to be orthodox, or at least not unorthodox. "I serve the Soviet Union!" Chernenko exclaimed.

Mouradian spoke into the voice tube to the bomb bay so Sergeant Suslov would know what was going on. "Just tell me when," Suslov said. "I'll drop 'em right down the whore's cunt." He even talked like the Chimp.

Shove the stick forward. Watch the nose drop. Not too steep, or you'd never pull out again. This *wasn't* a dive-bomber. When the airframe groaned, you needed to listen to it.

The ship swelled from bathtub toy to full-sized fearsomeness much too fast. Blue-clad Japanese sailors ran every which way like angry ants. Antiaircraft guns started filling the sky around the SB-2 with puffs of black smoke with fire at their heart.

"Five degrees to the left, Comrade Pilot. I say again, five degrees left." With business to attend to, Chernenko was a competent professional. Mouradian obeyed without question. "*Da,*" Chernenko said. "That'll do it." Stas thought so, too—they'd pass over the ship from bow to stern. A near miss from a shell shook the SB-2. The copilot ignored it, calling through the tube, "Be ready, Innokenty! At my order!"

"Ready, Comrade Bomb-Aimer! Let's fuck 'em!" Suslov answered.

"Now!" Chernenko shouted.

As soon as the bombs fell free, Mouradian pulled back sharply on the stick, climbing away from the antiaircraft fire. He heard soggy thumps when the bombs went off. When he could see the ship again, smoke rose from the stern. "We did something to it, anyhow," he said, although it was still steaming.

"We should have done more." Chernenko sounded absurdly disappointed. "I wanted to *sink* the son of a bitch."

"We'll have more chances." Mouradian was just glad they'd got away in once piece. He'd never dreamt a ship could throw that many shells. It almost tempted him to go after the next one from several thousand meters up. Almost.

COLONEL OTTO GRIEHL looked out at the men of his black-clad regiment. The black-clad panzer crewmen stood waiting. Theo Hossbach absentmindedly scratched an itch. Next to him, Adi Stoss puffed on a cigarette. Nobody seemed very excited. They all—even Theo—had a good idea of what was coming next.

Griehl scratched, too, at a scar on his chin. He was lean, almost hawk-faced, with hollow cheeks and close-cropped gray hair. Like his men, he wore pink-piped black collar patches with a silver *Totentkopf* in each one. The skull and crossbones had been the panzer emblem for as long as Germany'd had armored fighting vehicles.

"Well, boys, it's time," Griehl said. "We came into this fight by dribs and drabs, and then we had to put up with the worst winter even an old man like me can remember." Theo wasn't sure the colonel's face had room for a grin, but it did. It made him look years younger—though still old, of course. It didn't last long. He sobered as he went on, "But now we're here in the East in proper force, and now the ground and the weather . . . aren't too bad." That was as much praise as he would dole out to Polish conditions. "And so—it's time to show the Ivans what we can do."

A low hum ran through the *Panzertruppen.* Here and there, men nodded: Adi did, and so did Sergeant Witt. Theo just stood, listening. He was ready, but he wasn't eager. He knew what could happen when things went wrong. If he was ever tempted to forget, the missing joints on his ring finger reminded him.

"We're going to drive them out of Poland," Griehl said matter-of-factly. "Once we take care of that—well, we'll see. I don't know what the *Führer* and the High Command will want us to do then. One thing at a time, though. Let's talk about our immediate objectives."

And he did, detailing the routes the regiment would take as it pushed east and north from the vicinity of Bialystok. He talked about artillery and air support, and about the infantry who would move forward with the panzers.

"Most of them are Polish units," he said. "Remember that, for God's sake, and don't shoot them by mistake. They wear a darker, greener khaki than the Russians, and their helmet is almost like the Czech pot—it doesn't have a brim like the Russian model."

"Tell us something we didn't know," Adi muttered. Theo heard him, and maybe Witt did, too, but nobody else. Theo was patient with these lectures. One reason you walked barefoot through the obvious was that people *did* forget, especially when other people were trying to kill them.

"Give the Poles a hand where you can," Griehl said. "They're good troops. They're brave troops. The only thing that's really wrong with them is, they don't have as many toys as we do. Infantry, machine guns—they've got those. But they're light on artillery and panzers and planes. That's why they called us in to help against the Reds. So we'll do it." He grinned again. "It's not like the *Führer* hasn't got his own reasons for going after Russia. If you've read *Mein Kampf,* you'll know that."

He got more nods. Hitler's book was Holy Writ to the Party. Theo had looked at it, found it bombastic and badly written, and put it aside. But you didn't have to have gone through page by page to know he talked about Russia as Germany's *Lebensraum.* Stalin doubtless had a different view of that, which didn't bother the *Führer.*

"We go at 0430 tomorrow," the colonel finished. "Good luck to every one of you. Believe you me, Ivan will never know what hit him."

When the big push in the West started a little before Christmas 1938, officers promised men the showgirls and bars of Paris. They didn't quite deliver; Theo lost the end of that finger in the last failed effort at a breakthrough. Maybe this time everything would work out the way Colonel Griehl said. Theo had his doubts. He didn't voice them. For one thing, what was the point? For another, he hardly ever voiced anything.

He was in the panzer before the appointed hour. He squeezed meat paste from a tinfoil tube onto a chunk of black bread. Not the kind of breakfast he'd eaten before conscription called, but he didn't raise his voice to complain, either. And that meat paste was one of the best rations the Germans had. Tommies on patrol stole tubes of it from dead *Landsers.*

Where he sat, he couldn't see what was going on. All he could see were his radio set, the machine pistol next to it, and the panzer commander's behind and legs. He didn't care. He had his own little world. He heard the order to go forward, and relayed it to Hermann Witt. And, through the Panzer II's armor and through his earphones, he heard the thunder of the German artillery as it pounded Soviet positions to the east. Stukas would be screaming out of the sky to take out strongpoints too tough for artillery. Theo couldn't hear them, but he knew how an attack worked.

No. He knew how an attack should work. Things always went wrong. Neither side had really known what it was doing when the *Wehrmacht* drove into Czechoslovakia. A good thing the Czechs were as thumb-fingered as the Germans, or that one might have failed. On the Western front, they'd tried to go too far too fast. Looking back, he could see that. At the time, it seemed easy—until, all of a sudden, it didn't any more.

Now . . . The Panzer II squashed barbed wire under its tracks. Foot soldiers, whether in *Feldgrau* or dark Polish khaki, would be able to follow. Sergeant Witt sprayed short bursts of machine-gun fire ahead of the panzer. If the Russians had to keep their heads down, the infantrymen with the German armor would have an easier time disposing of them.

Rat-a-tat-tat! Except is wasn't *rat-a-tat-tat!,* or not exactly. It was *clangety-clangety-clang!,* as if somebody were attacking the panzer with a rivet gun. Machine gunners couldn't resist panzers. They also couldn't hurt them, if you didn't count scaring the crew half to death.

"Panzer halt!" Witt shouted. Adalbert Stoss obediently hit the brakes. The panzer commander fired a three-round burst from the 20mm main armament. "All right," he said. "Drive on!"

Forward they went, with a whine of protest from the overstrained engine. A moving target was harder to hit, and the Panzer II's armor, especially on the sides, wouldn't keep out anything more than small-arms fire. Theo knew from experience what happened when something got through. His crewmates didn't, and he hoped like hell they didn't find out. He'd got away from his murdered first panzer in one piece. Too many guys weren't so lucky. If he never smelled that thick reek of burnt pork . . .

"Enemy panzers ahead—two o'clock!" Witt shouted. Theo's balls crawled up into his belly, not that that would save them. From what he'd seen, Russian panzer gunners weren't very good, but they only had to be competent, or even lucky, once to slaughter a crew. But then Witt shouted again, in glad surprise: "Cancel that! They're ours—Czech machines!"

No one but Theo heard his own sigh of relief. Of course the *Wehrmacht* had commandeered all the surviving Czech panzers it could. They were better than German Panzer Is and IIs, if not up to the standards of the new IIIs and IVs. But the new German panzers were still in short supply. Military administrators had got the Skoda works up and running again, turning out more of the Czech models for the *Reich*.

And if you were looking for the enemy, you'd see him whether he was there or not. Theo was happy Witt hadn't opened up. One of war's dirty little secrets that nobody liked to talk about was that you could kill friends as easily as foes. Friends could kill you, too. They'd be sorry afterwards, not that that did you a hell of a lot of good.

There *were* Russian panzers up ahead. Theo got the word on the radio, and relayed it to Witt. Then he heard the fearsome *clang!* of a round from a cannon smashing through hardened steel. It wasn't his panzer, which was the only good thing he could say about it. That crew would never be the same.

"Panzer halt!" the commander ordered. Halt it did. He fired another three-round burst from the 20mm gun. "*Got* the fucker!" he yelled. "Drive on!"

On they went. Theo tried to figure out what was happening from the endless stream of radio reports he heard. They made up for not being able to see out. Everything seemed to be moving according to plan. Germans and Poles stormed forward. Russians fell back or died. Germans and Poles were dying, too. Theo knew that, but the radio didn't talk about it.

Chapter 9

Colonel Borisov eyed the flyers in his squadron. He coughed a couple of times, like a man who'd smoked too many cigarettes. He probably had, but that wasn't tobacco roughening his throat. Sergei Yaroslavsky would have bet gold against pig turds it was embarrassment.

Just a couple of weeks before, Borisov had been loudly certain this year's fight against the Nazis in Poland would look the same as last year's. Well, not even a colonel was right all the time. Coughing once more, Borisov said, "The situation at the front has developed not necessarily to our advantage."

He sounded like Radio Moscow. As it had when Vladivostok fell, the radio was doing its damnedest to make things sound better than they really were. Like the other SB-2 pilots, Sergei had flown over the front. He'd done everything he could to slow down the Germans. The radio would have faced a bigger challenge had it tried to make things out to be worse than they were.

"In certain places, the Nazis and their Polish running dogs have penetrated our lines to some degree," Borisov went on. "Our assignment is to help whip them back to their kennels so the Red Army can resume—excuse me, can continue—its victorious offensive."

No one laughed in his face, which proved discipline—or fear of the NKVD, assuming the two weren't one and the same—ran deep. From the sky, you could see that the dark gray German tanks hadn't just "penetrated" the Soviet line. They'd torn through, and were rampaging loose in the Russians' rear. Enemy infantry moved up with them and behind them to finish off the pockets they carved out.

"Groundcrew men are fueling and bombing up our planes," Borisov said. "We shall strike hard for the *Rodina*! We serve the Soviet Union!"

"We serve the Soviet Union!" the flyers echoed. They left the big tent in which he'd harangued them and hurried to their SB-2s. Sergei wondered whether he'd be able to land at this airstrip when he came back from the bombing run. The way the Germans were moving, it was almost in range of their guns. One more thing to worry about.

"Does he truly believe what he says?" Vladimir Federov asked in a troubled whisper.

Sergei would have whispered a question like that, too. "He does while he's saying it, anyhow," he answered, also quietly. "You can't contradict the Party line."

Off in the distance—not far enough in the distance—German artillery rumbled. It might have been distant thunder. Unfortunately, it wasn't, not on this bright, sunny day. No thunderheads in the sky: only a few little white puffs. Federov jerked his head in the direction of the sound. "*That* contradicts the Party line."

Sergei didn't feel like arguing with him. "Well, we'll dispose of the contradictions, then, won't we?"

He climbed into the cockpit. Sergeant Kuchkov was already at his station in the bomb bay. The Chimp didn't worry about contradictions in the Party line. He'd drop the bombs. He'd shoot at whatever tried to attack the SB-2. He'd get back to the airstrip and he'd drink and swear and try to get laid. He hadn't come down venereal yet, but not from lack of effort.

Nothing looked bad on the preflight checks. The engines started up right away. The familiar roar and vibration filled Sergei. Groundcrew men pulled out the chocks in front of his wheels. He taxied down the dirt runway and took off. The heavily laden SB-2 wasn't a hot performer, but it flew, it flew.

It hadn't flown far when antiaircraft guns opened up on it. "Are the Nazis this far east already?" Federov shouted through the din.

"No—these are our guns, dammit," Sergei shouted back. "The stupid *muzhiks* down below see anything in the air, they think it has to belong to the Germans."

The Germans *had* come farther east than they had on the last mission the SB-2 had flown, the day before. Fire and smoke did a good job of announcing where their panzers were—where Soviet forces were in trouble, in other words. And so did antiaircraft fire of a sort entirely different from what the Red Air Force bombers had got a few minutes before. When the Nazis started shooting, the shells burst all around the SB-2s. Every one of them seemed much too close.

One scored a direct hit on a bomber in front of Sergei. The last third of a wing parted company with the rest of the plane. Fire raced up the wing root toward the fuselage. The SB-2 lurched out of formation and tumbled downward. Sergei looked for parachutes, but didn't see any.

"*Bozhemoi!*" Behind the oxygen mask, Vladimir Federov's face was white as milk. "They're murdering us!"

"Well, we need to pay them back, then." Sergei found what he was looking for: Nazi flags spread out on the ground. Both sides used their national emblems to keep from getting hit by their own aircraft. But the recognition signals could also turn into targets. Sergei pointed through the cockpit glass. "There. That's what we want."

"All right." No matter how shaken Federov was, he had a job to do. *And the sooner he does it, the sooner we drop our bombs, the sooner we can get the devil out of here,* Sergei thought.

But before the bomb-aimer could line up the SB-2 on the swastika flags far below, a frantic shout dinned in Sergei's earphones: "Messerschmitts!"

"Drop the bombs, Kuchkov!" Sergei ordered at once. "Right now!" They'd come down on somebody's head: with luck, on some German's. He wanted the plane as light as he could make it. He also didn't want machine-gun bullets tearing into all those explosives. That was asking to turn into a fireball in the sky.

"Bombs away!" the Chimp yelled, sending them earthward with some choice obscenities. Then he asked, "Nazi cocksuckers jumping us?"

"*Da,*" Sergei said. He still hadn't seen any 109s. But, one after another, three SB-2s spun toward the ground, two burning, the other out of control—maybe the pilot was already dead. With the bombs gone, he had no reason to stick around any more. He had no desire to, either. He swung the bomber into as tight a turn as he could manage and gave it full throttle back toward the east.

A 109 shot across his path. He had two forward-facing machine guns in the cockpit. He squeezed off a long burst at the German plane. He didn't hit it. He hadn't really expected to. He did want to warn it he was alert and ready to fight. Let it go after some sleepier pilot.

It must have worked. Kuchkov, in the dorsal turret now, didn't start shooting at anything. And no bullets came ripping up through the bomber's now empty belly. Sergei looked wildly around the sky. Some of the other SB-2s had also escaped. One of them had a starboard engine that trailed smoke. He hoped it would keep flying till it found the airstrip.

"That was . . . very bad." Federov seemed to be trying his best to stay calm, or at least to seem calm.

Sergei respected him for that. You had to do it in combat. Showing how scared you were didn't do any good. Everybody was scared. You had to keep going anyway. If you didn't, you only made getting yourself killed more likely.

Sergei wondered whether Stukas would have cratered the airstrip. He didn't want to try to land on a highway or in the middle of a field of new-planted barley.

He didn't have to, to his vast relief. He taxied into a revetment. Groundcrew men covered the SB-2 with camouflage netting. In the gloom, he reached out and set a hand on Federov's shoulder. "We made it. One more time, we made it."

"But how often can we keep getting away with it?" the copilot asked. "I know the plane used to be able to run away from fighters, but not any more. The idea is for us to hurt the enemy, right? Not for him to shoot us down? How many of our guys didn't come back today?"

"Too many. Maybe some landed at other strips, but too many any way you look at it," Sergei answered.

"One of the planes that went down was Colonel Borisov's," Federov said.

"The squadron commander's? Are you sure? I didn't see that." Sergei wasn't sure what to think about it, either. Borisov had too much apparatchik in him to get close to the men he led, but he was a good administrator and a brave enough pilot. He had been, anyhow.

"I'm positive," Federov said.

"One more thing, then," Sergei said wearily. He unhooked his flying harness. "Well, let's go report to . . . whoever we report to."

"BROAD STREET STATION!" the conductor bawled as the train down from New York City slowed to a stop. "All out for Broad Street station! Philadelphia!"

"Oh, my God!" Peggy Druce dabbed at her eyes with a tissue she pulled from a purse. She didn't need the fellow in the kepi yelling at her. That Gothic pile of brick, granite, and terra cotta couldn't be anything else. It meant she was home. She wouldn't have believed it, but it was true. More than a year and a half after she set out on what was going to be a month in Europe, here she was.

If I ever, ever set one toe outside the borders of the US of A again, somebody ought to whack me in the head with a two-by-four, she thought. She'd almost been whacked with plenty of worse things in too many different places in Europe.

People were getting up and heading for the door. Lucky for them, too, because she would have stepped on them if they weren't moving the way she wanted to go. A liner back to New York from London. No sign of U-boats, for which she thanked God. Not the smoothest passage, but not the choppiest, either. She was a good sailor. She didn't lose any victuals.

Almost all the clothes she brought back she'd bought on the other side of the Atlantic. What she'd brought with her hadn't been meant for staying away so long. That interested the hell out of the American customs inspectors. Even after she explained what had happened to her—

backing everything up with the stamps and visas in her passport—they didn't want to listen. All they wanted to do was collect duty, and collect they did. The Nazis couldn't have been more inflexible.

But she wouldn't think about the goddamn Nazis now. After all, she'd crossed the Atlantic so she wouldn't have to think about the Nazis again, or deal with their arrogance. And so she'd dealt with American arrogance at customs instead.

"Watch yo' step, ma'am," a colored porter said as she descended. He touched a callused finger to the shiny brim of his cap. She nodded back at him. She hadn't seen any Negroes all the time she was in Europe. This chubby fellow was just one more reminder she was back where she belonged.

Down three wooden steps and onto the platform. Husbands and wives, boyfriends and girlfriends, parents and children were all milling around and falling into one another's arms. They were hugging and squealing and kissing. They were . . .

"Herb!" Peggy let out a squeal of her own. She might have been a bobby-soxer getting all excited about the latest skinny crooner from Hoboken, not a respectable woman of middle years running toward a prosperous gent in a gray pinstriped suit and a fedora whose band and brim told the world it wasn't quite the latest style.

"Peggy!" He squeezed the breath out of her. He wasn't usually one for public displays, but then she didn't usually get stuck in the middle of a world war. He smelled of aftershave and American cigarettes—good smells, familiar smells, she'd almost forgotten about in her crowded time overseas. And he smelled of himself, which was even better and even more familiar.

"Oh, Lord!" she said when they got done kissing out there in front of everyone like a couple of newlyweds. "I missed you so much!"

"Well, I'm not exactly sorry to see you back, either, sweetheart." That sounded more like Herb. He might not have majored in understatement at Villanova, but he sure must have minored in it.

He took a pack of Pall Malls from a jacket pocket, tapped one against the palm of his left hand, and stuck it in his mouth. As he was lighting it, Peggy said, "For God's sake give me one of those, will you? I've been smoking like a chimney—I mean like a steel-mill chimney—

since I got back to New York. What they use for tobacco in Europe shouldn't happen to a dog."

"Here you go." He lit it for her. She smoked greedily. She hadn't been kidding, not even a little bit. Herb let her take a few puffs. Then he said, "Come on. Let's rescue your suitcase, and then we'll go home."

"You have no idea—I mean, darling, you have *no* idea—how good that sounds." Peggy charged toward the baggage car like a panzer on the attack. Thinking of it in that particular way told her she wasn't the same person she had been when shells started falling around Marianske Lazne.

Herb tipped a redcap to carry the suitcase out to the Packard. When they got to the station door, the man said, "Suh, this here's as far as I'm supposed to go."

Without missing a step, Herb handed him another fat silver half-dollar. "I didn't hear a word you said. Did you hear anything, Peg?"

"Who, me?" she said. The porter's grin showed a mouthful of gold teeth. He lugged the bag out to the car and waved when he trotted back toward the station.

Philadelphia traffic took getting used to. So did everything else about the city. It didn't look shabby. People in the street weren't nervous or fearful. Or, if they were, it was from personal, private concerns, not because they worried that dive-bombers would scream down out of the sky and blow them into ground round.

There was so much in the shops! Gasoline was so cheap, and so many cars used the roads. "You don't know how lucky we are," Peggy said. A cop at a street corner was directing traffic. That was all he was doing. Peggy pointed his way. "Look! He isn't asking people for their papers."

"They'd spit in his eye if he did," Herb answered. "And who needs papers, anyway? Unless you're going overseas, I mean."

"I was mighty glad to have my American passport. Oh, Jesus, was I ever," Peggy said. As for the rest of it, though, her husband had the straight goods. If you lived in a free country, why did you need anything that proved who you were? Wasn't your word good enough? Peggy pointed again, almost at random. "No soldiers! No uniforms! Not one, except for the policeman."

"Well, who needs 'em?" Herb said.

She remembered Germany, where everybody this side of ragpickers put on an outfit that let him show off who he was and what he did and why everybody else should salute him. And she wouldn't have been a bit surprised if the *Reich* had mandated rank badges so people could tell a Ragpicker First Class from a lowly Ragpicker Second.

They lived not far from the Main Line, on a street that had been lined with elms till Dutch elm disease killed them. They had more house than they needed most of the time.

Herb parked the car in front of the place. Was he grayer than he had been the last time she saw him? And was he wondering the same thing about her? A year and a half! Lord!

"You don't know how good it is to have you back," he said.

"You don't know how good it is to be back!" Peggy said. She leaned over and kissed him on the cheek. "You have no idea. And count yourself lucky you don't."

"Maybe I do, a little," Herb answered, and left it right there.

Peggy started to tell him he was talking through his hat. She didn't do it, though. Maybe making it to middle age meant she thought before opening her big trap. Sometimes, anyhow. Herb had gone Over There in 1918. He'd seen combat; Peggy knew that much. Even after all these years, she knew very little more. Whatever he'd seen and done in France, he'd never talked about it once he came back to the States. This was almost the first time he'd suggested he might have run into an unpleasantness or three while working for Uncle Sam.

And so, instead of laughing at him, Peggy said, "I could use a drink—and if you want to spell that with a U, I don't mind."

"Motion seconded and passed by acclamation." Herb got out of the Packard, came around, and opened the passenger door for her. The suitcase stayed on the back seat. Peggy didn't need anything in it right away, and nobody would steal it, not in this eminently respectable neighborhood.

Herb opened the front door. He took half a step to one side so Peggy could walk into the foyer ahead of him. When she did, she was greeted by shouts of "Surprise!" and "Welcome home!" and enough cheers for a Sunday doubleheader at Shibe Park. Everybody she'd ever met seemed to be crowding the house.

She rounded on her husband. "*You* did this!" she said—half accusation, half delight.

"Darn right I did," he answered. "You don't come back from a war every day."

"I'm going to have that drink, or maybe that drunk, any which way," Peggy declared.

"Good. I'll help," Herb said briskly. She did, and so did he.

VACLAV JEZEK PUT a helmet on a stick and cautiously raised it up above the level of the trench in which he crouched. That was probably the oldest sniper's trick in the world, which didn't mean it didn't work. The German lines were most of a kilometer away, separated from his position by mines and barbed wire. All the same, a rifle shot rang out over there.

The helmet rang, too, like a bell. He jerked it down. It was a French model. Now it had a bullet hole a centimeter or two above the French crest soldered onto the front.

Sergeant Benjamin Halévy eyed that precisely placed hole. "Well, you were right," he said. "Fucking Nazis have a sniper of their own running around loose."

"Happy day," Vaclav said morosely. "I've done this before. I don't want to do it again, goddammit." When a sniper annoyed the enemy enough, he did his best to get rid of the annoyance. Vaclav had already won a couple of duels with a German sharpshooter. Now the *Landsers* were back for another try.

"They must have noticed when you murdered that mortar guy and the armored cars," Halévy said.

"Happy day," the Czech repeated, even more gloomily than before. The pile of dirt and ore and whatnot where the mortar crew had set up was behind the line now, not in front of it. Clearing all the Germans away from it had cost more lives than it was worth. And the boys in field-gray still had plenty more of those industrial hillocks to use as firing positions.

"Maybe a shell from a 105 will blow that son of a bitch right out of his marching boots," Halévy said.

"And then you wake up," Vaclav said, fumbling in his tunic for a pack of Gitanes. He was wearing a French one; the Czech tunic he'd had for so long had finally gone the way of all fabric. The pockets weren't in the right places—they weren't where his fingers automatically went, anyhow. Once he had the cigarette going, he added, "You can afford to be cheerful. The bastard isn't trying to put one in your earhole."

"He wouldn't turn me down if I did something stupid," Halévy said.

"No, but you'd just be part of his job. When two snipers tangle, it's personal," Vaclav said. That made it worse, as far as he was concerned. When you shot whoever you saw in the enemy's uniform, it was war. When you tried to kill one guy in particular, it was something different, something even older and more primitive.

Halévy hit that nail on the head when he said, "Fine. Once you plug this Nazi, cut his liver out and cook it. It'll probably be fat, like a force-fed goose's."

"Heh," Vaclav said nervously. The way the French got their nice fatty livers for paté made his stomach want to turn over. The idea of eating a German liver, on the other hand, disgusted him less than he thought it should. Still . . . "He's probably some lousy *Feldwebel* left over from the last war, and tougher than shoe leather."

"Wouldn't be surprised," Halévy said. "Long pig isn't any more kosher than regular pig, either. Too bad."

"It wouldn't stop you, not the way you gobble down all the ham you can find," Jezek jabbed.

The Jewish underofficer shrugged. "Food is food. When you get some, you eat it. You can be sorry afterwards. I'm always sorry afterwards. I'm usually sorry there wasn't more."

Vaclav snorted. Before he could give Halévy a hard time, a young French officer came up to them and started jabbering away in his own language. Vaclav spread his hands. He really didn't speak much French. And feigning even more incomprehension kept him from having to do what eager young officers had in mind. A couple of times, that might have kept him from getting killed.

Halévy could interpret, of course—if he felt like admitting he understood French. Sometimes he did, sometimes he didn't. Sergeants often mistrusted officers' schemes . . . and often had good reason.

But this fellow wouldn't be put off so easily. "Wait," he said in nasal German. "I was told you followed the *Boche*'s tongue."

However much Jezek wanted to deny it, he didn't see how he could, not without landing himself in more trouble. "*Ja,*" he said resignedly. "*Was wollen Sie, mein Herr?*"

"I will tell you what I want," the Frenchman said. "We have found the spot from which the German colonel in charge of the regiment opposite us is in the habit of making reconnaissance. He is a capable officer. If you eliminate him, very likely his replacement will be less so."

"*Foie gras,*" Halévy remarked. The French officer gave him a look that mingled annoyance and curiosity. The Jew did not explain.

In his boots, Vaclav wouldn't have explained, either. "I must see the place, sir, and find a spot from which to shoot," he told the officer. His own German was rusty, but it served.

"*Aber natürlich,*" the Frenchman said. "Come with me." He started to straighten.

Vaclav grabbed him before he could. "Be careful, for God's sake," he said. "The Nazis have their own sniper over there."

"Oh, really? Is that so?" Maybe the young officer was being ostentatiously brave. Then again, maybe he was being ostentatiously stupid. Vaclav took no needless chances. He wanted to live to get old and fat and lazy. If he settled down here and married a Frenchwoman, that wouldn't be so bad, even if it meant he'd finally have to buckle down and learn the lousy language.

Antitank rifle clunking against his back at every step, he followed the officer down the trench. He made sure he didn't show himself. If the German marksman was watching through field glasses or a telescope, he could recognize the rifle's long, thick barrel. Better—much better—not to let him do anything about it.

"Here is our lookout position," the officer said after most of a kilometer. Vaclav lowered the rifle and kept walking. The Frenchman spluttered. "You are insubordinate!" he declared, a word only an officer would bother learning *auf Deutsch.*

"No, sir," Vaclav said stolidly as the Frenchman trailed after him. "Think the Fritzes don't know where you look from? Maybe a sniper can't put one through your loophole there, but I don't want to find out the hard way."

The officer grunted. Speaking German, Vaclav sounded as authoritative as he did. Speaking German, anybody could sound authoritative. That was one of the few things the language was good for. With any luck at all, the Nazi with the scope-sighted Mauser would figure he'd stopped at the observation post. Two or three hundred meters farther on, he raised his helmet above the level of the parapet. When no gunshot came his way, he slowly lowered the helmet, put it on again, and peered across toward the German position.

"Now," he said, "tell me where the German colonel looks from. Don't point or anything. Just tell me."

"You know your business," the officer said, coming up beside him to look east. He sounded surprised, and more respectful than he had before.

"I'm still breathing," Vaclav answered, which covered everything that needed saying on that score.

"Do you see the burnt-out automobile, a little to the right of the broken brick fence?" the Frenchman asked. His right arm twitched, but he didn't point. "That is where the *cochon* does his reconnaissance."

Vaclav did see it. It was a long shot from here. He wasn't sure of a kill, but he had a chance. "*Sehr gut,*" he said. "I will come back before sunup, so I can get ready without the Germans seeing me do it."

"You will know what you require," the French officer said stiffly. He gave Vaclav a jerky little nod, then hopped off the firing step and down into the trench again.

The Czech *did* know what he required. By the time the eastern sky started getting light, he'd placed his rifle and covered most of the barrel with branches he tore from bushes. His helmet was covered with leafy branches, too, held in place by a rubber strip he'd cut from an old inner tube. He'd seen Germans use that trick, and he liked it well enough to steal.

Once he was set, he had nothing to do but wait. Wait he did, and wait, and wait some more. He wanted a cigarette, but he didn't smoke. He didn't know if the enemy was watching this spot, and he didn't want to do anything to draw his notice. A couple of *poilus* near the lookout post shot at the German line. They drew answering rifle and machine-gun fire. Vaclav smiled. If the Germans got all hot and bothered by those fellows over there, they weren't worrying about him.

Halfway through the morning, he was bored. He needed to take a leak. He *really* wanted a cigarette. He waited. That was half the battle, or more than half, for snipers.

And he got his reward. Here came a fellow in a *Feldgrau* greatcoat, with an officer's peaked cap on his head. He stationed himself near that dead motorcar and began a leisurely examination of the Allied position.

It seemed to Vaclav that the German was looking straight at him when he pulled the trigger. Did the fellow see the muzzle flash? Did he just have time to realize what it was before the bullet hit him? Because it did hit him—he went down like a marionette when the puppeteer drops the strings.

As soon as Vaclav saw that, he ducked and scurried away. The German sniper on the other side of the line would know he'd scored again. The bastard would want to meet him . . . in a manner of speaking. So many other things could kill or maim him, too. But he was still alive. He might stay that way a while longer.

ANOTHER MISERABLE SUPPER. Sarah Goldman's mother was a good cook. When you had so little to work with, though, what could you do? Pharaoh had ordered the Children of Israel to make bricks without straw. Hanna Goldman faced the same problem, thanks to the orders of Germany's latter-day Pharaoh. When root vegetables and turnip greens were all you could make, when salt was your only flavoring, you were licked.

After supper, Father turned on the radio. He didn't usually bother any more. "What's up?" Sarah asked.

"I want to hear the news," he answered.

"Good God—why?" Sarah exclaimed. "Same old rubbish."

"Probably." Samuel Goldman rolled a cigarette from newspaper and tobacco scrounged from dog ends. It wasn't a professorial skill, but he had it. Maybe he'd picked it up in the trenches in the last war. More likely, he'd acquired it since exchanging his university post for one in a labor gang. Jews got no tobacco ration of their own any more. After he lit the nasty cigarette, he went on, "I heard something interesting from somebody who said he heard it from someone you can trust. I want to see if the regular broadcast covers it."

Sarah had no trouble translating her father's opaque phrases. He'd been talking with someone who listened to the BBC, or possibly to Radio Paris. That was, of course, against the law, and the Germans jammed enemy stations as hard as they could. People tuned in to them anyhow. The Goldmans would have, even if it was doubly risky for Jews. But, with Saul still on the run from what the Nazis called justice, it was ten times doubly risky for them. If they got caught, they'd go straight to a concentration camp, and so they abstained.

Treacly music came out of the radio set once it warmed up. It was still ten minutes in front of the hour. Father shrugged and made a wry face. "I wish it were a classical program," he said. "Bach, Beethoven . . ."

"Wagner?" Sarah suggested.

His mouth twisted even tighter. "Well, maybe not."

Mother came out of the kitchen to listen, too. They endured the music, and the advertisements for things they weren't allowed to buy (most of which Aryan Germans couldn't really get their hands on these days, either), and the exhortations to turn in scrap metal and purchase war bonds.

At last, the announcer said, "And now, the news." He paused importantly, as if certain everyone was hanging on the sound of his voice. He might not have been so far wrong, either. "In the east, the *Wehrmacht* and the *Reich*'s Polish allies continue to punish the Jew-Bolshevik Red Army. The Asiatic hordes who follow the Soviet red star cannot hope to stand against our brave, well-disciplined troops."

"He'll have us in Moscow in a couple of weeks," Father said dryly.

Nothing much was happening in the west. In what was happening there, the front line was moving toward the German border, not away from it. Unless you listened with an atlas in hand, you'd never know it from what the newsreader said. By the way he made things sound, panzers would roll through Paris any minute now—maybe even ahead of the ones rolling through Moscow.

He claimed enormous numbers of English and French terror

bombers—they were always terror bombers—shot down the day before. No alarms had sounded over Münster. Had the other side's bombers not come here? Or was the newsreader making things up? How could you tell? You couldn't. He went on to claim even more enormous numbers of Russian terror bombers destroyed in the east. And he gloated about the dreadful things German bombers were doing to military targets—only to military targets, of course—in London and Paris and half a dozen Russian cities, some of which he had trouble pronouncing.

Wasn't he trying to have things both ways? It seemed so to Sarah. By her father's ironic eyebrow, it seemed so to him, too.

The announcer also bragged about Japanese raids in Siberia, and about the signing of a new German-Swedish economic agreement. "Thus we preserve Sweden's neutrality, as we preserved Denmark's and Norway's," he declared. He sounded perfectly serious about it. Father's eyebrow quirked again anyhow.

Then the fellow went on to condemn an economic agreement between France and the United States. The enemy sought to drag America into their unjust war—at least if you listened to him. Sarah thought her father's eyebrow would jump right off his forehead. It was only radio, so she couldn't see the newsreader's face. How could he possibly hold it straight? But even if he was grinning, he sounded as if he meant what he said.

"I now turn to the occupied regions of Bohemia and Moravia," he went on in portentous tones. That was what German authorities were calling the conquered part of Czechoslovakia, the part that hadn't turned into the puppet state of Slovakia. "Despite all warnings, Jews in these regions have continued in their anti-German activities. As a result of their vicious folly, the *Führer* and the *Reichsführer*-SS see that they have no choice but to implement appropriate countermeasures."

Sarah and her father and mother all stared straight at the radio. What did that mean? Whatever it meant, it didn't sound good. What *had* Hitler and Himmler come up with?

The newsreader proceeded to spell things out: "The Jewish bacillus in the occupied territories of Bohemia and Moravia must be quarantined. Accordingly, the *Führer* has ordered all Jews in the aforementioned occupied territories to be transferred to the town of Teriesenstadt, where they may be concentrated, observed, and guarded against. Personnel under the command of the *Reichsführer*-SS will facilitate the transfer and supervise the just distribution of any property abandoned in the process."

Father's eyebrow didn't quirk this time. Both brows came down and together in a frown that might have suited Jove's awesome visage. "It's a ghetto, that's what it is," he said heavily. "A hundred years after we got out of them, they're shoving us back in again. Western civilization!" He made the words into a curse.

"He talked about abandoned property," Mother added. "What do they give the Jews? One suitcase apiece?"

"Or maybe just the clothes on their backs," Father said.

"How many Jews in Czechoslovakia?" Sarah asked.

Her mother and father looked at each other. She shrugged. He spread his hands. "Not as many as there are in Poland—that's all I can tell you for sure," he said. "The ones there are lucky their government is on the Nazis' side, or they'd get the same or worse."

"Some luck," Sarah said.

"It is," Father insisted. "Poland has millions of Jews—I know that. I've never had much use for *Ostjuden.* Sometimes they seem almost as backward and barbarous to me as they do to Hitler. They'd sooner pray than think, if you know what I mean. But when push comes to shove, they're my people. The Nazis have said so all along, and they've finally convinced me they're right."

"What can we do to help the Czech Jews?" Sarah asked.

Her father spread his hands again. "Nothing I can think of, not unless you want the SS visiting us again. We can hope the Germans don't decide to throw *us* into ghettos, too." He hesitated. When he spoke again, he sounded surprised at himself: "We can *pray* they don't decide to do that. I always thought the *Ostjuden* prayed too much. Could it be we don't pray enough?" Hearing that from such a secular man as Father told Sarah more clearly than anything else how much the times had changed.

Chapter 10

As a Welshman, Alistair Walsh did not have a high opinion of eastern Scotland. The terrain was low and flat and full of Scots. Dundee couldn't have been duller if it rehearsed. Walsh said so in several pubs. He couldn't even get into a good fight. Too many of the other soldiers stranded in those parts agreed with him.

But, all things considered, he could have been worse off. The Germans might have sunk the ship that plucked him out of Namsos. He might not have got out, in which case he would be languishing inside barbed wire in a POW camp. Yes, there were all kinds of interesting and unpleasant possibilities.

And he was on leave, while the great military bureaucracy tried to figure out what to do with him and his fellow survivors. He tried to pick up barmaids. The Scots girls were pretty, but they seemed depressingly chaste. He hired a bicycle and rode out into the countryside. Going someplace where no one was trying to kill you or even give you orders had its points.

The only thing better than traveling in a place like this by himself would have been traveling in the company of a friendly young lady.

Since he wasn't having much luck on that score, he went alone. Soldiers he saw too often anyhow. Getting away from them was more fun than going out with them would have been.

He'd had almost two decades of peacetime service between the wars. A year and a half of the genuine article was enough—no, far more than enough—to make all that seem to belong to another, and very distant, lifetime. The hired bicycle creaked and squeaked under him. He didn't care. All he heard except for the bike were the wind, an occasional crow's caw, and the even more occasional rattle of a passing auto. Not many motorcars were on the roads, not with petrol so savagely rationed.

His ears drank in the quiet. You didn't realize how badly war abused them till you got away from the racket of gunfire and explosions for a while. He suspected he'd be deaf as a stump when he got older. The prospect bothered him less than it might have. The way things were going, living long enough to grow old and deaf didn't seem half bad.

A farmer out in the middle of an emerald field of new-sprouted barley waved to Walsh as he pedaled past. Cautiously—he hadn't been on a bicycle in a while, and the road was bumpy—the sergeant lifted a hand from the handlebars and waved back.

He rode on. Another farmer came up the road perched on a wagon pulled by two mismatched horses. Did he have a motorcar he couldn't drive because he couldn't get fuel for it? Walsh wouldn't have been surprised. You made do with what you had. He'd seen as much on the Continent. He wasn't surprised to see it in Britain, too. This time, he waved first. The farmer gravely returned the courtesy.

When Walsh first heard the buzz of airplane engines, he thought his ears were ringing because they weren't used to so much silence all around. Before long, though, he decided the sound was real. Then, for a few seconds, he believed it was coming from an RAF plane. But that wasn't right, either. The engines sounded a different note, one that made the short hair at the nape of his neck prickle up.

"Bugger me blind if that's not a German," he muttered as he pulled to a stop on the grass at the edge of the road. He peered up at the sky, shielding his eyes against the sun. "What the bleeding hell is Fritz doing here?"

A bombing raid on Dundee from Norway? A *daylight* bombing raid?

Was Fritz that stupid? Walsh didn't think so. And the noise in the sky didn't sound like squadron after squadron of bombers. *One* plane was up there, no more. Walsh's ears had been abused, but he was sure of that.

Then he spotted it. He recognized it right away. German planes mostly had sharper angles than their RAF counterparts. This one was . . ."A 110!" Walsh had no doubt. He'd been strafed several times by the two-engined fighters roaring along at just above treetop height. This Bf-110 flew quite a bit higher, but its shape was unmistakable.

He scratched his head. He wasn't lousy any more—that was something. But why on earth would a lone 110 fly over Scotland? Had some Nazi pilot poured down too much schnapps and taken off on a bet, or full of drunken bravado? That was madness, but so was everything else Walsh could think of.

Then the madness got even crazier. A parachute popped open. Whoever'd been flying that plane was coming to earth apart from it. Why, in the name of heaven? Walsh didn't think anything was wrong with the airplane. Even after the fellow inside bailed out, the 110 flew on as if nothing had happened. The engine note never changed. It hadn't changed before the flyer hit the silk, either.

Walsh got a crick in his neck. The descending 'chute was almost overhead. Walsh started to duck, imagining himself getting clopped by the German's boots. But the breeze carried the fellow a few hundred yards into the field through which the road ran.

Walsh trotted toward him. He'd closed about half the gap before he wondered how smart he was. German pilots commonly carried pistols, while he was unarmed. But he was in his own country, for Christ's sake. The German would have to be daft to plug him. Of course, the German had to be daft to come here like this in the first place, so what did that prove?

"Hands up!" Walsh yelled. *"Hände hoch!"* He spoke little German, but most British soldiers learned that one.

The flyer had a knife. He used it to cut himself free of the parachute shrouds. The canopy tumbled off across the field. The man slowly got to his feet. He favored one ankle a little. Walsh shouted at him again. With a smile, he let the knife drop to the ground and raised his hands. He was in his mid-forties—very old for a pilot—with bushy black eyebrows and a chin that stuck out. He looked oddly familiar.

"Do not fear me," he said in good English. "I come in peace."

"In a Messerschmitt-110? Sure you do, mate," Walsh retorted.

"I am Rudolf Hess," the man said.

And damned if he wasn't. No wonder he looked familiar. In how many photographs had Walsh seen him at Hitler's elbow? Half the time, his hand would be upraised in the stupid Nazi salute. To save his hide, Walsh couldn't remember exactly what Hess' title was. He was one of the biggest of the Party big shots, though. So what the bleeding hell was he doing in the middle of a Scottish field, still wearing a parachute harness? Walsh asked him, in lieu of standing there with his mouth hanging open like a stupid clot.

"I am come to confer with your government," Hess answered, as if it were the most obvious thing in the world. Maybe he saw that Walsh wondered whether he was out of his skull, because he added, "Unofficially, of course."

"Oh, of course," Walsh said. "Confer about what?"

He guessed Hess would tell him it was none of his damned business. But Hess didn't. "Why, about ways to end this unfortunate war between Germany and England and France, *natürlich.*"

"*Natürlich,*" Walsh echoed in a hollow voice. "You could start by telling your soldiers to quit trying to kill me."

"This I wish to do. We waste our time fighting one another," Hess said seriously. "Better we should all fight the Russians together. So I feel. So feels the *Führer* also."

All of a sudden, Walsh stopped wondering if Hess was a nutter. The staff sergeant had no idea whether Neville Chamberlain's government would make a deal like that, or whether France would go along if it did. But the government might. It might. The breeze felt chillier—or did the cold come from inside him? He had to force words out one by one: "I'd better take you back into Dundee."

"*Danke schön.* This would be good," Hess said.

Back they went. It was several miles. They took turns walking and riding slowly on the bicycle. Hess spewed out a million reasons why England and France should turn on the Bolsheviks. At last, Walsh got sick of listening. He said, "Look, pal, I'm only a bloody sergeant. I can't do anything about it one way or the other." The German subsided into wounded silence.

When they got into Dundee, Walsh had a devil of a time convincing his superiors that Rudolf Hess was Rudolf Hess. They were even more certain than he had been that Hess wasn't about to arrive in Scotland by jumping out of a Bf-110. Then they *did* believe him, and that might have been worse, because they started having kittens right before his eyes. They whisked Hess away in a swarm of military policemen.

"You will forget about this," a captain barked at Walsh. "It never happened. You have no knowledge of it. Do you understand me?"

"Yes, sir." Walsh judged that was the only possible answer that would keep him out of a military jail. The bloke who said a little knowledge was a dangerous thing knew what he was talking about. To show he understood what the captain meant, Walsh added, "I won't tell a soul."

"You'd better not." The captain sent Walsh a hard look, as if wondering whether to jug him like a hare on general principles. Walsh tried to exude innocence: not easy for a man of his age and experience. After a long, long pause, the captain jerked a thumb toward the door. "Get out." Walsh had never been so happy to obey an order in his life.

JULIUS LEMP WAS used to getting strange orders from his superiors, and even to attracting them. He was still paying for sinking the *Athenia.* Chances were he'd go on paying for the rest of his career, unless he did something wonderful enough to cancel out the screwup. Offhand, he couldn't think what that might be. Finding Jesus walking barefoot across the swells of the North Sea might do it. Anything short of that, no.

When you were in the U-boat business, strange orders were liable to get you killed. (So were ordinary orders; it was that kind of trade. But with strange orders your odds were worse.) If that bothered his superiors in the *Kriegsmarine,* they went out of their way not to show it.

And so the U-30 cruised slowly through the chop off the east coast of Scotland. Not very far off the Scottish coast, either: land was clearly visible to the west. One of the ratings on the conning tower with Lemp said, "If they've got a 105 on the beach, they can hit us with it. We can hit 'em back with the 88 on deck, too."

"I know," Lemp replied. "But even if they do have a 105 there, chances are they won't shoot with it. They're bound to think we're one of their own U-boats, not a German machine. No German boat would be mad enough to show itself so close to their coast."

"Sure, skipper," the rating said, as if humoring a lunatic. "So what the hell *are* we doing here?"

"We are carrying out our orders," Lemp said, which was literally true. "We are searching for any signs of wreckage or survivors from a Messerschmitt-110 that may or may not have gone into the North Sea in these waters."

"Sure," the rating said again. "But why?"

"Martin, you never ask that question," Lemp answered patiently. "Because they told us to, that's why."

Martin only sniffed. The hell of it was, Lemp had a hard time blaming him. He wondered why they were looking for bits and pieces of a Bf-110, too. However much he wondered, he didn't know. The hard-faced captain back in Kiel hadn't looked the sort who was much inclined to answer questions. In fact, he'd looked the sort who would bite your head off if you had the nerve to ask any. Sometimes the best thing you could do was salute, go "*Zu befehl!*", and get the hell out of there. Lemp had judged that to be one of those times.

Had he been wrong? If the Royal Navy or the RAF decided the U-30 wasn't an English U-boat, the enemy owned all the advantages here. Cruising along in broad daylight was all very well. *Audace, audace, toujours l'audace,* the French said. Well, yes, but when the fellows on the other team trumped all that audacity with depth charges . . .

He scanned the gray-green sea. This close to the coast, all sorts of rubbish floated in it. He hadn't seen anything from a German fighter plane, though. He wondered if some important officer's son had been flying the 110. That might account for a search like this. He couldn't think of much else that would.

One of the things floating in the North Sea was a basket of the kind and size that might have held a baby. Martin said, "Sir, with all this shit around, how are we supposed to recognize stuff from a 110 even if we do come across it?"

"We've got to do the best we can," Lemp answered, by which he meant he didn't have the faintest idea.

Martin, unfortunately, understood him much too well. "Right," the rating said, and scratched the side of his jaw. Gingery stubble sprouted there. Lemp didn't shave when he was at sea, either. Like a lot of U-boat men, from the lowliest "lords"—ordinary seamen—to skippers, he trimmed his whiskers when he got back into port.

"What do they do when we send them the message that we can't find what they're looking for?" another rating asked.

"We don't send it." Now Lemp's voice grew sharp. "We're ordered to maintain radio silence throughout this cruise. I will make the report orally when we return to Kiel. Have you got that?"

"Yes, skipper. Sorry," the rating said. Lemp didn't usually come down hard on his men, but he had to be sure no one fouled up here. Somebody's head would roll if the U-30 broke radio silence. He knew whose, too: his.

Like the rest of the men on the U-boat, he wished he knew what was going on. He didn't like getting sent out on wild-goose chases. He especially didn't like it when he had to wear a blindfold while hunting his wild geese.

All of which had nothing to do with anything. They'd given him his orders. He was following them. If he found no wreckage—or even if he did—he was to return to Kiel after four days of searching. It made no sense, not to him or to the men he commanded. Maybe that was because the officers set over them knew more about what was going on than they did. Or maybe the geese had got uncommonly wild lately.

The U-boat performed the ordered search. It found nothing from a Bf-110. For that matter, it found nothing from any airplane. Lemp wasn't sorry to order the boat away from the Scottish coast. He counted himself lucky not to have been spotted. The Royal Navy must not have believed the *Kriegsmarine* would give any of its boats such an idiotic assignment. Well, he wouldn't have believed it himself if he hadn't got stuck with it.

No English planes happened on the U-30 as it hurried back across the North Sea. The farther Lemp put the British Isles behind him, the happier he grew. He was downright delighted when the boat got back to Kiel. But his pleasure chilled when armed guards on the pier kept anyone but him from going ashore. "We have our orders," said the chief petty officer in charge of the detachment. That was a sentence unchallengeable in any branch of any military service the world around.

More sailors with Mausers escorted Lemp to the office where he was to make his report. He wasn't astonished to find Rear Admiral Dönitz there waiting to hear him. Whatever was going on, it was going on at levels far over his head.

He came to attention and saluted. "Reporting as ordered, sir. My news is very simple: we saw nothing and found nothing."

"Very well," Dönitz said. "That makes it more likely the 110 reached England, then. Scotland, I should say."

"Sir, did you *want* it to do that?" Lemp asked.

The admiral looked through him. "Don't worry about it, Lieutenant." In his mouth, Lemp's rank might as well not have existed. A word from him, and Lemp's rank wouldn't exist.

"Yes, sir," Lemp said. "But you can't wonder if I'm a little curious. Everyone on my boat is a little curious, or more than a little."

"It has to do with high policy. You can tell them that much," Dönitz answered. "And you can tell them not to push it, not if they know what's good for them." His eyes were gray-blue, and at the moment frigid as the North Sea in February. "The same goes for you."

Lemp could take a hint. "I understand, sir," he said quickly.

"I doubt that. The scheme surprised *me* when I heard about it," Dönitz said. "If it works, everything changes. And if it doesn't, we've lost very little."

What was *that* supposed to mean? One more quick look at Dönitz's face discouraged Lemp from asking. He saluted again. Then he asked, "May my men go ashore for liberty now?"

"After you let them know they'd better keep their mouths shut," the admiral said. "Anyone who makes a mistake will regret it. Is that clear?"

"Yes, sir," Lemp said. *Clear as mud,* he thought. Maybe events would answer his questions for him one of these days. Or he might spend the rest of his life wondering. You never could tell.

CHAIM WEINBERG COULDN'T believe his eyes. Was he really seeing this? Damned if he wasn't. Half a dozen French tanks clanked up to the stretch of line the Abe Lincoln Battalion was holding outside of Madrid. These weren't slow, ancient Renaults—leftovers from the last war. They were brand-new Somua S-35s, the best medium tanks the French made. The Spanish Republic had got a few—only a few—in 1938. Chaim didn't know France had turned any loose since.

But here they were, painted a pale grayish green that put him in mind of olive leaves. It was a good color for operating in Spain. It would be even better once they got dusty and dirty. The Italians and Spaniards painted theirs khaki. The German tanks of the *Legion Kondor* were mostly dark gray, which made them stand out more. That mattered only so much. If you couldn't stop them, so what if you saw them coming?

He wasn't the only guy who got a charge out of seeing these—nowhere near. And he wasn't the only guy who could see what they meant. The Abe Lincoln Battalion, like the International Brigades generally, was full of people who found politics a game more exciting than baseball, bridge, or chess.

"We're going to knock Sanjurjo's cocksuckers into the middle of next week," somebody said gleefully. "The froggies must've decided Hitler ain't gonna do 'em in, so they can turn loose of some of their toys."

"About fuckin' time, ain't it?" Chaim said. "Been a year now since the big German push fell short. They woulda given us these babies back then, we coulda started cleaning out the Nationalists that much sooner."

"Piss and moan, piss and moan," the other Abe Lincoln said. "We've got 'em now. That'll do it."

Maybe it would. Each tank had the Republic's flag—horizontal stripes of red, yellow, and purple—painted on the side of the turret. The crewmen were Spaniards. They all seemed as enthusiastic as the men from the International Brigades. They knew what the tanks meant. In a word, victory.

So it seemed to Chaim, anyhow. The next interesting question was, could victory and *mañana* coexist? The Abe Lincolns were wild to hit the Nationalists in front of them as soon as the tanks arrived. The attack was ordered—but nobody bothered to tell the artillery, which stayed quiet. Even with tanks, you couldn't go forward without artillery support. Well, you could, but they didn't. Things got pushed back a day.

Then one of the tanks broke down, and the driver to another caught influenza, which spread to the rest of his crew the next day, to two other crews the day after that, and to the Abraham Lincolns the day after *that.* "Germ warfare," an International said dolefully, in between sneezes. "The fucking Nationalists are trying to make us too sick to fight."

If they were, they made a good job of it. Chaim lay flat on his back, weak as a kitten with aches and fever, for five days, and felt as if one of the fancy French tanks had run over him for a week after that. The tanks, meanwhile, sat out in the open. No one seemed to wonder whether the Nationalists were watching.

At last, everything was ready again. The attack was scheduled for 0600. The artillery barrage was scheduled for 0500. It actually started at 0530. By Spanish standards, that was a masterpiece of punctuality.

At 0618 on the dot, the tanks rumbled forward. The Abe Lincolns trotted along with them. Nothing like putting all those tonnes of hardened steel between yourself and the other fellow's machine guns.

Chaim loped with his buddies. He wasn't a hundred percent yet, despite enough aspirins to make his ears ring. He wished he were still in bed—with luck, with La Martellita, but even alone would do. But he'd improved to the point where he could carry a rifle without falling over. He went forward. Plenty of other Americans—and the foreigners and Spaniards who filled out the battalion—were in no better shape.

One of the fancy French machines stopped so the commander, who doubled as the gunner, could blast a machine-gun nest to ruin. Which he did. But, while he was doing it, a Nationalist soldier popped up out of a foxhole next to the tank and chucked a wine bottle filled with blazing gasoline through the open hatch. Flames, greasy black smoke, and screams rose from inside the tank. The Republicans shot the brave Nationalist, but the damage was done.

"Fuck," Chaim said, eyeing the pyre the tank had become. The Republicans had invented the infantryman's antitank weapon. The Nationalists had christened it the Molotov cocktail. Now both sides used it. So did foot soldiers everywhere who had to fight tanks without antitank guns.

Another Nationalist threw a Molotov cocktail at the back of a Somua S-35. Flaming gasoline dripped down through the louvers over the engine. Before long, the engine started burning, too. The crew got out, but that tank wouldn't go anywhere ever again.

"Assholes," an American near Chaim said. "Don't they know how expensive those goddamn things are?"

"I wonder how the Republic *is* paying for them," Chaim said.

"IOUs," the other Abe Lincoln said. They both laughed. The Spanish Republic might not have thought it was so funny. Spain's gold reserves had gone to the USSR for safekeeping, and to pay for Soviet aid in the dark days when no one else thought the Republic was worth helping. Would that gold ever return from Moscow? Chaim might be a loyal—if talkative, even argumentative—Marxist-Leninist, but he wasn't holding his breath.

Whang! That was a big shell hitting, and devastating, a tank. The machine brewed up at once. You could kill tanks with artillery, but most antitank guns were of smaller caliber than the monster that fired that round. The Germans made an 88mm antiaircraft gun. Being Germans, and thorough, they also made an armor-piercing shell for it. Chaim would have bet that was what had put paid to the French tank.

And another round from the same gun, whatever the hell it was, blew the turret clean off another S-35. "It's like the bastard tipped its hat when it got hit by that one," Chaim said. It wasn't a bad joke . . . as long as you didn't happen to be inside the turret when the big shell hit. If you did, you were too dead to appreciate the wit. You were, in fact, scorched raspberry jam.

The last two surviving tanks decided they wanted to go on surviving. They wheeled around almost in their own length and hightailed it for the rear. One tank used the thick black smoke rising from another that had been killed as a smoke screen for its own getaway.

Chaim had trouble blaming the crews, though he knew people in positions of authority might have no trouble at all. Going forward into certain death was a losing proposition. *And what about going forward into likely death?* his mind gibed. Advancing without armor support sure made death more likely. His own death, for instance.

Not surprisingly, the Republican attack bogged down. Chaim wasn't the only Abe Lincoln who could see that Sanjurjo's soldiers would slaughter them if they banged their heads against a stone wall without tanks to smash it down. They'd gained a few hundred meters before things went south. Okay, fine. Chaim pulled a fancy entrenching tool off his belt (some Italian who'd taken Mussolini's orders would never need it again) and started improving the hole in the ground in which he huddled.

Dirt flew from more holes and bits of shattered trench as other members of the battalion imitated him. Or, more likely, he was imitating others. He doubted he was the first one who'd decided the Abraham Lincolns had gone about as far as they could go. You didn't need to belong to the German General Staff to figure it out. No more tanks equaled no more advance. If that wasn't one of Euclid's axioms, it should have been.

Now . . . would the Nationalists counterattack? Not right away, anyhow. They might have feared the tanks would come back or more would show up. Chaim knew better, but he wasn't about to tell them. He kept on digging. He'd spent a lot of time in foxholes. If you worked at it, you could make them nearly bearable. Work he did.

CORPORAL BAATZ GLOWERED at Willi Dernen. "Let me see that paper one more time," he said suspiciously.

"Sure." Willi handed it over. Did Awful Arno think he could have forged a certificate of leave? He might have, if he'd thought he could get away with it. But he hadn't. This one was legitimate. Could Baatz make the same proud claim?

Still unhappy, the underofficer handed it back. "If you're even one minute late returning to duty, your ass is mine," he declared.

"Sure, Corporal," Willi repeated. He would have said anything to get Awful Arno out of his hair. "Can I go now?"

"Yeah, go on. Get out." Baatz wasn't about to do anything so bourgeois—so human—as to wish him a good time. That wasn't his style. Why one of his own men hadn't shot him . . . *Why haven't I shot him?* Willi wondered. *Easy to do in combat. I probably wouldn't've got caught.*

All he wanted to do now was get away from Baatz, get away from the war. He gave his Mauser and grenades to the *Feldwebel* in charge of the company's weaponry. The senior noncom told him to have fun on leave. They weren't all shitheads. Some of them sure were, though.

Out of the line. Away from Awful Arno. Then the chain dogs were on him. So *Landsers* called military policemen because of the metal gorgets they hung around their necks. Once more, his papers passed muster. The *Kettenhunde* never cracked a smile, but they waved him on.

Antiaircraft guns stuck their snouts into the sky around the train station. The stationmaster was also a *Feldwebel*—and, at a guess, a veteran of the last war who'd been called up to help run the military trains. Willi showed him the leave papers. "All right, son," the gray noncom said. "Where do you want to go?"

"Breslau. That's where I'm from," Willi answered. Homesickness, long swallowed, welled up inside. "All the way over on the other side of the *Reich*."

"Thought so, by the way you talk." By his own musical, half-Scandinavian drawl, the *Feld* came from Schleswig-Holstein, up near the Danish border. He puffed on a pipe and nodded to himself. "Well, we can do that."

And he did. Along with the leave permit, which he returned, he gave Willi a round-trip ticket to Breslau. "Do I have to pay anything?" Willi asked.

The *Feldwebel* looked affronted. "Don't be silly. You're in the service of the *Reich*. If we can't take care of our own, what are we good for?"

Luxurious that care wasn't. Willi's seat was hard, and the car packed with soldiers getting away from action for a while. The stink of so many bodies that hadn't washed lately would have bothered Willi . . . had he noticed it. He fell asleep almost as soon as the train started rolling. The hard seat and crowding bothered him no more than the thick fug. He'd slept in plenty of worse places. Nor was his the only snore rising to the low ceiling—far from it.

When he woke, he was back inside Germany. The train was rolling through countryside that hadn't been bombed or shelled. It looked abnormal to Willi. He'd been at or near the front too goddamn long. He wanted to say something to somebody about it, but he had no friends sitting close by. Half a dozen soldiers in the car were still sawing wood, too. He kept his mouth shut. It wasn't as if he didn't have practice. When Awful Arno ordered you around, biting your tongue became a matter of self-preservation.

A few of the towns through which the train rolled showed bomb damage. The locals probably thought they'd survived disaster. They didn't know how lucky they were. If they stayed lucky, they wouldn't find out.

More chain dogs came through the cars at a stop, checking people's papers. Willi showed his without hesitation. Why not? They were good. Farther back in his car, the military policemen caught somebody whose papers weren't good, or who didn't have any. They dragged the poor bastard away. "I can explain," he kept saying. If he couldn't, he'd landed in more trouble than he knew what to do with.

Willi had zwieback and a tube of butter in his pockets. Hoping the dining car would give him something better, he made his way to it. The stew was cabbage, potatoes, and tripe rubbery enough to use as a tire retread. The coffee was German ersatz, not spoils taken from French houses. It tasted bad and had next to no kick. All things considered, butter smeared on crackers might have been better.

Because the train traveled slowly and made many stops, he took almost a day to cross the country and get to Breslau. People got on and off. Some of them were civilians. Some of the civilians were women. Hearing women talking in a language he could understand was a treat he'd forgotten.

Breslau was a city of bridges, set right in the middle of the Silesian plain. It was also a city of many smokes. There was coal nearby, and iron, so factories worked round the clock. And it was a city of many Jews. Willi had known that before, but he hadn't thought about it one way or the other. Riding the streetcar out to his folks' block of flats, he got his nose rubbed in it. The yellow stars on the clothes of people on the street leaped out at him. No yellow stars on the streetcar passengers, though. Public transport was for Aryans only.

No one sat near him. People stood up instead, as far away as they could. He realized he really could use a bath. He was a little embarrassed, but only a little. If they couldn't figure out he was just back from the front, too bad.

Even if he was ripe, his mother squealed and almost squeezed the breath out of him when he knocked on the door. "Why didn't you wire that you were coming?" she demanded.

"I thought I'd surprise you," he said.

"Think? You didn't think." But Klara Dernen didn't sound angry. "Now where am I going to get my hands on a nice, fat hen?" She winked. "There are ways that don't cost ration points. Magda owes me. If she's got one, or knows where to get one . . ."

"Sure, *Mutti*," Willi said. You could always find a way around rules you didn't like, whatever they happened to be. He'd seen that.

A hot bath! When was the last time he'd had one? He couldn't remember. It had been a while, though. He put on civilian clothes when he got out of the tub. The pants were too big through the waist, but all his shirts felt tight at the shoulders. He was in better shape than he had been before the *Wehrmacht* got him.

His younger sister, Eva, and his kid brother, Markus, both squealed when they got home from school. They told him about Russian air raids and running for the cellar. "That's just like fighting, huh?" Markus said.

"Pretty much." Willi left if there. Markus was only thirteen. The war would be over—the war had better be over—by the time he got old enough to fight.

Sure enough, Mother got her fat hen. She'd make a better chicken stew than the thumb-fingered soldiers who cooked in the field. It filled the flat with a savory smell. Father came home not long before the stew was ready. Herbert Dernen worked in a factory that had made clocks before the war and was turning out gauges and dials for panzers and planes these days.

He'd fought in France in the last war. After a long, measuring look at Willi, he slowly nodded at whatever he saw. "Well, son, now you know" was all he said, and it seemed more than enough.

"Now I know," Willi agreed. No, they needed not another word on that score.

Father understood. So did other men of his generation, and other soldiers on leave. Willi couldn't find anyone else in Breslau who did. He felt like a stranger, or maybe even a Martian, in his home town. That didn't stop him from seeing—and kissing, and doing his best to feel up—the girls he'd been friendly with before conscription called. But they were either like his brother and thought they knew all about war because some bombs had fallen here, or they wanted him to explain what the fighting in France was like.

And he couldn't. If you hadn't done it, you'd never get it. In that, it was more like screwing than anything else. He said so once. He thought it would get his face slapped. Instead, it got him laid. Even afterwards, though, he couldn't tell sweet Susanna what shooting and being shot at and getting shelled and bombed were like. They weren't *like* anything.

He couldn't tell her about the camaraderie, either, not in any way that would make sense to her. But, when his leave was up, a big part of him was glad, or at least relieved, to head west once more. He was a real, for-sure *Frontschwein,* all right. *God help me,* he thought, but it was true.

Chapter 11

Luc Harcourt had just found a good place to crap when the sniper got him. It really was perfect. The bushes screened him from sight—or he'd thought so, anyhow. And the leaves were young and soft and green. This side of a goose's neck, you couldn't get a better substitute for paper.

He dug a little hole with his entrenching tool. He undid his belt, dropped his pants, and squatted. The shot rang out. "*Aiii!*" he howled, and sprang straight up. If the Olympics had a record for a high jump from a squatting position, he broke it by thirty centimeters.

At the same time, he clapped a hand to the wounded part. It came away bloody. Sure as hell, he'd got shot in the ass. Trousers still at half mast, he rolled behind a big, thick elm. Bullets could penetrate an amazing amount of wood, but he didn't worry about that. All he wanted was to keep the lousy *Boche* from seeing him any more. Besides, that last bullet had penetrated *him*.

He pulled up the khaki trousers. He didn't bother with the belt. Holding the pants up with one hand, he hobbled back to the encampment. He'd never tried walking with a wounded *gluteus maximus* before. It wasn't one of the experiences you sought out for the sake of having it.

Lieutenant Demange greeted him with the sympathy he'd come to expect: "The hell's the matter with you? You look like you just tried to hump a donkey, only the donkey didn't like it." Wordlessly, Luc turned around to display the bloody seat of his pants. Demange didn't care. "If you're on the rag, couldn't you find a pad?"

"Fuck you!" Luc snarled. Enough was too much.

"That's 'Fuck you, *sir*!' " Demange said easily. "All right, go on back and have somebody patch you up. Welcome to the club, if it's worth anything to you." A German had shot him in 1918.

"Not a goddamn thing." Luc made his slow way back to the aid station.

A male nurse who smelled of garlic and cologne gave him a shot of novocaine and a tetanus shot, then sutured the wound and bandaged him. "It's only a crease, not through-and-through," the fellow said. "You can go back to your unit. They'd skin me alive if I wasted a cot on you."

"Thanks one hell of a lot," said Luc, who'd hoped for some leave. "What do I do when the numbing wears off? It'll hurt even worse then, on account of the stitches."

Plainly, the male nurse was about to say it wasn't his problem. Whatever he saw on Luc's face made him think twice. Instead, he handed over a vial of white pills. "Codeine," he said. "It won't make things stop hurting, you understand, but it can take the edge off. And it constipates you. You won't need to go into the bushes so often for a while."

"Oh, hurrah," Luc said in distinctly hollow tones. Then he asked, "You have any pants around here that aren't all bloody?" If he waited for the quartermasters to issue him a new pair, he'd keep wearing these for God knew how long. But if he could manage things informally . . .

Sure as hell, the nurse said, "Some poor *con* stopped one with his face. I don't know why they bothered bringing him back. He wasn't breathing by the time he got here—I know that."

The dead man had bled a little on his trousers, but nowhere near so much as Luc had on his. The pants were loose and too long, but a belt and some sewing would fix that. The people at the aid station, or maybe the stretcher-bearers, had already emptied the poor guy's pockets. No surprise there. They'd missed an aluminum-bronze franc. Luc added the inheritance to his small store of cash.

When he got back, Lieutenant Demange said, "Fucking took you long enough. I thought they were cutting off your cheek, like the old lady in that story."

Luc had run across *Candide.* He was surprised Demange had; the veteran seemed unlikely to read anything that didn't have photos of naked girls in it. You never could tell.

"So you'll sleep on your stomach for a while, eh?" Demange went on.

"I guess," Luc answered. "Got any other good news for me, or are you through?"

"Well, I was gonna have you lead a raid on the *Boches* tonight . . ." Demange raised an eyebrow to see how that went over. Luc looked back at him without expression. He didn't jump up and down and yell and scream, the way Demange obviously wanted him to. The older man made a disgusted noise. "Ah, fuck off. You're no goddamn fun."

"Poke somebody you've never nailed before, if you want to watch him pitch a fit. In the meantime, let me bum a butt off you."

"What? You get your own shot off, then you want a replacement?" But Demange pulled the ever-present pack of Gitanes out of his tunic pocket and handed Luc one.

In due course, the novocaine wore off. When it did, the wound started hurting worse than it had when Luc first got it. The spot where he got the tetanus shot was sore, too, and it made him feel feverish. He took two codeine pills, then two more. Instead of leaving him sleepy and dopey, they made him feel as if he'd just had four cups of strong coffee. He wanted to *do* something, even if he couldn't figure out what.

The Germans solved that. They pulled a trench raid of their own, a couple of hundred meters off to the left of Luc's position. He ran to the Hotchkiss gun and fired off strip after strip of ammo at the *Boches* as they fought and as they retreated. Joinville couldn't feed the machine gun fast enough to suit him. The piece's cooling fins glowed a dull red. But it was a reliable piece of machinery. No matter how hot it got, it kept working.

Luc stayed awake all through the night. When the sun came up the next morning, he saw five dead Germans not far in front of the French lines. The regimental commander was a lieutenant colonel named Jacques Soupault. He had a mean, skinny face, a hairline mustache, and greasy black hair combed straight back. His eyes were black, and cold as a corpse's. All that notwithstanding, he folded Luc into an embrace, brushed cheeks with him, and made him a sergeant on the spot.

"Without your promptness, the enemy attack might well have succeeded," he said. "Prisoners we took couldn't talk about anything but 'that damned machine gun.' At least three men called it the same thing."

By then, Luc was desperately tired. He'd already taken more codeine, to try to keep himself going and to ease the pain in his backside. "Thank you, sir," he muttered, hoping Soupault would dry up and blow away. The drug wasn't hitting him so hard this time.

At last, the officer left. Lieutenant Demange grinned at Luc. "See? You should get shot more often."

"You're trying to make me lose my temper again," Luc said. "Take another crack at it after I grab some sleep."

"Yeah, you were bouncing off the walls, all right," Demange said. "I dunno what kind of dope the doc gave you, but whatever it was, I want some, too."

"Wasn't even a doc. Only a nurse," Luc replied.

"She have big jugs, at least?"

"He needed a shave."

"Boy, you had all the luck yesterday, didn't you? Except for the dope, I mean."

"Yeah. Except for the dope." Luc yawned. "I *am* going to sleep. Why not? I'm a sergeant now—Soupault said so. What else do sergeants do?"

"Now you're trying to get a rise out of me," Demange said accurately. "I'd make you sorry, but you did a good job last night, even if you had some help from the pills."

When was the last time Demange had said something like that to him? When was the last time Demange had said something like that to anybody? The veteran was far quicker to show scorn than praise.

"Since you *are* a sergeant, you may have to give up your precious gun," Demange said. "You can tell more people what to do now."

"Don't want to." Luc yawned again, wider. "I have a slot I like. I'm good at it, too. So why would they take it away?"

"Because you're lucky, that's why. That's how you get promoted: do something cute while the officers are watching. Go on, curl up somewhere. They won't yank you off the piece till you wake up."

"The way I feel right now, that'll give me another month. At least." Luc headed off to find somewhere he could rest.

Lieutenant Demange's laughter followed him. A sergeant! He wouldn't just have to shorten his new trousers. Eventually, he'd get a yellow hash mark to replace the two brown ones he wore now. More work with needle and thread. *After I sleep,* he told himself. *I've earned it.*

"SOMETHING'S COOKING," Herman Szulc declared.

Pete McGill warily eyed his fellow Marine. He had to get along with Szulc. The number of Americans—and of leathernecks in particular—in Shanghai was too low to let what you thought about somebody show too much. But Pete hadn't liked him or trusted him since he tried to say Vera was out for what she could get and that she hadn't really fallen in love the way McGill had.

"You bet something's cooking," Max Weinstein said. "The proletariat is rising up against its imperialist oppressors." How you could be a pinko and a Marine at the same time was beyond Pete, but Max managed. Pete didn't know how good a pinko he was, but he made a damn good Marine, even if he drove other people nuts sometimes.

"Thank you, Josef Stalin," Szulc said. Weinstein flipped him the bird. Ignoring it, Szulc went on, "Nah, what I heard was that the Chinamen were gonna make things hot for the Japs here in Shanghai."

"That's what I told you," Max pointed out. "Whoever said Polacks were dumb knew what he was talking about."

"Same guy who said sheenies were cheap, I bet," Szulc said, which shut Max up with a snap. Into the sudden silence, Szulc continued, "What people are sweating about is, the Chinks're gonna give white people the most grief, see if they can get us or England or France mad enough to jump on Japan."

"You think that's true?" Pete asked, interested in spite of himself.

"All I know is what I read in the newspapers." Herman Szulc was about as far removed from Will Rogers as a human being could be. And none of this was in the Shanghai papers, whether in Chinese, English, French, German, Russian, or Japanese. Japan censored everything. Editors crossed the military government at their peril. For public consumption, everything in Shanghai was just fine.

Max tried again: "I believe it. We're the ones who cause trouble around here, so we're the ones the oppressed proletariat's gonna go for. Only stands to reason."

"*We're* the ones? White men are the ones?" Szulc said incredulously. "How about all the slanty-eyed shitheads who bow down to Hirohito?"

"They're only imitating what the Europeans and Americans taught 'em," Weinstein answered.

"We cause trouble? How about vaccination? How about newspapers?" Pete said.

"I think the first one was discovered here. I know goddamn well printing got invented here," Max returned.

Pete couldn't have said whether that was true or not. Max would bluff when he talked, the same way you'd bluff playing poker. Do it every so often and it helped your game. Do it too much and you looked like an asshole. But Pete had more cards to play: "Chinks didn't invent steamboats or railroads or cars or movies or phones or planes or the stuff that goes with 'em. They didn't invent your Commie bullshit, either. What's-his-name—Groucho Marx—did."

"Karl, for Chrissake." That crack genuinely pained Max, where the rest rolled off his back. His ears turned pink. Thinking about Marx, Pete found that funny. The Jewish Marine went on, "The Chinese proletariat has the sense to see what a good thing Marxism-Leninism is—which is more than I can say for a couple of dumbfuck leathernecks."

"More than a couple. You're about the only Red Marine God ever made," Pete said. "What are you doing in the Corps, anyway? Boring from within? Is that what they call it?"

"He's boring, all right," Herman Szulc said. They looked at each other in surprise—they weren't used to agreeing.

Two days later, the Chinese bombed a movie theater full of Japanese soldiers. Maybe the Chinese had invented gunpowder, but a Swede came up with dynamite—Pete did happen to know that. As for who first found the idea of taking swarms of hostages and slaughtering them, well, it had to be as old as the hills.

The Japs were good at it, though. The flat cracks from firing squads' rifles went on day and night. Soldiers didn't just kill with rifles, either. They used swords and shovels and picks and iron bars and whatever else they could get their hands on. People who knew about the Rape of Nanking a few years earlier said this wasn't so bad as that, but it sure wasn't good.

Wailing and moaning and shrieking from the Chinese who made up the vast majority of the people in Shanghai filled the air. Everything at the American consulate went straight to the devil. It didn't pass go. It didn't collect two hundred dollars Mex. All the cooks and maids and laundry men and sweepers stayed home. You couldn't blame them, not when they were liable to get murdered if they were dumb enough to show their faces on the street.

You didn't have to be Chinese to buy a plot, either. A Japanese soldier bashed in two French businessmen's brains with a spade and broke three ribs on another Frenchman before his friends could drag him off. The way Pete heard the story, the friends didn't try very hard to stop him. He believed it; that sounded like the Japs he thought he knew and didn't love.

"So now what'll happen?" Pooch Puccinelli wondered out loud. "The Japanese government gonna pay France an indemnity, like they did with us after they blew up the fuckin' *Panay*?"

"That'll make the dead guys happy, all right. Fuckin' A it will," Pete said. He didn't give a rat's ass about a couple of Frenchmen. He was worried about Vera. He hadn't been able to get word to her since the Japanese clamped down, and he hadn't heard from her. He hadn't heard that anything bad had happened to her dance hall, but he didn't know that he would. For the time being, the Marines were confined to barracks. He'd never been so tempted to go AWOL.

Max Weinstein also didn't sympathize with the dead Frenchmen, but he had different reasons: "You're a capitalist, the only reason you come to China is to exploit the local workers and peasants. You do that, you deserve whatever happens to you, far as I'm concerned."

"You're a sweet old boy, Max—yeah, a real SOB," Pooch said. "Wasn't the Chinks who did for 'em, remember. It was the Japs."

"They got it on account of they came out here. If they'd stayed home where they belonged, they wouldn't have," Max said stubbornly.

"No, the Nazis would've blown 'em up instead," Pete put in.

"If you want to see everything that's wrong with capitalism, and I mean everything, all you gotta do is look at Hitler's Germany and the Moose's Italy," Weinstein said. "There it is, naked."

"You start talking about naked, I don't want to talk about Nazis," Szulc said. "I want to talk about broads."

"That's 'cause you're a dickhead," Max told him. "You think with your dick, and now you're talking with it, too."

Had anybody said that to Pete, he would have tried to murder the guy. Herman Szulc puffed out his chest and looked proud of himself. "I'd sooner talk with my dick than with my Red asshole like you any day," he said.

Max surged to his feet. "You stupid fuckin' Polack—"

"Yeah, Yid?"

There they went again. Other Marines got between them. Everybody was as jumpy as a cat in a bar full of Dobermans. The Marines were only a symbolic presence in Shanghai, as they had been in Peking. The real action in these parts was between the Japs and the Chinese. When they started going at each other hammer and tongs, it reminded the Americans of their futility. Nobody liked having his uselessness exposed.

Pete wasn't even sure he could protect his woman. If anything in the world felt worse than that, he didn't know what it would be. Other Marines had had to keep him from going after Herman Szulc, too. Herman had a big mouth, and liked to hear himself talk. One of these days . . . *But not yet. Not yet, dammit,* Pete thought, not without regret.

ALISTAIR WALSH HAD his own opinions about politics. He was the staunchest of Tories: a Winston Churchill supporter who put up with Neville Chamberlain only because he might be marginally better than whatever Labour put up to oppose him.

Of course, Walsh was also a soldier. He was actively discouraged from doing anything about his views. The last thing Britain wanted was Bonapartism, and soldiers doing anything about their political opinions seemed to the powers that be a long step in the wrong direction. And so, but for mouthing off in barracks and barrooms and foxholes, Walsh had stayed as politically innocent as his superiors could have wanted.

Staying politically innocent after Rudolf Hess almost literally fell into his lap wasn't easy, though. You couldn't keep a thing like that secret. The Army and the government did their best, and failed. Too many people saw and recognized the German big shot when Walsh brought him back into Dundee. And Hess' Bf-110 crashed into a barn farther inland, killing several cows and a horse and just missing the farmer himself, who'd tended the animals in there a few minutes earlier.

They took Hess down to London, presumably to tell the government about what he'd already told Walsh. They brought Walsh along, presumably because they didn't know what else to do with him. After all, he already had the vision of *Landsers* and Tommies and *poilus* marching into Russia shoulder to shoulder implanted in his brain. If they didn't get him out of sight, he might start telling people about it before they decided what the people ought to think.

He knew what he thought, not that anyone asked a staff sergeant's opinion. Walsh would have been shocked had the tight-lipped young officers from the Ministry of War and their even tighter-lipped colleagues from the Foreign Ministry done any such thing. The way they kept eyeing him made him wonder if he would suffer an unfortunate accident before he made it to the capital.

He didn't. But he worried when they put him up in a posh hotel instead of with his mates. "You may do as you please, so long as you don't leave your room," one of the tight-lipped captains said.

"Meals?" Walsh asked.

"They'll be sent in. Order what you please from room service," the officer replied, an extravagance Walsh had never enjoyed before. But he didn't really enjoy it now, either. It came at too high a price: four armed guards outside the room made sure he wouldn't amble down the corridor. It was six floors up; he couldn't very well leave by the window, either.

"Gets a bit dull here, all by my lonesome," Walsh hinted. The captain only shrugged, as if to say that wasn't his worry. Walsh decided to be more direct: "If you're spending all that filthy lucre on room service, can you lay out a bit more and get me a girl? I'll have better things to talk about with her than Rudolf bloody Hess, by God—I promise you that."

The officer's lips got tighter, and paler, than ever. "I shall have to take that under advisement," he said, and got out of there as fast as he could.

No girl knocked on the door. Walsh hadn't really expected one would, but asking didn't hurt. The food was pretty good, and room service would send up beer and whiskey when he asked for them. Things could have been worse. He kept reminding himself of that. They could have stuck him in a cell somewhere and lost the key.

But he couldn't talk to anybody. That was why they kept him here. They didn't want reporters asking him questions. They didn't want other soldiers asking him anything, either. They knew how news flashed through the military. Soldiers and sailors were worse than women when it came to gossip.

He could step out into the hall. The guards would only shake their heads if he spoke to them, though. And, while he could go into the hall, those guards wouldn't let him take more than a couple of strides along it. They had old-fashioned bayonets—the long ones—fixed to their rifles. By all appearances, they were ready to use them if he looked like getting out of line. He didn't; he owned a well-honed sense of survival.

Like any prisoner, he suspected changes in routine. What were they going to do to him *now*? Find that cell and drop him into it? Or bump him off as if he'd never existed to begin with? They could do that, if they decided to. They could do anything they damn well pleased. Who'd stop them?

What would happen if the Nazis sent bombers over London? Would the guards escort him to the cellars, perhaps with a gag on his mouth so he couldn't blab to anyone? Or would they leave him up here, staying themselves to share his fate? He didn't want to find out, and was glad the *Luftwaffe* seemed to be staying away.

Even if the alarms outside didn't go off, the ones inside his head did when somebody knocked on the door one night at half past eleven. His heart pounded as he walked over to it. Was this the moment? Had they decided to imitate the Fascists and the Reds and dispose of him at midnight?

If they had, he could do damn all about it. Defiantly, he threw the door wide. There in the hall stood a short, portly man in his mid-sixties, with a round red face—a wrinkled, irascible baby face, it was, although he smoked a large and decidedly unbabyish cigar.

Walsh recognized him right away. Few Britons wouldn't have, of course. "Winston!" he blurted.

"At your service," Winston Churchill replied, his voice familiar from the wireless but more resonant now that he was here in the flesh. "May I come in?"

"How can I say no?" Walsh stepped back to let the politician enter, then closed the door behind him. He pointed to a whiskey bottle on the sideboard. "I could use a drink, sir. Would you care for one?"

"How can I say no?" Churchill repeated, blue eyes twinkling. Moving as if in a dream, Walsh poured for them both. He gestured toward the siphon-equipped soda bottle beside the whiskey: a silent question. Churchill shook his head. Walsh was just as well pleased. He wanted something potent himself.

Churchill raised his glass. "The King!" he said. Walsh echoed the toast. They both drank. Churchill smacked his lips. "Not bad. They *are* treating you satisfactorily?" The six-syllable word sounded natural in his mouth, though more often than not he was the most plainspoken of politicos.

"Yes, sir." Walsh finished his whiskey at a gulp—he needed it. "Did you come here to ask me that?"

"I did not," Churchill rasped. "I came to ask you this: how would you and your comrades in arms like to march with the Germans and against Russia?"

That was as plainspoken as a man could get. Walsh poured himself a refill. Churchill held out his glass, and Walsh filled it as well. "I don't care to speak for anyone but myself, sir. . . ."

"Then by all means do that. Your reluctance does you credit."

Shrugging, Walsh said, "I don't know anything about that. What I know is, I'm damned if I want some Nazi general giving me orders. And that's what it comes down to, isn't it? We'd be helping Hitler do what he already wants to—hell, what he's already started doing. He couldn't lick us, so now he wants us to join him. I've fought against Fritz twice now. I don't want to be on his side. He makes a fine enemy, but I doubt he'd prove such a good friend. If he's after the Russians now, there's more to Stalin than I looked for."

The words poured out of him, fueled more by nerves than by whiskey. Once he ran dry, he wondered whether he'd just doomed himself. If the government had already decided to throw in with Adolf . . .

But the wrinkles smoothed out of Churchill's face as he smiled. "God bless you, son. I thought you'd say that—I hoped you would—but I was far from sure. Even if you're too modest to say so, I feel sure you spoke for most British fighting men. And, most eloquently, you spoke for me as well."

"Good Lord!" Walsh did not expect ever to win the VC. Aside from that, he couldn't imagine a finer honor. He dared a question of his own: "Is it decided? What we'll do, I mean?"

"Decided?" Churchill snorted and shook his head. "Not likely! Neville Chamberlain couldn't decide to change his drawers if he shat in them." That made Walsh blink. Then he remembered Churchill had fought in the Boer War and commanded a battalion on the Western Front in the last big go-round. Some of it must have stuck—he knew how soldiers talked, all right. He went on, "No, Sergeant, it's not decided. But I daresay you've helped put a spike in *Herr* Hess' wheel. That you have." This time, he poured the whiskey. He raised his glass. "Down with Hitler!"

"Down with Hitler!" Alistair Walsh had never heard a toast he was gladder to join.

RUMORS. ALWAYS RUMORS. Vaclav Jezek didn't like the ones he was hearing lately. "That's what they're saying," Benjamin Halévy told him. "There's supposed to be talk in Paris about throwing in with the Germans."

"They can't do that!" Vaclav exclaimed in dismay verging on horror.

"Tell me about it," the Jewish sergeant said. "But the trouble is, they damn well can. And the *poilus* think they're going to."

Most of the time, Vaclav found speaking next to no French an asset. If he didn't understand an idiot officer, he didn't have to follow idiotic orders—unless the fellow knew German, as some of the bastards did. Now, though, he wished he could pick up the trench rumors at first hand instead of relying on Halévy to pass them along.

"Some of the *poilus* want to fight. Some of them don't, though." Vaclav put that as politely as he could. He didn't want to offend the sergeant, who was at least as much Frenchman as Czech (and, to Jezek, more Jew than either).

He needn't have worried. Because Halévy was more Jew than anything else, or Jew first and everything else later, he was all for giving the Nazis one in the nuts. "Too right they don't. How'd you like to take on the Russians instead?"

"Oh, so it works like that, does it?" Vaclav said. Halévy nodded. Vaclav didn't need to think it over. "No, thanks. Not me. Russia tried to help Czechoslovakia when Hitler jumped us, and that's more than anybody else can say—France included."

Once more, the challenge turned out not to be one. "Yes, I know," Benjamin Halévy answered. "We did as little as we could to technically honor our treaty."

"Aren't there a lot of Reds in the French Army?" Vaclav said. "What'll they think about fighting for Hitler and against Stalin?"

That made Halévy pause, at any rate. "Interesting question," he said at last. "I'm not sure. We'll just have to find out, if that's what the big wheels decide to do. Most of *them* would sooner throw in with the Nazis—you can bank on that."

"Oh, sure," Vaclav agreed. "France really *would* have done something when Germany invaded us if your government didn't halfway wish you were in bed with Hitler."

He wondered if that would make Halévy angry, but the redheaded noncom took it in stride. His only response was "I'm glad you said 'halfway.' "

"What are we supposed to do while the boys in the cutaways and the striped pants figure out which way to jump?" Jezek asked.

"Ha! That I can tell you: same as we'd do any other time. We keep on killing the assholes in *Feldgrau* and do our goddamnedest to keep them from killing us."

"Sounds like a plan," Vaclav allowed.

The Germans wanted to kill him in particular. They knew too much about him, too: they knew he was a Czech, not a Frenchman. Their imported sharpshooter (or maybe he was homegrown—Vaclav didn't know for sure) started singling out men who wore the domed Czech helmet rather than the crested Adrian style that made *poilus* look as if they were still fighting the last war. This was a better Adrian helmet than the old model. It was stamped from a single piece of manganese steel instead of being built up from two pieces of lower-quality ironmongery. But it still *looked* old-fashioned. And it still was made of thinner metal than the Czech pot.

Not without regret, Vaclav switched to a French helmet. He'd done that before; doing it again didn't bother him too much. He wanted to hang on to the Czech helmet he was abandoning, but he didn't. The antitank rifle meant he lugged around extra weight as things were. He didn't need another kilo or kilo and a half.

Somewhere over there, off to the east, that German sniper lurked in the trenches. Or maybe he wasn't in the trenches any more. Maybe he sprawled in a shell hole between the lines, or inside the carcass of a dead automobile, or under a smashed-up rubbish bin. You could sneak out under cover of darkness. One shot would be all you needed. Odds were nobody would see where it came from. When night came, back you'd go. In the meantime, you could amuse yourself by carving another notch into your rifle's stock.

You could if you were a nice, thorough German, anyhow. Vaclav wouldn't have cared to be captured carrying a rifle that bragged that way. If you were, your chances of seeing the inside of a POW camp ranged from slim down toward none. He chuckled sourly when that crossed his mind. The weapon he carried was a hell of a lot more conspicuous than any ordinary rifle, notched or not.

He began looking with a new eye at possible hiding places out in no-man's-land. The way he went about it made him laugh once more, on as dry a note as he'd used earlier. Was this how ducks scouted for hunters' blinds in the marshes at river's edge as they flew down to land and feed?

There was a difference, though. Unlike the ducks, he could shoot back.

He suddenly laughed again, this time in real amusement. He imagined flocks of mallards or pochards or smews with machine guns under their wings and cannon in their beaks. By God, you'd think twice—three times, if you had any sense—before you went after one of those!

"All right. What's so funny?" Benjamin Halévy asked. Vaclav explained his conceit. The Jew gave him a peculiar look and found another question: "Are you sure you're a Czech?"

"Damn straight," Jezek answered proudly. "How come you're asking such a stupid thing?"

"On account of Czechs aren't usually crazy like that. Even Frenchmen aren't usually crazy like that. You sure you're not a Yid in disguise?"

"Damn straight," Vaclav repeated, still proudly. Had someone not a Jew asked him that, he would have decked the son of a bitch. As things were, he added, "Nobody's gonna get near *my* dick with the gardener's clippers."

"That's not how it's done," Halévy said. "Or I don't think it is. I was only eight days old when it happened to me, so I wasn't taking notes."

"No, huh? Doesn't it bother you not having a foreskin?"

"Why would it? Does having one bother you?"

"Nope," Vaclav said. "What bothers me is that Nazi shithead. He's out there somewhere, and he wants to punch my ticket for me."

"Do unto others before they do unto you," Halévy said. "It may not be just what Jesus said, but that doesn't mean it's bad advice."

It was, in fact, damn good advice. Vaclav had already been following it, even if he hadn't phrased it so well. He decided he'd better head out into no-man's-land himself. If he didn't nail the sniper, he'd have a better shot at other German soldiers.

Maybe they'd pick the same nook. Wouldn't that make for a cheery meeting in the dark?

He spent the rest of the day scouting places to hide. Some of the ones that looked best lay several hundred meters in front of the line

Czech and French troops shared. The very best one, or so it seemed, was behind or perhaps under a rusted-out French armored car that had probably been sitting there since the big German advance a year and a half before. The Fritzes would have taken whatever parts and weapons and tires they could use and left the shell to gather dust . . . and, now, snipers.

When he told Halévy of his plan, the Jew said, "Well, you can do that if you want, but I sure wouldn't."

"How come?" Jezek yelped indignantly.

"You already answered your own question: it's been sitting there the past year and a half. You think the Germans haven't noticed it? You think they haven't booby-trapped it six ways from Sunday?"

Vaclav paused to find out what he did think. After a few seconds, he said, "Aw, shit." After a few more, he added, "Thanks." Nothing came harder than admitting the other guy was right. But Halévy was, sure as hell. The sergeant nodded back. Vaclav started looking for a different place to hide.

Chapter 12

Peggy Druce had been through things none of her friends and acquaintances in Philadelphia could match. The more she talked about them, the plainer that got. She'd changed, and they hadn't. She was convinced that she'd changed for the better, and that they needed to move in the same direction as fast as they could. They seemed disappointingly dubious.

Herb always listened to her. A good thing, too, or she would have gone round the bend in a hurry. Even as things were, more than a few of those friends and acquaintances would have said she'd already done it.

"For crying out loud," she told her husband after finding that even more people didn't want to pay any attention to her, "it's like I'm the only one who knows what love is, and everybody else thinks I'm lying when I talk about it. What am I supposed to do? Besides haul off and belt somebody in the chops, I mean."

He clicked his tongue between his teeth. Doing his best to keep a judicious tone—Peggy recognized the tone, and the effort—he answered, "Well, it might help some if you didn't sound so much like a missionary out to convert the heathen Chinee."

The nineteenth-century phrase made her smile . . . for a moment. But only for a moment. Then she got mad—not at him, but at everybody deaf to her blandishments. That meant, basically, at almost everyone she knew on this side of the Atlantic. If Herb had also thought she was a crank, she didn't know what she would have done. Thank God, he didn't.

"For crying out loud," she said again, "the way a lot of people sound, they're halfway to being Nazis. More than halfway. It's terrible! The way they go on, they *want* England and France to line up behind Hitler and knock Russia flat."

"Stalin's no bargain," Herb said: once more, judiciously.

"Yes, *dear.*" Peggy's own oversweet tone was redolent of I-expected-better-from-you-of-all-people. "Next to Hitler, though, he's George Washington and Abe Lincoln rolled into one."

"I'm sure he would agree with you," Herb remarked.

"So what?" Peggy said. "Next to Hitler, Attila the Hun is a bargain. I ought to know. I've talked to the man."

"To Attila?" her husband asked, not innocently enough.

Peggy sent him a severe look. "Hitler. As. You. Know. Perfectly. Well." She bit off the words one by one, as if from a salami.

"Okay, okay," Herb said. "Did you ever talk to Hess, too, or meet him?"

"I saw him a couple of times. I never really met him," Peggy answered. "Do you think he parachuted out over London or Paris or wherever it was, the way people are saying?"

"Stranger things have happened."

"Oh, yeah? Name two."

"Mm . . . There were the Braves in 1914."

"That's one," Peggy said.

Her husband said nothing for some little while. Then he spread his hands, as he might have done after turning over a bad dummy at the bridge table. "Maybe I can't think of anything else that peculiar. But it's been a pretty crazy war any way you look at it, hasn't it?"

"Think so, do you? I'll tell you something." Peggy took a deep breath, then proceeded to do exactly that: "America's even stranger than all the crazy places I saw in Europe. The ostrich with his head in the sand is wearing an Uncle Sam top hat."

"Honey, *I* don't want to see us in the war," Herb said. "I went Over There. I saw the elephant. That's what my granddad would have called it, anyway: what he *did* call it after he came home from the Army of the Potomac. The only reason I've ever been glad we couldn't have kids is that a son of mine would be draft age right about now. Some of the things I did, some of the things I saw . . . I wouldn't wish them on my son."

"Herb—" Peggy didn't know how to go on. They hardly ever brought up the subject of children; it was too raw and painful. In the early days of their marriage, she'd miscarried three times in the space of two years. After that, her doctor warned her that any more tries probably wouldn't succeed, and would put her life in danger. So she and Herb had relied on French letters and on techniques some people called perverted, and remained fond of each other's company to this day.

If something was necessarily missing, well, what could you do? *Something* was missing from everybody's life. Peggy had more leisure—and more money—with which to travel. Most of the time, she and Herb could look on the bright side of things.

(She hadn't worried about any of that when she ended up letting Constantine Jenkins into her bed in Berlin. She'd been so sloshed, she hadn't worried, or thought, about one goddamn thing then. She'd guessed the embassy undersecretary was queer. She'd been pretty sure, in fact. If he was, he sure could switch-hit every now and then. Only luck he didn't put a bun in her oven. And wouldn't *that* have fouled up her life?)

She took a deep breath. "Somebody's got to stop Hitler. If that means us, it means us, no matter what it costs."

"Maybe," he said. Unlike her, he held back a lot of what went through his mind. Most of the time, she thought that made him easier to live with. Most of the time, but not always. After a moment, he added, "But if Chamberlain and Daladier are pushing him forward, who's going to ask us to hold him back?"

The question was painfully good. The only reason the USA had gone into the last war was to pull England and France's chestnuts out of the fire. Still, Peggy found a possible answer: "Stalin?"

Her husband snorted. "He may ask, but who'll listen to him? Not enough Russian votes—or Red votes, come to that—to get FDR's bowels in an uproar, especially with this third-term boom. Most people don't want a war. They can finally see the end of the Depression, or they think they can, and they just want to stay under their own vine and fig tree."

Peggy's strict parents had sent her to Sunday school every week till she got big enough to put her foot down and quit going. Bits and pieces of it stuck to this day. She could come out with chapter and verse from Micah (in the King James version, of course; her folks seemed to think that was what God had used to talk to the Hebrews): " 'But they shall sit every man under his vine and under his fig tree; and none shall make them afraid.' " She sighed wistfully. "Boy, that'd be swell!"

Herb smiled, whether at the quotation or at the old-fashioned slang she couldn't tell. "It would, wouldn't it? The way it looks to most people, we've got the Atlantic and the Pacific instead of the vine and the fig tree. With all that water between us and trouble, why worry?"

As usual, he sounded calm and reasonable. And Peggy usually liked him to sound that way, which only proved the old saw about opposites attracting. "England thought it was safe behind the Channel, too, till Hitler started bombing London," she snapped.

"Kaiser Wilhelm did the same thing the last time around," Herb answered. "The more it changes, the more it stays the same."

"It's not," Peggy insisted.

"What's the difference?"

"Hitler hits harder." Listening to herself, Peggy thought she might have come up with a campaign slogan for the *Führer.* But Hitler didn't need to worry about campaign slogans any more. That was one of the advantages of being a dictator. Now everybody else had to do the worrying.

"I'm not the person you need to tell. Roosevelt is," Herb said.

"Well, I'll do that, then," Peggy declared. She'd met the President before; his New York background was not so very different from hers here in Philadelphia. She couldn't hop on a train to Washington and walk into the White house with the confident expectation that he would see her right away. If she wrote him a report on what she'd seen and what she thought about it, though, she did think it would reach him.

What he'd do afterwards, and whether he'd do anything . . . That, she'd just have to find out. Her parents had also made sure she could type. There'd been other crashes before this latest one. Somebody with a salable skill always had an edge. She sat down at the family Royal and began getting the past year and a half down on paper.

A RUSSIAN PRISONER staggered, stumbled, slumped to his knees, and then, with a small groan, rolled over on his side. The Japanese guard tramping along fifty meters or so in front of Hideki Fujita walked over to the skinny, filthy man on the ground. He shouted at the luckless fellow. The Russian only lay there. The Japanese soldier kicked him: once, twice, three times.

The prisoner groaned again, louder. He tried to stand but could not. He looked up at the guard. His hands spread in a hopeless last appeal.

Hopeless indeed. Not even wasting a bullet, the guard bayoneted him in the throat. The Russian thrashed his life away. It didn't take long; he had little life left to lose.

Sergeant Fujita trudged past the still feebly writhing body. He didn't spare it so much as a sideways glance. It wasn't as if he hadn't seen plenty of others just like it. And it wasn't as if plenty of the Red Army men who'd surrendered outside of Vladivostok but still managed to shamble along through Manchukuo wouldn't keel over themselves pretty soon.

One of the prisoners—a man shaggy as a bear, because he hadn't shaved or trimmed his hair since the surrender—caught Fujita's eye and stretched out an imploring hand, palm up. "Food, please, soldier-*sama*?" the Russian said in bad Japanese. *Lord soldier*—the fellow knew which side his bread was buttered on.

It didn't help him, not here. "They'll feed you soon," Fujita said roughly. The prisoner's blank stare said he didn't understand. Fujita simplified things even more: "No food now. Food later. Keep marching."

Keep marching. That was the essential command. Fujita was glad he had the pair of fine Russian boots he'd taken from a dead soldier in the Siberian woods. They were much easier on his feet than the clodhoppers the Japanese Army issued. What the Russians didn't know about leather wasn't worth knowing.

Few prisoners had any boots at all. They'd been plundered after they gave up. Well, of course they had. As soon as a man surrendered, he stopped being a man. He was just a beast, a thing, to be used as his captors found convenient . . . or amusing.

Fujita had put a few fallen prisoners out of their misery. Couldn't have them slowing up the column, after all. But he'd never fired into a mass of Russians just to watch them go down. When he had to kill, he killed quickly and cleanly, as the guard in front of him had done. He saw no sport in gutshooting men or bayoneting them so they died a centimeter at a time.

But he said not a word to the Japanese soldiers who enjoyed doing things like that. It wasn't as if standing orders forbade mistreating prisoners of war. During the last fight against the Russians, such orders had been in place. Japan wanted to show the European powers and America she'd built the same kind of civilization they already had.

Now, by all the signs, the people who ran the country didn't care what the European powers and America thought. Surrender had long been a disgrace in Japan. If the captors of soldiers who gave up felt like mistreating them or even killing them, no so-called laws of war stood in the way.

And Japan had never ratified the Geneva Convention. The Europeans' silly rules weren't going to hold back the Empire, either. Nothing was, not any more.

Peasants in the fields—maybe native Manchus, maybe Chinese settlers—stared at the column of white men in ragged khaki. None stared from close range, however. Not only was the column unfamiliar and therefore alarming; it was guarded by Japanese soldiers, and so doubly alarming.

Yes, Manchukuo was Japan's ally—Japan's puppet, if you wanted to be unkind about it. But the local peasants didn't see Japanese soldiers as allies. They saw them as plunderers, as locusts. Fujita had served in Manchukuo for some time now. He knew the peasants had their reasons for seeing his comrades that way. On the other hand, they *were* peasants. No doubt they would have kept their distance from Chinese soldiers (or, for that matter, from Brazilian soldiers), too.

Lieutenant Hanafusa strode by, a one-man parade. Being an officer, he wasn't burdened with a rifle and a heavy pack. He could afford to waste energy showing off. (And he too wore a pair of supple Russian boots, so his feet would be happy.) "Sir, may I ask you a question?" Sergeant Fujita called to him.

"What is it?" Hanafusa returned.

Fujita got the idea that, if the lieutenant didn't care for the question, someone would be unhappy immediately thereafter. He also had a good notion of who that someone would be. Well, too late to back off now. "Have you heard yet, sir, just where we're supposed to be going with all these miserable prisoners?"

To his vast relief, Hanafusa nodded. "As a matter of fact, I have. There's a camp—or some kind of facility, anyhow—at a place called Pingfan."

"Where would that be, sir?" Fujita knew he was pressing his luck. He bowed to the officer. "Please excuse me, but I've never heard of it."

"Well, I hadn't, either, when somebody told me about it," Lieutenant Hanafusa said, with more generosity than he usually showed. "It's about twenty-five kilometers south of Harbin."

"*Ah, so desu!*" Fujita exclaimed. He knew where Harbin was, all right. Any Japanese who'd spent some time here would have. Not only was it one of the biggest cities in Manchukuo, it also looked more like a Western town than most places here. That sprang from the strong local Russian influence, which persisted even now. And it was a major rail center; you went through Harbin if you needed to get anywhere in Manchukuo. Fujita had done it several times. He tried one more question: "What will they do with them there?"

"Beats me. That's for the damned Russians to worry about," Hanafusa replied. "All I know is, we're taking them to something called Unit 731. The people who run it want prisoners. Now that we've taken so many, our job is to deliver the sorry bastards to them."

"What are they going to use them for? Or will they use them up?"

"Beats me," Hanafusa repeated cheerfully. "That's for the Russians to worry about, too. Maybe after we make the delivery I'll go back up to

Harbin and screw a blond Russian whore—one more reminder that we beat them."

"Yes, sir. That sounds good, sir." Fujita grinned.

Hanafusa started to strut off, then caught himself. "Oh, that reminds me, Sergeant. You *were* vaccinated for smallpox when you went into the Army, weren't you?"

"I sure was!" Fujita winced at the memory. "It took. I was sick for a couple of days. My arm swelled up like it was poisoned, and I got a big old blister full of pus."

"I had the same thing happen to me. Not much fun, was it?" But Lieutenant Hanafusa nodded, as if satisfied. "That's all right, then."

"What's all right, sir? Why do you need to know a silly thing like that?"

"It ties in with what people say about Unit 731," the lieutenant said. The answer might have made sense to him, but it didn't to Fujita. The sergeant was going to ask him to explain, but Hanafusa did hurry away this time. Fujita had already pushed him as far as a noncom could reasonably push an officer, and maybe a little further besides.

He'll come back. It's still a long way to Harbin. If he's in a good mood, I can find out later on, Fujita thought. He rubbed his arm. It felt fine now, but he still wore a nasty scar from the vaccination. And he remembered how little sympathy the doctors had shown. One of them told him, *You'd be a lot sicker than this if you really came down with smallpox.*

Fujita knew that was true. One of his grandfathers had a pocked face, and mourned a younger brother who hadn't survived the disease.

"Food, please, sir?" another Russian prisoner whined in bad Japanese.

"No food now. Food later," Fujita answered. Idly, he wondered whether the white man had ever been vaccinated.

THEY'D REMOVED THE CANNON from Hans-Ulrich Rudel's Stuka for this mission. He wasn't shooting up Russian panzers today. His plane and half a dozen others would try to take out a railroad bridge over the Dnieper near Borisov.

Colonel Steinbrenner nodded to the pilots he'd chosen. "I picked you boys for a reason," he told them. "You're the best I've got. That bridge has got to go. The Reds are hauling all kinds of crap over it. Don't let me down. Don't let the *Reich* down, either."

The flyers nodded. Hans-Ulrich noticed that the wing commander didn't say anything about not letting the *Führer* down. He didn't make a fuss about it, but he noticed. How could you help noticing such things when everybody'd got so maniacal about security and loyalty these days? Yes, the powers that be thought Steinbrenner was all right. He wouldn't have replaced Colonel Greim if they hadn't. But you never could tell whether they'd change their minds.

"Questions?" Steinbrenner asked after he finished the briefing. One of the other pilots stuck up his hand. The colonel nodded. "What is it, Franz?"

"Borisov is in Russia, *nicht wahr*?" Franz Fischbach said.

"In Byelorussia, actually. But yes, inside the Soviet Union, if that's what you meant," Steinbrenner answered. "The gloves are off. I'll say that again, to make sure you get it. *The gloves are off.* The Reds have been bombing us whenever they found the nerve. Now we get to show them what they bought. Don't you like it? If you don't, I'll find somebody else to go instead."

"Oh, no, sir. Don't worry about me," Fischbach said quickly. Any other reply and he could have kissed his flying career good-bye. "I just wanted to make sure the brass bothered to check the map."

That got a chuckle from the wing commander. "Yeah, you never can tell with the fellows with the fancy shoulder straps. . . . Other questions?" He looked surprised when he got one. "What's on your mind, Peter?"

"Are we knocking the Reds around to help persuade England and France to throw in with us?" Peter Tannenwald inquired. "That's what you hear everywhere."

"I've heard it, too. I don't know if it's true or not," Colonel Steinbrenner said. Hans-Ulrich had also heard it. He hoped it was true. It would make life easier. Steinbrenner went on, "You'd do better asking somebody from the Foreign Ministry, not me."

"Oh, sure, sir." Tannenwald grinned at him. "Only you're right here, and those clowns are back in Berlin."

"That's true, but they know the answer, and I just wish I did. All I know is, you've got to go get that bridge," Steinbrenner said. "Good luck to you all. I hope to see every one of you back here before very long."

Hans-Ulrich hoped that would happen, too. The Germans and Poles had just about cleared the Red Army out of Poland. They'd pushed into the northern Ukraine from southeastern Poland. The Pripet Marshes, which lay on the Polish-Byelorussian border, slowed their advance in that part of the front. No German panzers were anywhere near Borisov, not so far as Hans-Ulrich knew.

Franz Fischbach summed up what that meant: "We don't want to get shot down behind the Russian lines, you're saying."

"Not unless you've got a big insurance policy and you need your next of kin to cash it in right now," Steinbrenner agreed dryly. By all the signs, the Russians cared little for the Geneva Convention. They hadn't signed it. That meant the Germans didn't need to follow its rules when dealing with Red prisoners. But it also meant the Russians did as they pleased with Germans they captured. You heard stories about foot soldiers ingeniously mutilated, maybe after they were dead, but maybe not, too. Some pilots made sure they always kept a round in their pistol, to keep the Russians from having fun with them if their luck soured. Hans-Ulrich hadn't worried about such things before. Flying against Borisov . . . *I'd better see to it,* he thought.

After the meeting broke up, Sergeant Dieselhorst asked him about what was going on. Hans-Ulrich explained the mission. Dieselhorst nodded impatiently. "*Ja, ja,*" he said. "But what about the Western powers? Are they going to come to their senses, or will they go on fighting us instead?"

"Peter asked Colonel Steinbrenner the same thing."

"And . . . ?"

"And the colonel said he should talk to the fellows in striped trousers, 'cause they might know and he didn't."

Dieselhorst snorted. "Those fairies don't know their ass from their elbow. Sure would be a lot easier if we didn't have to worry about the Western front."

"You're right. It would. But the colonel can't do anything about that, and neither can we. All we can do is bomb the snot out of the Ivans, so we will."

"Sounds good by me." The sergeant sent him a crooked grin. "And then you can try and get back to Bialystok and see your half-Jewish girlfriend."

Rudel's ears heated. "Sofia's not my girlfriend." That was true, although not from lack of effort on his part. "I don't know what kind of *Mischling* she is." That was also true. She was maddeningly vague about herself. She might have been almost a full-blooded Jew. Or she might just have been an uncommonly swarthy Pole. In these parts, half the time nobody was sure what anybody else was.

Flying the mission seemed easier than facing Sofia, anyhow. The Russians could only kill him in the air or torture him and then kill him if they caught him on the ground. They couldn't humiliate him, make him feel he was twelve years old again, and at the same time make him feel more electrically alive, more sparky and sparkly, than he'd ever felt before.

As soon as his Stuka crossed over into territory the Reds still held, they started shooting at him. They opened up with everything they had: not only antiaircraft guns but also machine guns and rifles. That small-arms fire would fall far short of the plane. All they were doing with it was putting themselves in danger. A bullet falling from a couple of thousand meters could kill you if it landed on your unprotected head. The Germans wasted much less ammo like that: not none, but much less.

He droned along behind and to the left of Peter Tannenbaum's plane, the flight leader. If Peter didn't know the way to Borisov, they were all shafted. Hans-Ulrich kept an eye peeled for Soviet fighters. Messerschmitt pilots scorned the biplanes and flat-nosed monoplanes the Red Air Force threw against them. But a fighter all but helpless against a 109 could hack a Stuka out of the sky with the greatest of ease.

"See anything, Albert?" Rudel asked through the speaking tube.

"Only the rest of our boys," Dieselhorst answered. "I wish they'd given me two heavy machine guns back here instead of one ordinary piece. Then I'd really stand a chance against whatever came after us."

Roughened by static, Tannenbaum's voice came through Hans-

Ulrich's earphones: "I see the target ahead at one o'clock. Everybody have it?"

That ribbon of water through the flat landscape had to be the Dnieper. And those steel curves marked the bridge. It looked as graceful as most in Germany. Given Russian slovenliness, that surprised Rudel. It was so all the same. "Got it," he said, his confirmation intermingled with the others.

One by one, the Stukas flipped a wing in the air and dove on the target. The Ivans knew how important the bridge was. Their flak sent up puffs of black smoke all around the bombers. Most of the shells burst behind them. Gunners often underestimated how fast a diving Stuka could go. But Franz Fischbach shouted in pain and despair and fear. His Ju-87 plunged faster than any of the others, and didn't pull up. An enormous explosion and a pillar of black smoke marked where it slammed into the ground.

Hans-Ulrich released his bombs and hauled back on the stick for all he was worth. The climb was the real danger point, not the dive. The Stuka wasn't very high, and it moved slower and slower as it shed the momentum it had.

"Somebody got the bridge," the backwards-facing Sergeant Dieselhorst reported.

"Good," Rudel answered. "I hate it when our men go down." Another flyer would have talked of friends going down. Hans-Ulrich had precious few friends in the *Luftwaffe.* The other pilots had come to respect his skill and courage. Like him? That seemed to be asking too much. But he had more urgent things to worry about, starting with staying alive.

And, with the bridge down, maybe he could ask Colonel Steinbrenner for a short furlough in Bialystok. He wasn't sure Sofia liked him, either. Whether she did or not felt at least as important as whether he kept on breathing. Why not? If Sofia liked him, he'd have something to go on breathing for.

GERMAN AND FRENCH lines ran close together in front of Luc Harcourt's position. When a Fritz came out in front of his side's trenches,

Luc could have potted him easy as you please. But the soldier in field-gray carried a couple of items that made him think twice. One was a large white flag of truce. The other, even more curious, was a megaphone.

Luc wondered where the hell he'd found it. Did the Germans issue them, say, one to a battalion? That took thoroughness to what struck him as an insane degree, but you never could tell with the *Boches.* Or had this fellow liberated it from the little French town whose ruins lay right behind the line?

Wherever he'd got it, he raised it to his lips and bellowed through it in gutturally accented French: "We would like a cease-fire! We won't shoot if you don't! We should all fight the Russian Jew Bolsheviks instead!" After repeating himself several times, he waved to the *poilus* on the far side of the barbed wire, gravely lowered the megaphone, and withdrew back to some place where things were apt to be safer.

"Give 'em a burst, Harcourt," Lieutenant Demange rasped. "They came out with that same horseshit while they were squashing Czechoslovakia, remember? Then it was our turn, so they kicked us in the nuts instead."

Luc did remember the eerie, almost unnatural quiet on the Western front till the German onslaught a couple of weeks before Christmas 1938. With some surprise, he realized he and Demange were two of the very few left in this company who could recall that quiet at firsthand. So many new fish in, so many veterans dead or wounded or down with one frontline sickness or another . . .

He squeezed the triggers on the Hotchkiss gun. Yes, for the moment it was still his baby, even if he wore a gold sergeant's stripe. Half a strip's worth of ammo roared toward the Germans' line. Demange hadn't told him to try to kill anybody, so he fired high. In war's rough language, he was saying no without being rude.

Even if he was polite, he expected the *Boches* to shoot back. But they didn't. The silence from their side of the line might have been a pointed comment about his burst.

"Be damned," Joinville muttered. "Maybe they mean it this time."

"Fuck 'em. Fuck their mothers. Fuck their grannies." Villehardouin spoke only a little French, almost all of it filthy. He went on in Breton.

Luc understood Breton no more than he understood Bulgarian, but it sounded vile. Joinville had picked up scraps of Tiny's native tongue. He whistled and clapped his hands. Whatever Villehardouin said, it must have been juicy.

After sundown, German planes rumbled overhead. Searchlights and antiaircraft guns hunted for them, without much luck. But no bombs whistled down from the planes. They dropped leaflets instead. The leaflets carried the same message the *Landser* had shouted out. They also showed a cartoon: a wolf with a Jewish face and a Soviet officer's red-starred cap attacking a pretty blonde labeled CIVILIZATION. A knight called WESTERN EUROPE was coming to her rescue with a sword.

The paper was cheap, brownish pulp. All the same . . ."Not the worst asswipe I've found lately," Luc said. "And it's a better present than most of the ones the *Boches* try to give us."

"Boy, you've got that right," Demange agreed. "I wonder if Hitler bit off more than he could chew over there on the other front."

"Could be," Luc said. "Germans never tried to make that kind of deal in the last war, did they?"

"I hope to shit, they didn't," the middle-aged veteran answered. "They knew we would've told 'em to stuff it. You've got to figure the fucking Nazis aren't serious this time around, either."

"How come? They sure are putting a lot of effort into it. I bet they've got guys yelling and planes dropping leaflets up and down the whole front."

"Oh, sure. But so what?" Demange said. "The way it looks, they just want us to throw in with them on account of they're so fucking cute, y'know? They aren't saying they'll pull out of France or the Low Countries. They aren't saying they'll turn loose of Denmark and Norway. They want to rape us, *and* they want us to come while they're doing it. Shitheads should live so long."

Luc grunted. Demange had a way with words—not always a pleasant way, but a way. Being nasty didn't make him wrong. Luc hadn't heard anything that made him think the Nazis were willing to pull back from what they'd grabbed. Thoughtfully, he said, "I wonder if any of that's occurred to our diplomats, or to the English."

"Don't hold your breath," Demange advised. "Our boys are a bunch of hyenas in top hats and cutaways. And as for the English . . . *Merde alors,* the English fucking boil bacon. Anybody who does that can't be long on brains."

Luc hadn't thought of it like that, which again didn't mean the foul-mouth reluctant lieutenant didn't have a point. "Any which way, I'll be happy as long as this cease-fire holds."

"Well, so will I," Demange answered, lighting a fresh Gitane from the stub of his old one. Luc looked wistful, so Demange, muttering, handed him a cigarette, too. Then he continued, "We'd better not go to sleep like we did after old Czecho got it. *Boches*'re liable to be piling up tanks behind their line, ready to give us another clop in the teeth as soon as we squat over the slit trench with our pants at half mast."

"You'd think our recon would notice something like that," Luc said.

Demange laughed raucously. "Yeah, you would, wouldn't you? And you'd think those *cons* might've noticed something the last time, too. Did they? Not fucking likely! So how far can you trust 'em now?"

"I've learned not to trust the *Boches,* either—except to trust them to be sure to cause trouble," Luc replied with dignity.

"Good job! Maybe you're not as dumb as you look. Maybe." Demange's seamless scorn for all mankind had plenty of room to include Luc.

Come the next morning, the Germans still didn't fire. They did show themselves, as if confident the *poilus* wouldn't shoot at them without provocation. As Luc had seen many times before, German discipline was a formidable thing. He wondered if any of the *Landsers* walking around within easy rifle shot had given their officers a nasty look when they were ordered to come out from their nice, safe trenches. He knew damn well he would have.

He waited for Lieutenant Demange to tell him to open up on the *Boches.* If Demange gave the order, he would obey. He didn't want to face French military justice, a contradiction in terms if ever there was one. But he also didn't want to start the fighting up again without orders.

And the orders did not come. Neither hard-bitten Demange nor any of his superiors seemed eager to provoke the enemy. Their attitude looked to be that they could fight if they had to, but that they weren't going to start anything. Luc felt the same way.

The fellow with the megaphone came out again: "We will trade beer for wine, or tubes of meat paste for good tobacco."

"Nobody answer," Demange commanded. Informal commerce did happen now and again. The Germans knew their enemies liked that meat paste. And everybody knew the Fritzes made better beer but worse wine than people on this side of the Rhine. Lieutenant Demange wasn't about to let such bargaining come out into the open, though.

"Beer tastes like stale piss anyway," opined Joinville, like most men from the south of France a confirmed wine-bibber.

"How do you know what stale piss tastes like?" Luc asked. Joinville gave him a dirty look. Luc grinned back. Even in a cease-fire, you had to make your own fun.

Chapter 13

Every time the morning news came on the radio, Sergei Yaroslavsky tensed. He wasn't the only flyer who did—far from it. The Germans and the Poles were giving the Red Army and Air Force all the trouble they needed and more besides. If the rest of the decadent capitalist powers lined up behind the Hitlerites, the homeland of the glorious October Revolution would be in deadly danger once more.

"Moscow speaking," came out of the radio at the appointed hour. The pilots and bomb-aimers gathered in the officers' quarters all leaned toward the set. What new disasters would it announce? Which ones would it try to sugarcoat? The only thing Sergei was sure of was that there would be some.

"First, a report on the fighting in Poland," the newsreader said. Unfortunately, several of the towns he mentioned weren't in Poland, but in Byelorussia or the Ukraine. The average Soviet citizen—especially the average citizen who didn't live near the USSR's western border—probably wouldn't know that. Such was bound to be the official hope.

As always, Radio Moscow made things sound as good as they possibly could, or else a little better than that. Again, only someone expert at reading between the lines—or someone in the middle of the Soviet retreat—was likely to notice. How many people did that include? It was hard to gauge, not least because admitting you noticed anything out of kilter about the broadcasts would win you a quick one-way trip to the gulag.

Lately, though, the fighting hadn't been the only thing Sergei was worrying about, even if it was going worse than Moscow cared to admit. He waited till the announcer got done listing the Polish (and, sadly, Soviet) towns that had changed hands lately. After that . . . After that, the man switched to a report on the desultory fighting that went on in the Far East. Vladivostok was lost. The USSR wouldn't get it back any time soon. What else needed saying?

Something, evidently. "Through reliable sources, the Soviet Union has learned that the Japanese are barbarously mistreating our prisoners of war," the newsreader announced. "The peace-loving and humane government of the USSR has warned the Japanese Empire through neutral channels to cease and desist from this practice at once. All regimes are liable to punishment for violating the laws of war."

That sounded good. The only trouble with it was, Japan hadn't signed the Geneva Convention. She wasn't obligated to treat POWs according to its rules. And, for that matter, neither had the USSR. Sergei wouldn't have wanted to be a German or Pole who had to surrender to the Red Army. He wouldn't have wanted to yield to a German or Pole, either. Since the USSR hadn't signed the convention, her enemies in the west didn't have to follow it with Soviet prisoners, either.

But all that was swept away when the newsreader got to what Yaroslavsky and the rest of the Red Air Force officers were really waiting to hear. The man's voice deepened and saddened as he said, "The ominous lull on Fascist Germany's western front continues. The reactionary capitalist states will regret throwing their troops against the peasants and workers of the Soviet Union alongside and under the orders of the Hitlerite hyenas if they make that fatal mistake. General Secretary Stalin has stated, 'We shall resist any and all aggression with the courage and iron determination suited to the workers' revolutionary vanguard. We shall resist, and we shall triumph.' Stormy applause greeted his remarks to the Supreme Soviet."

Nobody in the officers' lounge seemed to want to meet anyone else's eye. The USSR was having all it could do to hold off Germany and Poland. Poland was . . . not much. However reactionary England and France might be, they were great powers. If they came after the Soviet Union with the Nazis, what would happen next? Nothing good, not so far as Sergei could see.

The newsreader went on in somewhat brighter tones: "In England, Winston Churchill continues to speak out strongly against the proposed misalliance with the Nazis. While a reactionary himself—he tried to strangle the glorious Red Revolution in its cradle—Churchill is not blind to the dangers of Hitlerism. 'The lamb may lie down with the lion,' he said, 'but only the lion will get up again—full.' "

That sounded good even after being translated into Russian. Most foreign gibes lost their flavor once they left their native tongue. Churchill must have seemed uncommonly witty in English.

"Although Churchill is a member of Prime Minister Chamberlain's Conservative Party, Chamberlain has gone out of his way to assure the English Parliament that Churchill does not speak for him or his government," the newsreader said portentously.

"Chamberlain is playing with his dick again," one of the pilots said in disgust. The Chimp couldn't have put it any more plainly—and probably would have put it about the same way. The news didn't sound good. If Chamberlain was criticizing Churchill, and Churchill was criticizing cutting a deal with the Nazis . . . What was the likely result? Trouble for the *Rodina,* that was what.

More trouble for the Rodina, Sergei mentally corrected. The Soviet Union already had as much country as any self-respecting country needed.

After music replaced the news, Major Konstantin Ponamarenko—Colonel Borisov's replacement as squadron leader—said, "You men will know—not everything that happens comes on the radio right away."

Heads bobbed up and down, Yaroslavsky's among them. The main purpose of Radio Moscow news was to hold up morale on the home front. Sergei had thought as much himself not long before. He hadn't looked for the new squadron commander to acknowledge it so openly.

Ponamarenko went on, "You will also know that the situation in the field is developing in a way that might possibly be better."

He waited for more nods. He got them. Sergei admired him. The pilot had rarely heard a more graceful way of admitting the USSR was getting the snot knocked out of it.

"Don't waste time worrying about those French and English whores," Ponamarenko said earnestly. "They can't get at us yet, and we can't get at them, either. Worry about the German cocksuckers, and about their Polish lap dogs yapping along behind them. We can hit back at them, and we damn well will."

Sergei nodded one more time. You had to show you agreed. Somebody was always watching you. No: somebody always might be watching you. You always needed to stay on your guard. It was all right to remember that Stalin had started the fight with Poland the winter before, looking to pick up Wilno on the cheap. If the General Secretary hadn't, the Soviet Union would still be at war with Germany, but only in a formal sense, since neither side could have struck at the other without violating some buffer state's neutrality. Well, now the USSR had done just that, and this was what the Soviet workers and peasants got for it.

Yes, it was all right to remember Stalin might well have outsmarted himself. But it wasn't all right to show you remembered such things. You never could tell who might notice, and report. You never could tell when you might disappear.

"What I'm saying is, we are going to be flying missions inside what was Soviet territory before the war," Ponamarenko continued. "We will try to drop our bombs only on the heads of the Fascist jackals, of course. Of course." He bore down on the repeated phrase. "But accidents happen in war. I don't have many virgins here. You know that. And I need to tell every one of you—don't worry about them. Some of our explosives may do a little harm to Soviet citizens. If the rest of our loads help drive the invaders out of the Motherland, though, that's a price worth paying. Do you hear what I'm telling you, Comrades?"

By the way the flyers' heads moved, they might have been on springs. This also was nothing that hadn't occurred to Sergei before. He didn't want to hurt his own people. He'd never dreamt such a dreadful thing might be possible when he first put on the uniform he wore.

However dreadful the possibility might be, it was here. And Ponamarenko had it right. If the bombers hurt the invaders worse than the locals, their strikes were bound to be worthwhile in the long run. A surgeon cut you up to make you healthier in the long run.

But you still had a scar after the operation. And it still hurt while you recovered from it. Sergei wished he hadn't thought of any of that.

EVERY ONCE IN A WHILE, war seemed easy, even to someone like Theo Hossbach who knew better most of the time. When the German panzers smashed through the Low Countries and into northern France, it was obvious the *Wehrmacht* was playing a faster, deeper game than the Dutch and Belgians, the English and French, who tried to slow it down. Unfortunately, the enemy caught on just before Germany managed to slam the sword all the way home.

Now, again, the panzers rolled forward as if nothing in the world could slow them down. The experienced German troops outclassed the Ivans as effortlessly as Adi Stoss had outclassed the infantrymen he played against on that snowy Polish football pitch.

Maybe—probably, even—an individual ground pounder was in better shape than Adi. Russian panzers were often better than German machines. But when Stoss got the ball, he knew what to do with it. And even when he didn't have it, he knew where to go so he might get it, or so he might keep the guys on the other side from causing trouble.

The Germans were like that as they pushed from Poland into Byelorussia (and into the northern Ukraine, too, but Theo knew about that only by rumor and by brags on Radio Berlin). The panzers struck, then sped on, leaving it for the German and Polish infantry slogging along in their wake to clean up the Ivans they'd shattered.

And the Ivans couldn't figure out what to do about it. It was as if their manager had to shout in directions from the touchline to get them to move. Left to themselves, they would defend in place till they got smashed up, but they maneuvered only slowly and awkwardly. They might have those formidable panzers, but they didn't know how to use them.

The Germans did. They took advantage as quickly and eagerly as a guy trying to screw his girl. And they were screwing the Russians, all right. People talked about Smolensk and Vyazma. When people got excited, they talked about Moscow and Leningrad.

Theo talked . . . very little. When he sat in the bowels of the Panzer II, he relayed orders from the platoon CO, the company CO, regimental HQ, division HQ . . . Whatever came in through his earphones, he faithfully passed on to Hermann Witt. And he sent back the panzer commander's responses. Witt had to needle him only every once in a while to make sure he exercised his voice enough to do that.

"Don't keep it all to yourself, Theo, my dear," he would say. "They put that set in there for a reason, you know."

And Theo would nod. And he'd do better for a while. But only for a while. He was too much a creature of the deep silences inside his own head ever to grow comfortable with the racket of the outside world.

While they drove, while they fought, he didn't have much to do with Adalbert Stoss. How could he, when they had their places at opposite ends of the Panzer II's fighting compartment? Adi talked to Theo—who didn't?—but he wasn't a guy who yakked all the time for the sake of yakking. And his job needed him to pay attention every single second, which Theo's didn't.

When they rolled into bivouac at the end of one of the midsummer days where the sun never wanted to set, Theo sometimes felt Adi's eye on him. The driver rarely went beyond commonplaces when they talked, but Theo figured there was more to him than he let on. What would he say if he spoke up? Something like *You don't have to pull in your head like a turtle to hide,* perhaps. Or perhaps not. Theo knew his own imagination and guesses sometimes ran away with him.

He didn't know what he could do about it. Adi seemed happy thundering up and down the pitch with everybody else. Goalkeeper suited Theo better. Most of the time, the action was far away, so he could daydream. There were the stark moments when he had to make the save or botch it, but they were mercifully few and far between. Even if he did botch one, he could get by as long as he didn't screw up too much more than anyone else would have. Sometimes you just couldn't do anything about a shot.

Unfortunately, that also held true on the battlefield. Burnt-out carcasses of Panzer Is and IIs and IIIs testified to the truth there. The Ivans didn't play the game very well, but they played goddamn hard. They played so hard, in fact, that infantrymen and panzer soldiers on the pitch were as nothing beside it. Germans with a football played rough, but it was only a game. The Russians were playing for keeps. When you played like that, all the rules flew out the window.

Back in the West, when something went wrong you had a chance of surrendering. When you did surrender, you had a chance of living till you got to a POW camp—not a guarantee, but a chance, often a decent one. The Russians usually got rid of prisoners instead of bothering to send them back.

The panzers clattered forward again the next morning. There inside his armored cave, Theo listened to what was going on. Every so often, Witt would order Adi to stop the panzer. He would fire a few rounds from the 20mm or a burst from the machine gun, and they would go on. Now and then, a rifle round or a few bullets from a Russian machine gun would make everyone inside the panzer jump, but that was all. Anything more than small-arms fire . . . No, Theo didn't want to remind himself of that.

"We will slow down for the village ahead. We'll go around it and shell it from the outside." Not the voice of God, but the company commander's: close enough. It was the first Theo had heard that a village lay anywhere close by.

He relayed the order to Witt, who was standing up in the turret as usual. The sergeant said, "*Ja.* Makes sense," and passed instructions on to Adi. The Panzer II slowed and swung to the left, presumably to go around the village. Theo also thought skirting built-up areas made sense. You didn't want to give some Russian the chance to pop out of nowhere and chuck a bottle full of burning gasoline through your hatch. Molotov cocktails, the Germans called them: a name the *Legion Kondor* had brought back from Spain.

But slowing down carried risks of its own. A rifle cracked outside the panzer, much closer than usual. Witt dove—fell, really—back into the fighting compartment, blood streaming down his face. "Jesus Christ!" he yelled, dogging the hatch behind him. "There's a motherfucking Ivan on the panzer!"

"What happened?" Theo asked, the words jerked from him.

"He should've blown my head off," Witt answered. "I'm just creased—I think." He raised his voice: "Adi! Shake him off if you can!"

Stoss didn't answer, but the panzer sped up and jerked wildly, first to one side, then to the other. It didn't work—Theo could hear the Russian scrabbling around on the machine's armored carapace. Wounded or not, Witt had the presence of mind to slam the observation ports in the turret shut. The bastard out there wouldn't be able to drop a grenade inside . . . Theo hoped.

He grabbed the Schmeisser that hung on a couple of iron brackets. He'd never needed it before, not inside the panzer. He wished to God he didn't need it now.

The Russian stood up on the engine decking and worried at something on the turret. It wasn't the radioman's escape hatch. Maybe the Ivan didn't even realize that was there. If he didn't, he was about to find out. Theo yanked it open and fired off the whole magazine the instant he caught a glimpse of khaki. There was a wild scream and a thump, as of a heavy weight falling back onto the engine louvers. A moment later, the panzer shifted again, as if that same heavy weight had fallen off.

Theo sucked in a deep breath, which reminded him he hadn't been breathing before. He took a wound dressing out of its belt pouch and turned back to Witt. "I'll bandage you up."

Witt had already started trying that with his own wound dressing. He was making a hash of it, since he couldn't see what he was doing. Theo wrapped cotton gauze around his head—he had a ten-centimeter gash in his scalp. But it seemed to be only a crease, as the panzer commander had said.

"Thanks," Witt said when Theo was done. "Way to get the son of a bitch, too. You want to take my seat for a bit? Sorry, but I can't see straight right now. And it hurts a little bit."

If he admitted it hurt a little, it doubtless hurt a lot. Theo didn't want to command the panzer, even for a little while. He saw he'd have to, though. He made himself nod. "All right." The first thing he did after that—even before he scrambled into the turret to trade places with Witt—was to stick a fresh thirty-two-round box on his machine pistol.

LEAVE IN MADRID. Chaim Weinberg couldn't have been happier. Sure, he'd left New York City, come to Spain, and joined the Abe Lincolns to fight Fascism. When he first got off the boat, he'd been raring to shoot the enemies of the working class every hour of every day of every week.

But that was three years ago now. One of the big differences between a rookie and a veteran was that the vet developed a sense of proportion. Chaim still wanted to kill Fascists. Every hour of every day? Well, no. For one thing, that increased the chances that the Fascists would kill him instead. And, for another, there was more to life than killing people, no matter how much they deserved it.

A hot bath. Delousing. Clean clothes. A shave with hot lather from a barber. Hell, with any lather. In the field, Chaim just scraped his face with a straight razor when he bothered to shave at all.

And then . . . Madrid! Wine—usually not good wine, but he wasn't fussy. The lousy Spanish beer would also do. Women—usually not good women, either, but who needed an excessively good woman when you were just back from the front? Song—either in a cantina or coming out of the speakers at a movie house. Sitting in a comfortable chair in the dark for a couple of hours, watching beautiful people do things that had nothing to do with war, was not the least of pleasures . . . at least, if the air-raid sirens didn't start to scream right when the flick was getting to the good part.

The food was better in Madrid, too. It also cost more. This particular leave, Chaim wasn't inclined to complain. He'd come away from the trenches with money in his pocket. A dice game with an optimist had redistributed some wealth. *From him, according to his abilities. To me, according to my needs,* Chaim thought happily.

So, clean and smooth-cheeked and even fragrant to the extent of a splash of bay rum, his belly full, enough *vino* in him to help him ignore what a jackass he was being, he sat in some late-afternoon shade outside Communist Party headquarters and waited for the revolutionary vanguard to knock off for the day. If he'd drunk a little more, he might have sauntered right on in. And the Reds in there likely would have thrown him out on his ass. Sometimes waiting was better.

He didn't want to do anything strenuous, not in the ferocious summer heat. Even the pigeons that begged for crumbs begged in slow motion. They retreated in a hurry, though, if he moved in a way that looked dangerous. During harder times, Madrileños had eaten a lot of their cousins. The survivors were the wary ones. Darwin had known which end was up, all right.

Because of the afternoon siesta, Spanish offices let out late. Chaim didn't mind; he was used to the rhythm of life here, and liked it better than the way things worked in the States. Except for pissing off the pigeons because he had no crumbs, he was happy enough to wait.

People started to come out about when the blast-furnace heat began easing off. Spaniards either worked or dozed while it was hot outside. Once it got nicer, they did what they wanted to do instead. A damned civilized arrangement, when you got right down to it.

There she was! The adrenaline stab Chaim felt reminded him too much of a near miss from a machine-gun bullet. *You can still chicken out,* he reminded himself. But himself was already getting up and walking toward her. Had he ever stormed into a Nationalist trench so happily? He didn't think so. Then again, he hadn't had such incentives storming trenches.

"*¡Hola! ¿Qué tal?*" he said. His accent grated in his own ears.

No doubt it sounded even harsher to La Martellita. She was so pretty, Chaim didn't care. That hair! That mouth! It made him imagine things thoroughly illegal back in good old New York—which didn't mean people there didn't do them, and enjoy doing them, as much as they did anywhere else.

She was tiny, but that didn't bother Chaim, either; he wasn't very tall himself. Her shape was everything it should have been, and a little more besides. Her eyes . . . looked at him as if he'd come out of the wrong end of one of those wary pigeons.

"Oh. You," she said. Her *nom de guerre* meant *The Little Hammer,* the way Molotov's meant *Son of a Hammer.* And if she'd had a sickle to go with it, she would have cut Chaim down at the ankles. "What do you want?"

"I have some leave. I was hoping"—Chaim heard himself butcher the participle—"you would teach me more about proper Party doctrine." He couldn't just say, *I want to tear your clothes off and jump on you.* Well, he could, but he knew she'd kill him for real if he tried. Dinner and a movie were long odds, too. If she had any kind of weakness where he was concerned, ideology was it. She thought *his* ideology was weak. Wasn't it her duty to instruct the ignorant and backward? He sure hoped it was.

Her gull-wing eyebrows rose. "You were?" Then those eyebrows came down and together, as if she were aiming a rifle at his *kishkes.* "I thought you were proud of your errors."

"Not me." Chaim denied everything. When Peter denied knowing Jesus Christ, he probably did it with an eye toward laying some broad in Jerusalem who thought old J.C. was nothing but a windbag. A stiff dick had no conscience.

"Why should I do it?" La Martellita demanded. "Doesn't the Abraham Lincoln Battalion have a Party cadre?" She knew damn well the Lincolns did.

Humbly, Chaim answered, "You were the one who showed me my mistakes. You must be the one who knows them best." No, no conscience at all.

She looked at him—looked through him. "Is that all you want me to do?"

"*No entiendo,*" Chaim lied. He understood her much too well, and she understood him much too well, too.

Was it possible to sound too innocent? Evidently. She stuck her elegantly arched nose in the air. "You can find someone else, I'm sure," she said, and walked away. Any football ref in America would have given that walk a backfield in motion penalty.

"Doesn't it matter that I'm fighting for the Republic?" Chaim called after her.

She paused and turned back to him. "It matters to the Republic. It matters to Spain. To me . . ." She didn't even bother finishing that. She just turned again and went on walking away.

"Wait!" Chaim cringed at the desperation in his voice.

To his surprise, she did stop once more. "If you need to find a whorehouse so badly, I can tell you where they are."

She might have torched his ears with a Molotov cocktail. "Never mind," he muttered.

"*Bueno.*" Her shrug of victory was magnificent. "I'm sure you can get to one with no help from me. *Hasta la vista.*" Away she strode, like a long home run off the bat of Jimmy Foxx or Hank Greenberg: going, going, gone.

Chaim stared after her till she rounded a corner and disappeared. Then he kicked at the battered sidewalk. A tiny pebble skittered away from his boot. A pigeon pecked at it, discovered it wasn't food, and sent him a stare full of bird-brained reproach. He hardly noticed. "Ahh, shit," he said in English.

And then, with nothing better to do, he did go find a brothel. It was the lousiest good time he'd ever had in his life. Yeah, he had his ashes hauled, but he left the place gloomier than he'd gone in. You couldn't get too much of what you didn't really want to begin with.

He got drunk. Finding a bar in Madrid was even easier than finding a brothel. He got into a brawl. An equally drunk Spaniard pulled a knife on him. He kicked it out of the guy's hand—which he probably couldn't have done sober (or wouldn't have been stupid enough to try)—and pounded the crap out of him. That satisfied Chaim no better than the whore had.

Still plastered, he wandered Madrid's blacked-out nighttime streets. No moon tonight—only a lot of stars. They were beautiful, but they shed next to no light on things. They might as well have been La Martellita. Or had she shed altogether too much light? That seemed much too likely.

Lurching through the warm darkness, Chaim burst into tears. A woman he couldn't see said "*¡Pobrecito!*"—poor little one! But he wasn't even one of those. He was only a drunk on leave, and somewhere down inside he knew it.

JULIUS LEMP WORE a clean uniform—he'd even had it pressed after the U-30 came into Wilhelmshaven. He'd shaved off his at-sea beard. He stood at ramrod-stiff attention before the engineering board and barked out "Reporting as ordered, sir!" to its head. He might almost have served in the *Kriegsmarine*'s surface fleet. Almost: he hadn't replaced the stiffening wire in his white-crowned officer's cap. A limp cap marked a U-boat skipper every time.

"At ease, Lieutenant," the boss naval engineer said. Lemp sagged out of his brace, but not very far. The senior engineer was a rear admiral. Neither his gold-encrusted sleeves nor his craggy, weathered face encouraged subordinates to relax. He checked some papers on the table in front of him. After a moment, he nodded to himself. "It seems your boat has been using the *Schnorkel* longer than any other."

"Yes, sir," Lemp answered woodenly. As if the head of the board hadn't known that without looking at his precious papers! And as if he and his almost equally distinguished colleagues didn't know why! *You were the fuckup who got stuck with the experimental gadget!*

But the rear admiral didn't say anything like that. He just stared at Lemp over the tops of his reading glasses. "And what is your opinion of it?" He raised a hand before Lemp spoke. "Be frank, please. No one is taking written notes or rating you on your response. We really want to know what you think."

"Sir, I've been frank in my reports," Lemp said. "The thing is useful—no doubt about that. I'm faster underwater with it than without, I can get closer to my targets without being spotted, and I can charge my batteries without surfacing. Those are all good cards to have in my hand."

"Drawbacks?" one of the other men on the board inquired.

"It'll suck all the air out of the inside of the boat and feed it to the diesels if the antiflooding valve closes," Lemp answered dryly. "That leaves the crew trying to breathe exhaust fumes."

"And you recognize this when it starts smelling better inside the U-boat, eh?" the rear admiral asked, his voice bland.

Lemp opened his mouth, then closed it again. For all his forbidding appearance, the senior man owned a sense of humor after all. Lemp tried to make himself seem as naive as he could. "Sir, I don't know what you mean."

All five men on the board chuckled, though a couple of the noises sounded more like coughs. "The devil you don't," the rear admiral said, wrinkling his beak. He glanced at the papers again. "And how's this Beilharz, the puppy who came along with the snort?"

"He's about two meters' worth of puppy, sir," Lemp said.

"That should be fun on a U-boat," the senior man observed. "How often does he hit his head? Has he got any brains left at all?"

"He wears a helmet—but he is pretty good about ducking," Lemp replied. "He's pretty good all the way around. I wanted a second engineering officer the way I wanted another head when he came aboard—meaning no offense to you gentlemen, none at all, but we're crowded enough as is."

"And you wanted the *Schnorkel* the way you wanted another head, too," the rear admiral said. He did understand why Lemp's boat had it, then. Well, anybody with three working brain cells would.

"That, too, sir," Lemp agreed. "But he's worked out well. He keeps the snort going—and when it isn't going, he keeps the regular engineering officer posted so we don't end up asphyxiating ourselves."

"All right. That's good to hear. I said we wouldn't take notes, but do you mind if I write that down so it goes in his promotion jacket?"

"Of course not, sir," Lemp said. "I'll put it in writing myself, if you like."

"Never mind." The rear admiral scribbled. "If he gets promoted away from you, will you still be able to use the *Schnorkel*?"

"Oh, absolutely, sir. He's trained a couple of my petty officers. They don't quite have his feel for it—he acts like he grew up with it—but they can take care of it well enough and then some."

"Good." The rear admiral didn't say *I was hoping you'd tell me something like that.* He'd assumed an officer smart enough to command a U-boat was smart enough to see that an important piece of equipment shouldn't depend on one man's mastery of it. And he'd been right. Lemp shuddered to think what would have happened to him had he confessed to the board that only Beilharz could make the snort behave.

One thing he didn't have to worry about, anyhow. But there were others that he did. A captain who hadn't spoken before said, "This isn't an engineering question, but it is important to the performance of your boat and crew."

"Sir?" Lemp did his best to project attentive interest.

"Are your men thoroughly loyal National Socialists, ready to follow the *Führer*'s lead with iron determination?"

That was the last question Lemp had expected. But even Clausewitz had defined war as the extension of politics by other means. And politics, more and more, got extended *into* this war. If the rumored deal with England and France came off . . . *Worry about that later,* Lemp told himself. He answered the question as simply as he could: with a crisp, "Yes, sir!"

But the captain didn't seem satisfied. "How do we know they are?" he pressed.

Because they didn't mutiny and take the boat to England. Lemp swallowed the flip comeback. These people, and the people set over them, would only hold it against him. He said, "Sir, we were ashore here when the traitors tried to strike against the *Führer.* Not a man went over to them. Not a man said a word anyone could imagine disloyal."

"We have reports that there is grumbling during cruises," the captain declared.

Lemp cast his eyes up to the heavens. Whatever this fellow might have done, he'd never made a wartime cruise in a submarine. "Sir, they're U-boat men," Lemp said, hoping the other officers on the board had some idea of what he was talking about. In case they didn't, he spelled it out: "They're crammed into the pressure hull. The food is bad. No one has a bunk or any privacy at all. Nobody washes much. The heads don't work all the time. Oh, and the lads're liable to get killed. I'd worry about them if they *didn't* piss and moan."

"About the *Führer*?" The captain sounded disbelieving.

"About anything and everything," Lemp answered, as firmly as he could.

"This cannot be permitted."

"I don't know how you can stop it."

"Summary punishments might do the job."

"Maybe, sir, but I think they'd help the enemy more than us, and I'd be surprised if you found any other U-boat skippers who told you different."

The board members looked at one another. Maybe they *had* heard the same thing from other U-boat commanders. If they hadn't, Lemp's comrades in arms had missed the chance of a lifetime to speak truth to the powers that be.

At last, the captain who acted like the National Socialist loyalty officer spoke in a grudging voice: "We have received no complaints about *your* dedication to the *Reich,* Lieutenant Lemp."

"I'm glad to hear it, sir." In half a dozen words, Lemp spoke his own truth, the whole truth, and nothing but the truth. If the higher-ups suspected him, they wouldn't just beach him, not the way things were since the failed coup against the *Führer.* They'd fling him into a camp, and things would roll downhill from there.

Maybe something of that abject, alarm-tinged relief got through to the rear admiral who headed the board. A smile stretched his face into angles that looked unnatural. "This is secondary, Lieutenant. The data on the *Schnorkel* are what we needed most. After your refit and liberty, we'll give you something new to try."

"Sir?" Lemp said: a one-word question.

He wondered if the senior man would deign to explain. Rather to his surprise, the rear admiral did: "Things are heating up in the Baltic. The Ivans need their ears pinned back." He spoke with unveiled contempt. Lemp only nodded. The Baltic's shallow, narrow waters would be different, all right. But any place where he didn't need to worry about the Royal Navy sounded goddamn good to him.

Chapter 14

Summer in Münster. A lot of the time, it seemed a contradiction in terms. It could be cool or rainy or foggy in July as easily as not. It could be, but it wasn't always. Not today, for instance. The sun shone down from a blue, blue sky. It was about twenty-five degrees: warm but not hot. You couldn't ask for more.

A blackbird hopping through the long-unmown park grass fluttered away from Sarah Goldman as she and Isidor Bruck came toward it. He carried a picnic basket. Even when times were hard for everybody and harder for Jews, a baker's son could come up with enough rolls and such for a Sunday-afternoon lunch.

Other picnicking couples and families dotted the grass. It was so tall, you could hardly see some of them. "If we don't sit too close to anybody, they won't notice our stars," Sarah said.

"How about over there?" Isidor pointed. "It's by the trees, so we can go into the shade if we start to toast."

"Do you have to talk about your work all the time?" Sarah teased. They both laughed. She hurried toward the spot he'd suggested. It was a good one, so good she was surprised nobody else had taken it. She spread out a couple of towels and sat down on one. The grass rustled. It got mowed less often than it had before the war, because most of the gardeners wore *Feldgrau* these days. Something small and green and many-legged jumped onto her knee. She yipped and brushed it away.

Isidor sat down beside her. He opened the basket and took out rolls and ripe plums—where had he come up with those?—and a real treasure: a tin of sardines. Sarah's eyes widened. Her stomach rumbled. She couldn't remember the last time she'd seen any, let alone tasted them. A couple of bottles of beer to wash things down, and . . .

"I'll explode!" she said. "Did you rob a bank?"

"Two of them," Isidor answered. She giggled. Every moment where you could forget the big things and enjoy the little ones was a moment won. A hundred meters away, a little blond boy ran beside a yapping dog. He didn't even know about the big things yet. The little ones were all he had. Sarah envied him.

Even now, the big things intruded. The plane buzzing overhead was a Bf-109. Sarah didn't need to think to recognize the shape and the engine note. By the way Isidor raised one dark eyebrow, he knew what it was right away, too. Who in Germany wouldn't, these days? Sarah took another swig and emptied her bottle. She didn't *have* to think about it, or about anything else that wasn't right here.

"Is there any more of that beer?" she asked.

"There sure is." Better than a stage wizard pulling a rabbit out of a hat, Isidor pulled another bottle out of the basket for her. She drank eagerly. Beer helped blur the big things. Isidor produced a fresh bottle for himself, too. By the way he drained it, he didn't care to see them clearly, either.

They both tensed when a policeman wandered through the park. Sarah didn't look especially Jewish, but Isidor did. But the man in the black uniform with the swastika armband didn't even notice them. He ambled away.

Along with the afternoon heat, seeing him prodded them to move over under the shade of the trees. They'd be less noticeable in the shadows—and the grass was even longer there. Most of the picnickers went on basking in the sunshine; they knew it might not last. If their hides were red and tender tomorrow, well, so what?

Isidor put his arm around her. She snuggled against him. The two of them against the world? Not quite—but, although the big things blurred, they didn't go away. When he kissed her, she responded with a fervor that probably astonished both of them. If the beer couldn't do it, maybe this would let her forget everything that wasn't right here, at least for a little while.

They lay back on the blankets, and the world did seem to disappear—in green. Anyone could come up and see them. Anyone could, but no one did. Isidor reached under her skirt. He'd tried that before, but she'd always slapped his hand away. Now . . . Now she discovered she didn't want to. Before long, he got where he was going, and gently began to rub.

And, amazingly soon, Sarah got where she was going, too. He was still kissing her when she did, which muffled the noises she made. As she came back to herself, she stared at the boughs swaying in the breeze above her head. It was like what she sometimes did in the dark—like, but altogether different.

"You're crazy," she whispered.

"Crazy for you," Isidor answered, also in a low voice. "This crazy." He took her hand.

The bulge he set it on was like nothing in her nighttime aloneness. "What do you want me to—?" she asked.

He undid his fly. There it was, in the open between them. If anybody came by now, they wouldn't get in trouble just for being Jews—although whoever came by would know he was. "Take it and—" he said. Awkwardly, she did. He gasped, but after a minute or two he told her, "It helps if you spit in your hand." So she did. She didn't know if it helped her, but it sure seemed to help him. He gasped again, on a different note, and grunted. None of the mess he made got on her clothes, for which she was duly grateful.

She wiped her hand as clean as she could on the grass. She didn't want to use even an old towel for that. Isidor quickly set himself to rights. She sat up and looked around. No one was rushing toward them—or running off to bring the policeman back. They'd got away with it.

All the same, she said, "I think we'd better go home."

"Whatever you want," Isidor said. If she'd told him he was on fire, he would have agreed as readily. He beamed at her. "You're wonderful—do you know that?"

He thought so because she'd made him happy. She still had a little sticky stuff on her fingers to prove it. Well, he'd made her happy the same way. She hadn't known ahead of time she would let him do that, but it was way too late to worry about those little details now, wasn't it? "I think you're pretty wonderful yourself," she replied, and while she said it it was true.

As they were walking out of the park, she saw a bench with a sign: NO JEWS HERE. Isidor saw it, too. "Who needs a dumb old bench, anyway?" he said. Sarah squeaked. Could everybody see her ears were on fire? But she laughed at the same time, because it wasn't just scandalous; it was scandalously funny.

The park was closer to the bakery and the flat over it than to her house, but he walked her all the way back anyhow. The picnic basket was lighter now, which helped. He kissed her decorously on the cheek outside her front door. Did his feet touch the ground at all as he went out to the sidewalk?

"Have a good time?" Father asked when she came in. Samuel Goldman was reading a volume of Dio Cassius in the original Greek. She didn't think anything a Roman historian had written almost two thousand years ago accounted for the grim look on his face. Had Isidor been so obvious that Father guessed what had happened?

"It was very nice," Sarah said. "But what's wrong?" If it was going to come out, better to have it come out now than let it fester.

Father's mind was a million kilometers from what had gone on in the park, and from Dio Cassius as well. "Winston Churchill is dead," he said heavily. "I heard it on the radio less than an hour ago. He was crossing a street in London, and a Bentley ran him down. The driver is supposed to have been intoxicated." By the way he said it, he didn't believe that for a minute.

Sarah had to shift mental gears. "That's . . . bad, isn't it?" she managed.

"It's about as much worse than bad as you can get," Father said. "Churchill was the main fellow fighting the alliance against Russia. And to die like that—!" He shook his head. "That's how Hitler or Mussolini—

or Stalin—gets rid of people. They don't play politics like that in England. Or they didn't . . . till now." He stared down at the open pages of Dio Cassius. "Except for the Bentley, Septimius Severus might have handled it the same way."

"Maybe it really was an accident," Sarah said.

"Oh, yes. Maybe it was." But Samuel Goldman laughed harshly. "And maybe *Herr* van der Lubbe set the *Reichstag* fire all by himself, too."

That heated Sarah's ears again, and not in such a nice way as Isidor had. No one with a pfennig of sense believed the half-witted Dutch Red had torched the German Parliament without plenty of help from the Nazis. But he was the one who'd lost his head for it. And the fire gave the Nazis whatever excuse they needed to go after the Communists inside the *Reich* for all they were worth.

"What do you think will happen in England now?" she asked in a small voice.

"I'm going to pretend I didn't hear you, because what I think and what I hope are so different," Father answered. After that, there didn't seem to be much point to saying anything more. Besides, she still needed to wash her hands.

"WAFFENSTILLSTAND!" the French officer shouted across the lines. Willi Dernen supposed that was what he was shouting, anyhow. He had a horrendous accent. But the word for *truce* wasn't easy to mistake for any other.

And the *poilus* around here seemed to think the war was over. The Germans had been shouting at them not to shoot, and they mostly hadn't. Till now, though, they'd kept out of sight so the Germans couldn't shoot at them. Willi understood that. He hadn't shown himself, either. Trust a Frenchman? Not likely!

But it looked as if France and England really were going to join the German crusade against Russia. Willi was just glad he'd stayed on this front instead of getting sent east. Army rumor said the Reds might not be very skillful, but they were goddamn mean.

"Friends!" the French officer yelled. He did a little better with *Freunde!* Pointing east, he added, "To hell with the Communists!"

"Dip me in shit," Corporal Baatz said reverently. "The *Führer*'s gone and done it again."

Willi would have been happy to do just what Awful Arno suggested. He wasn't so sure about the other part of what Baatz had to say. "I wonder what kind of deal we cut to make the enemy go for it," he remarked.

"Know what I hear?" the corporal said.

"No, but you're gonna tell me, aren't you?" If Willi sounded resigned, it was only because he was.

The corporal nodded, not noticing the resignation. Awful Arno failed to notice all kinds of things. Doing his best to sound important, he said, "*I* heard Rudolf Hess flew to England all by himself to set up the deal, like."

"Everybody's heard that." Willi rolled his eyes in disgust. "It's been on the news, for crying out loud."

"*Ja, ja.*" Awful Arno nodded again. "But I *also* heard he put the Englishmen up to finally giving Churchill what he deserved."

"All right. That's new, I guess." Willi hated to admit it, but didn't see that he had much choice.

"And now he'll come back a hero, and the *Führer* will pin the fanciest medal in the world on him. The Knight's Cross with oak leaves, swords, and diamonds." Baatz sighed. "Can you imagine it? What could be better?"

"I'm not sure he was doing us a favor, you know," Willi said.

"Huh? What d'you mean?" No, Awful Arno didn't get it. Willi wasn't much surprised. Baatz had a great head—for a cabbage.

"The Tommies and the froggies aren't shooting at us any more, right?" Willi said, trying to see how long the corporal would need to work it out.

"You can see they aren't," Baatz answered. "They're going to join with us against the goddamn Ivans instead."

Willi made small, soundless clapping motions. "Very good. *Very* good."

"You can't talk to me that way, you pigdog." Awful Arno turned dull red.

He was already pretty dull, all right, as far as Willi was concerned. "Well, then, take a hint," Willi said. "They're going to help us fight the

Ivans—you just told me so yourself. That means we've got to go fight the fucking Ivans ourselves. Is that what you really want to do?"

"Oh," Baatz said, his mouth a black circle of dismay. He tried to rally: "They can't be worse than what we've been facing."

"Oh, no? Since when?" Willi retorted. "You get in trouble here, maybe the Frenchies won't plug you when you give up. What about the Russians? You want them to get their mitts on your carcass? They'd eat you up, I bet."

Awful Arno was chunkier than most German soldiers. He was sensitive about the extra kilos he carried, too. His complexion went from dull red to fiery. "They don't do things like that," he said, but his voice lacked all conviction.

"They don't fight fair. They're Russians. They're Bolsheviks. I don't want 'em capturing me, by God," Willi said.

Instead of arguing any more, Baatz changed the subject. That should have meant Willi had won. He supposed it did, but he still wasn't happy about it, because Awful Arno said, "If we're on the same side now, England and France'll have to give back the German prisoners they took. If your asshole buddy Storch did run over there after all, he can tell the *Gestapo* all about it." Now he sounded sure, all right, and full of gloating anticipation.

"Oh, give it a rest. I think that French bombardment blew him right off the map," Willi said. As a matter of fact, he knew damn well Storch had gone to surrender to the French. The blackshirts would have grabbed him if he hadn't. So would they get a second crack at him now? That seemed horribly unfair. Fair and unfair, though, had precious little to do with the price of beer.

Another *poilu* came up out of the French trenches. "Who wants to buy tobacco? Who wants to buy booze?" he shouted. Wherever he'd learned his German, he didn't speak badly at all.

And he knew what the *Landsers* wanted, all right. Before long, field-gray and khaki mingled between the lines. Because of the favorable rate of exchange the occupation set, many Germans had more francs in their pockets than French soldiers did. Everybody went away from the deals happy.

Everybody, that is, except people like Arno Baatz. "It's fraternizing with the enemy," he fumed. "There are regulations against things like that."

"There's a truce," Willi said. "If they're going to fight the Russians with us, they aren't really the enemy any more, are they?"

"Don't play barracks lawyer with me, Dernen," Awful Arno snapped. "I'll have that chickenshit pip off your sleeve so fast, you won't know which way to look for it."

"*Zu befehl!*" Willi said.

"That's more like it," Baatz growled. Fortunately for Willi, he completely missed the irony in that *At your orders!*

After a few days, the cease-fire began to seem more natural. Soldiers from both sides met and tried to talk with one another. They shared smokes and drinks. As best they could in each other's languages, they swore at the officers who'd set them shooting at one another.

Willi had never particularly hated, or even disliked, France and England. His father came home from the last war with high respect for the *poilus* he'd fought. Even now, France seemed more . . . in the way than anything else. And the Tommies were as tough as anybody.

"Be funny, us fighting on same side," said a French soldier who could muddle along in German. "Take orders from your generals. Funny, *ja.*" And he stumped around as he imagined a German general would walk.

To Willi, he looked like a self-important rooster. That wasn't Willi's take on his own generals, but it was funny. His French was much worse, so he stuck to German: "We'll all clean out the Russians together."

"Well . . ." A long pause from the *poilu.* "Maybe," he said at last.

"What's the matter?" Willi asked. "What else are we going to do? Why did you guys join up with us if that isn't what you've got in mind?"

The *poilu* looked at him. "You don't know me. You never find out who I am, *ja*?" He seemed to be talking more to himself than to Willi.

"Sure, buddy." Willi nodded anyway.

"You Germans, you do for your Communists." The French soldier slashed a hand across his throat to show what he meant. Willi nodded again. The fellow in grimy khaki went on, "Us, we still have 'em. Not want to go fight against Russia." He eyed Willi from under shaggy eyebrows. "Not want to fight for Hitler, neither. Fuck Hitler, they say."

Had he been talking to Awful Arno, Baatz would have tried to deck him, and maybe started the war up again. Willi only shrugged. "What can you do about it?" he asked, wondering if he'd hear something his officers needed to know about.

But the *poilu* shrugged, too, a gesture more expressive, less impassive, than Willi's. "We all find out, *ja*?" he said.

CROSS THE SOVIET UNION to fight Japan. Cross the country again, going the other way this time, to fight Poland and Germany and England and France and, for all Anastas Mouradian knew, Uruguay as well. He'd predicted that it would happen. Being right didn't make him especially happy. On the contrary—it told him the people running the country had no more idea of what they ought to be doing than he did. The fate of the USSR didn't pivot on his ideas. On theirs? That was a different story.

As far as he could tell, the Soviet government's main business these days was bellowing defiance against the world. Whenever the Trans-Siberian Railway train (the *almost* Trans-Siberian Railway train, one wag put it) stopped to let passengers get out and stretch their legs, loudspeakers blared out promises of death and destruction to the Fascists and their reactionary capitalist running dogs. Posters, strident in red and black, showed angry clenched fists and determined workers in cloth caps carrying rifles.

It would have been impressive, had people paid more attention to the patriotic foofaraw. But the Soviet authorities had been yelling at the workers and peasants at the top of their lungs for the past generation. Who got excited about one more propaganda campaign?

The authorities seemed uneasily aware that they might have a problem. Mouradian's train had almost reached the Urals when he saw new posters on walls and telegraph poles: REPORT COUNTERREVOLUTIONARY ACTIVITY! and BEWARE WRECKERS! Stalin and his henchmen suddenly seemed to realize some people might see the invaders from the West as liberators, not conquerors.

There was another Armenian on the train, a pilot named Hagop Balian. The two of them had enjoyed speaking their own language with each other. Mouradian was fluent in Russian, but that didn't mean he liked using it. Russian, for him, was like a car that wouldn't engage its top gear. He could get around with it, but something was missing. Balian felt the same way.

No matter how they felt, they both went back to Russian as soon as they saw those security posters. Stas didn't want ethnic Russians staring at him while he used a language they couldn't understand. They might decide he was plotting against the Soviet Union, or even that he was speaking German. That would be good for a trip to the gulag archipelago, all right! And some ethnic Russians were more ignorant—and prouder of being ignorant—than anyone had any business being.

The propaganda campaign only got louder and more strident as the train neared Moscow. Some of the men on the platform at every stop belonged to the NKVD. They so obviously belonged to the security apparatus, they would have been funny if they couldn't have ruined a man's life with a single gesture. The arrogant stare, the aggressive, forward-thrusting posture . . . They should have come out of a bad movie, but here they were in real life.

"Your papers!" one of them barked at Mouradian when he got out to buy food.

"Here you are, Comrade." He showed the man his military ID card and the orders that sent him to Moscow.

The Chekist looked them over, then grudgingly handed them back. "Well, be on your way," he said, his voice gruff.

"Thank you, Comrade," Mouradian said as he stashed away the precious documents. A soft answer turned away wrath . . . except, of course, when it didn't. He bought a fatty sausage in a roll and got back on the train.

"All right?" Balian asked—again, in Russian.

"Well, sure," Mouradian replied in the same tongue. They didn't need to look at each other. There was a certain tone to which Russians seemed deaf. People from the Caucasus and Jews and other semitrusted associates of the largest clan in the USSR could use it to say what they wanted right under their masters' noses.

Of course, the NKVD was full of people from the Caucasus and

Jews. The masters needed to have men who could hear that note around them, even if (no, especially since) they couldn't do it themselves.

When they got to Moscow, they reported to a Red Air Force office in the shadow of the Kremlin. A bored lieutenant shuffled through papers till he found Mouradian's dossier. "You served in the SB-2 in Czechoslovakia, in Poland, and against the Japanese," he said.

Stas nodded. "That's right."

"And you were a pilot when you served in the Far East?"

"Yes, I was."

"What do you think of the SB-2?"

There was a question Mouradian hadn't expected. Cautiously, he answered with the exact truth: "It's getting old for frontline action against modern fighters, but it can still do the job."

The lieutenant grunted, which might have meant anything or nothing. He made a check mark on a form. Mouradian couldn't read it upside down, so he worried. Had he come all this way to get purged because of an honest response? The man on the other side of the table looked up at him with eyes so pale, the irises were hardly darker than the whites—Russian eyes, eyes he never would have seen among his own people, dangerous eyes. "So," the other fellow said, "you would prefer an aircraft with higher performance?"

If he said yes, was it off to the gulag for insulting what the Soviet Union already had? Dammit, he *did* want a plane like that, though. Still picking his words as carefully as he could, he said, "If such an aircraft is available, yes." There were rumors that new bombers were in the works, but, so far as he knew, rumors didn't yet translate into airframes.

Or did they? The other lieutenant checked a different box on that maddeningly upside-down form. "Very well," he said. "You are assigned to pilot training on the new Pe-2 medium bomber. Go out the door you came in. Turn right. Go past two doors and into the third room on the left. They'll take care of you there."

"I serve the Soviet Union!" Stas said dazedly.

He went out. He walked down the hall. He went into the room to which the pale-eyed lieutenant had sent him. Several other Red Air Force officers sat in there. Most of them were smoking *papirosi.* A couple sipped from glasses of tea. Stas went over to the samovar in the corner and got one for himself. It gave him something to do.

Another man walked in a couple of minutes later. "The Pe-2?" the new arrival said, as if he had trouble believing it. Only when the officers already in there nodded did he—and Mouradian—start to relax.

Hagop Balian came in, too. He looked as anxious as Anastas must have before. "It's all right," Stas said, and hoped he meant it. Even now, the NKVD could be lulling a room full of suspects.

Then a short, squat lieutenant colonel strode into the room. "You are men who have been chosen to fly the new Petlyakov bomber," he declared. "Be proud, for you serve the Soviet Union in a new way. This machine makes the SB-2 look like it just got its dick knocked off."

He was a Russian. *Mat* came naturally to him. Most of the pilots in the room were Russians, too. The sudden crudity only made them grin. Stas followed *mat* but hardly ever used it himself. You had to be a Russian to do it right.

"Well, what are you waiting for?" the lieutenant colonel said. "Come along with me, and you'll see what's what."

They went. Trucks waited behind the building. Again, Stas wondered if they would head to a camp instead of an airstrip. He got into one anyhow. The only other choice was running, and he couldn't do that . . . could he?

The trucks rattled out of town. His rear end knew when dirt replaced paving. He couldn't see out except through the back. Most of what he saw was the snout of another truck right behind his.

After an hour and a half or so, the truck stopped. The senior officer had ridden up front with the driver, on a more comfortable seat. He jumped down and yelled, "Everybody out!"

Out Stas came. He smiled happily—it *was* an airstrip. The NKVD hadn't nabbed him yet. Only after that thought was out of the way did he notice the planes there. They had to be Pe-2s—they sure weren't anything he'd ever seen before. And . . . they made the SB-2 look like it just got its dick knocked off.

They were lean and long-nosed. They looked more like German Bf-110s than any other plane Stas could think of off the top of his head, and they weren't much bigger. They'd be fast, the way the SB-2 had seemed fast when it was new. And they'd pack a punch, too. All of a sudden, Stas wished he could do that pale-eyed lieutenant a favor, because the fellow had sure done one for him.

EVEN THOUGH SHANGHAI lay under Japanese occupation, Hollywood movies still reached the theaters. Not right away, of course: *The Wizard of Oz* must have been out in the States for a year before it crossed the Pacific and the Sea of Japan. But here it was at last.

By himself or with his buddies from the Corps, Pete McGill would have chosen a Western or a gangster movie, or maybe a French flick with a bunch of chorus girls high-kicking in their scanties. Holding hands with Vera like a lovestruck teenager . . . the Scarecrow and the Tin Woodman and the Cowardly Lion seemed a better bet.

He knew the story; he'd read the Oz books, and had them read to him, when he was a kid. Most Americans had. Vera hadn't, so she didn't. And she gasped when Kansas black-and-white turned to the Technicolor Land of Oz. Well, Pete almost gasped, too. That and the trick photography and the song-and-dance numbers were pretty amazing, even if it wasn't a movie he would have chosen for himself.

"This Wizard in the Emerald City, he will help them?" Vera whispered in Pete's ear. She'd got into the spirit of it, all right.

He cared more about the feel of her warm, moist breath than about all the wizards in the world put together. Smiling, he whispered "You'll find out" back at her.

Down the Yellow Brick Road capered Dorothy, with Toto and their unlikely companions from Oz. In the distance lay the Emerald City. Its palaces gleamed against the painted sky. If you couldn't find what you were looking for in a place like that, you probably couldn't find it anywhere. And they were on their way.

The bomb in the theater went off just before they got there.

One second, Pete was listening to swelling, cheerful music and watching colors brighter than any he'd see in real life. The next, there was a roar and a crash. The theater went dark in the same split second as two walls and part of the ceiling fell in.

As soon as Pete heard the explosion, he tried to throw himself flat and to sweep Vera down with him. He reacted at a level far below conscious thought—he was a trained Marine. He was halfway to the grimy, threadbare carpet when something clipped him behind the ear and darkness deeper than the one inside the movie house engulfed him.

Some while later—he never knew how long—he came back to himself without fully realizing he'd been knocked for a loop. He kept trying to yank Vera down to the deck. Only then did he notice she wasn't in the circle of his left arm any more. And only after that did he notice that every square inch of himself, with the possible exception of the soles of his feet, hurt like hell. He couldn't account for why, not at first. Had a bunch of Japs decided to stomp him? This felt even worse than he thought that should have.

Then memory, as opposed to reflex, came back. He'd been watching the movie. There'd been warnings the Chinese underground was getting frisky. One of the things they shouted at you over and over while you were a boot was *Anything that can happen can happen to you! Be ready for it!* He hadn't been ready enough.

Or had he? He was still here, anyhow, wherever here was. "Vera?" he said—or tried to say. Only a croak emerged. His mouth was full of blood and what he guessed was plaster dust.

When he spat, a chunk of tooth came out with all the glop. That, at the moment, was the least of his worries. "Vera?" he said again. This time, he could more or less understand himself.

A face appeared above him. One second, it wasn't there; the next, it was. So it seemed to him, anyhow. He was still drifting in and out of consciousness. The face wasn't Vera's. It belonged to a skinny, middle-aged Chinese man. Next thing Pete knew, the fellow's hand was in his pocket, grabbing for his wallet. He tried to knock it away, but his right arm didn't want to do what he told it to. The Chinese man disappeared. So did Pete's cash.

Then another Chinese looked him over. This guy spoke to him in bad French. "Don't get it," Pete managed.

"Ah," the Chinese man said, and tried again in English: "You hurt? Where hurt?"

"Fucking everywhere!" Pete said. He tried to use his right arm to point. The pain almost drove him under. "Arm especially," he gasped.

To his surprise, the Chinese man produced a syringe from a small leather case and gave him a shot. He felt better right away. If that wasn't morphine, he didn't know what it would be. As he drifted toward sleep on a warm cloud of contentment, the Chinese man started bandaging him. *A doc,* was Pete's last clear thought. *How about that?*

When he really came back to himself, he was inside the American consulate. The shot was wearing off. Every nerve screamed. The Navy doc who took care of the Marines didn't want to give him more dope. "You aim to end up a junkie?" the white man asked.

"Right now, buddy, I don't give a fuck," Pete said fervently. Muttering, the Navy doctor stuck him. This time, Pete didn't go away as the pain receded. "Where's Vera? How's she doing?" he asked as soon as he could think of anything outside his own torment.

"The woman you were with unfortunately did not survive the explosion," the doctor answered, his voice disapproving. "I was told she must have died very quickly and did not suffer."

Pete wailed. Even drugged, even with his own hurts still tormenting him, he yipped like a puppy taken from its mother. Tears poured down his face. He wanted to kill the doctor for telling him something like that. He wanted to call the man a liar, too. He wanted that more than anything, but he knew he couldn't have it.

"She can't be dead," he said. "I loved her."

"I'm sorry, son." The Navy doctor didn't sound one bit sorry. "You ask me, the Chinese aren't doing themselves any good with these terror bombs. The Western powers will just decide Japan can do whatever she wants to put down maniacs like that. I bet the Chinks are a bunch of Reds, trying to give Stalin a helping hand."

Pete hardly heard him. He'd just betrayed his own hopes. *I loved her.* Morphine didn't keep him from noting the dreadful finality of that past tense. He believed Vera was gone. How could he live without her? He had no idea. He didn't much want to try. He wailed again.

That made the doctor give him another shot. This one wasn't morphine. It knocked him for a loop, whatever it was. When he woke up, it was the following afternoon. He didn't want to believe that, but the strips of sunlight coming in through windows he knew faced west gave him no choice.

He looked around the sick bay. He was the only guy in it. If any other Marines had been watching *The Wizard of Oz,* they'd either got off scot-free or they'd bought the whole farm.

The doctor walked over to him when he saw him awake. "How are you doing?" the man asked.

"Awful," Pete said honestly.

"I believe it. Fractures, abrasions, contusions . . . You're lucky to be here."

"Some luck." Pete wanted to wail again, not for himself but for his lost love.

"I am going to recommend that we evacuate you to Manila," the doctor said as he stuck Pete once more. Now he wasn't going on about addicting him. He'd had a better chance to see how badly hurt Pete was. And maybe he hoped the morphine would help dull the pain in Pete's soul along with the one filling his battered carcass.

That was a forlorn hope. "What's wrong with the hospitals here?" Pete asked. "I want to be near—" He couldn't go on. He choked up instead.

"You can't do anything for her here," the doc said. "You've got to know that. It isn't like you two were married or anything. And besides, any excuse that lets us get our personnel out of here, we take. Hospitals here are still here, and we can't protect you if you're in one of them."

Protect him from whom? More Chinese bombers? The Japs? Himself? No, they couldn't protect him from any of those, and he couldn't protect himself, either.

Chapter 15

"All right." It wasn't all right, not even slightly, but Luc Harcourt wasn't about to admit it till he found out what the hell was going on here. Since he didn't know, he asked: "What the hell is going on here?"

One of the *poilus* in front of him had a fat lip. The other had a mouse under one eye. They glared at each other as if they would sooner have tangled with machine guns than with fists. Fat Lip jerked a thumb at Mouse. "Sergeant, this *con* is a filthy Communist. He says he doesn't want to fight the Russians no matter what kind of orders we get."

"*Merde,*" Luc said wearily. He'd been waiting for this kind of crap to break out. The only thing that surprised him was how long it had taken. "Did you really say that, Boileau?" *Were you really that dumb?*

"You bet I did, Sergeant." The man with the shiner sounded proud of his own stupidity. He gave his accuser a withering glance. "And Paul here isn't just a squealer. The fairy wants to suck Hitler's cock."

"Listen to me," Luc said. "Listen hard, because this is your first, last, and only chance. You can't make a mutiny. You can't disobey orders or tell other people to disobey orders. If you do, they'll shoot you. Have you got that through your thick wooden head? Well? Have you?"

"I hear you," Boileau answered. "I know you have to come out with that kind of garbage. But you're a proletarian, too, right? Where's your class consciousness? I bet one man in three won't follow orders to attack the heartland of the glorious Socialist revolution. Your precious government can't shoot all of us. To the barricades!" He thrust a clenched fist in the air.

"Quit trying to sound like Victor Hugo," Luc said, which earned him a wounded look.

"You ought to have the military gendarmerie take him away, Sergeant," Paul said. "He's talking sedition!"

Boileau thrust his arm in the air again, this time in a Nazi salute. Paul jumped on him. They fell to the ground, slugging and swearing. "Cut it out!" Luc yelled. "Cut it out, goddammit!" When they didn't, he kicked them both with savage impartiality.

For a bad moment, he wondered if that would make them gang up on him. Fortunately, it didn't. They separated. Now Boileau had two black eyes, while Paul, whose last name Luc couldn't—and didn't want to—remember, was bleeding from the nose.

"Save it for the enemy, will you?" Luc snapped.

They might have been doing a vaudeville turn out in the provinces. Their timing impeccable, they pointed at each other and chorused, "*He's* the enemy!"

"No. *Nom d'un nom,* no," Luc said. "We're all Frenchmen together. We do what the government tells us, or we're all screwed together."

"We do what the government tells us, *and* we're all screwed together," Boileau said. The Communist soldier walked away, rubbing at sore ribs.

"Are you going to let him get away with that?" the rightist soldier demanded indignantly.

"Paul . . ."

"Yes, Sergeant?"

"Why don't you fuck off?" Luc made it a friendly suggestion. Under it, though, lay the warning that he would whale the kapok out of Paul if the private didn't fuck off. Paul eyed him, considering. The sergeant's hash mark didn't change Paul's mind. Luc's look of anticipation was a different story. Muttering, Paul departed—not in the same direction Boileau had chosen. That was good, anyhow.

It was the only good thing Luc could see about the situation. He did what he did when he didn't know what else to do: he hunted up Lieutenant Demange. If anybody was above (or maybe below) politics, Demange was the man. He hated the whole human race, white, black, yellow, brown, and Red.

Luc poured out his tale of woe, finishing, "How many sergeants are trying to deal with this shit right now, all over France? What can I do about it? What can anybody do about it? We're liable to have a civil war on our hands!"

"Yeah, I know," Demange said, the perpetual Gitane in the corner of his mouth twitching as he spoke. "You aren't the first guy who's come to me up in arms about it, either."

"What can I do?" Luc asked again.

"Sounds like you did what you could—and I hope you booted both those assholes good and hard," Demange said. "As long as they remember they're soldiers and do what you tell 'em, we're all right. If they don't . . ." His ferret face screwed up in a nasty grimace. "If they don't, it's gonna be worse than 1917."

"Ai!" Luc winced. Any Frenchman would have. Things in 1917 had got mighty bad. After one more failed offensive against the *Boches,* whole divisions of the French Army had mutinied. A combination of executions and granted privileges kept things below the point of full explosion, but barely. The army was useless for the rest of the year. The Germans could have walked over it in the spring or summer if they'd ever learned about the mutinies. Somehow, they didn't. Germans could be blind in the most peculiar ways.

Demange glanced east. German soldiers wandered around out in the open, confident the cease-fire would hold. Part of the deal was that they would evacuate France once the French and English went into action with them against Russia, but they were still here now. "Want to find out what they think about it?" Demange asked with a sour sneer.

"I already know. They're laughing their nuts off," Luc said bitterly.

"You don't want to fight alongside 'em, either, do you?" Demange said.

"No more than you do," Luc answered. "I don't mind shooting Russians. Plenty of Russians nobody'd miss for a minute, I bet. But son of a bitch, Lieutenant! Marching with the fucking Nazis?"

"It's like you said to your privates—if they tell us, 'Do it,' we've got to do it," Demange said. "Will I jump up and down about it? Not a goddamn prayer I will. But maybe it'll turn out for the best—I dunno."

"Fat chance . . . sir," Luc said.

"Sorry, kid. I don't know what else to tell you," the older man said. "This is what they've cooked for us, and we've got to eat it."

"Even if it tastes like shit?"

"Even then." Demange sounded disgusted, but he nodded. "No matter how crappy it tastes, mutiny'd taste worse. They'd beat on you for causing trouble, and then they'd make you do what you mutinied to try and get out of."

That struck Luc as much too likely. All the same, he said, "Not if the mutineers won."

Demange laughed in his face. "Good fucking luck!"

"It happened in 1789," Luc said stubbornly.

Demange laughed some more. "And what did they end up with? The Revolution, and the Terror, and Napoleon. And Napoleon, he was the Hitler of his day, by God! He marched 'em all over everywhere, and they got their balls shot off while they were yelling, '*Vive l'Empereur!*' Pretty fucking lucky, right?"

"Thank you, Lieutenant," Luc said. Demange raised a questioning—or more likely a challenging—eyebrow. Luc explained: "Whenever I feel lousy, you can always find a reason I should feel worse."

Demange's brief grin showed irregular, smoke-yellowed teeth. He took off his helmet and bowed with a flourish, as if he were a nineteenth-century musketeer doffing a plumed, beribboned broad-brimmed hat. "At your service, *mon petit ami*."

Luc made gagging noises. The lieutenant chuckled, coughed, and chuckled again. "You're stuck with it. You may as well enjoy it as much as you can."

"That's what you told her, right?"

This time, Demange laughed out loud. Luc was proud of himself; he could count on the fingers of one hand the times he'd really amused the veteran. That thought swung him in a new direction. He was a veteran himself, and had been for a while now. And what had it got him? More worries—that was all he could see.

THE DIVISION TRAMPED EAST, back toward the German border. The men went proudly—it wasn't as if they were defeated troops. Out in front of each regiment, bandsmen with swallow's nests on their shoulders played marching tunes with tubas and trumpets and drums. Some of the men sang as they marched.

Willi Dernen remembered his father talking about the endless singing as the Kaiser's army headed for the last war. Those poor bastards hadn't known what they were getting into, though they found out pretty damn quick. Willi had already been through the mill. He didn't feel like making noise.

Besides, Awful Arno made enough racket for the whole squad, maybe for the whole platoon. Baatz couldn't carry a tune in a wheelbarrow, but he loudly insisted on trying. He was trying, all right—trying to everybody who had to listen to his godawful noise. Short of taping Baatz's mouth or his own ears shut, Willi didn't know what to do about that.

They marched and sang their way through a French village. No one came out to bid them farewell. Willi didn't care. He was as glad to see the last of the place as the villagers were to see him gone. As long as nobody opened up on the departing Germans with a long-hidden varmint rifle, he was happy.

Under the singing, he remarked on that to the fellow marching beside him. The other *Landser* nodded. But sure as hell Arno Baatz owned a pair of rabbit ears. Despite everyone's singing—including his own raucous efforts—Awful Arno heard the low-voiced remark. He stopped caterwauling the tune to speak in pompous tones: "Don't be silly, Dernen. Security forces confiscated all the French firearms. Lists of registered weapons at the police stations made it easy." Without waiting for an answer, he started abusing the music again.

Willi wouldn't have answered him anyway, except perhaps with a snort of derision. The *Gestapo* might have got most of the registered weapons, but what about the ones that weren't? There were bound to be some, and probably lots. Weren't the froggies people like everybody else? There'd be guns they wanted to keep quiet about, either because they didn't feel like dealing with the police or because they used those guns in ways the *flics* wouldn't fancy.

And so he wasn't very surprised when a couple of *francs-tireurs* took potshots at the regiment in front of his from the woods off to one side of the road. The officers in charge of that outfit didn't seem surprised, either, even if Awful Arno was. They sent a whole company into the woods to dig out the obstreperous Frenchmen.

When the Germans came back empty-handed, Willi also wasn't very surprised. The Frenchies would have had a line of retreat worked out, or else a hiding place good enough for them to trust their lives to it. You didn't open up on a regiment unless you figured you could get away with it.

Optimistic amateurs opened up on the soldiers twice more before they got to the border. The second time, the Germans did hunt down one of them. Two *Landsers* dragged his body out of the woods by the feet. They tied it, upside down, to a stout tree branch as a warning to others. If the French were on the Germans' side now, they needed to act like it.

Willi didn't breathe easy till his unit crossed back into Germany. It wasn't far from where he and Wolfgang Storch had scouted out the hesitant French invaders going on two years ago now. He looked around for someone to tell that to. The only other man close by who'd been there then was Arno Baatz. Willi kept his mouth shut.

When they marched through a village in the *Reich,* schoolchildren waving swastika flags cheered from the sidewalk. Willi would rather have looked at older girls, but what could you do?

They took the *Landsers* to a barracks hall. "*Gott im Himmel!*" Willi said. "Everything's so clean!"

"And so neat!" another soldier added.

Fresh white paint gleamed on the walls. It was a new coat; Willi could still smell it. The cots and footlockers were laid out as if they were part of a study in geometry and perspective. The cots' iron frames had got a fresh coat of black paint. Not a single light fixture held a burnt-out bulb.

It almost seemed wrong to have real, live soldiers—dirty, smelly men in grimy uniforms all torn and patched, foulmouthed lazy smokers and snuff dippers and spitters—profane a place as sterile as an operating theater. That didn't keep them from claiming cots and plopping packs on the dark wool blankets.

They stripped off their uniforms and headed for the communal showers. Willi wrinkled his nose at the soldier next to him. "Are those your feet, Konrad, or did somebody die in your boots?"

"It's your auntie's twat, is what it is," Konrad answered. Laughing, they went off to clean up.

The *Landsers* splashed one another and flicked towels at behinds like the boys they'd been not long before. But few boys came with the many and various scars the soldiers wore. Few boys came with the lines on their faces, either, or the eyes that seemed to look everywhere at once.

"What are they going to feed us?" somebody asked, and that was the next good question.

"Dead Russian," somebody else said. The laughs that followed were nervous. It sounded like a joke, but not enough like one.

What they did end up getting was the usual army swill: potatoes and sauerkraut and smelly cheese and sardines. There was plenty of it; Willi patted his belly after he finished. But field kitchens scrounging off the French countryside turned out better chow. So did soldiers heating up rations and leftovers and whatever the hell for themselves. To the cooks, it was just another job. They cared about getting it over with, not about making it good.

As a *Gefreiter,* Willi didn't have to worry about getting tapped for washing dishes or any of the other enjoyable duties doled out to lowly privates. He flopped down onto the cot and made the world go away simply by closing his eyes. One of the lights blazed right above his head. Other soldiers were playing cards and talking and generally making nuisances of themselves. He didn't care. He was sound asleep less than two minutes after his head hit the pillow.

The regiment had four days' furlough in the little village. Willi got drunk at the *Bierstube.* The lager was weak, but that only meant you needed to drink more and piss more. He tried to pick up a blond barmaid. She laughed at him. Awful Arno was more direct: he grabbed her ass. She hauled off and slapped him hard enough to spin his head around. The soldiers packing the place clapped and cheered. Everybody loved the corporal.

Willi was nursing a headache when they marched away. One of the other soldiers said, "I wonder if the froggies'll be using that hall now that we're clearing out."

"They're welcome to it, as long as they come shoot Ivans with us," Willi said. "I just wish I could hang around and watch one of 'em try to feel up that gal at the tavern."

"Silence in the ranks, Dernen!" Awful Arno shouted furiously. He hadn't cared about anyone else talking in the ranks. And even the routine order didn't satisfy him—he scowled at Willi and added, "Shut the fuck up!"

"Yes, Corporal," Willi said. Sometimes the smartest thing you could do was exactly what they told you.

Along with everybody else, he climbed aboard a train. As far as he knew, this was the same route he'd taken when he went home on leave. Sure as hell, the train rolled through Breslau. Most of the men came from these parts. Some of them waved out the windows, not that it was likely anyone who'd recognized them would see.

This time, the train didn't stop at his old stomping grounds. It kept going, up to the Polish border and beyond. At the border, one Polish soldier came aboard each car, as if to say *This is our country.* Poles were proud, touchy people. Willi'd seen that in Breslau; a lot of them lived there.

It might be their country, but more and more it was Germany's fight. What would come of that? *A bunch of dead Germans,* Willi thought, and hoped like hell he wouldn't end up one of them.

WINSTON CHURCHILL GOT a hero's funeral. That didn't make Alistair Walsh any happier about the politician's demise. If anything, it only threw petrol on his suspicions.

Assorted Conservative Party dignitaries walked behind the hearse and a riderless black horse with polished black boots reversed in the stirrups. At the politicians' head strode Neville Chamberlain. The Prime Minister reminded Walsh of nothing so much as a gray heron with a black bowler and an umbrella. The day was sunny, but the umbrella seemed at least as much a part of him as, say, his small intestine.

Walsh shook his head. Everybody knew the PM always had his umbrella. Whether he had guts wasn't nearly so obvious.

Why were the Tories laying on a memorial like this for a man most of them couldn't stand? Come to that, how and why had Churchill walked in front of a speeding Bentley? Important people didn't do such things . . . did they? Not very often—Walsh was bloody sure of that.

Guilty consciences, he thought unhappily as the slow funeral procession passed him. *That's what it smells like to me.*

He wondered if there wasn't also a touch of guilt in the way the authorities hemmed and hawed about returning him to duty. He wouldn't have stayed in London to watch the funeral procession if they'd been sure what to do with him. *Why the devil did I have to be the one who saw Rudolf Hess come down? Somebody had to, but why me?*

Quite a few men in Army khaki, Royal Navy deep blue, and RAF blue-gray lined the route of the procession. Like Walsh, many of them doffed their caps in silent tribute when the hearse rolled by. They weren't so silent when Chamberlain followed. Several hisses floated through the warm, damp summer air. So did calls of "Shame!"

Chamberlain might have been oblivious. His small head, set atop a long neck and tall, thin, angular frame, only made him seem the more birdlike. Had he suddenly thrust forward and straightened up again with a wriggling fish clenched in his jaws, Walsh wouldn't have been surprised.

But no. The Prime Minister passed close enough to let Walsh see a small muscle under his left eye twitch. Walsh wouldn't have believed Chamberlain had been issued a conscience at birth, but he might have been wrong.

Behind the PM walked Lord Halifax. If Chamberlain looked like a heron, Halifax resembled a walking thermometer. He was tall—even taller than the Prime Minister—and lean, with a big bald head that looked like a rugby ball standing on end. He smiled at something the man next to him said. Assuming he'd ever come equipped with a conscience, it wasn't troubling him now.

Not all the spectators were military men—not even close. There were many ordinary civilians: housewives and greengrocers and shopgirls and chemists and secretaries and clerks. Almost all of them wore somber black to pay their respects to the dead man. Some of the women dabbed at tears behind dark veils. Churchill had always been more popular among the people than the gray men who held the reins of power. Unlike them, he was a recognizable human being. Having met him, Walsh knew how very human he was.

And, because he was a recognizable human being, he roused dislike as well as admiration. A furlong or so down the street from Walsh stood a knot of Silver Shirts, supporters of Oswald Mosley's British Union of Fascists. They were in uniform, something Walsh hadn't seen since war was declared. He thought there was a law against it, but he wasn't sure. If there was, the authorities were looking the other way.

The Silver Shirts bawled organized abuse as Churchill's body rolled past them. The man standing to Walsh's right nodded. "That's telling the daft old bugger," he declared.

"Think so, do you?" Walsh asked in conversational tones.

"Well, yes, as a matter of fact I do." The man was younger and larger than Walsh. "What about it, sport?"

Walsh slugged him in the jaw. He was a veteran of the front and of years of bar fights. Nothing in his expression or the direction in which he looked warned that he was about to do anything at all. The chap who liked the Silver Shirts better than Churchill never knew what hit him. He toppled as if all his bones had turned to gravy.

A bobby rushed up. "'Ere, what did you go and do that for, Staff Sergeant?" He was about Walsh's age. No doubt he'd done a tour in the trenches the last time around, to recognize the noncom's rank emblem so readily.

"He spoke ill of the dead," Walsh answered quietly.

"That's right—he did," a woman behind Walsh said.

"Like that, was it? Spoke ill of Winnie, did 'e, with 'im on 'is way to the grave?" The bobby clicked his tongue between his teeth. "I'll let you off with a caution, then, but take yourself somewhere else before 'e comes to, like."

"Obliged, Officer." Take himself elsewhere Walsh duly did. He steered clear of the band of Silver Shirts. He would only have got into another fight, and against so many he wouldn't have come off well.

Another man of about his own age, this one wearing the uniform of a chief petty officer, came after him. "Will you let me buy you a pint, friend?" the Royal Navy man said. "Or a shot, or whatever your pleasure may be? If you hadn't coldcocked that bastard, I'd've landed on him with you."

He looked like a good man to have on your side in a fight. He was strong and stocky and plainly knew his way around. Walsh gave his name and stuck out his hand.

The CPO took it. He had a grip like a vise. "Douglas Green, at your service. The cheek of those Mosley maniacs, to heckle Churchill when he's not even in the ground! I'd like to break all their heads, I would."

"Save a few for me, by God," Walsh answered. "If we are where I think we are, there ought to be a pub around this corner and half a block down."

They were. There was. The two veterans went in together. Walsh ordered a pint of bitter, Green a whiskey. They raised their glasses together. "To Winston!" they chorused, and they both drank.

"Amen," the bartender said. "He was a right good one, he was, not like the cabbageheads running things nowadays." He had to be over sixty; his bushy mustache was white as fine flour. "You blokes mind if I turn up the wireless a bit? They've got the ceremony on, and I don't hear so good when other folks are talking at the same time as what I'm listening to."

"Go ahead," Walsh said. "I know what you mean." Age hadn't dulled his hearing, not yet. Countless bullets going off near his ear had, though.

In hushed tones, a BBC broadcaster said, "The cortege now approaches St. Paul's. Inside, after the customary prayers and a sermon from the Archbishop of Canterbury, the Prime Minister will say a few words."

"Oh, Winston'd love *that,* he would," the barman said.

"If he wasn't already dead, it'd kill him," Walsh agreed.

"Bore him to death," Douglas Green put in. The man behind the bar liked that so much, he gave them the next round on the house. Walsh drank up, though none too happily. The last funeral the BBC had broadcast was George V's, four and a half years earlier. Like the rest of the obsequies, this worried Walsh instead of comforting him. Churchill hadn't been in power. Why were the present rulers making such a show of these rites, if not to make the public look away from them? *See how sorry we are he's dead?* they might have been saying. They might have been, but Walsh didn't think they were.

Prayers and sermon were almost invincibly conventional. William Cosmo Gordon Lang, senior prelate of the Church of England, couldn't have been duller if he were Neville Chamberlain. Or so Walsh thought, till Chamberlain took the microphone.

"England has lost a patriot," the PM said, "and we shall go on to accomplish his desires." That almost made Walsh choke on his beer. How was Chamberlain going to justify such an enormous lie? He did his best: "Early on, Winston Churchill recognized the dangers and evils of Bolshevism. After the last war, Britain attempted to nip the canker in the bud. Sadly, we failed then, despite Churchill's best efforts. This time, with God's help, we shall succeed."

His claque in St. Paul's applauded. "God's help? What about Hitler's?" Green said.

"Churchill knew Germany was dangerous before anybody ever heard of Bolsheviks," Walsh added. "Will Chamberlain say anything about that?"

Neville Chamberlain said not a word.

"HEY, YOU! SERGEANT! Yes, you! Whatever your name is."

"Fujita, sir!" Hideki Fujita sprang to attention and saluted. "At your service, sir!" He hoped he wasn't in trouble.

Evidently not. The captain had been at Japan's research center at Pingfan longer than Fujita had—how much longer, the sergeant had no idea. But the man, who seemed to be a doctor or scientist as well as an officer, wasn't especially harsh. Now that he had Fujita's attention, he said only, "Fetch me two *maruta,* right away."

"Two logs! Yes, sir!" Fujita saluted again. Then he asked, "Do you need a particular kind of log, sir, or will any of them do?"

"Good question." The captain actually smiled at a noncom, which had to prove he didn't come out of the Regular Army. "Let me have a couple from the ones you just brought here."

"Right away, sir!" With one more salute, Fujita hurried off.

The size, the scale, of the Pingfan complex astonished him. It was six kilometers square. Before he got here, people were calling it a village. There had been a Chinese village named Pingfan here. Japanese authorities had driven off the natives, except for the ones whom they'd put to work building what they needed.

This wasn't a village any more. It was a city, with its own railroad spur. It had a swimming pool and even a geisha house (not for the likes of him: for the officers). And it had the tightest security he'd ever seen anywhere.

The outer fence was electrified with killing voltage. So were the compounds that housed the *maruta.* Each compound—and the outer perimeter—also boasted plenty of barbed wire, and machine guns atop towers that could sweep wide areas with fire. The relatively weak gates—by the nature of things, they couldn't be electrified—had large guard contingents at all times.

And all that was just the outer reaches of Pingfan! The citadel where the scholarly captain worked had a solid wall five meters high, so no one on the outside could see what went on within. More barbed wire and electrified wire topped the wall. Nobody inside could come out without permission from those in authority. It also worked the other way around.

Fujita didn't know what went on inside that citadel. Asking questions was strongly discouraged—which understated things. As Fujita had seen elsewhere, there were things about which it was better not to get too curious.

He approached the lieutenant in charge of one of the gate garrisons. Saluting, he said, "Sir, Captain—I think his name is Sugiyama: please excuse me, but I'm new here—well, anyway, he needs two Russian logs right away."

"Captain Sugiyama." The lieutenant slowly nodded. "Yes, I know him. All right, Sergeant. Wait here. I'll get them for you."

"Thank you very much, sir."

After a brief colloquy with the lieutenant, one of the men from the garrison shouted into the POW compound in Russian. A couple of the prisoners Fujita had helped escort from Vladivostok shambled up to the gateway. They were scrawny, filthy, and shaggy—hardly human beings at all, to the sergeant's eyes. No wonder the Japanese called the prisoners here logs.

At that, the POWs who'd made it to Pingfan were the lucky ones. Ravens and vultures and foxes and flies feasted on the flesh of the thousands of Russians who'd died along the way. The Japanese had marched them hard and fed them little. Why take pains for men who'd surrendered?

Two squads of soldiers aimed their rifles into the compound as the pair of volunteers came forth. No one who wasn't authorized would come out . . . and the prisoners wouldn't try a mass escape.

As soon as the two *maruta* emerged, the Japanese soldiers closed the gate again and snapped all the locks shut. The posts to which the locks were affixed were steel, and were mounted in concrete. Nobody without a bulldozer, or more likely a tank, could knock them down.

One of the Russians gave Fujita a doglike grin. Pointing to the inner citadel, he spoke in broken Japanese: "Good food in, *hai*?"

"*Hai.* Good food," Fujita agreed. For all he knew, it was true. Plenty of supplies went in there. Maybe the *maruta* got their fair share of them. Who could say for sure? No one on the outside. And the hope helped keep the Russians docile. He gestured with his rifle. "You go now."

Go they did. The one who knew some Japanese translated for his companion. Even if he hadn't, the gesture should have been unmistakable. Neither of the large, smelly men gave Fujita any trouble. That was all he cared about.

An armored door to the citadel opened. The Russians went inside. The door closed in Fujita's face. He couldn't even see anything interesting beyond the wall. Khaki canvas screened whatever was in there away from prying eyes.

Not all the prisoners in the outer area were Russians. There were also pens full of Chinese *maruta.* Some of them were soldiers who'd been taken in battle; the war between Japan and China dragged on and on, no end in sight. But others were prisoners from jails in Manchukuo and Japanese-occupied China. And there were pens full of women and children. Where they came from, Fujita didn't know. He did know the men in the citadel sometimes called for female logs.

And he knew how the Chinese arrived: in big black vans without any windows. Every so often, one or more of them would pass through the outer perimeter and disgorge the people it carried. Some of the Chinese were in bad shape when they came out. That didn't bother Fujita. As far as he was concerned, the Chinese deserved everything they got.

One day, a fancy black Mercedes convertible—not at all the kind of car anyone would expect to see on Manchukuo's wretched roads—pulled into Pingfan. Out jumped a tall Japanese in colonel's uniform. He wore an upswept mustache, as if he came from the Meiji era.

Everyone fussed over him and all but kowtowed before him. *So this is Colonel Ishii,* Fujita thought, impressed in spite of himself. Unit 731 at Pingfan was Colonel Shiro Ishii's creation. He was a bacteriologist, a water-purification expert, and a Regular Army officer. This was the first time Fujita had seen him; he was just back from a trip to Japan.

"Let's see how things are going!" he shouted, and took off on a whirlwind inspection tour. Junior officers hurried along in his wake.

This was a doctor? Most of the physicians Fujita had seen—and Pingfan was crawling with them—were shy, self-effacing, quiet fellows. Not Ishii! He had a big, booming voice and an abrupt, aggressive manner. He went here, there, everywhere, always barking out questions. When he liked the answers he got, he grinned and patted a subordinate on the back. When he didn't, he glowered and shouted and shook his fist in people's faces. He acted a lot like a sergeant dealing with privates, in other words. Fujita wouldn't have been surprised had he actually belted somebody, but he didn't, or not where the real sergeant could see him.

No real sergeant would have hurled around the technical terms Colonel Ishii used. He talked about infection rates and vectors and plague and cholera and typhoid and paratyphoid. He talked about rodent breeding and insect breeding. He talked about anthrax and glanders and horses and cattle and spores. Much of it flew straight over Fujita's head, except that he recognized it as scientific.

Ishii talked too much, as far as Fujita was concerned. But how could a sergeant say something like that to a senior officer? Simple—he couldn't.

"I may be going off again before too long, either back to Japan for another lecture or off to south China to see what happens when we put some of what we've learned into action," Ishii told his men. "Even when I'm gone, though, I know you'll carry on with the work. Isn't that right?"

"*Hai!*" they chorused.

"We are protecting Japan. We are serving the Emperor. Isn't *that* right?" Ishii shouted.

"*Hai!*" the men repeated, louder this time.

"Good. Very good." The colonel who was also a bacteriologist nodded, apparently satisfied. "Any country foolish enough to make Japan angry will regret it for ten thousand years! And isn't *that* right, too?"

"*Hai!*" everyone yelled again.

Chapter 16

The next time Chaim Weinberg ran into La Martellita, it wasn't because he was looking for her. It was because he got a pass to go back into Madrid and happened to walk into the bar where she was already drinking. Madrid had a lot—a devil of a lot—of bars. It was just dumb luck. After the way she'd sliced him to pieces outside Party headquarters, he was damned if he thought it was good luck.

His wounds were still fresh enough to hurt. He didn't go over to her or try to pick her up. He just ordered a beer and some olives and crackers and sat down at a little table where he could look at her without making a pest of himself doing it.

She was already drunk, and getting drunker. No doubt hoping to take advantage of her, the guy beside her set a confident Spanish hand on her knee. Chaim wanted to do things like that so confidently. He wanted to flap his arms and fly, too.

Confident or not, the Spaniard misread the signs. La Martellita picked up his beer mug, threw the beer in his face, and broke the mug over his head. "*¡Madre de Dios!*" he shrieked, beer and blood running down his cheeks and dripping from his nose and chin. "What did you do that for?"

"To teach you to keep your hands to yourself, you shitheaded motherfucking no-balls faggot," she answered, and went on from there. Spanish was a good language to swear in, and Chaim realized he was listening to a modern master.

Like the beer and his own blood, it all rolled off the Spaniard. With immense dignity, he accepted a towel from the bartender and patted himself dry. When he saw how much blood splotched the towel, he mournfully shook his head. He got to his feet, which impressed Chaim. After a clop like that, the guy might have had a fractured skull.

He actually bowed to La Martellita. "You don't need to worry about that any more, not with me," he said. "You may be a whore, but you are a frigid whore." He turned and walked out. He was taking a chance—she might have knifed him in the back or chased after him and beaten him to peanut butter. All she did, though, was give him more details on where to go and how to get there.

Then, to Chaim's alarm, she picked up her glass of whiskey or brandy or whatever the hell it was and carried it over to his table. Unlike the hard-headed Spaniard, she wobbled when she walked. She plopped herself down across from him with a warning glare. "Don't *you* start anything," she snapped, breathing high-proof fumes in his face.

"What? You think I'm *loco*?" he said. "I like my head. It's the only one I've got. I don't want you to break it for me."

"You'd better not," she said fiercely. Then she took another big swig from her glass. How many times had she already emptied it? Quite a few, if Chaim was any judge. She slammed the glass down, slopping a little booze over the edge. And then she started to cry.

Weeping belligerent shikker *women, care and management of* was a manual Chaim hadn't read. Hell, he didn't even know where they issued it. "What's the matter?" he asked. "You still mad at that guy?"

She stared at him as if she thought he was even more cretinous than usual. "Claudio? Oh, no. He's just an asshole," she answered. "But the revolution in Spain is ru-ru-ruined." She had to try three times before she could get the word out. It made her cry harder than ever. Eyeliner and mascara dribbled down her face. She dabbed at her eyes with a dirty handkerchief.

Chaim wanted to cuddle her and comfort her and tell her everything would be fine. He would sooner have tried it with a rattlesnake. All he said was "We're doing fine. The Nationalists haven't beaten us yet, and they won't."

The look she gave him then made him think he'd have to study to be a cretin. "Where will our munitions come from?" she said. "England and France have jumped into bed with the Nazis. Do you think they'll keep sending arms to the progressive elements here? It will be even worse than it was before the big war started."

If she was right, the Spanish Republic was, to use a technical term, screwed. But Chaim only shrugged. "They weren't sending us much before," he said. "They were using the stuff themselves."

"They kept the Sanjurjo junta from getting any, though," La Martellita said. She hiccuped, whether drunkenly or because she'd been crying Chaim couldn't tell. "Now they won't."

He shrugged again. "If Germany is fighting the Russians right next door, she won't have much to spare for the half-assed Fascists way the hell over here."

This time, she eyed him like a floating spar in the middle of the ocean. "Do you really think so?" she asked. He wondered if he could get plastered on her breath. *What a way to go*, he thought dizzily.

"Sure," he said with yet another up-and-down of the shoulders. "You wait. We'll whip the bastards yet."

Instead of answering, she upended the glass and waved peremptorily for a refill. Chaim recognized the brandy bottle the barman brought to the table. That shit was a distilled artillery barrage. She'd regret it come morning. Jesus, would she ever! But she poured down some more. With muzzy suspicion, she said, "Maybe you're trying to soften me up so you can go to bed with me."

"No," he said, and the regret in his voice was plangent. "I don't want you to kill me, and I don't want Sanjurjo's *pendejos* to kill me, either."

"That's what you say." But even La Martellita couldn't make herself sound too angry at him.

He nodded. "Yes. That is what I say. What can you do after you get killed?"

She considered his foolishness with drunken gravity. Then she thrust out an accusing forefinger at him. "You were very silly there, outside the Party offices. You looked like a boy who couldn't get the candy he wanted."

"*Así es la vida.*" Chaim used that one a lot. When you spoke a language badly, clichés came in handy. And *So it goes* was better than bursting into tears the way she had. He thought it was, anyhow.

La Martellita wagged the finger his way. "You still want the candy."

"Well, so what?" He hadn't drunk a lot of beer, but he could feel his temper fraying. She'd drive a saint to armed robbery. Not without bitterness, he added, "Who wouldn't? You're smart, you're beautiful, you're—" He stopped. Dammit, he didn't know how to say *sexy* in Spanish. What the hell? He said it in English instead.

She understood it. He saw that right away. He wondered if he'd get a faceful of brandy with a glass chaser, the way she'd baptized luckless Claudio with beer. "But you don't try groping me," she said, and drank some of the vicious stuff instead of flinging it.

Yet another shrug. "Not American style. Not my style. Just coming to see you took all the nerve I had."

La Martellita got to her feet. Chaim was amazed she could. "I am going home," she announced, as if challenging him to doubt her.

He scrambled out of his chair. "I'll help you get there."

"I don't need nobody's—*any*body's help!" She swayed, caught herself, and giggled. "Well, maybe I do."

Out into the blacked-out night. There was a moon, which helped . . . some. He hoped like hell she remembered where she lived. He also hoped it wasn't far. She lurched like a schooner in contrary winds. Once all that brandy kicked in, she was going to keel over.

He didn't grope her, except incidentally, but by the time they got to her block of flats he was pretty much holding her upright. He didn't quite carry her up the stairs to the third floor, but close. Then along the hallway. "This one," she said. He hoped she was right. Otherwise, whoever lived in there would think he was getting burgled.

The key worked. They went in. Nobody screamed or opened fire. La

Martellita swiped at a wall switch. By some miracle, she hit it. A blackout curtain kept the light inside. The flat was tiny: a bed, a chair, a chest, a small bookshelf with a radio on top, a sink, a hot plate. The toilet and bathtub had to be down the hall. Chaim had lived in places like that.

She made it to the bed, fell onto it, and smiled at him, or maybe at the low ceiling. She was gassed. Lord, was she ever! A gentleman would have left, and hated himself ever afterwards. As Chaim had told more than one Spaniard, he was no gentleman. And, no matter how drunk she was, she wouldn't have brought him here if she didn't think he would try something . . . would she?

Only one way to find out. He turned off the light and advanced on the bed. She might hate him in the morning. In the morning, though, she'd hate the whole goddamn world. Whatever happened in the morning, he'd worry about it then.

ALONG WITH THE REST of the forces of the Czech government-in-exile, Vaclav Jezek stood at attention a couple of kilometers behind the now-quiet line. A French major was going to address them. It wasn't as if the son of a bitch spoke Czech. That would have been too much to hope for. Sergeant Benjamin Halévy stood at his elbow to translate.

The major had the grace to look faintly embarrassed. He coughed into his hand a couple of times before beginning. "Gentlemen, the Republic of France owes you a debt of gratitude. When times were hard, you came to our aid."

"And now you're going to sell us down the river, you piece of shit!" a man not far behind Vaclav shouted.

Sergeant Halévy translated that for the major, though probably not all of it. The Frenchman coughed again. "Well, you see, gentlemen, the situation has changed recently," he said.

More jeers from the Czechs: "You're fucking Hitler now—he's not fucking you!" "The Russians really helped us! That's more than you ever did!" And a rising chorus that drowned out all the individual insults: "Shame!" Vaclav joined in, baying the word at the top of his lungs.

"We do not abandon men who have helped us," the French major said stiffly. "Under no circumstances will we allow the Germans to take control of you. We understand that your authorities are still at war with them, even if that, ah, no longer obtains for us."

Halévy was a good translator. He even put in the officer's hems and haws, and imitated his tone very well. But so what? The bottom line was, even if the Nazis didn't get hold of this battered detachment, France would screw the Czechs for them.

The major proceeded to explain just how France would screw them: "If you wish to remain in France as civilians, you may do that. If you wish to be interned in Switzerland, which remains neutral, you may also do that."

He didn't say France would do anything for the Czechs. Stay here? Vaclav didn't know the language, and didn't much want to learn. More likely than not, he'd starve before he could. Switzerland? He'd already been interned in Poland. The Swiss would probably be friendlier about it—like most Czechs, he didn't think Poles were nice people—but even so . . .

"Or there is another possibility," the French major went on. "This would have to be done unofficially, you understand. Despite altered circumstances, we still maintain diplomatic relations with the Spanish Republic. You would need to enter on tourist visas issued by your government-in-exile, and we would have no formal knowledge of your doing so. But if, once you were there, you continued to uphold your cause, we would be able to say with a clear conscience that it was none of our doing."

Now that they were licking the Germans' boots, they didn't want to piss off the people wearing said boots. That was what it came down to. Even a corporal like Vaclav Jezek didn't need field glasses to see it.

"Suppose we go after you traitors instead?" another Czech yelled.

Vaclav wondered if Sergeant Halévy would translate that. He evidently did, because the major performed a classic Gallic shrug. He spoke briefly. Halévy put it into Czech, also briefly: "That would be unfortunate—for you."

Vaclav found himself nodding. He didn't want to, but he also didn't see that he had much choice. The Czechs had numbered about a regiment's worth of men when they went into action in France. They'd taken more casualties than replacements since. They had no tanks, or even armored cars. They could annoy the French if they rebelled, but that was about all.

Spain. He spat in disgust. It would be another losing war. The Republic was fucked the same way the Czechs were. Politics had got ahead of it, and now it was going under in the backwash.

What were the Nazis doing to Prague? What were they doing to the rest of Bohemia and Moravia? Next to no news came out of Czechoslovakia these days, but the answer had to be *nothing good.*

"God will punish you for selling out freedom!" another Czech shouted, shaking his fist at the major.

It had nothing to do with God. Vaclav understood that very well. France had decided that getting out of the war with Germany would work to her advantage. England had reached the same conclusion. And so they'd gone ahead and done it. The Czechs were just a minor problem to be cleaned up. By their standards, the French were being generous. They could have put their now-useless allies behind barbed wire. Or they could have handed them to their new friends, the Nazis. That would have been sweet, wouldn't it?

Calmly, the French major answered, "I am prepared to take my chances. Any man who claims he knows what God will do only proves he has no idea what he is talking about."

Sergeant Halévy went back and forth with the major in French. The officer shrugged once more, but nodded. Halévy turned back to the gloomy French soldiers standing before him. "For whatever it's worth to you bastards, I'm coming with you. The French Army has let me resign, and the Czech government-in-exile has let me enlist. It needs people—even Jews—and the French authorities can see I won't make a good little cog in the machine now that Hitler's at the controls."

What would the major have said had he understood Halévy's claim that Hitler was running the French war machine? Something interesting and memorable, without a doubt. But Czech was only noise to him. Being a small nation, Czechs realized they needed to learn other people's languages. Being a large and proud one, the French expected other people to learn theirs.

Vaclav didn't know about the other Czechs, but he was glad to have Halévy along. He didn't know that the Jew spoke Spanish, but he also didn't know Halévy didn't. He did know he wouldn't have been surprised. And he knew Halévy made a damn good soldier. He wouldn't have figured that when they first met. Everybody knew Jews weren't fighters. Here as so often, what everybody knew proved nothing but bullshit.

The officer brayed out some more French. Again, Halévy did the honors: "He says we're supposed to march to the nearest train station. They'll take us over the Pyrenees, so they don't have to think about us any more. That isn't what he says—it's me. But it's what he means."

March Vaclav did. He hadn't done a route march in quite a while. Picking them up and laying them down was no more fun than it had been the last time. If anything, it was worse, because his antitank rifle weighed at least twice as much as an ordinary piece.

He wondered what the Spanish Republicans would make of a sniper with an elephant gun. From what he'd heard, neither side down there had much in the way of armor. Well, there'd be plenty of—what did they call the assholes on the other side? Nationalists, that was it—plenty of Nationalists who needed killing.

There'd probably be plenty of Republicans who needed killing, too. He hoped not too many of them tried giving him orders. The enemy . . . You could deal with the enemy. You knew what he was, and you knew where he was. But you were stuck with your so-called friends.

Benjamin Halévy fell in beside him. "I wish this turned out better," the Jew said.

"Fuck it. What can you do?" Vaclav said. "Spain'll be another balls-up, won't it?"

"Well, I don't know for sure," Halévy answered. "But whenever the brass are willing to send you somewhere, you've got to guess they aren't doing you a favor."

"If they want to do me a favor, they can all drop dead."

"There you go." They marched on, away from one stalemated war that had suddenly flipped upside down and towards another.

AS FAR AS THEO Hossbach could see, Byelorussia looked a hell of a lot like Poland. Maybe it was a little shabbier, or maybe that was his imagination. He understood little bits and pieces of Polish, as a lot of Germans from Breslau did. Byelorussian sounded different, but not all that different. And a lot of villages had Jews in them. They could manage with German, and he could do the same with Yiddish.

The biggest change was in the signs. Polish and German used the same alphabet. Sometimes he could guess written words he didn't know. But the Soviet Union's Cyrillic script was almost as incomprehensible as Chinese would have been.

Adalbert Stoss said very much the same thing. When he did, Hermann Witt gave him a wry grin and answered, "We didn't come here to read, Adi."

"Ah, stuff it," Adi said. They both laughed.

So did Theo. If Heinz Naumann had said something like that to Stoss, the driver probably would have come back with the same response. But Heinz wouldn't have been grinning, and Adi would have meant what he said. That the other panzer commander and Stoss hadn't got along was an understatement. Naumann was dead now, though, and the feud buried with him in a badly marked grave back in Poland.

Witt attacked the engine with screwdriver and wrench. After liberating the carburetor, he held it up in triumph . . . of sorts. He delivered his verdict like a judge pronouncing sentence: "This thing sucks, you know?"

"Now that you mention it, yes," Adi said. "We clean out the valves, it'll do all right for a while—till it decides not to, anyway."

"That's about the size of it," Witt agreed. "I wonder if the carb on the Panzer III's any better."

"I'd sure like to find out," Stoss said.

Theo nodded. No matter what the carburetor was like, everything that counted was better on a Panzer III. Thicker armor, a cannon that could fire both high-explosive and armor-piercing rounds, a machine gun in the turret and another one in the hull . . . What was there not to like?

He could think of two things. The turret cannon and machine gun took a loader and gunner, which meant there would be a couple of new people to get used to—never his favorite pastime. And, more to the point, the *Reich* still didn't have enough Panzer IIIs to go around, so he was worrying about getting used to a pair of imaginary soldiers.

Back when Naumann commanded the Panzer II, the carb also misbehaved. He and Adi had quarreled about it. Witt didn't seem to want to quarrel with anybody except the Ivans. Theo approved of that.

The next morning, the promotion fairy sprinkled magic dust on the panzer's crew. Adi became a *Gefreiter,* and Theo himself an *Obergefreiter.* Witt slapped him on the back and said, "They'll pull you out and turn you into a real noncom pretty soon."

"Doesn't matter to me," Theo answered. The *Wehrmacht* had one more grade below *Unteroffizier* or corporal. After that, you had to go to training classes to get rid of the emblem on your sleeve and acquire an *Unteroffizier*'s shoulder-strap pip. Theo had had enough of training classes in basic to last him the rest of his life and twenty minutes longer.

Witt laughed. "Might do you good. It'd make you come out of your shell a little bit, maybe."

"Maybe." Theo didn't believe it for a minute. He could no more come out of his shell than a turtle could escape from its. It was part of him. If anything, he wished he came equipped with a Panzer III's armor, not a Panzer II's.

Heinz Naumann would have gone on giving him grief about it. Witt didn't. All he said was "You keep living through fights, they'll make you an *Unteroffizier* whether you like it or not."

"Oh, boy," Theo said. The panzer commander laughed again. Had Theo been the kind to come out with what he was thinking, he might have added that he'd never run into a better reason to get killed. He hated the idea of giving other people orders. He didn't like getting told what to do himself, either. He was, perhaps, not ideally suited to the *Wehrmacht.*

That, of course, bothered the *Wehrmacht* not a bit. Round peg? Square hole? Drive the damn thing in anyway. Hit it hard enough and it'll stay in place. Then we can hang some more stuff from it and get on with the war.

Adi Stoss was thinking of other things. "You know what?" he said. "Winter in Russia's liable to make winter in Poland look like a Riviera holiday."

"Try not to sound so cheerful about it, all right?" Witt said. "Besides, we'll have the Poles and the French and the Tommies shivering right beside us. Oh—and the Ivans, too, of course."

"*Aber natürlich,*" Adi agreed with more sardonic good cheer. "But the Ivans do this every year. They're used to it, poor devils. The rest of us aren't, except maybe the Poles."

"You're jam-packed with happy thoughts today, aren't you?" Witt said. "Why don't you gather up some firewood?"

"I thought *Gefreiters* didn't have to do shit like that," Stoss said. "Isn't the whole point of getting promoted not needing to do shit like that any more?"

"Like I told Theo, getting promoted means you didn't get blown up," the panzer commander answered. "If you figure out how to pack a servant into the panzer, he can gather firewood for us. Till then, somebody's got to do it, and right now that's you."

"Come the revolution, you won't be able to abuse the proletariat like this." Adi went off to collect sticks and boards.

Witt looked after him, shaking his head. "He sails close to the wind, doesn't he?" he murmured, perhaps more to himself than to Theo. "If somebody who takes the political lectures seriously heard him, he'd go on the rocks faster than a guy with the shits runs for the latrine."

Theo shrugged to show he'd heard. He did his share of fatigues, even though he was now an exalted *Obergefreiter.* For that matter, so did the sergeant. Adi knew as much, too; he was just making trouble for the fun of it. A panzer wasn't like an infantry platoon, with plenty of ordinary privates to do the dirty work for everyone else.

They rolled forward again the next morning—but not very far forward. The Russians had laid an ambush, with panzers hidden in a village and antipanzer cannon hiding among the fruit trees off to one side. The Germans pulled back after a couple of Panzer IIs brewed up and another lost a track.

Maybe the Ivans thought they'd halted their enemies. If they did, they soon learned better. Stukas plastered the orchard with high explosive. One of them, with cannon under the wings in place of bombs, dove on the village again and again. The columns of greasy black smoke rising into the sky spoke of hits.

Adi and Hermann Witt watched him swoop in the distance. They whooped and cheered and carried on. Theo watched the dials on the panzer's radio set. He could see the machine pistol on its brackets near the set and, if he turned his head, the back of the chair in which the panzer commander sat. Since Witt wasn't sitting now, Theo could also see his legs. It wasn't an exciting view. Theo didn't care. He wanted excitement the way he wanted a second head.

And, while the Stukas kept the Russians who'd set the trap hopping, more German panzers raced around their flank. The Ivans skedaddled; they were always nervous about their flanks. Theo's panzer company, or the survivors thereof, rolled past the village where they'd been held up. They didn't roll through it, a plan Theo liked. Nobody knew for sure whether all the Red Army men had abandoned the place. They might be waiting in there with Molotov cocktails and antipanzer rifles and whatever other unpleasantnesses they could come up with.

German and Polish infantry tramped along behind the panzers. Before too long, the ground pounders would come through here and clear out whatever Russians remained behind. In the meantime, the panzers would motor ahead and bite out another chunk of territory for the infantry to clear.

This was how things worked when blitzkrieg ran according to plan. When things went wrong, you outran your infantry support and the enemy concentrated against you where you couldn't outflank him. That had happened in France. There was a lot more space to play with in the Soviet Union. Maybe it wouldn't happen here. Theo hoped not. He wanted to win. More than anything else, though, he wanted to go home.

ANASTAS MOURADIAN would have liked more training on the Pe-2 than he got. No matter what he would have liked, he and his classmates went into action as soon as they figured out the controls and took off and landed a few times.

He did have a better plane than he'd flown before. The SB-2 had been a fine bomber in its day, but its day was done. In a couple of years, no doubt, something newer and snazzier would also replace the Pe-2.

Till then, Mouradian was happy to fly one against the Soviet Union's enemies.

Was Sergei Yaroslavsky still hauling his old SB-2 around the sky? For his sake, his former bomb-aimer hoped not. The Pe-2 was close to a 150 kilometers an hour faster. It could fly higher and carry more bombs. All that meant it had a better chance of coming back from its missions.

Three of his classmates at the airstrip outside of Moscow never got the chance to fly the new bomber against the Nazis. One of them botched a takeoff and crashed—or maybe an engine failed. Either way, he was dead. So were the two who flew their planes into the ground instead of landing them. Flying was an unforgiving business. If the Germans didn't get you, a moment's carelessness and you'd do yourself in.

His bomb-aimer and copilot was a Karelian named Ivan Kulkaanen. He was as blond as Anastas was dark, and spoke Russian with an odd accent. "Don't worry—I think you sound funny, too," he told Mouradian.

"When I talk Russian, I know I sound funny," Stas answered. "But you should hear me in Armenian."

Whereupon Kulkaanen gabbled out a couple of sentences in what Mouradian presumed to be his native tongue. Whatever it was, it meant nothing to him. "Finnish," the blond man explained.

"If you say so." Mouradian couldn't contradict him.

Back in the bomb bay was a Russian sergeant called Fyodor Mechnikov. Like the other bombardiers Stas had known, he was brawny and foul-mouthed. "They took me off a farm," he said, his grin displaying several stainless-steel teeth. "I've got the muscle. I don't scare easy. For the shit I do, who needs brains?"

"Can you read? Can you write?" Stas asked.

Mechnikov shook his bullet head. "Not a fucking word, sir," he answered, not without pride.

"I'll teach you if you want."

"Nah." Mechnikov shook his head again. "I've gone this long without it, I wouldn't know what to do if I could all of a sudden. And I remember real good. I start writing shit down, I bet I start forgetting like a son of a bitch."

He might well have been right. Stas had dealt with more than a few illiterate enlisted men in his time. Russia was full of them. In Western Europe, they said, almost everybody could read and write. It wasn't like that here. And illiterates did tend to have better memories than people who could read and write. They needed them.

The newsreaders on the radio tried their best to give the impression that everything at the front was fine. Their best might have convinced civilians who hadn't seen German soldiers or had German bombs fall on them yet. But if everything was as wonderful as the radio wanted people to believe, why was the Red Air Force rushing half-trained Pe-2 pilots to the front as fast as it could?

Stas didn't think anything was as wonderful as the radio wanted people to believe. He never had. Soviet propaganda was primarily aimed at Russians, and Russians, as seen through the jaundiced eye of a man from the Caucasus, lacked a certain subtlety. So did Soviet propaganda, at least to Mouradian. Stalin was a man from the Caucasus, too. Chances were he chuckled cynically at the stuff he had his propagandists put out. Which didn't mean the stuff didn't work.

And the new bombers worked, too—at least if you didn't crash them trying to get them to work. The pilots flew their planes and aircrews west toward the border between Russian and Byelorussia. That they landed at airstrips still inside the Russia Federation gave the lie to the swill that poured out of radio speakers. No, things weren't going nearly so well as the Soviet government wanted people to think.

English and French reinforcements for the Nazis hadn't got here yet, either. What would happen when they joined the Germans and Poles? Nothing good, not if you were a Soviet citizen.

Lieutenant Colonel Tomashevsky seemed to know his business. He wasn't a drunken blowhard like Colonel Borisov or a hopeless loser like the fellow who'd briefly given Mouradian orders in the Far East.

"The Nazis are still coming forward," he told the newly assembled men of his newly assembled squadron. He didn't bother mentioning the Poles. In his place, Stas wouldn't have, either. Tomashevsky went on, "We can't stop them all by ourselves, but we can hurt them. That will give the Red Army a better chance to do *its* job."

Was he saying the Red Army wasn't doing its job? Would some political officer rake him over the coals for telling the truth? Such things happened all the time. That was a shame, but they did.

"One more thing," he added. "The best way to become a Hero of the Soviet Union isn't to try and dogfight the 109s. The Pe-2 may have started out as a heavy fighter, but it's a bomber now. It's a good bomber, but it's still a bomber, dammit. The best way to become a Hero of the Soviet Union is to finish your mission, come back, and fly your next one and the one after that. That's what heroes do: what needs doing. Go take care of it."

Thus encouraged, they hurried to their planes. Antiaircraft guns' snouts stuck up around the airstrip. Stas hadn't seen any bomb craters, though. The Germans hadn't found this place, then. Not yet.

Groundcrew men bombed up the squadron's Pe-2s. Fyodor Mechnikov was ready. "Let's blow the living shit out of these Nazi cunts," he said.

"I couldn't have put it better myself," Stas replied.

Up they went. After the more sedate SB-2, takeoff in the new machine was like a kick in the pants. "I could get used to this," Ivan Kulkaanen remarked.

"Let's hope so," Stas answered. Kulkaanen gave him a sidelong look. Stas didn't know about Karelians in general—he hadn't met many—but his bomb-aimer had an ear for the little things . . . if they were little. If the aircrew didn't get used to these takeoffs, they'd probably be too dead to care.

They droned west. Orders were to hit the Germans outside of Mogilev, on the Dnieper. When they got there, they discovered the enemy was already ten or fifteen kilometers over the river. They bombed the biggest concentration of Germans they could find. Antiaircraft fire came up at them from the ground, but it wasn't too bad. Mouradian had flown through plenty worse. No Messerschmitts seemed to be in the neighborhood. Nobody could anger Lieutenant Colonel Tomashevsky by pretending the Pe-2 still was the fighter it had originally been intended to be.

Once the bomb bay was empty, they sped back to Russia—Mother Russia to Mechnikov, if not to Mouradian or Kulkaanen (although it was to Tomashevsky: by his name, he was a Russian). Stas taxied into a revetment and killed the engines. As soon as the props stopped spinning, groundcrew men spread camouflage netting over the plane. The Germans wouldn't have an easy time finding this airstrip.

Unless, of course, they followed the Red Air Force planes and watched where they landed. Maybe that was what happened. Any which way, the antiaircraft guns around the airstrip suddenly all seemed to go off at once. Mouradian, Kulkaanen, and Mechnikov scrambled out of the Pe-2 and sprinted for the nearest slit trench.

One after another, Stukas dove on the field. The first one flattened what had been a *kolkhoz* supervisor's office and was now Lieutenant Colonel Tomashevsky's headquarters. Stas hoped Tomashevsky hadn't got back in it yet. Two other dive-bombers planted 500-kilo bombs right in the middle of the runway. Nobody would fly in or out till those holes got filled. And a fourth German bomber blew up a Pe-2 in spite of the netting that covered it. The flak didn't get any Stukas. As they roared off to the west, Mouradian only wished he were more surprised.

Chapter 17

Claustrophobia was foolish. Julius Lemp kept telling himself so. It helped . . . some. The Baltic was a couple of hundred kilometers across. But he was used to the greater elbow room of the North Sea and the vast freedom of the North Atlantic. Here in these enclosed waters, he felt as if he had land at his elbow every way he looked.

"Oh, good, skipper. I'm not the only one, then," Gerhart Beilharz said when Lemp complained out loud.

"You'd best believe you're not," Lemp agreed. If anyone on the U-30 was entitled to feel cooped up all the time, it was Beilharz. With his size, it wasn't as if he were wrong.

"Not a whole lot of traffic out there, either," the engineering officer said. "I hope we're not just wasting our time."

"Me, too," Lemp said. "Well, at least it's a war."

His voice sounded hollow. If he could hear it, no doubt Beilharz could, too. And he had his reasons for keeping enthusiasm on a tight lead. You could foul up all too easily in the Baltic, and foul up your career, such as it was, while you were at it. In the North Atlantic or the

North Sea, he could assume any surface ship he saw was bound for England or France.

Here . . . Suppose he sank a Swedish freighter bound for the *Reich* with a load of iron ore. That would torpedo any hopes he might still have for moving up the chain of command. Would it ever! He'd survived sending one ship to the bottom by mistake. Nobody could get away with being wrong like that twice.

Even if he spotted a gunboat, it might not belong to the Ivans. It might be Swedish or Finnish or Polish or Latvian or Lithuanian or Estonian. He'd wondered if Stalin would gobble up the Baltic republics the way Hitler had seized the Low Countries. No sign of it yet. Like drowning men with life preservers, the little nations in these parts clung to neutrality for dear life. As soon as one side invaded them, the other would, too. Whichever big power won the war, Latvia, Lithuania, and Estonia would lose.

So he had to be careful. Airplanes might belong to one of the neutrals, too. He couldn't shoot it out on the surface with one unless it fired at him first. Since that would be just exactly too late, he dove as soon as anybody spotted anything flying. Once, what turned out to be a Russian flying boat dropped depth charges on him—fortunately, with bad aim. They rattled his teeth and made the sailors use some amazing profanity, but did no damage.

"Are we going into the Gulf of Finland?" Beilharz asked one afternoon on the conning tower, in much the same tones a patient might use when asking his doctor if a biopsy had come back malignant.

"That's where Leningrad is. That's where the Russians go in and out," Lemp answered. Beilharz only sighed. Well, Lemp felt like sighing himself. The Baltic was narrow. The Gulf of Finland wasn't more than a good piss wide. If something went wrong while the U-boat was there . . . The technical term for that was *screwed.* But Lemp went on, "When somebody asked that American gangster why he robbed banks, he said, 'Because that's where the money is.' "

"Hey, even if we got a boatload of rubles, we couldn't spend 'em in Germany anyhow," Beilharz said.

Lemp was a pretty fair submarine driver. He hadn't been blessed with the sharpest or quickest sense of humor, though. He was about to snap at Beilharz for missing his point when he realized, in the nick of time, that the *Schnorkelmeister* was joking. "Heh," he managed—not the merriest or most sincere laugh that ever rang out on the U-30, but a laugh all the same.

Estonia owned the lower jaw to the Gulf of Finland, its namesake country the upper. Soviet territory lurked back deep in the throat. Minefields shielded that territory from visitors like Lemp's U-boat.

He respected those minefields without fearing them. He had good charts of where they lay. He didn't know for sure, but he would have bet the Finns had contributed a lot to those charts. They didn't love the enormous neighbor who'd ruled them till the Russian Revolution, and they needed to worry about the minefields, too, if their fishing boats and freighters were to stay safe.

But the Russians also sowed mines through the gulf at random. They'd sneak out under cover of darkness in fast attack craft, dump a few in the water, and run away again. They denied everything, of course. When one of those floaters blew a Finnish steamship sky-high, the Russians insisted the Germans must have placed it.

There *were* German mines in the Gulf of Finland, to make things difficult for the Soviet Union's Baltic Fleet. Lemp also had charts showing their positions. Sometimes, of course, a mine would slip its mooring cable and go drifting with wind and wave. You might not think any bobbed close by, but you had to keep your eyes open.

At least one Soviet battleship, the *Marat,* lurked inside the minefields. If she came out, she could cause all kinds of trouble . . . for a while, anyway. How long she'd last against U-boats and bombers was anybody's guess. *Not very long* was Lemp's. The *Marat* was a dreadnought built before the last war: a dinosaur, in other words. New and more deadly predators prowled these days.

No monster from wars gone by put the U-30 in trouble. Another damned flying boat did. It came out of the sun, so nobody on the bridge saw it till it was almost on top of the submarine. The first clue Lemp had that it was there was tracers snarling past his face.

"Jesus Christ!" he yelled. Then he heard the growl of the Beriev MBR-2's engine. The flying boat zoomed overhead no more than thirty meters above the sea. Bombs fell from under the wings. They didn't hit the U-30, but went off close enough to her hull to knock Lemp down on the conning tower and almost drown him with two enormous gouts of seawater.

Coughing and spluttering and trying not to puke, he pulled himself to his feet. One of the ratings who'd been on the tower with him was down and moaning. His hands clutched his belly. Blood poured out between his fingers—a fragment must have got him. The moans turned to shrieks a moment later.

Curses and shouts of surprise came from inside the boat. How much water had suddenly flooded down the hatch? Much too much, by the noises from down there. But that, at the moment, was the least of Lemp's worries. The MBR-2 was turning for another pass.

They couldn't get down fast enough to escape it. The only thing they could do was bang away at it with the 37mm antiaircraft gun. "Take off the tompion!" Lemp shouted. Both the antiaircraft gun and the 88mm deck cannon had bronze plugs protecting the inside of the barrel from seawater. If you tried to fire one without removing that protector, you'd be very unhappy—but not for long.

Off went the tompion. It dangled from the barrel by a chain so it wouldn't roll into the ocean. The gun roared. The flying boat fired back with its machine gun. Lemp had hoped the gunfire would scare it off, but no such luck.

Then he cheered when smoke and fire spurted from the Russian plane's engine. The MBR-2 came down in the Baltic. Lemp hoped it would cartwheel and break to pieces. Again, no such luck. There it sat, on the water, and it went on shooting at the U-boat. Bullets clanged off the conning tower. Some bit through it. Those holes would have to be patched before the boat could dive again.

"Man the deck gun!" Lemp yelled down the hatch. He had to jump back as sailors sped up the steel ladder inside. The antiaircraft gun was still trading fire with the flying boat's machine gun. Chunks flew from the plane's metal wing and wooden hull, but the Ivans inside kept up their fire. No one could say they had any quit in them.

Then the deck gun roared. It wasn't identical to the 88mm antiaircraft piece that was also a fearsome antipanzer weapon, but it came close enough. No plane could take that kind of pounding. A couple of rounds into the cockpit and the enemy machine guns went quiet.

Two more sailors were down, one at the flak gun, the other at the 88mm. The latter had taken one through the head. They'd bury him at sea, along with the poor devil with the belly wound, although that unlucky fellow might be a long time dying. The other wounded man had a neat hole through his leg. He'd probably live.

"Good Lord!" Lemp said, deeply shaken. "I hope we never have to do *that* again!" Everybody up on deck with him nodded. Several ratings crossed themselves. Lemp was no Catholic, but he felt like doing the same thing.

PEGGY DRUCE HAD already voted for FDR twice. She had every intention of voting for him again. If ever anyone deserved a third term, Franklin D. Roosevelt was the man. It looked that way to her, anyhow.

Most of her Main Line friends and acquaintances were rock-ribbed Republicans. Rock-headed Republicans, as far as she was concerned. They seemed convinced the world ended right where good old American beaches gave way to the ocean. The sole exceptions they recognized were shopping trips to London and Paris and gambling junkets to Havana.

The only thing Peggy wished was that Roosevelt weren't so coy about the chances the USA would get into the war. "On which side?" one of her friends asked, altogether seriously.

"Whichever side isn't Hitler's," Peggy answered without the least hesitation.

"But—!" The other woman stared at her in horror undisguised. "That would mean fighting *for* Stalin and the Bolsheviks!"

"So what?" Peggy answered. "Winston Churchill said that if Hitler invaded hell, he'd try to give the Devil a good notice in the House of Commons."

"He's dead," her friend reminded her. "He's dead, and England doesn't want to fight for Stalin. You ask me, Chamberlain's no dope."

Peggy didn't blow up. She'd already had this argument more than once. By now, she was resigned to it. People who hadn't been to Europe and seen what Nazi Germany was like for themselves didn't—couldn't—believe it. Russia was the devil they knew, the radical state that wanted to bury capitalism forever. To most head-in-the-sand Americans, anything that wanted to smash the Reds seemed swell.

Her friend went on, "I only wish Willkie didn't sound so much like That Man in the White House. He ought to give the New Deal a good, swift kick, is what he ought to do."

"If you say so, Blanche," Peggy said.

"I just did," Blanche replied. "And I tell you, we're getting some very *different* people donating to Bundles for Britain these days. Not everyone quit after the Big Switch the way you did." She raised her nose in the air—only a little, but it got through. It also let Peggy see the sagging flesh under Blanche's chin. Since her own jawline was still pretty good, she soaked up some *Schadenfreude* on that score.

"I'll bet you are," she said, feeling the need for a saucer of cream. "The ones who stand up and whinny when the band plays '*Deutschland über Alles,*' I suppose."

"It's not like that." Blanche's voice went shrill. "But it is a different crowd. Hardly any of those people come in any more."

"Why don't you just call them Jews? The *Führer* does. 'The Jews are our misfortune!' " She did her best to thunder like Hitler on the radio. It wasn't very good. That had to be just as well. She didn't want people jumping to their feet and screaming "*Sieg heil!*" every time she opened her mouth.

"I suppose they have to live somewhere, but I wish they were better at knowing their place," Blanche said.

"They do in Germany. One of them made a mistake—he sold me something when he shouldn't have. Then some brownshirts went into his shop and beat him up. He won't do anything that rude and pushy any time soon," Peggy said.

"Oh, come on. I don't mean that. You know what I mean," Blanche said.

"I know what Hitler means, too," Peggy answered. Outside the café where they were not enjoying time together, well-dressed, well-fed people hurried by. Shop windows promised the moon—and they'd deliver if you put down enough cash. Cars—so many cars!—whizzed up and down the street. Dealers were gearing up to start selling 1941 models. You could buy as much gas as you wanted, and for next to nothing. Rationing? Nobody on this side of the Atlantic had ever heard of rationing.

Blanche did have the grace to turn pink, if not red. "I don't want to go as far as the Germans do."

"I'm sure those people would be so glad to hear it," Peggy said. The scary thing was that, in spite of being sarcastic, she was also right. Jews, these days, were pathetically grateful for any crumbs you threw them. Considering what they got in the *Reich* in place of crumbs, they had reason to be. Peggy smiled sweetly. "No yellow stars or anything?"

This time, Blanche really did redden. "I don't know what to make of you any more. You've changed since you came back from Europe. *I* haven't. The rest of our crowd hasn't."

Fools never do. It sat on the tip of Peggy's tongue, along with the last bite of a really good BLT. You couldn't get anything like that in Berlin! But she swallowed the bite, and she swallowed the mean comeback, too. That might have been mature wisdom. Or it might just have meant she was too tired to argue all the time. She hadn't given up. She was getting better at picking her spots.

She looked at her watch and stood up. "I've got to run."

"So good to see you," Blanche said with transparent relief. Peggy tossed two dollars on the table—you paid for atmosphere at this place—and got out as fast as she could with any manners, or perhaps a little faster than that.

Out on the sidewalk, she waved for a cab. She got one in nothing flat, and another taxi driver drove off with a scowl because he'd missed the fare. The guy behind the wheel was about twenty-five. "Where to, lady?" he asked.

She gave him her address. He put the Plymouth in gear and pulled back into traffic. In almost any country in Europe, he would have been in the army. His cab wouldn't have been on the road any more, either. People in Berlin had stared at the one that took her from her hotel to the train station.

Shop windows, billboards, and neon signs all shouted at her as the taxi went along. *Buy!* they screamed. *Buy! Buy! Buy!* And people listened to them. There was a boy eating an ice-cream cone. There was a woman with her arms full of packages. There was a man in a sharp suit walking past shiny new cars at a Packard dealership while a salesman in a loud plaid jacket followed, a hungry smile on his face.

"So much stuff," Peggy murmured. Anyone on the other side of the Atlantic who'd been making do with what he had since the war started would drop dead if he could see this. And the politicians over there who'd made people live like that would count themselves lucky if they didn't get hanged from the closest lamppost.

"Wadja say, lady?" the cabbie asked.

Peggy was embarrassed; she hadn't meant him to overhear. But she repeated herself, louder this time, adding, "I got back from Europe a little while ago. Seeing everything all lit up, people buying and selling like nobody's business, still seems strange."

"Boy, I bet," the guy said. "Makes you glad you're an American, huh?"

"Sure," Peggy said, but she wondered how much she meant it. Maybe she'd stayed over there too long. No, for sure she'd stayed over there too long, but she wasn't thinking of the usual reasons now. A couple of years in Europe made the good old USA's displays of greed and abundance feel vulgar.

She could at least laugh at herself for her sudden attack of Puritanism. There was no inherent virtue in an empty belly, in a suit coat out at the elbows, in streets empty of cars because your country was using all the gas and steel and rubber it had to murder its neighbors. She saw that. But she also saw all this, and the excess turned her stomach.

The taxi pulled up in front of her house. Even the old familiar place seemed ridiculously large. Why did she and Herb need all this space? It wasn't so much that they did need it. But they could afford it, and so they had it.

"Eighty-five cents, lady," the driver said. She gave him a dollar. He started to make change. She waved for him not to bother. He nodded. "Thanks."

She got out. He drove off. She walked up to the front door. She was home. As she fumbled in her purse for the key, she wondered if she'd ever feel at home anywhere again.

MANILA. It wasn't as if Pete McGill had never been here before. Any leatherneck who'd been in the Corps for a while had come through the capital of the Philippines. It was like a halfway house between what you'd grown up with and the real, no-shit Orient. The wide streets and stately Spanish buildings reminded you of an American—or, more likely, a European—city. After more than a generation of U.S. rule, a lot of the natives understood English. You could buy burgers and Cokes.

But those natives were little and brown and had narrow eyes. Most of the time, they gabbled away in a language that sounded like barking dogs to Pete. Away from the wide thoroughfares, they lived in tiny tumbledown huts. What they ate when they weren't cooking for you or shining your shoes had nothing to do with hamburgers—no, sirree!

And it was hot. And it was muggy. All the time—spring, summer, fall, winter. There was a rainy season and a less rainy season, and that was about as far as seasons went. But Jesus God, it was so green! If you turned your back on a bamboo plant, it would be six inches taller when you turned around again and gave it a second look. Armies of little brown gardeners kept the stately Spanish buildings from being swallowed by jungle.

Yeah, when you got to Manila, you realized you weren't in Kansas any more. Or in the Bronx, which Pete had called home till the recruiting sergeant convinced him he'd get a better deal if he signed on the dotted line. He hadn't needed much convincing. Anything that would get him the hell out of high school and pay him a little bit besides looked mighty goddamn good.

So now he was back in Manila, in the military hospital, under a lazy ceiling fan that did exactly nothing to fight the heat and humidity. He'd got himself wrecked on account of a terrorist bomb. He'd got the woman he loved killed. And all he could do was lie here and stew.

He wanted to murder the Chinamen who'd planted the bomb in the movie house. And he wanted to murder the Japs who ground down the Chinese till they started doing things like planting bombs in movie houses. Give him a machine gun and enough ammo, and there wouldn't be a Jap or a Chinaman left alive.

He even glared at the Filipino nurses who helped the Americans take care of him. They hadn't had anything to do with the bomb, of course. The rational part of his mind understood that. But they were little and brown and had narrow eyes. They didn't exactly look Chinese or Japanese, but he wasn't inclined to be picky, not right then.

They gave him crutches and encouraged him to hobble down the hospital hallways. Hobble he did; he was looking for anything to do besides lie there like a sack of dried peas. Staying on his pins—and on the additional wooden pins with which he was fitted out—took everything he had in him. While he was upright, he was too busy concentrating on staying that way to have time to brood about Vera.

One of the American nurses looked a little like his lost love. That, of course, only rubbed salt in his wounds. What made it even worse was that Mary Anne wouldn't shut up about her fiancé, an Army captain named Harold. Whether that was first name or last Pete wasn't sure.

He didn't bother asking. He hoped Harold ran into a wall facefirst. He hoped the Army man caught the pox in a Filipino whorehouse and gave it to Mary Anne. He hoped war started and the Japanese captured Harold and treated him the way they'd treated the swarms of Russians they'd captured in Manchukuo. Marched to death, beaten, shot on the road . . . The horror stories got more and more horrible as time went by.

All that because the nurse already had a fellow and was happy with him. Anybody who heard about Pete's thoughts would have opined that he was a few turns around the bend. But nobody heard about them. When the doctors asked him how he was feeling, all they wanted to know was how badly his knitting bones still hurt. That, he told them. The other? Torture wouldn't have dragged it out of him. The only thing more unmanly than talking about his emotions would have been putting on a dress and high heels.

As he had in Peking and Shanghai, he listened to ball games from the States on shortwave radio. The Indians and Tigers and Yankees were taking turns knocking one another out of first place. The Yanks had won four pennants in a row. Pete wanted the fifth one. You could take the kid out of the Bronx, but you couldn't take the Bronx—or the Bronx Bombers—out of the kid.

The radio didn't talk about China much. The Japanese were supposed to be making gains south and west of Peking. But some kind of hideous disease had broken out in those parts, so Western reporters were even less eager to see for themselves than they would have been otherwise. Was it typhoid or typhus or plague or cholera? Nobody seemed to know for sure, or to care very much. Why worry? It was only killing Chinamen, and maybe Japs.

Pete wouldn't have been sorry to hear that the whole Japanese Army had come down with the plague. He wanted to get news from Shanghai, but he never heard any. Hell, he hadn't even been able to arrange a proper burial for Vera. He'd been too torn up to do anything at all, which was why they'd sent him here.

He hoped somebody'd taken care of it. Maybe the owner of the Golden Lotus, the club where she'd danced. He was a Jew; Pete knew that. She'd spoken of him with amused respect—he was ugly, but he was smart. Was he a good enough guy to reach into his pocket for what needed doing? Pete couldn't begin to guess.

Most of the men on the ward with him were Army and Navy files from the Philippines. Like him, they figured a war with Japan was coming. Unlike him, they expected it to be easy.

"Piece of cake," said a pilot who'd fractured this, that, and the other thing crash-landing a Boeing P-26 Peashooter. The fighter was obsolete, which didn't mean the Army Air Force here wasn't still flying it. Despite that, Frank Houlihan didn't lack for confidence. "They make their shit out of tin cans and baby buggies. They try us on, we'll wipe the floor with 'em."

"They've been pounding the crap out of China. They've taken Vladi-watchacallit away from the Russians. They're tougher than you think," Pete said.

Houlihan didn't want to hear it. "Slant-eyed little monkeys with stupid round glasses and buck teeth? Don't make me laugh, man—it hurts when I do."

"Yeah, yeah. I heard all that crap, too. You ever see 'em in action?" Pete said. "I'm telling you, those guys don't know how to back up."

"Hot damn," Houlihan said. "If they don't, we'll teach 'em."

The less the other guys on the ward had actually seen of the Japanese, the more certain they were that the United States would clean the clocks of Hirohito's finest. Pete didn't like Japs, which was putting it mildly. But anybody who didn't think they were tough . . . well, as far as Pete could see, that fellow was getting too many pain shots.

You had to know your enemy. The men on his ward didn't, and didn't want to. Maybe that meant nothing. Pete couldn't say for sure; he was only a lousy two-striper himself. But what if American admirals and generals had the same attitude as the men they led? That wouldn't be so good.

He did know for a fact that the Japs were interested in everything America did. People said they only imitated. Okay—fine. Say their equipment wasn't quite as good as the stuff Uncle Sam handed his boys. If the men using the gear were better, didn't that wipe out the difference?

Pete was a Marine. The Marines were based on the idea that you could kick the other guy's ass if you were meaner and faster than he was. They'd done it against the Germans in the last big wingding, and in half a dozen banana republics since. It wasn't always pretty, but it worked for them.

So why wouldn't it work for the Japs, too? No reason at all, not that he could see. But he couldn't explain it to the Army and Navy men who'd hurt themselves or come down sick. They believed in firepower the way Mormons believed in Joseph Smith. To them, the quality of the men holding on to the guns was just a detail.

"Okay, fine," he said to Houlihan at last, throwing his good hand in the air. "Have it your way. I hope to God you're right, to tell you the truth. But I've got news for you—if you're wrong, we're in deep shit." Houlihan and the other guys laughed at him. He wished he thought it was funny, too.

NOBODY WAS BOMBING Münster any more. Sarah Goldman liked that fine. Rationing went on, of course. The war was still going. If you took the newspapers seriously, it was going hotter than ever. Of course, if you took the newspapers seriously, you needed to have your head examined.

Troop trains rattled through town, all of them going from west to east. The papers said some of them held French and English soldiers on the way to Russia to help the *Wehrmacht* against the Bolsheviks and the Jews who ran the Soviet Union.

"I wonder how many soldiers on those trains are Jews," Samuel Goldman said at breakfast one morning. "I wonder what they think of the orders they have."

"Maybe some of them will . . ." Sarah didn't finish the sentence. They didn't talk about Saul and what he was doing. None of them really believed the house was bugged, not any more, but none of them believed in taking chances, either.

"Yes, maybe they will," Father agreed now, understanding what she was saying even if she hadn't said it. "That would be interesting, wouldn't it? Very interesting indeed."

"It would," she said. The idea that Saul might run into anyone with whom he didn't have to hide what he really was drew her on like a will-o'-the-wisp. How long could you live a lie? If your other choice was dying, as long as you had to. But living the lie here also involved the risk of dying, and not a small one. Papers printed black-bordered casualty lists every day. . . .

Father set a checked cloth cap on his head. "Away I go," he said as he stood up from the table. "What I do won't be very interesting, but it will remind the powers that be of my wonderful virtues and my strong back."

He stumped toward the door. His limp was worse than it had been. Unlike Saul, he didn't have a body made for hard physical labor every day. He should have stood in front of a classroom, chalking names and dates and Latin and Greek phrases on the blackboard. No matter what he should have done, this was what he did. It was what the Nazis made him do, and all they let him do now.

What would happen when the labor gangs ran out of work? Now that the bombs had stopped falling, wouldn't the workers get ahead of the rubble? Sarah shook her head. She was being silly. The bosses could always keep their laborers busy, even if they had to invent work for them.

They had labor gangs full of Jewish women, too. The only reason

Sarah and her mother hadn't got dragooned into them was Samuel Goldman's war wound. That was the kind of privilege it won: nothing to make anyone celebrate in sane times, but better than nothing when madness called the shots.

Or was it madness? The *Führer* had an amazing knack for getting exactly what he wanted. If England and France helped him finish off Stalin, he would bestride Europe as no man had since Napoleon. And then wouldn't he turn on them the first chance he got? How did they think they'd stop him when he did?

The day dragged along. In the late afternoon, Sarah went shopping. The Big Switch hadn't made things any better there. Soldiers from the Western democracies might cross the German frontier, but food didn't seem to. Hadn't England lifted the blockade? Maybe so, but food still meant war bread and cabbage and potatoes and turnips.

She got what she could at the grocer's, and precious little it was. A sign in his front window claimed he had plums, but they were all gone by the time Sarah and the other Jewish shoppers were allowed to buy. She would have been angrier had she been more surprised. Some of the cabbages and beets he was selling looked better than usual. Maybe the Aryan women had got so excited about the plums, they hadn't picked over the ordinary vegetables so carefully.

Her stringbag fuller than she'd expected it to be, she crossed the street to the bakery. BRUCK'S, it said over the door. On the window was taped a faded, swastika-bedecked sign: *German people! Don't buy from Jews!* Sarah smiled mirthlessly. She wasn't a "German person." The "Jew" stamped on her identity card proved as much.

As she'd hoped, Isidor stood behind the counter instead of his father. His face lit up when he saw her. "Hello!" There were other people in the bakery; he couldn't say everything he might have. By the way an older woman's eyebrow quirked, he'd said plenty with one word.

"Hi," Sarah answered.

"What do you need today?" Isidor did his best to sound businesslike and matter-of-fact, but his best wasn't very good.

"Two kilogram loaves," Sarah answered, also as plainly as she could.

"Coming up." Isidor took them off the shelf with as much ceremony as if they were fit for a king. They were plain, solid, black war bread; a king would have to get mighty hungry before he cut slices from them.

The other shoppers paid for what they'd bought and parted with ration coupons. After they left, Isidor reached under the counter. He pulled out half a dozen lovely purple plums, displaying them in the palms of his hands. "Where did you find those?" Sarah exclaimed.

"Across the street," Isidor answered. "Old Böhm at the grocery isn't such a bad guy. He'll trade this for that. If we're careful, we can get away with it." He gave her the fruit. "Anyway, these are for you."

"For me?" she squeaked. "No, Isidor. That's too much!" Half a dozen plums, and she was carrying on as if he'd given her a kilo of gold. It was silly—or would have been if she weren't what she was where she was.

"Hush," Isidor said firmly. "I can't get you the kinds of things I want to. They'd shoot me if I tried. Besides, nobody in Germany can get that kind of stuff nowadays except guys like Göring. So I do what I can. Today, it's plums. Next week, who knows? Maybe even lamb shanks or something."

He sounded a hundred percent serious. He was most of the time. Sarah had more whimsy in her. She wagged a finger at him. "Don't you know the way to a *man's* heart is through his stomach?" Even as she said it, she realized there were probably Jewish girls in Münster who would sell their body for half a dozen plums. The difference between bad and worse was far bigger than the difference between good and better.

"I know how you got to my heart," he answered, and her cheeks heated. He'd got to hers the same way, there hidden by the tall grass at the park. He glanced up toward the flat over the bakery. "If my folks weren't home right now . . ."

She nodded. Getting together when no one else was around wasn't easy, which was putting it mildly. Maybe that should have relieved her. If she were what people called a good girl, she supposed it would have. She must not have been, because it didn't. She wanted him to touch her again the way he had then. She'd touch him, too, even if that got messy. And if he wanted to do even more . . .

You lost your reputation when you did things like that. It would have been funny if it weren't so sad. As if a Jew in the Third *Reich* had any reputation worth losing!

"Maybe Father and Mother will go out one night before too long," Sarah said. "Curfew's not as tight as it has been. Neither is blackout. If they do—"

"Let me know!" he broke in.

"I will." She had to hide a smile. She'd expected him to be eager. She hadn't exactly expected him to be that eager. Everybody said men were like that when they thought they were going to get what they wanted. A lot of the time, what everybody said was a bunch of *Dreck*. Not here, evidently. Then she thought of something else, something different. "Can you give me some newspaper to cover up the plums? If people see them in my stringbag, they'll wonder how I got them."

"Sure." He handed her the front page from the day's paper. "Nice to think it's doing something useful, anyhow."

"I know. I'd say it was only good for wrapping fish, but when's the last time you had fish to wrap?" Sarah said.

"Been a while," Isidor said sadly.

"I know." Sarah nodded. "We'll, I'd better go. Thanks again." She felt his eyes on her as she left. It didn't bother her one bit.

Chapter 18

"Here you go, Rudel." Colonel Steinbrenner signed Hans-Ulrich's furlough papers with a flourish and handed them to him. "Do you know what you'll do?"

"Well, sir, I wasn't thinking of going anywhere very far," Hans-Ulrich answered. "Five days . . . That's not much time, and I don't want to spend most of it sitting on a train. I thought maybe, oh, Bialystok. It's a city, and it hasn't got smashed to the devil like the White Russian towns."

"Have a good time," the squadron commander said. "You've got a girl back there, don't you?"

And here Hans-Ulrich thought he'd been so casual! He coughed a couple of times. "Uh, not exactly, sir."

Colonel Steinbrenner seemed to riffle through a mental card file. "Oh, that's right," he said when he came to the card he wanted. "You're the one who was chasing that little Jew or half-Jew or whatever she is at the tavern. Go on, then. Have fun. I hope you catch her."

"Thank you, sir." Hans-Ulrich got out of there as fast as he could. He hoped he caught Sofia, too. Marrying a Jew, or even a half-Jew, would shoot down your career faster than flak from the Ivans. Laying one, though . . . If there were any regulations against that, he hadn't heard about them. And he would have, because he kept his ear to the ground.

The nearest railhead was in a town northeast of Minsk. Hans-Ulrich took the squadron's *Kübelwagen* to get there; one of the groundcrew men rode along so he could drive it back. As Hans-Ulrich hopped out, the noncom said, "Enjoy yourself, Lieutenant. Fuck that bitch till she begs for mercy."

"Um," Rudel said, and was spared the need for anything more because the groundcrew man put the *Kübelwagen* in gear and drove away. Did everyone in the whole wide world know he was interested in Sofia? Everybody in the squadron did, anyhow.

A *Feldgendarmerie* sergeant with a shiny gorget checked his papers and his ID before letting him board the train. "Go ahead, sir," the fellow said when he was satisfied. "You're you, all right."

"I hope so," Hans-Ulrich said. "I'm not likely to be anybody else, am I?"

"You'd be surprised," the military policeman answered. "Matter of fact, you'd be fucking amazed. Some of the guys who try to go west on bad papers or no papers at all . . . Makes you wonder whose side they're on, by God."

With such encouragement ringing in his ears, Hans-Ulrich climbed onto the train. It was already crowded, but he wedged his way into a compartment. He promptly fell asleep. Several hours later, shouts of "Bialystok! All out for Bialystok!" roused him and sent him staggering down onto the platform at the train station.

Yawning, he tried to figure out where Sofia's place of employment lay. East of the station—he thought. He started that way. If he couldn't find it, he'd ask somebody. Most Jews and some Poles here understood German.

Quite a few men in *Feldgrau* prowled the streets—fewer in his *Luftwaffe* gray-blue. Bialystok wasn't Paris or even Warsaw, but it wasn't the front, either. It had enough bars and brothels and cinemas to keep the Germans amused while they unwound after weeks nose-to-nose with Ivan.

He found the place without too much trouble. Since the signs in Bialystok were in two languages he couldn't read—one with an alphabet as meaningless to him as Hindustani—he took that for a good omen. The next interesting question was whether Sofia would be working when he walked into the tavern. Had he come all this way just to sit around and drink mineral water or coffee?

But there she was, small and dark and slim and maddening. "Oh. It's you," she said, as if he hadn't been away blowing up Russian panzers for weeks. "Well, come on over here and sit down."

She led him to a little table off in a corner. "What? I don't deserve a better seat than this?" he said, more or less joking.

Sofia, plainly, wasn't joking at all. She shook her head. "Why should you? You don't spend enough cash to make it worthwhile to put you anywhere else. Coffee! Fizzy water!" She rolled her eyes at what they did to profit margins. The expression and the logic behind it certainly made him think of her as a Jew. They didn't make her any less attractive, though, even if they should have.

Doing his best to sound reasonable, he answered, "I don't get drunk and tear the place up and break things, either."

"We can collect on that—sometimes, anyhow. I suppose you'll want coffee now." Without waiting to find out whether she supposed accurately or not, she bustled away. Hans-Ulrich admired her trim ankles. He'd never particularly cared about ankles before—things got more interesting as you moved north—but he made an exception here. Hers were turned on a superior lathe.

She came back with the coffee, set it down on the table, and stood there waiting. He gave her money. That made her turn to go again. Before she could disappear, he spoke quickly: "What time do you get off today?"

"Past your bedtime," Sofia said. Glancing at the steaming cup she'd brought, she added, "Past your bedtime no matter how much coffee you drink."

"But I came all the way back here to see you," Hans-Ulrich said. "There's sure nothing else in Bialystok that would have brought me back."

"Why is this supposed to be my problem?" Sure as the devil, Sofia specialized in being impossible.

"Because—" Hans-Ulrich hesitated. *Because I love you* would make her laugh in his face. *Because I want to go to bed with you* was more honest, but too likely to get him slapped. Hoping the hesitation wasn't too noticeable, he tried again: "Because you're the most interesting girl I've met since I don't know when."

A black eyebrow leaped toward her hairline. "You talk prettier than most of them, but you mean the same thing." Somebody with an empty beer stein banged it on the table and shouted for her. "I've got to go," she said, and she did.

Hans-Ulrich sipped the coffee. It was better than what a field kitchen made but, he thought, not so good as it had been the last time he was here. The war was rough on everybody, at the front or not.

He watched Sofia. He bought more coffee, and more coffee, and more coffee still. If she kept working till after his bedtime now, she'd be doing a twenty-four-hour shift and then some. He got rid of the used coffee in a crowded, odorous *pissoir* made more cramped still by the infantry sergeant passed out next to the urinal.

A panzer crew and some foot soldiers started punching one another. Hans-Ulrich helped break up the brawl and throw them out. Then he went back to his table.

After a while, Sofia came over with a fresh cup of coffee. She had his rhythm down, all right. Pausing, she said, "Why should I want anything to do with you? You're a German. That makes you trouble with a capital T."

He shook his head. "Nah. Germans in Poland are only trouble with a small t. That's what your government decided. Russians are trouble with a capital T."

"I don't care what the government decided. The government is stupid," Sofia answered, which could have sent her to a camp had she been overheard in Germany. "Germans are always trouble."

"This isn't about Germans and Poles or Germans and Jews or Germans and Portuguese, if you happen to be Portuguese," Hans-Ulrich said. "It's about you and me, that's all."

"Easier for the one who drops the bombs to talk like that than for the poor so-and-so they land on."

How did she know he dropped bombs? He supposed she could find out. Or she might have been using a figure of speech. Before he could find any sort of comeback, a shouted call for a refill sent her scurrying away. He sipped his coffee. His eyes were wide, wide open. Not quite benzedrine, but not so far away.

The tavern stayed crowded no matter how late it got. Sofia accidentally on purpose spilled a mug of beer on a German who tried reaching up under her skirt. The guy's friends laughed at him, so he couldn't get mad. He was drunk and hopeful, not really determined. Lucky for him, too, because Hans-Ulrich would have murdered him if he'd tried to take it out on the barmaid.

And then Sofia came to his table without a cup of coffee in her hand. "All right, *Herr* Hotshot. I'm off work," she said, her sharp chin lifted in defiance. "Now what?"

Hans-Ulrich sprang to his feet. He was so surprised and happy, he wondered why he didn't bounce off the ceiling. He offered her his arm. The way she took it was more challenge than anything else. He didn't care. All he cared about was that she took it. "Let's both find out," he said.

"NIGHT BOMBING." Lieutenant Colonel Ponamarenko spoke the words as if they tasted bad. "This is what we are reduced to until we can reequip with Pe-2s or some other new bombers. We serve the Soviet Union, of course." Plainly, he wished the squadron could serve the country some other way.

Sergei Yaroslavsky understood his superior's pride. He had trouble sharing it, though. Enough was enough. Enough, in fact, was too much. Against the *Luftwaffe*'s fighters, the SB-2 had had its day. It was as simple as that. Too many of the faces listening to Ponamarenko were fresh and new. Too many veterans who'd served as long as Sergei were dead, shot down by fighter planes they couldn't escape.

Yes, night bombing was second-line duty. But it was something the SB-2 could still manage. Finding enemy aircraft at night was largely a matter of luck. Bombing by night was also a matter of luck, with navigation and aim so uncertain. But what about it? The explosives were bound to come down on somebody's head, and the somebody would more likely than not be a Nazi.

Kerosene lanterns and men with electric torches marked the edges of the runway. "Should be fun finding this place again in the dark, shouldn't it?" Lieutenant Federov remarked.

Sergei had been thinking the same thing. To keep from dwelling on it, he told his bomb-aimer, "Well, if they lit it up like peacetime, the Germans would find it before we got back."

From Moscow all the way to Germany's western border, no one showed a light at night. You didn't want to give the other side a free shot at you, any more than you wanted to hand the other team a penalty kick in a football match. But the lights were on again in England and France. They didn't worry about German bombers any more. They didn't need to: the capitalists had made common cause with the Fascists to destroy the building workers' and peasants' paradise here.

It won't happen, Sergei told himself. *We won't let it happen.* The Red Army kept yielding ground, but falling back before the enemy worried him much less than it would have worried, say, a Frenchman. In France, you could fall back only so far till you ran out of real estate.

That wasn't a problem in Russia. Trading space for time had been a Russian specialty ever since invaders started coming out of the west—pretty much forever, in other words. Napoleon made it to Moscow, but much joy he had from his homecoming. Sergei didn't think the Germans would get that far, even with help from the other degenerate Western powers. And if they should, he didn't think they wanted to fight through a Russian winter.

Once they were airborne, an order came over the radio: "Switch off navigation lights!" Sergei flipped the switch. The command came sooner than he'd expected. He hoped the SB-2s wouldn't collide with each other in the darkness. He saw no bursts of flame or midair explosions, so he supposed they didn't. He would have waited longer than Lieutenant Colonel Ponamarenko had all the same.

The bombers droned west. A fat gibbous moon spilled milky light over the *Rodina* far below. There was the front. It couldn't be anything else. Those sullen fires down on the ground, the plumes of smoke climbing into the air . . . "Any target we hit from now on, it belongs to the Nazis," Federov said.

"Any military target," Sergei agreed absently. He was studying the compass. Out of the corner of his eye, he watched the copilot and bomb-aimer blink. If Federov was NKVD, as he'd wondered, should he have said that? Too late to worry about it now. And how many Byelorussians had the German hordes overrun? Millions, surely, and some Great Russians and Ukrainians as well.

Russians called Germans *Nemtsi*—the tongue-tied ones. To ancient Russian ears, the German language was sense-free, senseless babble. In German, *Slav* and *slave* both came from the same word. Even in the days when they were forming their speech, the Germans had thought their eastern neighbors fit only for doing what they told them to do.

All that went back more than a thousand years—how much more, Sergei didn't know. He did know not much had changed since.

The navigation lights were out, but he found he could still spot the flames in the exhaust from the other SB-2s' engines. No doubt they could see his plane the same way. That was good—he supposed. If he saw other ghostly shapes, other exhaust fires, coming out of the west . . . He shook his head, refusing to borrow trouble.

Compass and airspeed indicator were his only navigation tools. Calling that crude gave it too much credit. "We're about where we ought to be," he said at last, hoping he was right. "Let's give them our present and head back to the airstrip."

"Sounds good to me," Federov said.

Sergei shouted into the speaking tube: "Bombs away, Ivan!"

"Right!" the Chimp answered. The bombs fell free. The SB-2 got livelier. "Bombs fucking away!" Kuchkov reported.

"Then I'm getting out of here." Sergei hadn't seen any German night fighters, and he didn't want to, either. He hauled the bomber around in the sky and headed back toward the airstrip. Even more than he had on taking off, he hoped he'd be able to find it.

A moment later, he started hoping he'd get back to Russia *to* find it. German flak woke up all at once. The Nazis had no searchlights, the way they would while defending their own cities. They were firing by ear and by guess, gauging height and position from the sound of the bombers' engines.

Fire flashed on the ground as the antiaircraft guns went off. Red and yellow streaks were tracer rounds rising through the air. And the bursts reminded Sergei of the booms when skyrockets turned nights into magic. Here he was, in the middle of one of the fanciest fireworks shows he'd ever imagined.

A fragment clanged into the fuselage. The Germans might be guessing where his plane was, but they made goddamn good guessers. The longer the flak went on, the scarier it got. "You all right back there?" Sergei called to Sergeant Kuchkov.

"Bet your cock I am. Pussy missed me by twenty motherfucking centimeters, easy. Those bitches can't shoot any better than they can fart." Kuchkov swore as naturally as he breathed, and a lot more artistically.

"Well, good," Sergei said, making the bomber jink to help confuse—he hoped—the gunners' aim. "Any damage to the plane?"

"Nothing the groundcrew assholes can't fix pretty easy," the Chimp replied, and Sergei had to be content with that.

After crossing the front, Sergei picked up a little antiaircraft fire from his own side, but only a little. He'd been thinking about football before. Now he did again. *Come on, fellows. You don't want an own goal here.* What Ivan Kuchkov called the Russians manning those guns should have unmanned them from several thousand meters.

Sergei peered down toward the ground, looking for the rectangle of lights he'd left—or for any other rectangle of lights he happened to see. They wouldn't mark a football pitch, but an airstrip.

He almost yipped in surprise when he saw one. Was he that good a navigator, or just that lucky tonight? As he descended, he grew more and more convinced this really was the runway from which he'd set out. The lights were arranged the same way, anyhow, and he didn't think the authorities would have standardized that.

He lowered the landing gear and put down as gently as if the dirt strip were paved with eggs. Night landings were not for the faint of heart. He was proud of this one, and prouder when Federov said, "We've come in rougher than that plenty of times in broad daylight."

"We have," Sergei agreed. He tried to sound as if that were routine, but couldn't even convince himself that he managed it. If those bombs had actually hurt the Nazis, this would be a perfect run.

HANS-ULRICH RUDEL was happy in the way only a man who's wanted a woman for a long time and finally got her into bed can be happy. He was pretty much an idiot, in other words, but a sated and smiling idiot. This was the best furlough of his life. He was sure it was the best furlough of anybody's life. Yes, he was pretty much an idiot for the time being.

Sofia, he discovered after asking eight or ten times (definitely an idiot), was half-Jewish: a *Mischling* First Class, as the *Reich* classified racial categories. She thought of herself as a Jew, though. "My father's a miserable drunk," she said. "Why should I want to be like him?"

Sounds like a Pole, Hans-Ulrich thought, as if there'd never been a German drunk in the history of the world. Although an idiot, he wasn't quite an imbecile: he didn't say what he was thinking out loud. He did ask, "What does your mother do?"

"She went to Palestine," Sofia answered. "With the war, I haven't heard much from her the past year or so. After she broke up with my father, she got the Zionist itch. I think she was making up for marrying a *goy,* but try and tell her that." She rolled her eyes. "Try and tell my mother anything. Good luck!"

"And here you are with me," Hans-Ulrich said, running a hand along the smooth, warm length of her. She had a tiny flat a couple of blocks from the tavern where she worked. "Maybe you're not so different from her after all. Should I watch it if I try to tell you something?"

Not quite an imbecile, but absolutely an idiot. What woman wants to hear she's like her mother? "You'd better not start," Sofia replied with a bayonet-sharp edge to her voice. "And I haven't talked about marrying you, have I? *Gevalt!*"

"Well . . . no," Rudel admitted. He hadn't talked about marrying her, either. You could screw just about anybody, and your superiors wouldn't care as long as you didn't come down venereal. He tried to imagine a *Luftwaffe* officer marrying a *Mischling* First Class in wartime.

His superiors would care about *that.* Oh, yes, just a little! What better way to shoot your military career right between the eyes? You'd never see another promotion again. They'd probably take the *Ritterkreuz* away, too.

"All right, then. Don't be dumber than you can help," Sofia said, which, at that moment, might have been asking for more than Hans-Ulrich could give.

"How about this, then?" he said, and rolled on top of her. She squeaked with surprise, but not with dismay. He was amazed he could go this often. He was a young, healthy animal in fine physical condition. He had very few limits when it came to horizontal athletics.

Some little while later, after both their hearts stopped thudding so hard, Sofia asked him, "And what do you do when you're standing up?"

"It's been too long. I don't remember," he answered, deadpan.

"Braggart!" She poked him in the ribs. "You—man, you." An exquisitely timed pause. "But I repeat myself."

He did have the mother wit to realize he ought to ask her something personal (and he wasn't ready for another round [he didn't think he was, anyhow]). "What do you want to do with yourself?" he said.

"Live through the war," she said at once. "If I can't do that, nothing else matters, does it?"

"No," he said, wishing he'd come out with the question in a different way. His odds of living through the war were . . . well, not good. Stuka pilots went where things were already hot and made them hotter. That was a good way to win yourself a Knight's Cross. It wasn't such a good way to persuade your insurance man to write a fat policy on you.

Most of the time, Hans-Ulrich avoided thinking about that. What combat soldier didn't? If you started feeling the goose's footfalls every time it walked over your grave, how were you supposed to do your duty? You couldn't—it was as simple as that. And so you figured that everything had gone all right the last time, and that meant it would this time, too.

"You're going to forget me," Sofia said. "When you remember me, you're going to be embarrassed you had anything to do with me." Most women would have started weeping and wailing after they came out with a line like that. Sofia sounded no more excited than she would have if she asked him whether he wanted more coffee.

All the same, Rudel tried to deny everything. "I'll remember you forever."

"Oh, cut the crap," Sofia said. "You're going to remember me after you've got four kids and a blond Aryan wife? Don't make me laugh. You'll do your best to pretend nothing in Bialystok ever happened."

"How do you know I'm not married now?" he asked.

"You're the kind who'd wear a ring. And even if you didn't, you're the kind who'd get upset about cheating on his sweetie back home," Sofia answered. "It wouldn't stop you—does it ever stop anybody?—but you'd get upset about it anyway."

He twisted in the narrow bed so he could face her. The mattress creaked under him. It had been doing a lot more creaking than that lately. The sun was going down; shadows shrouded Sofia's features. "You don't much like people, do you?" he said.

She shrugged. The same excellent firm that did her ankles had also sculpted her collarbones. "I am one. What else have I got to like? I'm not one of those jerks who get a dog or a cat and pretend it's their baby."

"All right," he said. He tended to get sloppy over dogs, but not the way she meant. If Sofia were to get a pet, he had the feeling she'd choose a cat instead. Or maybe a viper.

She leaned up on one elbow. Her breasts were small, with broad, dark nipples, almost as if she'd already had a child. Maybe she had; there was a lot he didn't know about her. When he reached out to touch one, she knocked his hand away. "So," she said, "what's it like for a Nazi to fuck a Jew?"

He had no idea how to answer that, so he tried a counterquestion: "What's it like for a Jew to lay a Nazi?"

"My people already don't like me because of who my father is," Sofia replied. "You, though, you're different. What would your mother say if she found out who I was?"

His mother disapproved of everything that had anything to do with sex. She'd warned him about women before he had any idea what she was talking about. He was sometimes amazed he'd ever been born. His father must have been very persuasive one night—or just too horny to take no for an answer.

"I'm a big boy now," he said. "I don't have to worry about that any more."

"Fine." Sofia found a new place to stick in the needle: "What would your commanding officer say, then?"

"He teased me about having a girlfriend before I set out for Bialystok," Rudel answered. "I just hoped he was right."

She gave him a crooked smile. "What? You weren't sure you could sweep me off my feet?"

"I don't think anybody's ever sure of anything with you," he answered truthfully.

"I hope not." Sofia took that as a matter of course—and as a matter of pride. "When people are sure about you, things get boring."

Hans-Ulrich could imagine the two of them parting a lot of different ways. Heading the list was one—which hardly mattered—clanging the other in the ear with a frying pan. Other filmworthy melodramas also stood high up there. Getting bored with each other lay way down below something like being separated in an attack by flying orangutans.

He could imagine her finding a German protector useful. Poles didn't love the Jews who made up a tenth of their country's population. Perhaps because they had so many Jews, no laws restricting them were on the books here. The *Reich* had such laws, of course. Maybe Sofia feared they would come to Poland, too, and hoped a German could help her escape their bite. And maybe she was right in both fear and hope.

That might account for her taking a German into her bed. But what accounted for her taking a *particular* German, one Hans-Ulrich Rudel? He didn't ask her. He had a fear of his own: that she might tell him the exact and literal truth. Whatever her reasons were, he was glad she had them. Glad and more than glad . . .

"*Again?*" she said as he began to rise to the occasion. "I'm going to have to put some new minerals in your mineral water, I swear I am." But she didn't push him away or tell him no. Her arms closed around him, her lips met his, and he wished his furlough could last forever.

LIKE MOST OF the men in his division, Willi Dernen came from the Breslau *Wehrkreis*—near the Polish border. He knew a handful of Polish words, most of them foul. Till this campaign, though, he'd never crossed the frontier. He hadn't even fought in Czechoslovakia; his outfit had guarded the *Reich*'s western border against a French attack that never really materialized. A good thing, too. If the froggies had hit hard, they would have cracked the undermanned German defenses like a man breaking the shell on his breakfast soft-boiled egg.

And now Frenchmen and Tommies would help the *Wehrmacht* smash Stalin's so-called workers' paradise. Life—and who was diddling whom at any given moment—could get very strange sometimes.

Minsk, now, wasn't in Poland. Up until recently, it had been the capital of the Byelorussian Soviet Socialist Republic. Now it was where the Germans reorganized before sending units new to the east up to the fighting front. A lot of Jews and Red officials had fled the place before the Germans and Poles broke in. The Russians and White Russians who remained seemed resigned to the town's sudden change of overlords. The Poles in the population seemed delighted. They flew Polish flags, white over red, at any excuse or none.

Willi watched German engineers cart away larger than life-sized bronze statues of Lenin and Stalin. That wasn't just to show the locals that Minsk was under new management. There had to be at least a tonne of bronze in each statue. Germany was chronically short of raw materials. Pretty soon Vladimir and Josef would get shot back at the Ivans.

Even Corporal Baatz laughed when Willi remarked on that. Awful Arno hadn't been as awful as usual, at least not to Willi. He had to inflict his *Schrechlichkeit* on the replacements who filled out the company, and that took up most of his time and bad temper.

The bulk of the replacements also came from *Wehrkreis* VIII. The *Wehrmacht* tried to keep men from the same part of the country in the same outfit. It helped units hold together, and anything that did that looked good to the men who gave orders. If you'd gone to school with one of the new guys, or maybe with a cousin of his, you'd try harder to keep him in one piece, and he'd do the same for you. That was the idea, anyway.

Unfortunately, the high foreheads who'd come up with the idea had never heard of Arno Baatz. He was doing his best to make sure that all the replacements, regardless of which *Wehrkreis* they came from, hated his guts. And his best, as Willi had too much reason to know, was pretty goddamn good.

His latest target was a new *Gefreiter* named Adam Pfaff. The fellow was new to the company, that is; a wound badge and a slightly gimpy left leg showed he'd been around the block before. He seemed a good soldier. Normally, even Awful Arno would have had trouble finding something for which he could pick on him.

Normally. But, for reasons of his own, Pfaff had painted his rifle dark gray. The job couldn't have been neater. But Arno Baatz had never before seen anybody who carried a dark gray rifle. Like any other monkey, he made fun of the unfamiliar without even thinking about whether he ought to. He gaped and pointed and growled, "What the hell are you doing with that stupid thing? You aim to paint polka dots on it next?"

"No, Corporal." The calm way Pfaff answered made Willi guess he'd got grief from noncoms before. He patted the *Feldgrau* sleeve of his uniform tunic. "They make our clothes this color on account of it's hard to see. I figured I'd fix my Mauser up to match. It doesn't do any harm."

"It looks stupid," Awful Arno said, by which he meant *It had better not still be gray the next time I see it.*

"It doesn't do any harm," Pfaff repeated, by which he meant *Fuck you.*

There were plenty of things Arno Baatz didn't understand, but he got that, all right. His plump cheeks turned the color of iron in a blacksmith's forge. "Oh, yeah?" he ground out. "Well, let's just see what Major Schmitz has to say about that." He deployed the heavy artillery. Major Heinrich Schmitz commanded not just the company but the whole battalion.

But the barrage failed to obliterate Pfaff. "Fine with me," he answered easily. "He's already seen it. He told me he thought it was a pretty good idea."

"Whaaat?" Baatz stretched the word out to unnatural length. "You expect me to believe that shit? I'm gonna go talk to him right this minute, and if I find out you're lying—no, *when* I find out you're lying—your sorry ass is mine." Off he stormed, gloating anticipation splashed all over his face.

Pfaff lit a cigarette. "Boy, that was fun," he said to no one in particular. Then, catching Willi's eye, he asked, "Is that arselick always that bad?"

"Nah." Willi shook his head.

"That's good," the other *Gefreiter* said. "Must be on the rag or something, huh?"

Willi shook his head again. He hadn't finished yet. Now he did: "A lot of the time, Awful Arno's worse."

"About the third time I've heard people call him that," Pfaff said with a thin chuckle. "Everybody must love him to death."

"*To death* is right," Willi answered, rolling his eyes. "He's not yellow or anything like that, I will say. When the shooting starts, he's all right to have at your elbow. Any other time . . . It's like you said. He's the biggest asshole left unwiped."

He wanted to ask Pfaff whether he'd been bullshitting when he told Baatz Major Schmitz had given his *imprimatur* to the gray rifle. But he held his peace. As far as he was concerned, it was everybody in the world against Awful Arno. You didn't want to let on that you had doubts about someone on your own side. Not only that, but he'd also find out for himself, one way or the other, pretty damn soon.

When Baatz came back about twenty minutes later, he might have had a thunderstorm hanging from his wobbly jowls. He didn't come up to Adam Pfaff and admit that the new *Gefreiter* told the truth. That would have been the gentlemanly thing to do, which meant it was as far beyond Baatz's ken as the mountains on the back side of the moon.

Since the corporal couldn't take it out on the man who'd made him embarrass himself, he took it out on everybody else. He screamed at Willi, who'd heard him call Pfaff a liar when the replacement wasn't. Because Willi had heard all that, he endured the *Sturm und Drang* with a smile on his face. That only pissed Awful Arno off worse. He couldn't stick Willi with extra fatigues: the privilege the pip on Willi's left sleeve gave him. And so Baatz screamed some more. Anybody who could draw extra duty did. Willi's smile got wider.

"You have that fat clown's number, by God," Pfaff said, nothing but admiration in his voice, when Awful Arno finally went away. "How long have you been stuck under him?"

"Since before the shooting started," Willi answered mournfully.

"Oh, you poor, miserable son of a bitch," Pfaff said. Willi nodded; he thought of himself the same way. The other *Gefreiter* went on, "I bet he doesn't like your rifle, either."

Willi carried an ancient, beat-up Mauser. It shot pretty well, but it was ugly as Siamese-twin hippos. He'd had the fine sniper's rifle, but . . . "I was going to get out from under him. Swear to Jesus, I was. Then the sharpshooter who was training me got his head blown off, and I went back to ordinary duty. Arno made sure of that, and that I didn't get to keep my nice piece. He said it would shoot too slow with the downturned bolt, y'know? Thank you *very* much, Corporal Baatz."

"I'm glad you said he was good in the field. Otherwise . . ." Pfaff stopped right there. One more word could have landed him in trouble. Willi'd had those thoughts about Baatz himself. He'd never quite done anything about them—Awful Arno wouldn't be here for Pfaff to discover and admire if he had. But he'd had them. Oh, yes. He would have bet a year's pay against a sack of sheepshit there wasn't one single guy in the whole goddamn company who hadn't.

Chapter 19

"Weinberg! Hey, Weinberg!" The call was urgent, even imperative.

"Yeah? *Nu?* What's up? *¿Qué pasó?*" Chaim answered, wondering who the hell needed him and for what. He thought he knew the voice of every Yank and Spaniard in the Abe Lincoln Battalion. Whoever was taking his name in vain, he'd never met the guy before.

And he found out, because the fellow (a Spaniard) said, "You're wanted in Madrid. *Pronto.*" Chaim might know all the Abe Lincolns, but he damn well didn't know every one of the couple of million people left in Madrid.

"Wanted? By who?"

"The cops," put in one of the guys he did know.

"Funny, Hank, funny like a dose of the clap. Har-de-har-har. See? I'm laughing my ass off." Chaim switched from English to Spanish to ask his question again: "Who wants me?"

"Why, the Party, of course." The messenger seemed amazed he would need to ask about anything that obvious.

Patiently, he tried again: "The whole Party, or somebody in particular?"

Maybe he screwed up the grammar worse than usual, so the messenger didn't get it. Or maybe he owned more patience than the Madrileño, because the man just repeated, "*Pronto.*"

"All right, already. I'm coming," Chaim said with no great enthusiasm. He wanted to stay with his buddies. The Communist Party cared no more for what he wanted than for any other individual's desires. But he wasn't exactly brokenhearted about going back to the capital. With a little luck, he'd be able to see La Martellita after the apparatchik who'd pulled his card out of a box got done with him.

His blunt, pudgy features softened. "Magdalena," he whispered under his breath. That was her real name, Magdalena Flores. She'd been desperately hung over the next morning. She barely remembered making love with him while she was drunk. But he tended to her so well—aspirins, strong coffee, the hair of the dog, a very little mild but greasy food—that he convinced her he cared about her along with wanting her sweetly curved body. It wasn't quite that the road to her heart ran through her stomach, but it also wasn't very far removed from that. She'd let him back into her bed when she was sober. What more could any man not a fairy want?

And so he followed the messenger south through the zigzagging communications trenches. By the time they came out into the open, they were too far behind the line to need to worry about snipers. The messenger took charge of his own bicycle and another one reserved for Chaim. They pedaled into Madrid. No *mañana* here; *pronto* meant what it said.

To call Chaim's bike a piece of junk would have given it too much credit. "If this were a horse, I'd shoot it," he said.

"You can walk if you want to. Still a few kilometers to go, though," the messenger answered. Chaim shut up.

People on foot, people on other bikes, people on donkeys and horses, people on animal-drawn wagons and carriages, even a few people in cars: afternoon traffic in Madrid. Everyone who had a horn blew it. Everyone who didn't shouted or whistled instead. It made New York City seem not just sedate but sedated. Foul language and obscene gestures were all part of the show.

Chaim wasn't much surprised when the messenger led him to the building where La Martellita worked. He was summoned on Party business, and this was Party headquarters. But when the fellow said, "Report to room 371," he blinked. That was her office.

Why had she pulled him out of the line? Was she going to put him back on propaganda duty with Nationalist prisoners? He thought—in fact, he was sure—she didn't believe his ideology was pure enough to let him do that. Maybe one of her bosses had overruled her, and she was going to read him the riot act before she let him tell the POWs what a gang of fat, exploiting slobs their former bosses were.

That made more sense than anything else he could come up with. Which didn't mean it was right, of course. One way or another, he'd find out in a couple of minutes.

He climbed the stairs to the third floor (which would have been reckoned the fourth floor in the USA). The building had an elevator, and it worked. No one used it. It required an operator, and the Party had decided positions like that demeaned the proletarians who had to fill them.

La Martellita looked up from her paperwork when he walked into her cramped little room. Emotions chased one another across her face too fast to let him sort them out. All she said was, "Close the door, *por favor.*"

Close it he did. Had she summoned him so she could fool around right here, and on company time? The mere idea was enough to heat his blood. "What is it, my pretty one, my sweet one, my little dove?" he asked as he stepped toward her. Compliments sounded so much more, well, complimentary in Spanish.

Then he stopped in his tracks, as he would have when he saw a sign with skull and crossbones that warned of a minefield ahead. He recognized her expression now, all right: raw, red rage. "You goddamn stinking son of a bitch, I'm going to have a baby!" she screeched. So much for the closed door.

"Oof!" he said, as if someone had punched him in the pit of the stomach. Whatever he'd been expecting, that wasn't it. He wondered why not. The next time they used a safe would be the first. Condoms were hard to get here; despite the Republic's progressive social policies, Spain remained a Catholic country.

"What are you going to do about it?" La Martellita demanded.

"Seems to me I already did what I do," Chaim said. If looks could kill, they would have dragged him out of the little office by his feet after the one she gave him. Helplessly, he spread his hands. "Babies are a chance you take, you know." He made pregnancy sound like a social disease. Well, wasn't it the ultimate social disease? Without it, there wouldn't be any society.

La Martellita's glare did not abate. "You aren't helping," she said pointedly.

"What am I supposed to say?" he asked in what he thought of as reasonable tones. Odds were La Martellita thought he was hectoring her. Hectoring or not, he went on, "If you want me to marry you, I will."

Did that just come out of my mouth? he wondered dizzily. Damned if it didn't. He knew damn well it was dumb luck he'd ever got to sleep with her in the first place. She'd drunk herself sad—hell, she'd drunk herself tragic—and he happened to be in the right place at the right time. There'd never been a dull moment in the sack with her, whether she was drunk or sober. All the same, he'd always figured himself for the cat that fell into the cream pitcher. Before long, it would have to scramble out and lick its fur dry, and then it would have a memory to last forever.

But if he could keep right on bedding down with her . . . If he could see if he might make a go of it with this fierce, beautiful, eminently kissable creature . . . That would be joy beyond his wildest dreams—at least till she decided she'd rather murder him than live with him any more.

"Well!" she said, nodding slowly. "You *are* a gentleman after all. Yes, let's do that. It will give the child a name—and I can divorce you as soon as it's born." She sounded as if she eagerly looked forward to it, too.

She probably did. Divorce was easy in the Spanish Republic: easier than in the States, even in Nevada. Where Marshal Sanjurjo ruled, it was impossible. He and his followers took their religion seriously, or at least legislated as if they did.

Chaim took the bull by the horns. "Let's go find a judge," he said. If he was going to be married, he hoped to enjoy the privileges of matrimony for as long as he could.

La Martellita kept right on glaring. She didn't have to be Einstein or Freud to know what was in his beady little mind. "You only want to keep screwing me."

"Not *only,* my sweet," Chaim answered with such dignity as he could muster. "But a man has to be a *maricón* not to want to screw you. Even if he *is* a *maricón,* he'll think about it."

You never could tell what she'd like and what would piss her off. That, she seemed to like. She even laughed a little. "You're crazy," she said, not without admiration.

"*El narigón loco,* that's me," he agreed, not without pride. *The crazy kike:* a nickname he'd acquired by brawling in bars like a man who didn't care if he lived or died. Well, if marrying La Martellita wasn't a good reason to go on living, he couldn't imagine what would be.

And if she was going to have a baby, so was he. He hadn't left a wife and kids behind to come fight in Spain, the way some Abe Lincolns and a lot of other Internationals had. This would be his first time as a father. He liked that idea, too—maybe not so much as jumping on La Martellita's elegant bones whenever he felt like it, but he did.

"MOSCOW SPEAKING."

Along with the other officers in his squadron, Anastas Mouradian listened to the hourly news. When you were fighting a war, you only know how your own little piece of it was going. Often enough, you weren't even sure about that. If you were going to see the bigger picture, you'd see it through the radio and the newspapers.

"There is fierce fighting against the Fascist invaders near the border between the Byelorussian SSR and the Russian Federated SSR," the newsreader went on. Stas heard him rustle the papers from which he was reading. "And heavy fighting continues in the northwestern Ukrainian SSR."

Fierce fighting meant fierce fighting. *Heavy fighting* meant the Red Army was taking it on the chin. Nobody in the Soviet Union ever came right out and admitted things were going badly. You had to decode the news and read between the lines if you were even going to see through a glass, darkly.

"Lieutenant General Andrei Andreyevich Vlasov continues to distinguish himself in combat against the Hitlerites," the announcer said. "An entire German panzer division has been hurled back in confusion by his troops."

That was interesting. Except for Stalin and Marshal Zhukov, the news rarely mentioned generals by name. Maybe that was a hangover from a few years before, when so many of them got purged. Any which way, this Andrei Vlasov seemed to have evaded the restriction.

"There is also an important announcement in the field of foreign relations," the newsreader said. Mouradian tensed—and he wasn't the only flyer listening to the news who did. What had gone wrong now? Had Finland declared war on the USSR? Had the United States? The one would be a misfortune; the other, a catastrophe. But, for once, it wasn't *that* kind of announcement. The familiar voice continued, "Foreign Minister Litvinov will travel to Tokyo to confer with officials from the Empire of Japan about terms for ending the war in the Far East which Japan will find acceptable."

Mouradian and several other officers sighed on the identical note. Peace against Japan hadn't come cheap in the early years of the century, and it would be even more expensive now. Vladivostok would go, and with it the Soviet Union's main Pacific port. The Trans-Siberian Railway wouldn't go all the way across Siberia any more. The last war had cost Russia the southern half of Sakhalin Island north of Japan; this one would probably cost the USSR the rest of the place. And who could guess what else Japan would want to squeeze out of Litvinov?

On the other hand, the USSR desperately needed peace on the distant frontier, because it had a much bigger, much more urgent war much closer to home. When it came, the country could pay full attention to the Nazis and everybody else coming out of the west. Stas only hoped that would prove good enough to save the Soviet Union. Frighten all your neighbors and make them hate you, and this was the kind of mess you wound up in.

"President Franklin Roosevelt of the United States has offered to help mediate the dispute between the Soviet Union and Japan," the announcer said. "His cousin, Theodore Roosevelt, was President of the USA during the Russo-Japanese War, and helped work out the terms of the Treaty of Portsmouth, which ended it. General Secretary Stalin immediately accepted the American proposal. The Japanese, however, refused it, declaring that they doubted America was truly committed to peace. This being so, Japan and the peace-loving Soviet Union will pursue their talks bilaterally."

Some of Mouradian's colleagues scratched their heads, trying to work out what was going on there. He sighed inside his own mind; some people really shouldn't have been allowed to run around loose. Japan thought the USA would sabotage the peace talks, not help them along. That was obvious to Stas, if not to his comrades. As long as Japan was busy fighting the Soviet Union, she wouldn't also take on the United States—not if her leaders were in their right mind, she wouldn't.

But she was clearing the decks for the big fight, the important fight, no less than Stalin was. Knock America back on her heels and Japan was master of the Pacific. No one else could challenge her there. England and France were busy far closer to home. Holland, mistress of the resource-rich Dutch East Indies, lay under Nazi occupation. If Japan didn't have to worry about the USA . . .

The newsreader spoke of the anticipated harvest and by how much it would exceed the norms established by the agricultural planners. Only the planners had any real idea of how much grain came in across the country. If they cooked the books to make things sound better, who would stop them? Who else would even know? As long as people didn't start starving, nobody. And if people did start starving, it might be for reasons political rather than agricultural. Anyone who didn't believe that could ask the surviving Ukrainians.

"Stakhanovite shock brigades continue to increase steel, coal, and aluminum production," the newsreader said proudly. "Output rises even as factories are knocked down and transported east, out of range of the Hitlerite savages and their terror-bombing campaign."

"Good. That's good," murmured the pilot sitting next to Mouradian. It would indeed be good if it was true. That it could be true struck Stas as most unlikely. The less you said, sometimes, the better. He said not a word here.

The newsreader blathered on and on. He seemed to speak very candidly: everything was for the best in this best of all possible worlds. Mouradian smiled a little when that occurred to him. Too bad it was a joke he would have to keep to himself. Somehow, he didn't think the NKVD would find it funny.

When music finally came out of the speaker instead of the newsreader's perpetual optimism, Lieutenant Colonel Tomashevsky addressed the squadron: "Well, boys, you heard it yourselves. We're going to make nice with the little slanty-eyed shitheads for a while. One thing at a time, I always say. Once we give the Nazis what they deserve, we'll go back to the East and pay what we owe there. Oh, yes. You'd best believe we will."

Speaking of perpetual optimism . . . Did the squadron commander really believe what he was saying? If he did, Stas wanted some of whatever he'd been drinking. Or maybe not. Whatever it was, it was probably too full of sugar to be palatable for an ordinary man.

Then again, perhaps you needed that kind of spirit—and that kind of spirits—if you were going to keep serving the Soviet Union. They weren't flying from the airstrip they'd used when they first took their Pe-2s into action against the Germans and Poles. German bombers had worked that one over.

As far as Mouradian could see, the new Russian plane was better than any bomber the *Luftwaffe* used. It had at least as large a bomb load, and it was faster and more maneuverable than the German bombers. But that mattered only so much. Back in the day, the SB-2 really had been able to outrun the biplane fighters it met in Spain. Against the Bf-109, it turned into a death trap. If the Germans had chased the Pe-2 across the sky with Heinkel and Dornier bombers, everything would have been lovely. Sadly, the Messerschmitt fighter remained more than a match for the Petlyakov machine as well.

But the USSR was a big place—bigger, maybe, than the Nazis fully understood. They had only so many 109s: nowhere near enough to cover all of Soviet airspace all the time. The Pe-2s stood a much better chance of getting through and coming back than did the older, slower

SB-2s. Not for the first time, Mouradian hoped Sergei Yaroslavsky and Ivan the Chimp remained among those present.

PLENTY OF TRAIN LINES in southern France went down toward Spain. Only two actually crossed the border: one near the Atlantic, which led into territory loyal to Marshal Sanjurjo, and this one hard by the Mediterranean, which took the Czech soldiers who had fought for France against Germany into the Republic to fight Fascism now that France wasn't interested any more.

Vaclav Jezek made a sour face when Benjamin Halévy told him that. "So those French assholes could be shipping shit to Sanjurjo at the same time as they're giving us to the Republic?" he said.

"That's about the size of it," Halévy agreed. He was heading into exile, too.

Because he was, Vaclav saw fit to add, "Nothing personal."

"Don't worry about it," the Jew replied. "I think they're assholes, too." He wore a new uniform from the army of the Republic of Czechoslovakia, with a Czech sergeant's three dots on his shoulder straps replacing the French hash mark on his sleeve. Running a finger between his collar and his neck, he grumbled, "I'm still not used to the way this damn thing fits."

"If you're a Czech, you never fit in the way you're supposed to," Vaclav said. "You'd better get used to it."

Halévy raised a gingery, ironic eyebrow. "I think I can just about manage that, you know?"

"Yeah, I guess." Vaclav felt foolish. The only way Jews would ever feel at home anywhere was to get their own country. Fat chance of that! And even if they did, they'd probably kick Christians and Moslems around just because they could. They were human beings, weren't they?

Till Vaclav got to know Halévy, he wouldn't have bet a single Czech koruna that Jews *were* human beings. He'd scorned them, distrusted them, despised them for no better reason than that they had their own funny religion—and, as often as not, they were too goddamn smart for their own good.

Halévy was no dummy. He wouldn't put Einstein out of business any time soon, though. And he made a good noncom, even if he'd had his cock clipped. He took war seriously. He wouldn't be wearing a Czech uniform, he wouldn't be carrying Czech papers in his pocket, if he didn't. Even the French weren't dumb enough to try to make Jews fight on the same side as Nazi Germany. He could have sat out the war in safety. He could have, but he didn't want to.

On second thought, who said he was no dummy?

Over the border, Vaclav saw the last of the French tricolor. He was glad to see the last of it, even if the colors were the same as those of his conquered homeland. They stood for liberty, equality, and fraternity, and what did any of those have to do with fighting side by side with Adolf Hitler? Damn all, as far as he was concerned.

On the other side of the frontier flew the Spanish Republic's flag—another tricolor, this one of red, yellow, and purple. It was certainly gaudier than France's standard, or Czechoslovakia's. But the Republic hadn't turned its back on whatever those colors stood for. It wouldn't still be fighting if it had.

Marshal Sanjurjo's side had another flag yet. Well, to hell with him. This was the one Vaclav had chosen. It might not be his first or even his second choice, but it seemed better than anything else out there right now.

The train wheezed to a stop. At first, he thought it had broken down again. The French had given the Czechs going off to fight in Spain the worst rolling stock they had. Their good passenger cars and new locomotives were hauling French troops east to fight the Russians. That being so, breakdowns were almost a badge of honor.

But no. This was some kind of customs inspection. Normally, countries frowned on large bands of uniformed men importing weapons. These weren't normal times, though. Vaclav doubted he would live to see normal times again.

He stared when a Republican officer came into the car. He supposed this was an officer, anyhow—what else would the fellow be? But the man was bareheaded, and wore denim coveralls over a collarless worker's shirt. He looked more likely to repair a clogged drain than to give orders.

"Revolutionary chic," Benjamin Halévy whispered to Vaclav. After that, the fellow's outfit made more sense. He spoke a sentence in a language that wasn't French but sounded something like it. Vaclav couldn't even swear in Spanish. He was surprised, but not very surprised, when Halévy answered in what sounded like the same tongue.

After a bit of back and forth, the Republic officer grinned and nodded and went on to the next car. "I didn't know you spoke Spanish," Vaclav told the Jew in admiring tones.

"Not Spanish—Catalan. Kind of halfway between Spanish and French," Halévy answered. "And I don't speak it, but I can fake it some."

"Ah." Jezek nodded. He could make a stab at Slavic languages not his own. It didn't always work—he'd been reduced to speaking German with the Polish soldier who interned him. But it was usually worth a try. He hadn't thought that the Romance languages might work the same way. He found a more relevant question: "So what did the guy want?"

"To make sure we've come to fight for the Republic and against the Nationalist shitheads—I think that's what he called them."

"Sounds right to me," Jezek said. "What did you tell him?"

"That we were really here for a picnic, and to meet all the pretty Spanish gals," Halévy replied without changing expression.

"Ahh, your mother."

"She was a pretty gal, but not Spanish." Halévy seemed willing to tell bad jokes all day. Vaclav planted an elbow in his ribs, not hard enough to hurt but to suggest he should quit acting like a jerk. It was a forlorn hope, and Vaclav knew it. Still, you had to make the effort. Vaclav also knew all about making the effort despite forlorn hope. If he hadn't, would he have come to Spain?

Another officer strode into the car. This one wore khaki, and he had on a cap with a flat crown. If his pink skin, broad face, and pale eyes hadn't told which army he belonged to, the uniform would have. He greeted the Czechs not in Spanish but in Russian, which he confidently expected them to understand.

Vaclav caught the gist, anyhow. Most of his countrymen probably did. The USSR had helped Czechoslovakia when nobody else would. Now the Czechs were helping Spain, the Soviet Union's ally, when hardly anyone else would. He thanked them for that.

Had he left it there, everything would have been fine. But he went on to say something to the effect that now the Czechs would have to follow Stalin's orders like everybody else. That was what Vaclav thought he said, anyhow. The Russian took no questions. He went on to inflict his greetings on the next car farther back.

"Did he say what I thought he said?" Vaclav asked Halévy.

"I don't know," the Jew answered. "But what I thought he said, I didn't like it for beans."

"Neither did I," Vaclav said. "That probably means we both think he said the same stupid thing."

"What can you do?" Halévy said with a sigh. "He's a Russian. Without the Russians, the Republic would have lost the war a long time ago. Then France would have had to ship us to Paraguay or something when she switched sides."

"Is there a war in Paraguay? I hadn't heard about a new one, and I thought the old one was over," Vaclav said.

"For all I know, it is," the Jew replied. "The French government would ship us over there any which way. They're my people, too, and I know how they work. If nobody's fighting there now, they'd count on us to start something."

That had an appalling feel of probability to it. Vaclav said, "Me, I was thinking they'd send us to China if they didn't have Spain. Everybody hates the Japs, pretty much—even the Russians."

"You're right. They do," Benjamin Halévy agreed. "The Japs may play even less by the rules than Hitler and Stalin do." He threw his hands in the air in mocking triumph. "And they said it couldn't be done!"

The train chose that moment to jerk into motion again. On they went, deeper into Spain and a brand-new war.

PETE McGILL WAS GETTING to the point where he could move pretty well on crutches. He could even hobble fifty feet or so with just a cane. And he'd made it from his bed to a chair nearby with no artificial aids whatever, for all the world as if he were a normal human being. One of these days, the cast on his arm would come off, and then he could truly start working on getting his strength back.

He couldn't wait. He wasn't the only injured serviceman in Manila who wanted to get back into action as fast as he could, or else a little faster. When he listened to the radio or read a paper, he could add two and two and get four. He might have had trouble in school, but he sure didn't in the real world.

Russia had patched up a cease-fire with Japan. She was trying to fight Hitler with everything she had. Okay, fine, but that also meant the Japs wouldn't have any distractions any more. Oh, they were stuck in China, but they could lick the Chinks whenever they set their minds to it. Chiang Kai-shek's troops wouldn't parade through Tokyo any time in the next hundred years. And neither would Mao Tse-tung's, no matter how much Stalin wished they would.

Well, if Japan had gone and started clearing her decks for action, where would the action be? To Corporal Pete McGill, *right about here* looked like the best answer to that question.

It wasn't as if the prospect of a war between Japan and the United States was a first-class military secret. The exact plans for fighting it were bound to be secret, of course. But almost every Navy file and leatherneck could give the short version of those plans. (Pete wasn't nearly sure Army guys could do the same thing: a firm Marine Corps belief was that men who joined the Army were a few ice cubes short of a whole tray.)

When you got down to it, the thing looked simple. The U.S. Navy would steam west from Pearl Harbor. The Japanese Navy would steam east from Tokyo Bay. Wherever they bumped into each other, they'd start slugging away. The last fleet standing would go on and thump hell out of the other side till they got sick of it and gave up. Not subtle. Not pretty. But plans didn't have to be. They just had to work, and being simple sure didn't hurt.

Things like aircraft carriers did complicate the game. Pete assumed his side knew how many the Japs had so they could make more. That wasn't necessarily the wisest assumption, but Pete had never tried to persuade American taxpayers to fork over for national defense. What he didn't know could hurt him, but he didn't know that, either.

He figured the fight would look like Jutland from the last war, only bigger. Somebody'd described the English admiral at Jutland as the only man who could lose the war in an afternoon. Both the American and

Jap commanders in the next fight would wear the same mantle, whether they liked it or not—and chances were they wouldn't.

The logical place for the big smashup was somewhere in Philippine waters. Japan would want to clear the USA out of this colony so close to the Home Islands. Do that and you'd also deprive the U.S. Navy of bases within striking distance of Japan. And the Americans wouldn't be able to interfere with whatever Japan decided to do in China and French Indochina and the Dutch East Indies.

Which was why Pete wanted to get back to active duty as soon as he could. Every Navy ship had a Marine detachment. On battlewagons and cruisers, Marines served the secondary armament: not the great big guns in the turrets, but the next size down. Marines kept order on smaller warships, and did whatever else people told them to do. If the Navy was going to fight the big fight against the Japs, Pete wanted to be there and join in.

A physical therapist gave him exercises to help him heal faster. He performed them with a dedication that amazed and alarmed the man. "If you tear a tendon working out, you won't do yourself any good," the fellow said severely.

"Right," Pete answered. Take this guy seriously? Forget it! For one thing, he wondered if the therapist was a faggot. For another, he subscribed to the informal Marine Corps creed: anything worth doing was worth overdoing.

The therapist didn't need long to realize that Pete was hard of listening. "Why are you pushing yourself like that?" he demanded. "It won't change things by more than a few days one way or the other."

"Could be a big few days," Pete said stubbornly. "Could be the difference between getting a ship and staying beached."

That, the therapist couldn't very well misunderstand. "Even if you do get beached, Corporal, there'll still be plenty for you to do," he said. "Or don't you think the Japs will try to land troops in the Philippines when the balloon goes up?"

"Huh," Pete said: a thoughtful grunt. He'd worried so much about the big head-on collision between navies that he hadn't wasted time with what might happen on land. Maybe he should have.

Or maybe not. "Doesn't matter whether they do," he said. "That'll just be a watchacallit—a secondary engagement, like. I aim to be where the real action is. I owe those yellow sonsabitches plenty—better believe I do. The more I can give 'em back in person, the better I'll like it."

"Well, you won't like a torn Achilles' tendon, so take it easy, okay?" the physical therapist said.

"I'll . . . try." Pete couldn't have sounded more grudging if the man had recommended that he quit screwing for the next five years.

He'd had to quit screwing while he was laid up. He hadn't been interested, either, not while he was mourning Vera. It would have seemed disloyal to her memory. Come to that, it still did, which didn't keep him from noticing whenever he spotted anything female and under the age of fifty.

People told dirty stories about military nurses and about how they'd blow you or jack you off if you needed it and you didn't have anyone of your own to take care of things for you. Pete had hoped those stories were the straight goods. They weren't just dirty. They were . . . what was the word? *Therapeutic* came pretty close.

The next sign of their truth he found would be the first. Oh, the gals were one hundred percent nonchalant when they handled your John Henry in the line of duty. But none of them here showed the least bit of interest in doing anything with Pete's but shoving it in a bedpan. *Too bad,* he thought, and so it seemed.

Time hung heavy. Everything in the Philippines seemed to move as lazily as the ceiling fans that stirred the air without cooling it. There was talk of air-conditioning the hospital, but there seemed to be neither will nor money to get on with the job. The talk was as desultory as everything else. Best guess was that the system would be installed by 1949 or the day before Philippine independence, whichever came last.

People grumbled about the mere idea of Philippine independence. There was already a small Philippine army, under the command of Douglas MacArthur. He served the Philippines with the exalted rank of field marshal, to which he couldn't aspire in the U.S. Army if he stayed in till he was 147.

"Goddamn Filipinos can fucking well keep him," said a U.S. Army sergeant in Pete's ward. "When he ran the Bonus Army out of Washington, my old man and my uncle were two of the guys he rousted."

"That was chickenshit, all right," another Army guy agreed. "So how come you joined up if you already knew they'd screw you the same as they screwed your father and your uncle?"

A resigned shrug from the sergeant, who'd got hurt in a car crash. "Shit, man, it was nineteen-fucking-thirty-four. There wasn't no work nowhere. I knew they'd feed me long as I stayed in. Afterwards? I didn't give a rat's ass about afterwards. Crap, I still don't. Afterwards'll just have to take care of itself."

"Boy, I figured the same thing when I signed on the dotted line for the Corps," Pete said. "I was broke, I couldn't land a job . . . World had me by the short hairs."

"Has it let go since?" the sergeant asked.

"Not hardly," Pete answered in a high, squeaky voice. Everybody laughed, as if he'd been joking.

Chapter 20

Alistair Walsh approached the personnel office with more trepidation than he'd felt crossing some minefields. All the same, he opened the door, took his place in the queue inside, and worked his way forward. Most of the men in front of him were ordinary privates with ordinary problems. He envied them.

In due course, he presented himself at a window behind which sat a noncom with almost as much mileage as he had himself. "Yes, Staff Sergeant?" the fellow said. "What can I do for you this morning?"

"I should like to make the arrangements necessary for leaving the Army." Walsh shook his head. That wasn't right, and he wouldn't pretend it was. "No. I don't like it. I've never liked anything less—except the notion of staying in and fighting on Hitler's side."

He waited for the personnel sergeant to call him an unpatriotic clot or some other similar endearment. The man did nothing of the kind. Nor did he seem surprised. How many other soldiers had come before him with the same request? More than a few, if Walsh was any judge.

"Are you sure of this?" the personnel sergeant asked. "The Army needs men like you—men who know what's what."

"Yes, I'm sure. I'm not happy, but I'm bloody sure," Walsh answered. "And the Army may need me, but I don't need the Army any more. If it's going to do . . . this, it's not what I took the King's shilling for all these years ago."

"You understand, of course, that only a small minority of military personnel feel as you do?"

"No. I don't understand that at all." Walsh shook his head. "Blokes I've talked with, most of 'em are disgusted to have anything to do with the Nazis except over open sights. Only difference is, they aren't disgusted *enough* to want to leave. It's not the same thing, you know."

"Possibly not." But the personnel sergeant wasn't finished: "You also understand that, of the men who wish to resign, we permit only a small proportion to do so?"

"Urrh," Walsh said—as unhappy a noise as he'd ever made this side of a wound. He'd been afraid of that. He stuck out his chin. "I'll take my chances. I can't stomach it any more, and that's flat."

"How about this, then?" said the man on the other side of the desk. "You could stay in, with a guarantee from the Ministry of War that you'd never have to serve alongside the German Army."

"The Ministry of War . . . makes guarantees like that?" Walsh said slowly.

"Under some circumstances, yes. To some people, yes." After a moment's hesitation, the personnel sergeant expanded on that: "It makes the guarantee to men it judges valuable enough to the Army. By your rank and experience, you would be one of those men. And it makes that guarantee where it does not look for any sizable amount of publicity, if you take my meaning."

"If I blab about it in the nearest pub, the guarantee flies out the window." Yes, Walsh took his meaning, all right.

"Quite." The personnel sergeant smiled. "So what do you say to that?"

Regretfully, Walsh answered, "I still want out. It's not just that I don't fancy fighting alongside Hitler's goons. I don't want Britain fighting alongside them. It goes dead against everything the country stands for."

"The Government thinks otherwise," the other veteran said, his smile disappearing. Walsh could hear the capital letter.

"Bugger the Government." He gave it right back. "Churchill was *in* the sodding government. How did he come to die?"

"It was an accident, a tragic accident," the personnel sergeant said primly.

"Right, mate. Sure it was. And then you wake up," Walsh retorted. "You'd better wake up, any road, on account of if you believe that you'll believe anything."

"Oh. You're one of those," the personnel sergeant said, as if much was now explained. "Let me check something." He consulted a typed list. Walsh recognized his own name even upside down. The other man made a tickmark alongside it in pencil. His voice went as cold as Norwegian winter: "You still wish to leave his Majesty's service, then?"

What Walsh wished right at that moment was for a chance to punch the personnel sergeant in the nose. It would have to come some other time, though. Too bad. "Yes. I still want that," he said heavily.

"Well, we can accommodate you, then, and in jig time, too." The personnel sergeant reached into a drawer, pulled out forms, and shoved them across the counter at him. "Complete these, and we'll carry on from there."

"Right." Walsh bent to the task. When he came to the line that read *Reason for seeking discharge,* he couldn't help snorting. The personnel sergeant raised a questioning eyebrow. Walsh pointed to the line and said, "Looks like they want to know why I want the clap."

"Damned if it doesn't. Never noticed that before." The personnel sergeant would laugh at such foolishness. Walsh had trouble imagining a soldier who wouldn't.

He had no trouble giving his reason. *Adolf Hitler is the enemy of the UK*, he wrote. *I will not serve with German soldiers, or under German officers.* He thought for a moment. That covered most of it, but not all. He added, *It is wrong for any British soldier to do so.* He nodded. Better now. He'd taken care of why he didn't want to stay in even if they said he didn't have to go to Russia himself.

He'd expected that resigning from the service would take a lot of paperwork. He hadn't expected it to take as much as it did. He waded through one form after another. It all boiled down to *I've done my bit, and I don't want to play any more as long as I have to play on Adolf's side.*

"Here," he said at last. He signed his name for the final time—he hoped it was for the final time!—and shoved the sheaf of papers back across the counter at the personnel sergeant.

That worthy went through them to make sure Walsh had crossed every *i* and dotted every *t*. He didn't find anything missing, which seemed to disappoint him. When he'd examined the last form, he asked, "Have you any idea what you'll do after leaving his Majesty's service?"

"Not the foggiest notion," Walsh answered, more cheerfully than he felt. "Something will turn up before I land on the dole. I hope so, any road. If all else fails, maybe I'll go to Spain. I hear the Republic is still taking on men who want to fight for her."

The way the personnel sergeant curled his lip said what he thought of that. It also said he'd watched a lot of aristocratic officers and was doing his best to imitate them. It was the kind of sneer that tempted Walsh to say the hell with Spain and to go sign on with the Red Army instead. Any man who didn't turn a bit Bolshie when he saw a sneer like that wasn't worth the paper he was printed on.

"You'd sooner fight for a pack of wogs than your own country?" the personnel sergeant said. It was *that* kind of sneer. Oswald Mosley would have been proud of it—which was, in its own way, a measure of Mosley's damnation.

"No, I'd sooner fight for my own country, all right," Walsh said, wondering how long that punch in the nose could be delayed. "But I'm not about to fight for the *Führer.* They aren't the same thing, and it doesn't matter if the Prime Minister says they are. I know a damned lie when I hear one. I don't care who comes out with it, either."

Even under the rather dim bulbs that lit the personnel office, he could see the other sergeant go red. "It's just as well that you're getting out," the man said.

"You bet it is," Walsh agreed. He started to turn away, then paused. "When does it become official?"

"Oh, you're out. Don't fret yourself over that," the personnel sergeant said. "The gents who run things, they don't want your kind in. You can take that to the bank, you can."

For upwards of twenty years, officers had been telling Walsh that men like him were the backbone of the British Army. His fitness reports had shown the same thing. All the same, he didn't doubt the personnel sergeant for a minute. Men who were not only able to think for themselves but insisted on doing so were dangerous—at least to their superiors' peace of mind—in any army.

Walsh left the personnel office with his last fortnight's pay and his provisional discharge papers in hand. He wondered if London would look different now that he was a civilian. It didn't, not so far as he could tell. A crew of men in uniform was hauling down a barrage balloon. No one expected Russian air raids, and people didn't have to worry about Hitler any more. Wasn't life grand?

Part of it was: no one could give him orders now. On the other hand, he needed to start worrying about bed and board . . . and everything else. What *was* he going to do now? As he'd told the personnel sergeant, he hadn't the faintest idea. But he wouldn't do anything because some damn Fritz told him to. As far as he was concerned, that mattered most.

THE TRAIN ROLLED into Germany. German soldiers—or maybe they were just frontier guards; their uniforms looked funny—waved to the French soldiers inside. Some of the *poilus* waved back.

Luc Harcourt muttered in disgust. To hell with him if he'd do anything like that. Most of the fellows who waved were new fish. They hadn't come up against German tanks and artillery and machine guns and dive bombers and grenades and . . . The list went on and on. They hadn't come up against Germans, was what it boiled down to. Luc had. Politics might put him on the same side as the *Feldgrau* bastards, but politics couldn't make him like them.

Beside him, Lieutenant Demange chain-smoked Gitanes. He would have done that anywhere, probably including church. "I wish I never would have come along for this, you know?" Luc said.

"Yeah, yeah. Wish for the moon while you're at it." Demange gave out as much sympathy as he usually did: none. "You should have let the pox eat off your foreskin. Then they would have thought you were a kike and given you something else to do."

"You love everybody, don't you?"

"But of course." The cigarette in the corner of Demange's mouth jerked as he spoke. It always did. Somehow, it never fell out, even when it got so small the coal was about to singe his lips.

"Well, come on. Did you ever figure we'd be fighting with the Nazis and not trying to blow their heads off?"

"No, but I'm not that surprised, either. *Cochons* we've got running things, they were always scared to death of another war with Germany. That's how come we've got the Maginot Line. That's how come Daladier went to fucking Munich: to hand Hitler the Sudetenland. But Hitler went to war anyhow, so we got sucked in. The good thing about fighting the Russians is, they've got to go all the way through Germany before they can bother us."

"Oh, no, they don't. We're going to them," Luc said.

Demange waved that aside. "You know what I mean. Think like a Paris politico. If the Germans took the place, they'd grab your mistress and her flat, and you'd be stuck in the provinces with your wife." He rolled his eyes at the inexpressible horror of the idea.

"Wonderful. Fucking marvelous," Luc said. "I'd sooner be a politico stuck with a fat, fifty-year-old wife than a *poilu* on his way to Russia to get his dick shot off."

"But the politicos don't give a shit what you'd sooner." Demange pointed out that basic truth with a certain savage gusto all his own. "And they've got tough bastards like me to make good and sure you do like they tell you."

"You're on your way to Russia to get your dick shot off, too," Luc observed. "What good does being a politico's watchdog do you?"

"Hey, I still get to tell all the sorry *cons* under me what to do," Demange answered. "Now that the dumb fucks went and made me an officer, I get to tell more sorry assholes what to do than ever."

"Doesn't help when the artillery starts coming in," Luc said.

For once, he might have got under Demange's armored hide. "Ahh, shut up," the older man said. Because he was an officer and Luc only a sergeant, Luc had to do as he was told.

In due course, they passed from Germany into Poland. Luc had never heard French spoken with a Polish accent before. German-accented French was a joke—a nervous joke, but a joke. Luc remembered a prewar cartoon of Hitler holding out a French translation of

Mein Kampf and going, "*Barlons vrançais.*" The way he butchered the French for *We speak French* gave his words the lie. But French with a Polish twist sounded extra weird—along with odd pronunciation, the Poles put the accent for every multisyllable word on the next to last.

And Poland looked weird, too. It wasn't the people Luc saw from the windows as the troop train rolled through towns (well, except for the black-hatted, long-coated, bearded Jews, who seemed like refugees from another time). It wasn't even the towns themselves. None of them would turn into Paris any time soon, but no provincial French towns would, either. It was the countryside. There was too much of it, and it was too flat.

"What did they do to get it like this?" he asked Demange. If the veteran didn't know everything, he sure didn't admit it. "It looks like somebody ironed the whole place."

"We spent billions of francs building the Maginot Line, like I was talking about a few days ago," Demange answered. "How much do you suppose the Poles would have to lay out to make themselves some mountain ranges?"

Luc hadn't looked at it like that. After a moment's thought, he nodded. "Yeah, that's about what it would take, isn't it?" He clicked his tongue between his teeth as another kilometer of plain rolled by. "But what happens because they can't make mountains?"

Lieutenant Demange's lips skinned back from his teeth in a horrible grin. "What happens? I'll tell you what happens, my little cabbage." He made as if to pat Luc on the cheek. Luc knocked his hand away. Unfazed, Demange finished, "Germans and Russians happen, that's what."

"Mm." Luc nodded again. "Must be fun being a Pole, huh?"

"Well, some of the broads aren't half bad," Demange said, and Luc nodded one more time. Some of the women he'd seen were spectacular beauties, with more stuff to hold on to than you could shake a stick at. But, again, Demange wasn't done. He gave his verdict with the air of a judge passing sentence: "Except for that, you couldn't pay me enough to be a Pole."

Once more, Luc didn't care to try to tell him he was wrong. When the people running your country saw the Nazis as the lesser of two evils—and when they might well prove right—you were, not to put too fine a point on it, in deep shit.

Once they got east of Warsaw, they started passing through country that had been fought over. It all looked much too familiar to Luc: the wrecked farmhouses, the untended fields, the rusting hulks of tanks and trucks, the cratered ground, the occasional crashed airplane, the hasty graves marked by homemade wooden crosses or just by rifles topped with helmets. The farther east they went, the worse the fighting looked to have been.

Then things changed again. Without warning, signs stopped making any sense at all. Luc could no more understand Polish than he could fly, but he could try to sound out the incomprehensible words. Chances were he was botching them worse than Poles botched French, but he could try. When the alphabet itself stopped meaning anything . . .

When the alphabet itself stopped meaning anything, they weren't in Poland any more. They were in the USSR. The Germans had the same problem here. Luc saw quite a few of their signs importantly pointing this way and that, stark black letters on a snowy ground. He didn't read German, either, though more of the words looked familiar than they did in Polish. But even seeing letters he could understand felt oddly reassuring.

The train stopped. Luc expected silence outside the car now that the noise from the engine and the wheels was gone. Instead, he heard something like far-off thunder. Somebody's artillery was going to town.

Lieutenant Demange gave him that dreadful grin again. "Well, we won't have to go real far to find the front, will we?"

"No. What a pity," Luc said, for all the world as if he meant it. Demange's sour chuckle said he understood.

A German officer came up to the detraining Frenchmen and immediately started shouting orders—in his own language, of course. None of the soldiers in khaki moved. Luc knew that, even if he did speak German, he would sooner lose a nut than admit it. Apparently, he wasn't the only one here who felt that way.

His government could make him board a train. It could ship him east. But it couldn't turn him into a good ally. If the Germans didn't happen to like that, well . . . What a pity. For the first time since stepping down onto Soviet soil, he smiled.

A DORMOUSE MIGHT find room to sleep inside a Panzer II. An ordinary human being didn't stand a chance. Theo Hossbach and his crewmates did the next best thing: they dug out a space under the little panzer, using its armored chassis and tracks to protect them from anything the Ivans threw their way.

It was crowded under there, but less crowded than inside the machine. Not so many sharp metal corners to catch you in the knee or the elbow or the side of the head, either. And Theo and Adi Stoss and Hermann Witt got along pretty well. They shared cigarettes and food and, whenever they could liberate some, vodka.

"I didn't like those clouds late this afternoon," Stoss said as they were settling down. "Looked like rain."

"Smelled like rain, too. Still does," Witt put in, wrinkling his nose in the fading, gloomy light. "Wet dust—know what I mean?"

Adi nodded. So did Theo. One of the reasons you dug in under your panzer was to give the beast room to settle. If the ground was soft, it could settle enough to squash you flat unless you were careful. And, of course, it would settle more if rain softened things.

But they'd dug enough of a cave so they wouldn't have to worry about that. Which didn't mean Theo didn't worry. Theo always worried. He had reason to worry here, too. When the fall rains started in this part of the world, they didn't stop for six weeks or so. All the roads that weren't paved turned to bottomless lengths of ooze. The next paved road Theo saw more than a couple of kilometers outside a Soviet city would be the first.

That was on the panzer commander's mind, too. "You know, our maps eat shit," he remarked, not quite apropos of nothing.

"You bet," Adi Stoss agreed. "What they call main highways are horrible dirt tracks. And the secondary roads—the ones on the maps, I mean—mostly aren't there at all for real."

"The railroads suck, too," Witt said. Once soldiers started bitching, they commonly had a hard time stopping. "Why did the fucking Ivans pick a wider gauge than everybody else in Europe?"

"So we couldn't use our rolling stock on their lines when a war started," Adi answered. "It works, too."

By the same token, the Russians couldn't use their cars and engines farther to the west. Their planners must have been afraid they were more likely to retreat than to advance when they banged heads with Germany. On the evidence of two wars, those planners had known what to fear.

Theo pulled his blanket over his head. Adi and Hermann kept talking for a while, but they lowered their voices. Theo fell asleep as if sledgehammered. Anybody who said war wasn't a wearing business had never been through one.

He woke early the next morning to a soft, insistent drumming on the panzer overhead and on the ground all around. No wonder it had looked like rain the afternoon before. No, no wonder at all. His lips shaped a soundless word: "*Scheisse.*"

His comrades stirred a few minutes later. They swore, too, not at all silently. "Break out the soup spoons," Adi said. "The easy advances just quit being easy."

"Maybe things will pick up again after the hard freeze comes and we aren't stuck in the mud all the goddamn time." Witt tried to look on the bright side of things.

"Yeah, maybe." Adi didn't sound as if he believed it. Theo didn't believe it, either. Just then, a tiny rill trickled down the dirt they'd thrown up from under the panzer and into their little cave. Adi sighed theatrically. "Forty days and forty nights—isn't that right?"

It was right in the Biblical sense. It was also about how long the fall rains in Russia would last. The panzer crewmen glumly emerged into a world that had changed.

The rain pattered down out of a sky that reminded Theo of nothing so much as the bellies of a lot of dirty sheep. It cut visibility to a couple of hundred meters at best. Beyond that, everything was lost in a curtain of murk and mist. A hooded crow on the roof of a burnt-out barn sent the Germans a nasty look, as if to say the evil weather was their fault.

Sorry, bird, Theo thought. *It's not us. Our generals will be tearing out their hair—the ones who still have hair, anyhow. The rest will throw down their monocles and cuss.* His opinion of the *Wehrmacht*'s senior commanders was not high. His opinion of other armies' leadership was even lower.

Adi stooped and eyed the Panzer II's tracks. Sure as hell, it was getting muddy. Sure as hell, the panzer was sinking into the mud. The driver mournfully shook his head. "Going anywhere in this crap will be fun, won't it?" he said.

Witt nodded to Theo. "Get on the horn with the regiment," he said. "See what we're supposed to do today. If we're lucky, they'll tell us to hold in place."

"Right," Theo said. The panzer commander didn't sound as if he expected them to be lucky. Since Theo didn't, either, he just climbed into the panzer and warmed up the radio set.

When he asked headquarters what the day's orders were, the sergeant or lieutenant at the other end of the connection seemed surprised he needed to. "No changes since last night," the fellow back at HQ replied. "The advance continues. Why?"

"It's raining," Theo said. For all he knew, it wasn't back there. Or, if it was, the deep thinkers at headquarters might not have noticed.

"We go forward," the man at headquarters said. Theo duly relayed his words of wisdom to Witt and Adi.

"Well, we try," remarked the panzer commander, who had a firmer grip on reality than anybody back at HQ. He nodded to Adi. "Start her up."

"Right you are," Stoss said. The Maybach engine belched itself awake. It should have had more horsepower, but it was reliable enough.

The panzer should have had more armor. It should have had a better gun. It should have been a Panzer III, in other words. But there still weren't enough IIIs and IVs to go around, so the smaller IIs and even Is soldiered on.

Witt stood head and shoulders out of the cupola. He draped his shelter half so it kept most of the rain off of him and out of the fighting compartment. "We're kicking up a wake," he reported, sounding more amused than annoyed.

Theo, as usual, couldn't see out. He believed Witt, though. The engine labored to push the panzer through the mud. The tracks dug in hard. Even through the panzer's steel sides, Theo could hear the squelching.

And the going only got worse. Theirs wasn't the only panzer trying to use the road. The more traffic it took, the more ruts filled with water and turned to soup. "I wonder if we'd do better in the fields," Adi said.

"Try it if you want to," Witt told him.

"Damned if I won't," the driver said, and he did. The panzer picked up speed—for a little while. Then it came to a stretch that German or Russian artillery had already chewed up. Rainwater had soaked into the shell holes, producing little gluey puddles. Adi carefully picked his way between them. "We're using more gas than we have been, too," he grumbled.

Again, Theo believed him. The engine was working much harder than it had when the road was dry. How anyone was supposed to fight in weather like this . . . He consoled himself by remembering that the Russians would have just as much trouble seeing enemies and moving as his own side did.

That turned out not to be quite true. The Panzer II was fighting to get out of a mudhole when Witt let out a horrified squawk and all but fell back into the turret. He frantically traversed it to the left. "Goddamn Russian panzer!" he explained. "Fucker's plowing through the mud like it isn't even there."

How fast were the Ivans turning their turret this way? Theo's gut knotted. A 45mm shell slamming through the thin side armor might answer the question any second now. Witt started shooting: one 20mm round after another, as fast as the toy cannon would fire. Then he switched to the coaxial machine gun, and Theo breathed again.

"Bastard's burning," the panzer commander said. "I think the machine gun got one of the crew, but the rest are still on the loose." He laughed shakily. "Never a dull moment, is there? . . . How are we doing, Adi?"

"We're fucking stuck, that's how," Stoss answered. "We need a tow."

"Right," Witt said. "Theo, get on the radio. Let 'em know."

"I'm doing it," Theo said. He hoped whatever recovery vehicle the regiment sent out wouldn't bog down before it got here. And he hoped—he really, really hoped—no more Russian panzers would come along first.

RASPUTITSA. Russian had a word for the season of mud that came along every spring and fall. The spring *rasputitsa* was worse, because it didn't mark rain alone: the accumulated winter snow melted, making the mud deeper and gooier yet. But the fall mud time was bad enough.

No planes flew. During the winter, fighters and even bombers landed with skis in place of wheels. Even that didn't work during the *rasputitsa.* To get airborne and come down again, a plane had to use a paved runway. As far as Sergei Yaroslavsky knew, the Soviet Union didn't have any.

The Germans were grounded, too. Poland had a few all-weather airstrips, but the front had moved too far east for them to matter. Sergei chuckled sourly. Advantages to everything, even defeat.

For the next few weeks, the flyers had nothing to do but sit around, play cards, and drink. A Red Air Force man sober through the *rasputitsa* probably had something wrong with his liver. When the hard freezes came, when planes could take off and land again, that would be time enough to get your nose out of the vodka jug.

Now . . . Now Sergei ate and slept and drank and argued and listened to the radio and argued some more. Even drunk, he was careful about what he said. NKVD men got drunk too, but they had an ugly habit of remembering what they'd heard then even after they sobered up.

The war ground on even while Sergei and the rest of the Red Air Force men perforce vegetated. That was why he listened to the radio: to find out what was going on while he couldn't do anything about it. He pored over the copies of *Pravda* and *Izvestia* and *Red Star* that came to the airstrip, even if they commonly got there a week after they were printed, their cheap paper already starting to yellow.

No one wanted to come straight out and say so, but the Germans and Poles were still pushing forward—not so fast as before, but they were. The first sighting of French troops raised a fine fury on the radio and then, after the usual delays, in the papers, too. The Party line raised echoes of the civil war after the October Revolution when the capitalist powers allied with the reactionary Whites to try to murder the Soviet Union at birth. They'd failed then, and they would fail now . . . if you listened to Stalin's propagandists, at any rate.

Back then, Japan had joined with England, France, America, and the Whites against the USSR. For a long time, the radio had made this war with Japan seem more of the same thing. *We're attacked on all sides, so we need to fight and work twice as hard,* was the message.

That had been the message, anyhow. But a two-paragraph item in *Izvestia* that Sergei almost ignored said Foreign Commissar Litvinov was on a diplomatic mission to Khabarovsk. It didn't say what kind of diplomatic mission or with whom he was conducting his diplomacy. But still . . . Khabarovsk!

You had to know where Khabarovsk was for the story to make any sense. As it happened, Sergei did. When he was a little kid, some school lesson had praised Khabarovsk, the jewel of eastern Siberia. The so-called jewel was probably one more Soviet industrial town, a quarter of the way around the world from where he sat now. That wasn't the point.

The point was, why would Maxim Litvinov be conducting diplomacy in Khabarovsk if not to talk some more with the Japanese? He wouldn't meet British or French officials there—that was for sure. But Khabarovsk was pretty close to Japan—and even closer to Japan's recent Siberian conquests. Nothing else made sense.

Which proved . . . what, exactly? Not a damned thing, as Sergei also knew. He was only a flyer, making guesses from what the government deigned to tell the people. What the men who ran things knew that they weren't telling . . . He could guess about that, too, but he was much too likely to be wrong.

Only he wasn't wrong, not this time. One very wet, very muddy, very hung-over morning, the radio newsreader followed "Moscow speaking" with "I have the honor to present an important announcement from General Secretary Stalin concerning the course of the struggle against imperialism."

Sergei went over to the samovar and got himself a glass of hot, strong, sweet tea. Then he poured a hefty slug of vodka into it. Put that all together and it might take the edge off his headache. He wasn't the only flyer medicating himself that way, either—nowhere close. Some skipped the tea.

Then the newsreader said, "A definitive and lasting peace has been reached between the Empire of Japan and the workers and peasants of the USSR. The two nations, recognizing their common interests, have decided to make permanent the cease-fire to which they agreed when Foreign Commissar Litvinov traveled to Japan this summer. They will end their conflict on the basis of current positions. The new borders will be demilitarized on both sides to a distance of twenty-five kilometers. Each nation also pledges neutrality in the other's current and future conflicts. The Foreign Commissar has expressed great satisfaction as a result of the formal termination of hostilities."

"Good. That's good," Lieutenant Colonel Ponamarenko said. "In fact, very good. *Ochen khorosho.*" He repeated the last two words with somber satisfaction as he stubbed out one *papiros* and lit another. He seemed to be one of those people who thought nicotine eased a pain in the hair—a term Sergei'd heard from a fellow flyer who'd served in Spain. It fit, all right. He'd smoked a couple of cigarettes himself, but just because he smoked, not because he thought they made much difference to his morning-afters.

Several flyers nodded. Even under Socialism, you couldn't go far wrong agreeing with your squadron commander—and, more to the point, being seen to agree with him. Sergei only wished he could. But the newsreader had left too much out. He hadn't said where the new borders were, for instance. That argued that Japan had seized more of southeastern Siberia than anyone cared to admit in public. The announcer hadn't said anything about returning prisoners of war, either.

Maybe none of that mattered. With the Soviet Union officially able to concentrate on the west, Stalin probably planned to hang on here and renew the fight in the Far East when he saw the chance. He couldn't let Japan hold on to Vladivostok . . . could he?

And what would Japan do now? She could put more soldiers into China. She plainly thought of the vast, disorderly country the way England thought of India: a place to exploit, with plenty of natives to do the hard work for her.

Come to think of it, Hitler thought of Russia that way. What else was he doing here but grabbing land and slaves? If he won this war, he would get his way. The thing to do, then, was make sure he didn't.

Sergei took another swig of vodka-laced tea. His headache was backing off—some, anyhow. He couldn't fight the Nazis now, not with the best will in the world. The *rasputitsa* made sure of that. It left him feeling more than commonly useless.

It was hard to remember, but across the sea lay a country where none of this mattered. The United States was the greatest capitalist nation in the world, and it was at peace with everybody. That struck Sergei as most unfair—all the more so when he was hung over. The Americans just sat there watching the rest of the world tear itself to pieces. As far as the pilot could tell, they didn't care. Why should they? No matter who won, they got rich selling grain and guns.

Something should happen to them. It would serve them right, he thought. Then he laughed at himself. What could happen to the United States? The Americans had beaten their natives far more completely than the English had won in India or the Japanese in China. The Atlantic and Pacific shielded them from the slings and arrows of outrageous fortune. They even seemed immune to the inexorable working of the historical dialectic.

He brought himself up sharply. The Americans might seem immune, but they weren't. Nobody was. The revolution would come to the United States, too. The big capitalists and exploiters would go to the wall, as they had in the USSR. It would happen in England and France, too—and in Germany, no matter what the Hitlerites thought or how little they liked it.

But when? The dialectic didn't speak to that. For the USSR's sake, Sergei hoped it would be soon.

Chapter 21

Some of the Russian prisoners at the camp south of Harbin were quick to learn bits of Japanese. They spoke without much grammar, but they made themselves understood. One skinny, hairy fellow bowed to get Hideki Fujita's attention—they learned Japanese customs, too—and said, "Peace now Russia, Japan—yes, Sergeant-*san*?"

"*Hai,*" Fujita agreed. He couldn't very well deny it, not when the peace had at last been officially announced.

"We go home?" the *maruta* asked.

To that, the Japanese sergeant only shrugged. "I have no orders one way or the other," he answered. It was harder to think of the prisoners as logs when they became talking logs: not impossible, but harder.

"So sorry—don't understand," this Russian said.

"No orders," Fujita repeated. They might be talking logs now, but no, they didn't talk well. You had to keep things as simple as you could, as if you were talking to a retarded three-year-old.

The *maruta* got it this time. "*Arigato,*" he said. "When orders? Soon?"

Fujita shrugged again. "I don't know," he said again, and walked away. He didn't expect the orders the Russian wanted to come quickly, but he could see that admitting as much would only cause trouble. The Soviet government seemed to care about the men Japan had captured almost as little as the imperial government would have worried about Japanese prisoners. These Russians had lost Vladivostok, and so they were in disgrace.

It made perfect sense to Fujita. It made much more sense than most of the things the Russians did. It was, in fact, a very Japanese attitude. And if the Russians didn't care what happened to their prisoners, how could anyone expect Japan to care? Simple: nobody could. And nobody did. The prisoners became *maruta,* became logs, and whatever happened to them was their hard luck.

Muttering, Fujita rubbed his arm and his backside. He'd had more shots since coming to Pingfan than ever in his life before. So it seemed now, anyhow. He was inoculated against everything from smallpox (they'd poked him again, even though he'd been vaccinated not too long before) to housemaid's knee. Again, so it seemed to him.

But there were no inoculations against some of the diseases they used here. If you came down with the plague, odds were you would die. He'd never seen people so nervous about fleas as they were at this place. If you found one on yourself, you had to catch it and kill it and give it to one of the people from the inner compound so he could examine its guts under the microscope or whatever the devil they did in there.

Another *maruta* said, "Food? More food?"

That, Fujita could and did ignore. The prisoners got as much food as the officers in charge of such things said they should. He had nothing to do with it either way. If the officers wanted them plump and healthy, plump and healthy they would be. It happened. Sometimes the scientists needed to see what germs did to people who had nothing wrong with them but a particular disease. More often, though, the POWs went hungry, as POWs deserved to do.

"Why treat us like this?" yet another Russian asked. "Us people, too. What we do to you?"

How many Red Army soldiers had tried to kill Fujita? More than he could count—he was sure of that. But it wasn't the point. Japan would have treated—did treat—Chinese prisoners the same way. And she would have treated other Japanese who surrendered to their enemies the same way, too. Thousands of years of history proved that, too. Soldiers who gave up *weren't* people any more, not in the eyes of their captors they weren't.

Could he explain that to a blond *gaijin* with shaggy cheeks? He not only couldn't, he didn't feel like wasting his time trying. He grudged the Russian two words: "You lost." He felt the man's pale eyes boring into him as he walked away, but so what? Those eyes only further separated the prisoner from him. They should have belonged to a cat, not to a human being.

A few days later, some of the white-coated men from the inner sanctum came forth. They needed fifty Russians to test something or other they'd developed. And, of course, they needed guards to make sure none of the Russians got unruly or got away. A lieutenant, a sergeant, ten ordinary soldiers . . . Fujita was the sergeant.

"What do we do, sir?" he asked the lieutenant—a chunky man named Ozawa—who'd been at Pingfan when he got there.

"Whatever the scientists tell us to do, we do that," Ozawa answered. "They're the ones who run this place. We're here to make sure that whatever they need to have happen, happens. Got it?"

"*Hai,*" Fujita said quickly. He'd already figured out that much for himself. He was hoping the officer would tell him more. But if not, not. As long as a sergeant followed orders, he couldn't go too far wrong.

They let Fujita choose the soldiers who would come along to keep an eye on the Russians. One of the first men he grabbed was Superior Private Shinjiro Hayashi. "Yes, Sergeant-*san,* I'll do it," Hayashi said, as he had to. If he was pleased about the assignment, his face didn't show it. Neither did his voice.

Fujita could have just whacked him in the side of the head and told him to do his job. But they'd served together for a long time. To his own surprise, the sergeant found himself explaining why he'd chosen the junior man: "I need you. You've got good sense."

That was part of it, but not all. He needed Hayashi's education, too, because he came off a farm himself. But there were things you could say and things you couldn't. He said as much as he could. If Hayashi was so goddamn smart, he could figure out the rest for himself.

He nodded now, accepting if still less than thrilled. "All right, Sergeant-*san*. We'll see what happens."

Trucks growled up to haul the Russians, the guards, and the bacteriologists away from Pingfan. A rail spur . . . Motor transport laid on whenever they needed it . . . The people who ran things here had it good. They had it better than most of the ordinary units in the Kwantung Army, that was for sure. Fujita thought about all the shoe leather he'd gone through because nobody could be bothered with sending out a truck to pick him up.

Well, he was riding now, north through Harbin and then into the forests beyond the city. One of the things that had always struck him about Manchukuo was all the space here. To someone who came from crowded Japan, it was especially noticeable. These were woods where no one had ever logged. They might have stood here, untouched, since the beginning of time.

Or so he thought till the trucks stopped in a clearing gouged out of the woods a couple of hundred kilometers north and east of Harbin: not far from what had been the Siberian border, in other words. Wind whistled cold through the trees. Fujita had unhappy memories of fighting in country like this. So, no doubt, did Hayashi, and several other common soldiers. For all he knew, so did the Red Army men. Winter was on the way, all right.

The bacteriologists had memories of their own. They'd used this place before. Poles had been driven into the ground in rough circles around a central open space. One of the white-coated men spoke to Lieutenant Ozawa, who nodded and relayed orders to the other ranks: "We tie a Russian to each pole, facing toward the middle there."

"Yes, sir," Fujita said. He didn't have to do the tying himself. He just supervised: the advantage of being a sergeant. One of the *maruta* tried to run away. A soldier shot him in the back, then walked over and bayoneted him. The men in white coats scribbled in their notebooks: they would be working with forty-nine, not fifty.

They set up something that looked like a bomb casing made of pottery in the central open area. Then they put on gauze masks and handed one to each of the soldiers. At their orders, all the Japanese retreated to the edge of the woods. The scientists got behind trees. So did the soldiers, a beat or two later.

The bomb, or whatever it was, went off. It sounded louder than a hand grenade, softer than a bursting shell. "Now we take the prisoners back and await developments," one of the bacteriologists said. No one asked him what the developments would be. He did condescend to add, "You would be wise to leave your masks on. Yes—very wise."

Some of the Russian prisoners were wounded by flying pottery—mostly the ones close to the burst. The others didn't seem to have been harmed. The soldiers herded them all into the trucks again. They rolled south, back toward Pingfan.

They got there in the middle of the night. The prisoners went into the walled-off compound instead of back to the pens. "They won't come out of there—not alive, they won't," Senior Private Hayashi said in a low voice.

Sergeant Fujita nodded—the other man was bound to be right. "Well, who'll miss 'em?" Fujita said, and Hayashi's head went up and down in turn.

AS LONG AS THE WAR dragged on, Sarah Goldman was positive things wouldn't get any better for Germany's Jews. Rather more to the point, she was positive things wouldn't get any better for her or her family. And she was positive she would start screaming about that any minute now.

Of course, she'd been positive of the same thing ever since the war started. Two years ago! Was that really possible? It was, however much she wished it weren't: not only possible but true.

She nodded to remind herself that the war had been going on for so long. Neither the radio nor the newspapers mentioned the anniversary. When she did remark on that, her father said, "The powers that be don't want you to remember, because then they'll also remember the fighting hasn't all gone the way some people promised it would."

Samuel Goldman chose his words with care. Sarah feared he wasn't careful enough, not if the *Gestapo* really was monitoring what they said in the house. There'd never been any proof of that, not in all the time since Saul killed his labor-gang boss, but the worry never went away.

Hanna Goldman's view of things was less political and more pragmatic: "Ever since we really started banging heads with the Russians, rations have gone to the devil. They were bad before, but they're a lot worse now. When they start taking coupons for potatoes and turnips . . ."

"Did they do that even in the last war?" Father asked. "I was at the front, and there was usually enough there. It wasn't very good, but we got fed. And we took everything we could from the countryside. I'm sure some of the bunnies we stewed meowed, but we weren't fussy."

He'd brought home a rabbit from somebody in his work gang the year before. He'd hoped it was a rabbit then, anyhow. No matter what it was, he'd eaten it without a qualm. So had Sarah and her mother. Sarah's mouth filled with spit as she remembered the rich, meaty taste. She hadn't got to enjoy it much since.

"What happened to that fellow who sold you one here?" she asked. "Could you get more from him?"

"Gregor?" Regretfully, Father shook his head. "He disappeared not too long after I bought the last one. Well, maybe he disappeared and maybe he *was* disappeared, if you know what I mean. I couldn't tell you whether he's on the lam or in a camp."

"I hope . . ." Sarah paused and thought before she spoke. "I hope he's in a camp, getting what he deserves."

If some bored *Gestapo* technician did chance to be listening in on her right now, he was probably fighting nausea. She couldn't imagine anyone saying one thing while more obviously meaning the other. Father's eyes twinkled. "*Aber natürlich,*" he said. "So do I. So does any right-thinking person."

"That's the truth," Mother chimed in. They beamed at one another in companionable hypocrisy.

To Sarah's amazement, a few days later Father brought home not a rabbit but half a dozen dressed pigeons wrapped in bloody newspaper. He had to hold one arm pressed against his jacket to keep them from falling out. Together with the limp from his war wound, that made him seem more crippled than he was.

"Where did you get them?" Mother exclaimed when he set the prize package on the kitchen counter.

"You'd better not tell the Pigeon-Racers' Association, but it turns out there's a sly fellow who traps them," Father answered. "He lives out on the edge of town, so nobody's going to catch him at it. If I lived out there, I would, too. It can't be very hard. Pigeons aren't the smartest birds God ever made. A few bread crumbs and you can probably get as many as you want."

As she had with the rabbit, Mother asked, "What did you pay for them?"

As he had with the rabbit, Father looked pained and didn't give her a straight answer. "It's not as though we're spending money on nightclubs or Strength through Joy cruises," he said.

"Yes, yes," Mother said. "But we are spending money on food and fuel and rent, and we aren't made of gold. So what did you pay?"

"We won't go to the poorhouse tomorrow on account of them," Samuel Goldman told her.

"How about the day after tomorrow?" Sarah suggested.

Her father sent her a reproachful look. "Doesn't the Bible say something about 'sharper than a serpent's tooth'?"

"I'm not an ungrateful child," Sarah said. "I'll never be ungrateful when you bring meat home." She just hoped her rumbling stomach didn't embarrass her in front of her parents. If it didn't, that would only be because theirs were rumbling, too.

"All right, not ungrateful," Father said. "Difficult, though. Let's see you talk your way out of 'difficult.' "

"Why should she?" Mother said. "Only right that someone in the family should take after you."

"I don't know what you're talking about," Father replied with dignity.

But he did. Sarah was sure of that. So did she. Her mother was much more easygoing than her father. Saul was a purely physical being; strength and speed served him the way rational thought did for Father. Sarah was rational, or hoped she was. She was also prickly and impatient with other people's foolishness. That too marked her as her father's daughter.

So did her hunger. Eagerly, she asked her mother, "How are you going to cook them?"

"Does it matter?" Hanna Goldman said.

"As long as they're hot and not too burnt, no," Father said. Sarah nodded—that summed things up for her, too.

Her mother stuffed the squab with bread crumbs and roasted them. They were wonderful. "I don't dare tell Isidor how good that was," Sarah said after crunching through the smaller bones and sucking all the meat off the larger ones. "Bread may be the staff of life, but meat is the gold crown on the end of the staff."

Her father raised an eyebrow. "That doesn't come from the Bible or the Greek philosophers, but it sounds as though it should."

"Just out of my own mouth. Sorry," Sarah said.

"Don't be," Father told her. "Old wisdom gets—well, old. We need new wisdom, too. Here and now, we really need it."

"We have new wisdom. It comes from the *Führer*," Mother said brightly. "The *Führer* is always right. That's what everybody says."

"Well, yes, of course. I knew that myself, as a matter of fact." Father was also playing to the listener who might not be there. As soon as the words were out of his mouth, he made as if to gag. The SS might have planted microphones in the house. Putting secret movie cameras in there was beyond the Nazis' skill. They might want to, but they couldn't.

Sarah smiled at her parents. Somehow, the silly games they had to play made her happy. Jews in Münster had no business being happy. The *Führer* would surely have agreed with that. But, no matter what he wanted to decree, no matter what his minions tried to enforce, happy she was.

Father winked at her. "It's the meat," he said. "It does strange things—especially after so long without."

If she was the one most like him, no wonder he could guess what she was thinking. "Maybe it is. Whatever it is, I like it," she answered. The *Führer* wouldn't approve of that, either. Well, too bad for the *Führer*—that was all there was to it.

ONE OF THE RATINGS on the U-30's conning tower jerked as if a horsefly had bitten the back of his neck. He pointed to port. "Mine!" he said. "To hell with me if that's not a goddamn mine!"

Julius Lemp's binocular-enhanced gaze followed the German

sailor's outthrust index finger. Sure as the devil, the metal horns of a contact mine and part of the sheet-iron sphere itself stuck up out of the cold gray water of the Baltic. "Good job, Sievert," he said. The mine drifted a few hundred meters away, no great danger to the U-boat now. Still, nobody in his right mind wanted to leave one of those hateful things bobbing in the sea, waiting for a target.

"Shall we get rid of it, Skipper?" another sailor asked eagerly. What was it about things that went boom that got grown men as excited as a pack of kids at a fireworks show?

Whatever it was, Lemp had it, too. "You bet we'll get rid of it," he answered, and bawled an order down into the pressure hull: "Man the deck gun!"

The sailors from the gun crew swarmed up the ladder. They hurried to the 88mm cannon on the deck in front of the tower. One of them carefully removed the tompion from the muzzle and let it dangle on its chain. Lemp nodded to himself—he hadn't even had time to give the order. Nothing would ruin your day like opening fire without uncorking your gun.

He did give the order that swung the cannon toward the floating mine. The gun crew banged away with great enthusiasm and no great skill. The 88 was really an anachronism left over from the days of more gentlemanly warfare. It couldn't fight any kind of surface warship. The idea behind it was that a surfaced U-boat could stop a freighter, pause while the crew took to the lifeboats, and then sink the vessel with gunfire, saving valuable torpedoes.

But that didn't work in an age of escorted convoys and radio sets. If an enemy destroyer wasn't bearing down on you at top speed, the freighter was calling in bombers to blow you out of the water. Antiaircraft guns gave you a chance against those, and the U-30 did carry one aft of the conning tower. And it had the 88, too, as much from the designers' force of habit as for any other reason.

Blam! Blam! Blam! Flame burst from the gun's muzzle as each round went off. Brass cartridge cases clanged on the deck. Columns of seawater leaped into the air as shells burst all around the mine. But the damned thing went right on bobbing in the sea. Lemp waited for a hit with rapidly mounting impatience.

At last, when he was about to shout something sharp to the gunners, he got one. It yielded a much bigger *Blam!*—one that rocked him and the submarine even though the mine wasn't close. The gout of water that rose on high was much bigger and much less tidy than the ones the shells had produced.

At the 88, the ratings shouted and pumped fists in the air and capered like lunatics. "We killed it!" one of them yelled. A couple of others dug fingers into their ears. They'd be ringing, all right. Lemp's rang even though he stood up on the conning tower. That was part of the chance you took when you played with things that went boom.

"Very good, heroes," he called to the gunners. "You can go below now."

They pretended not to hear him. Or maybe, since they'd been playing with explosives, they weren't pretending. Lemp figured they were. Coming topside was a rare treat for a lot of the men cooped up inside his steel cigar. They could breathe fresh air. They could focus their eyes on something farther away than their outstretched hands. Why would they want to go down into the dim red light, the humid air, and the symphony of stinks that characterized any working U-boat? Wasn't it like descending into hell? Wasn't it much too much like that?

Lemp had to give the order again before the gun crew obeyed it. They resealed the 88 and climbed from the deck to the conning tower once more: climbed far more slowly than they'd rushed down to start shooting. The fun was over now, and their dragging steps said as much.

They were even glummer about climbing down the hatch and into the U-30. One of them wrinkled his nose. "I wish they could make a U-boat that didn't smell like a polecat three days dead," he remarked.

"Well, Martin, if you don't fancy it, you should have stayed in the surface navy," Lemp said sweetly.

That did the trick. Martin—bearded, grimy, in a uniform that hadn't been washed any time lately—vehemently shook his head, as if the skipper had suggested that he engage in some unnatural vice. "Not me, by God," he declared. "The surface pukes, they fuss about every little thing like they're on the rag or something." And he vanished into the U-boat's fetid bowels. His buddies followed without another word of complaint.

Julius Lemp smiled. It wasn't that he thought the sailor was wrong. On the contrary. He was a U-boat man himself, after all, not a surface puke. He remembered how horribly out of place he'd felt when Captain Patzig summoned him to the bridge of the *Admiral Scheer.* Aboard the U-30, he was lord of all he surveyed. On the pocket battleship, he felt like a poor relation, and a damn scruffy poor relation at that, even if he'd put on his best clothes for the visit.

"Skipper?" said the man who'd spotted the mine.

"Eh?" Lemp came back to the here-and-now. "What is it, Sievert?"

"Was that a Russian mine, or one of ours?"

"I don't know," Lemp replied after a moment's thought. "Considering where we are, it could be either. I sure couldn't tell through field glasses. And I've heard the Ivans just copied our model when they started making their own mines, so there might not have been much to tell from."

"You couldn't read the 'Made in Moscow' plate bolted to the shell, eh?" Sievert asked with a grin.

"Er—no." Lemp managed a chuckle of his own, even if it took some effort. It wasn't that he didn't have a sense of humor, but the poor thing did suffer from lack of exercise.

"Well, it won't take us out, and it won't take any of our surface ships out, and we'll do for any Russian ships we come across," the rating said.

"That's right." Lemp nodded. No jokes lurking in the underbrush there. He felt relieved.

The watchers on the conning tower had gone on scanning sea and sky even while the gun crew played with its big, loud toy. Lemp would have been furious had they let the fireworks distract them. In the Baltic's close confines, trouble was never far away. It could land on you all too fast even when you were lucky enough to spot it before it showed up. If you didn't . . . If you didn't, some flying-boat crew would go home to paint a U-boat silhouette on the side of their fuselage and then fly off to look for more unwary Germans.

I should have paid more attention, too, Lemp thought. He made a quick scan himself, first with the naked eye and then sweeping his binoculars through a quadrant of the sky. Nothing. His breath smoked as he sighed with gratitude aimed at a God Who didn't listen enough.

He remembered the horror that had coursed through him when he'd spotted a small silver speck in the sky not too long before. He'd been about to shout for a crash dive before he realized the planet Venus probably wouldn't strafe the U-30.

He made a more careful scan of the sea, looking for periscopes. No matter how much the *Kriegsmarine* and *Luftwaffe* harried them, Red Fleet U-boats did get out into the Baltic. Ending up on the wrong end of one of their eels would be embarrassing, to say the least.

Again, nothing. His boat might have had the sea all to itself. He was master of everything he surveyed: gray water and gray sky. A gull winging its way south didn't acknowledge his supremacy. Gulls never did. They were an ill-bred lot, scroungers and scavengers and ne'er-do-wells. They were quite a bit like submariners, in other words.

His nose flinched when he had to lay below after his watch ended. He logged the incident with the mine. His script was tiny, cramped, and precise. Things could have been better: he might have sunk a Russian battleship. But they could also have been worse: nothing at all might have happened on his watch. Or no one might have spotted an approaching enemy U-boat. He wouldn't have had to log anything then: he would have been a trifle too dead. The one small detail aside, he couldn't see anything to like about that.

FDR WAS COMING to Philadelphia. The election was only a few days away. Four more years? Peggy Druce hoped so. At least, she supposed she hoped so. Everything in the world seemed to have turned inside out and upside down since England and France did their spectacular backflip with Germany.

Before the big switch, Roosevelt had sent England and France as many planes and guns as American factories could crank out, along with a whole fleet of destroyers he said the United States didn't need any more. Wendell Willkie, the latest Republican to try to boot FDR out of the White House, hadn't yelled at him for that. He'd yelled at the President for not doing more and not doing it faster. A bunch of Republicans were isolationists, but not Willkie.

Trouble was, all of a sudden isolationism looked a lot better than it had even a few weeks earlier. If England and France were on Hitler's side against Russia, they weren't using the American guns and planes and ships against the *Führer,* the way FDR had had in mind. Nobody in Washington was (or, at least, admitted to being) in love with Stalin, but nobody much wanted to see all those weapons turned against him, either.

Willkie's trouble was, he agreed too much with Roosevelt. He was Tweedledum complaining about Tweedledee. After the big switch, some Republicans tried to boot him off the ticket and run somebody more in line with how they figured the party ought to think. Their only problem was, they settled on Alf Landon again: a man only a diehard isolationist Republican could love. (And even then, remembering how FDR had trounced him in 1936, it wasn't easy.) Landon's campaign mostly amounted to *I told you so.* He himself had no hope of winning. The more votes he stole from Willkie, the easier the time FDR would have.

"You ready?" Herb called to Peggy. "The rally starts at half past seven."

"Just about." Peggy patted each cheek with a powder puff one more time. Looking in the mirror made her sigh. It would have to do, but it was a long way from perfect. *Well, too goddamn bad,* she thought. *She* was a long way from perfect. Perfect would have been twenty-five—twenty-nine, tops.

They drove down into the city. Blazing street lamps and headlights and neon signs reminded Peggy she wasn't in Europe any more. She supposed they'd lifted the blackout in London and Paris. People there were probably happy as could be. You could buy happiness, all right—as long as you didn't care what you paid for it.

A valet—a kid, maybe still in high school, maybe just out—took charge of Herb's Packard in the parking lot. As Herb tipped him, Peggy reflected that he would be wearing a different kind of uniform on the other side of the Atlantic. The USA didn't know how lucky it was.

At the Arena on Market Street, Herb confidently said, "Druce—that's D-R-U-C-E," to an important-looking fellow with a clipboard.

The man ran his finger down a typed list. The moving finger suddenly stopped. "Oh, yes, sir!" he said, and then, to a younger fellow standing behind him, "Eddie, take Mr. and Mrs. Druce down front. Make sure they've got good seats."

"Sure thing, Mr. Terwilliger," Eddie said. "Come with me, folks."

They couldn't have got better seats unless he put them up on the podium. Peggy recognized most of the big shots who were sitting up there: Pennsylvania politicos and union leaders. Herb was neither, for which she thanked heaven.

He seemed happy enough with where Eddie put them. Peggy also recognized quite a few of the couples sitting near them. The men of the family were doctors, lawyers, accountants. Clothes and double chins said they'd done well for themselves. Several couples were obviously Jewish. Remembering what she'd seen in Czechoslovakia and Germany, Peggy felt better about being here because of that.

Senator Guffey introduced the President. He spent a few minutes laying into the Republicans before he did. If you listened to him, the Republicans had their nerve for running anybody at all against FDR, and even more nerve for trying to run two people. "The Donkey is always the Donkey," he said, "but over there it's like 1912 all over again. They've got the Elephant and the Bull—Something."

Peggy joined the laugh. She was old enough to remember 1912. Taft had run as a regular Republican, and Teddy Roosevelt (FDR's distant cousin) on the Progressive or Bull Moose ticket. Nobody in his right mind would call starchy, upright Alf Landon a Bull Moose. Guffey had to be thinking of something more like *Bullshit.*

He didn't say that, of course. You couldn't say anything along those lines in a public forum. But letting the audience fill in the dirty word for itself was even more delicious.

The house lights darkened. A tight spot played on Senator Guffey. It gleamed from the frames of his reading glasses. "Now, ladies and gentlemen, I have the great honor and high privilege to present the President of the United States, Franklin Delano Roosevelt!" he said, and stepped away from the lectern.

Next thing you knew, FDR was standing behind it instead. They must have wheeled him on while the only light in the house was the spot on Guffey. Roosevelt was sensitive about being seen—and especially about being photographed—in his wheelchair, and who could blame him? With heavy braces on his legs, he could stand and even take a few stiff steps, but he also didn't like showing them off. In back of the lectern, he didn't have to.

Where you could really see him only from the shoulders up, Roosevelt looked strong and vigorous. He waved to the cheering throng in the Arena. The cheers got louder. Then he waved again, in a different way, and they eased off. "Thank you, folks," he said, his voice booming out of the loudspeakers hooked to the microphone. "Thank you very much. I'm glad to be in Philadelphia. This is where our freedom got its start. This is where the Declaration of Independence was written, and where the Liberty Bell rang out before it cracked." More cheers. Smiling, the President waited them out. "And I want to tell you, liberty almost everywhere seems a little cracked, or more than a little, today."

No one applauded that. People leaned forward to listen to whatever FDR would say next. Peggy found herself doing it, and saw Herb was, too. The President didn't keep them waiting: "Up till very recently, the war in Europe was a war against liberty—liberty there and liberty everywhere. We weren't fighting, but we were involved, because what happened there was liable to happen to us next. And we acted accordingly, doing what we could for the countries that thought more like we did."

Sadly, he shook his big, strong-jawed head. "But Europeans are still Europeans. President Wilson, in whose Cabinet I had the privilege of serving as Assistant Secretary of the Navy, found that out the hard way after the last war. And now we discover it all over again. When the so-called democracies make common cause with the Nazis against the Communists, no one cares for liberty any longer. It returns to the same sad old story of the strong trying to steal from the weak for no better reason than that they think they can. And I say, and America must say, a plague on all their houses!"

The Arena went nuts. That has how Peggy put it when she talked about the speech later on. At the moment, she and her husband yelled and stomped and clapped as loud as anybody else. She was as disgusted by England and France's jump from war against Germany to war against Russia as she'd ever been by anything in her life. (Except, perhaps, her self-disgust at waking up in bed with Constantine Jenkins.

But wasn't waking up in bed with Adolf Hitler a thousand times worse?)

"And so," Roosevelt went on, "we are sending no more weapons to England or to France. And I have ordered the appropriate authorities to ensure that we sell no more oil or scrap metal to Japan until she ends her aggression against China. Governments must no longer see their neighbors as their prey."

He got another ringing round of applause. Peggy noticed that he didn't say anything about Japan's just-ended war with Russia. Chances were he didn't want to remind people. Even some of his supporters had been hoping the Communists would lose, as they did.

Roosevelt also didn't say what Japan—whose home islands didn't yield much past rice and tough little men—was liable to do when her access to raw materials she needed suddenly got cut off. *We'll all find out,* Peggy thought as she left the hall.

Chapter 22

London bubbled like a pot of oatmeal left too long on the fire. No one could prove the government had arranged for that Bentley to run over Winston Churchill. But if Neville Chamberlain did arrange it, he got precious little time to enjoy what he'd done. He went into the hospital for what were described as routine tests . . . and came out after surgery for cancer of the bowel.

It soon became obvious he could not go on as Prime Minister. He laid down the office and left Number 10 Downing Street for a stay in the country "to recover his strength," as the papers said. Alistair Walsh could read between the lines. Chamberlain was dying, and would never amount to anything again.

His backers still held a tight grip on Parliament, though. Despite much impassioned oratory from the men Churchill had inspired, Sir Horace Wilson succeeded Chamberlain as the head of government. Wilson was, if anything, even more bonelessly pro-Nazi than his mentor had been.

"We're bloody well out of it," Walsh said one cloudy afternoon over a pint of best bitter at the Lion and Gryphon, a pub not too far from Parliament that these days found itself full of men in ill-fitting civilian clothes they seemed uncomfortable wearing. It was, in other words, a place where veterans the armed services found politically unreliable congregated. Misery loved, and drank with, company.

Some of the disgruntled ex-soldiers and -sailors and -flyers nodded. But another man who seemed as out of place as Walsh in tweeds and linen said, "We shouldn't let them sideline us, by God. If the PM and the Foreign Office have gone off the rails, who's going to set 'em right but us?"

He spoke like an officer, with a posh Oxbridge accent of the kind much imitated by BBC newsreaders. He had an aristocrat's long, bony features, too, and an air that said he expected to be taken seriously.

But ranks didn't matter any more. They were all demobbed together. Anyone could take a potshot at anyone else, no matter which accent he had. Someone at the back of the room said, "Sounds like treason to me."

The aristo—he was too young to have fought the last time around—only shrugged. "Winston would have quoted that bit about treason's only being treason if it fails—if it prospers, none dares call it treason."

His easy use of the Christian name made Walsh ask, "You . . . knew Churchill?"

"I had that honor, yes," the younger man replied. "And you?" He was trying to place Walsh, as Walsh was trying to place him.

"I talked with him once," Walsh said. "He came to see me after they put me on ice here. For my sins, I was the bloke who met up with Hess in the middle of that Scottish field."

"The famous Sergeant Walsh!" the other fellow said. "Winston spoke well of you, if that matters. Said you rather wished you'd plugged the bugger instead of bringing him in."

Walsh didn't remember telling Churchill anything like that. Maybe he had. Or maybe Churchill worked it out from what they had said. "Might've worked out better if I had," Walsh said. "Couldn't very well have worked out worse. On the same side as the bloody Hun . . ." He drained his pint to show what he thought of that idea.

"Let me buy you a refill, if I may," said the man who'd known

Churchill. He nodded to the fellow behind the bar. "Publican, if you'd be so kind . . . ?"

"Coming up." The barman worked the tap. He slid a fresh pint across the smooth surface to Walsh.

"Obliged," Walsh said. "I'll do the same for you when you finish there. And, begging your pardon, but you're a step ahead of me."

"Oh, quite. My apologies." The younger man laughed. "The name's Ronald Cartland." He held out his hand.

Walsh shook it. The name rang a bell. "You're an MP!" he blurted.

Ruefully, Cartland nodded. "Afraid so. These days, I'm not what you'd call proud of it. But they couldn't drum me out of Parliament, and I'm not about to resign there, the way I did when they tried shipping me off to Byelorussia to fight alongside the same bastards I'd been shelling after they invaded France."

"Same with me, sir," Walsh didn't *know* Cartland had been an officer, but an MP serving in the ranks struck him as wildly improbable. And he liked the certainty of status rank gave. After so long away from it, the arbitrary, whimsical nature of civilian life confused him. "I'd just got back from Norway when the Hun came parachuting down."

Cartland upended his glass of whiskey. When Walsh signaled to the barman, the MP shook his head. "Another time. For now, why don't you come with me?"

"Come with you where, sir?"

"Some chaps I'd like you to meet. They'd like to meet you, too, believe me."

Walsh frowned. "I fancy the crowd I'm in with now."

"Well, I understand *that.* I wouldn't be here if I didn't feel the same way. But . . ." Cartland's voice trailed off, as if there were things he wanted to say but didn't want overheard. "Please, old boy?"

Wondering what he was getting into, Walsh stood up and lit a Navy Cut. "Lead on, sir. I expect I'll follow."

Once they were out of the Lion and Gryphon, Ronald Cartland let out a sigh of relief. "Bound to be people spying in there—maybe the tapman, maybe a customer, maybe the tapman *and* a customer, to make sure they don't miss anything."

"Who's *they*?" Walsh asked.

"People who report to Horace Wilson," Cartland answered. "Like Neville before him, he keeps tabs on anyone who disagrees with him and has a chance of doing anything about it. And he's smarter than Neville ever was, damn him."

"Why's he sucking up to the Nazis, then?" Walsh demanded.

"Because he's afraid of them. It's the only thing I can think of." Cartland walked on a few paces, then added, "Almost the only thing, I should say. He's jealous of them, too. Dictators are very popular these days, as Edward said before he got to be King."

"Did he really?" Walsh said. Crawford nodded. Walsh blew out a big cloud of smoke. "A good job he didn't stay King long, then."

"Yes, a lot of people thought so," Cartland said, and not another word, leaving Walsh to wonder whether Edward's passion for his American divorcée was the only thing that caused him to lay down the crown.

Cartland's case-hardened reserve would have effortlessly turned a question about that. Seeing as much, Walsh just asked, "Where are we going, sir? You can tell me now, eh?"

"Why, to Parliament, of course," Cartland answered in surprise. "I should have thought you'd work that out for yourself."

"Sorry to be so slow."

"Don't worry about it. It will all come right in the end . . . unless, of course, it doesn't." On that cheerful note, Cartland led him past the guards outside—who nodded respectfully—and into the Parliament building.

Everything was smaller and shabbier and lit worse than Walsh had expected. This was the fount of democracy in the modern world, wasn't it? Shouldn't it be bright and clean and shiny? Evidently not. It reminded Walsh of nothing so much as a down-at-the-heels club for veteran sergeants. The thought made him feel more at home than he'd dreamt he could.

Cartland rounded up several other MPs. Eden, Macmillan, Cranborne (who seemed to go by Bobbety) . . . Names washed over Walsh. He wasn't sure he had them all straight, or connected to the right faces. It seemed to matter little. The others were all at least as incensed with the government and its policies as Cartland.

"We have to take back the country's soul," one of them said; Walsh thought it was Macmillan, but he wasn't sure. The MP went on, "Whatever our sins, we haven't done anything to deserve *this.*" He waved his left hand. He didn't use his right arm much. Had he caught a packet in the last war? He was the right age.

"How do you propose to do that, sir?" Walsh asked. "Short of using soldiers, I mean? There's plenty who like what's going on—especially the blokes who don't have to fight the Fritzes any more."

Macmillan and his comrades all looked unhappy. "Ay, there's the rub," one of them murmured. "They think they can ride the tiger without coming back inside him."

You could get drinks in the commons, as you could in a club. The MPs did. Cartland put Walsh on his chit. He'd come up in the world a bit, all right. These men were as disgusted and furious as any of the veterans in the Lion and Gryphon. Whether they had any better idea about how to change things remained to be seen.

NOVEMBER 5, 1940, was chilly and gloomy in Philadelphia. It drizzled on and off. It wasn't cold enough to turn the water in the streets to ice, but it didn't miss by much. Peggy Druce would have been more disappointed if she'd been more surprised. Indian summer might linger this late, but more often than not it didn't.

Her polling place was at a school only a couple of blocks from where she and Herb lived. Every fence and telephone pole was plastered with Roosevelt or Willkie posters. Some had both. Some had Alf Landon posters, too. Some had one guy's stuck on top of the other's. Some had a bunch of different layers going back in time like the rock strata that confounded geologists. Whoever got there with his stack of flyers and pastepot won . . . till the other side's guys came by.

She marked her ballot for FDR and stuck it in the box. "Mrs. Druce has voted," intoned the snowy-bearded poll attendant. He didn't look old enough to have fought in the Civil War, but he might well have been alive through it.

She wondered if he'd ever seen Lincoln. One of her grandfathers had. She also wondered what Honest Abe would have made of the present sorry state of the world. If Lincoln could have found anything good to say about it, she would have been very much surprised.

After completing the little secular ceremony, she went out onto the street. The rain had started up again while she was voting, so she raised her umbrella against it as she started home.

Several men who looked like bums collecting a day's pay for booze called out Roosevelt's name. Several others made noise for Willkie. Pennsylvania had laws against electioneering within a hundred feet of a polling place, but it wasn't as if anyone took them seriously.

Peggy peeled off her galoshes when she got back. She was glad she'd worn them, even if they were ugly. She boiled water on the stove, poured it into a cup, and stuck in a bag of Lipton's tea. They laughed at such things in England, but for fast and easy you couldn't beat a teabag.

Her mouth twisted. She'd loved England and everything it stood for when RAF bombers unloaded on Berlin. They might have killed her, but she loved them anyhow.

Now . . . Now loving England wasn't so easy. She wasn't fighting Nazi tyranny any more. She was marching with it side by side. How could you say Horace Wilson—or Chamberlain before him—was any better than Hitler?

Oh, the English didn't censor their newspapers . . . too much. They didn't persecute their Jews . . . yet. Well, Mussolini didn't persecute his Jews, either, but how many people held him up as a paragon?

"Shit," Peggy said. Why not? Nobody was there to hear her, so the tree fell soundlessly in the middle of the forest. She poured some cognac into the hot tea. Maybe it would help sweeten her mood.

She drank the improved tea. It did warm her body the best way, from the inside out. Her spirit remained unthawed.

The radio might help. She turned it on and waited for it to warm up. The station it was tuned to gave forth with a quiz show so nauseating, she almost broke off the dial in her zeal to find a different one. Glenn Miller's orchestra blaring away pleased her more . . . for a little while. The Nazis couldn't stand jazz.

But her smile quickly slipped. Now that England was marching with Hitler, would it outlaw this "degenerate" music, too? And how about

France? How about Django Reinhardt? He wasn't just a jazz guitarist. He had the nerve to be a *Gypsy* jazz guitarist. The Nazis gave Gypsies as hard a time as Jews, though Jews outside of Germany made more noise about what happened to their kind. Would the French abuse Django to sweeten up their partners in greed?

A hell of a thing when you couldn't enjoy music without worrying about politics. But you couldn't. Once upon a time, she'd liked Wagner—not always in large doses, but she had. She couldn't listen to him any more without remembering how he made Hitler and the rest of the Nazi *Bonzen* stand up and whinny. The thought of that congealed her own pleasure.

And she couldn't hear Shostakovich—or Aaron Copland, for that matter—without thinking, *Oh, yeah. He's a Red.* Maybe the music would outlast the politics. Beethoven's had. Nobody cared any more about what had inspired him. All that mattered was what he'd conceived in his mind and set down on paper.

Commercials followed: Ivory Soap, White King detergent, Old Golds, and De Sotos. Thirty seconds a pop, with singing and music as professional as they'd be on a piece of music from Tin Pan Alley. No great surprise there: Tin Pan Alley songsmiths sometimes turned working girl and sold their talent to the highest bidder. So did musicians and singers who hadn't quite got to the top—and sometimes the ones who had. Neither the Nazis nor the Reds would have approved. Peggy wasn't so sure she did, either, but for reasons of taste rather than ideology.

What she wanted was news. It was a quarter to the hour. The next record was a lot duller than the Glenn Miller piece. It was duller than a couple of the ads, in fact. They couldn't all be gems. That was why some Broadway shows went dark after a week.

The news turned out to be mostly guesses about electoral turnout and reports of tornadoes ripping through the Midwest. Anything across the sea? Peggy would have done much better to turn on the shortwave set for the BBC or Radio Berlin or—less polished—Radio Moscow.

More commercials followed. Peggy didn't know whether to laugh or to cry. *This* was what she'd pined for all the time she was stuck in Scandinavia? As a matter of fact, it was, or at least some of what she'd pined for. The rest, the biggest part, hadn't come back from the office yet.

Peggy cast a longing look at the brandy bottle, but she didn't pick it up. She and Herb still hadn't had that heart-to-heart about who'd done what while they were apart for so long. She wondered if they ever would. A lot of married years had taught her that the best conversations were sometimes the ones you didn't have. But there was a difference between *didn't* and *couldn't. Couldn't* constipated things.

She thought so, anyhow. Maybe Herb did, too. Or maybe he didn't have anything like that to talk about. She just didn't know, and she didn't have the nerve to find out. She was pretty sure he would forgive her, but she didn't want to get any forgiveness unless she could dole out some of her own at the same time.

"Life's a bastard sometimes, you know?" she told the refrigerator. It didn't give her any back talk, for which she was duly grateful.

She had a beef stew going and close to ready when Herb walked through the front door. He fixed himself a stiff bourbon on the rocks. "Well, I voted," he said, in tones as thrilled as the ones he would have used to announce he'd had a cavity filled.

"Yeah, me, too," Peggy said. "Build me one of those, would you?"

"Sure." He suited action to word. As he gave her the drink, he said, "Not like the last couple of times, is it? Hard to get excited about what happens."

"Landon might win. Then we'd all leave town," Peggy said.

"Boy, you can sing that in church!" Herb exclaimed.

After supper, they sat around with more drinks and plenty of smooth American cigarettes and listened to the returns come in. Taken as a whole, the Republicans put up a better fight against FDR than they had in 1932 or 1936. They picked up seats in the House and in the Senate.

But, with Alf Landon siphoning votes away from Willkie, Roosevelt won the slot at the top of the ticket going away. State after state reported an FDR plurality, if not always an FDR majority.

"A third term," Herb said. "How about that?"

"How about that?" Peggy echoed. After a moment, she added, "It feels like it should mean more somehow, you know?"

"If England and France hadn't flipflopped, we'd probably be in the war by now," Herb said. Peggy nodded. They could talk about politics. That was easy. The other things, the harder things, still remained unsaid.

HANS-ULRICH RUDEL didn't think he'd ever been so happy to see snow fall, not even when he was a little boy and it promised him a white Christmas. The snow swirling around the airstrip promised him something even better: a chance to start pounding the Ivans again.

"About time!" he said, sticking out his tongue so snowflakes would land on it. "I was starting to wonder if the mud would ever freeze hard."

Sergeant Albert Dieselhorst chuckled wryly. "Everything happens if you wait long enough. The trick is not going nuts while you're waiting—and not driving everybody around you nuts, too."

"Did I do that?" Hans-Ulrich sounded less innocent than he might have wished he did.

"You said it, sir. I didn't," Dieselhorst answered, which could only mean *yes.* It was also pretty much the same thing Jesus told Pilate when asked if he was King of the Jews.

You shouldn't be thinking about Jews, Hans-Ulrich's well-trained National Socialist side insisted. But he didn't always listen to that side. At the moment, his *Schwanz* didn't want to listen to that side at all. *Sofia's only a* Mischling. *She's not a full-blooded Jew,* he told himself uneasily.

As if reading his mind—a trick good sergeants often gave the impression of owning—Dieselhorst asked, "And how's your lady friend in Bialystok?"

"Fine, as far as I know," Hans-Ulrich answered uncomfortably. "I haven't heard from her since the last time I went back there on furlough."

"Uh-*huh,*" Dieselhorst said, which could have meant anything at all. "You suppose she knows how to write you through the *Feldpost*?" Mail to military men got through almost no matter what. Even the *Frontschweine* got their letters from friends and family and lovers, sometimes under fire in the trenches.

"Well, I didn't tell her," Rudel said, more uncomfortably still. No one superior to him had said anything to him about having a half-Jewish girlfriend. What would happen if he started getting letters from her, though? Letters always made things seem more official, more permanent. They might force the powers that be to notice.

"Don't fuss." Dieselhorst's good cheer didn't go with his own worries. "If she wants to find out, I'm sure she can."

"*Danke schön.*" That wasn't what Hans-Ulrich wanted to hear. He changed the subject: "I wish they'd let us get airborne again now that we can." Sitting around through the Russian mud time had only given him more of a chance to stew in his own juices.

"Don't you worry. It'll happen soon enough, whether you want it or not." Dieselhorst shook his head in resigned amusement. "Somebody's been feeding you raw meat, hasn't he?"

By way of reply, Rudel said something he wished he had back the second it came out of his mouth. Instead of withering Sergeant Dieselhorst, it made the rear gunner and radioman laugh. Rudel retreated in disorder.

He was flying again the very next morning, against a concentration of Russian armor and infantry west of Pskov. Bursts of colored smoke from German artillery pointed out the village in which the Ivans had holed up. Without that, he might not have known which village it was. Nobody could say the Russians weren't masters at concealing themselves, no matter whether one tried to find them on the ground or from the air. Several *Wehrmacht* men had got their throats cut inside German lines, with no remaining sign of whoever'd done the dirty work.

But the huts in the village weren't big enough to hide panzers from the air. The enemy soldiers had done what they could, piling brush and whatnot over the parts that stuck out. That changed the houses' outlines, though, and gave the game away. "I'm going in on one," Hans-Ulrich told Dieselhorst as he tipped the Stuka over into a dive.

However much he wished he would, he didn't catch the Russians by surprise. Tracers from enemy machine guns leaped up toward the Ju-87. A bullet gouged his thick windshield but didn't get through. The panzer he'd picked as his own swelled beneath him.

His thumb hit the firing button. The Stuka staggered in the air as the underwing cannon went off. One round from each of them and Rudel was hauling back on the stick for all he was worth, yanking the dive-bomber out of its plunge by brute force.

"You got him!" Dieselhorst yelled through the speaking tube. "The son of a bitch is burning!"

"Good," Hans-Ulrich said. "Let's go around again and see if we can take out another one."

"You're the boss," Dieselhorst replied. If his tone implied that he thought Rudel was a few liters short of a full gas tank, the pilot didn't have to listen to him.

Listen Hans-Ulrich didn't. He fought for altitude. It took a while—the Ju-87 really did lose performance when it carried these 37mm guns. Then he dove again. This time, the Ivans were waiting for him but good. They fired off everything they had as his plane plunged toward the ground. But they had only machine guns and rifles. A Stuka was built to shrug off a good many small-arms hits and keep flying. Hans-Ulrich fired the 37mm guns again.

"He's burning, too!" Dieselhorst reported as the pilot pulled out of the second dive. "Burning like a motherfucker!"

Serving in the *Luftwaffe* had got Hans-Ulrich past stewing when other people swore, the way a pastor's son might have. That was between Dieselhorst and God, not between the sergeant and Rudel. So Hans-Ulrich only said "Good" before asking, "Did you see any more panzers in there?"

"Yeah, there was another one, south of the two you blasted," Dieselhorst answered.

That wasn't what the pilot wanted to hear—not even slightly. But he said what needed saying: "Well, let's go get it, then."

He half hoped—more than half hoped—Dieselhorst would try to talk him out of it. The rear gunner might not have had too hard a time. But Dieselhorst just repeated, "You're the boss." He still sounded as if he wondered whether Hans-Ulrich had all his oars in the water, but he sounded that way too often for Hans-Ulrich to worry about it now.

Hans-Ulrich did worry when a pair of flat-nosed Polikarpov fighters rushed straight at his climbing Stuka from out of the east. They were monoplanes, yes, but old-fashioned next to a Bf-109 . . . which did him not a bit of good. The Ju-87 was hideously vulnerable to fighters any old time—and all the more so when it lugged the pair of antipanzer cannon.

Running was pointless. They had 150 kilometers an hour on him. And so he tried what he'd done once in the west: he opened up on them at long range with the 37mm guns. And either he was a better shot than he gave himself credit for or he got lucky. One of those big shells tore the wing off the lead Ivan. A round designed to smash through a panzer's armor did horrible things to a fighter plane. The Polikarpov plummeted to the ground, flame licking along the fuselage. Hans-Ulrich didn't see a parachute. *Tough luck, fellow,* he thought.

After seeing what happened to his buddy, the other Russian decided he wanted nothing to do with the Stuka. He whipped his plane into an improbably tight turn and got the devil out of there. Rudel fired at him, too, but missed.

"What's going on?" Dieselhorst asked. Hans-Ulrich explained. "Well, shit," the rear-facing gunner said. "You'll be a fucking ace by the time the goddamn war's done. A Stuka ace! Who would've figured that?"

"That's not what they need me to do," Hans-Ulrich said. "It's just to stay alive."

"I like staying alive," the sergeant said plaintively.

"Well, now that you mention it, so do I," Rudel answered. "But I'm still going to take care of that other panzer."

Only he didn't. The Russians holding the village set as many fires as they could. By the way some of them smoked, the Ivans threw motor oil on them. He couldn't find the remaining panzer through those gray and black plumes, and neither could Dieselhorst. Bombs would still hurt the Red Army foot soldiers, but he didn't have any. Dieselhorst reported the situation by radio as they flew away.

One more mission, Hans-Ulrich thought. He'd done his job, and the Polikarpov made a nice bonus.

VACLAV JEZEK DIDN'T know what he'd expected when he agreed to go to Spain. He'd expected not to get handed over to the Nazis after France went and crapped out on him. He'd got that much, anyhow.

As a matter of fact, the Spaniards made a big fuss over the survivors of the Czech regiment. The mayor of some town along their route did some speechifying that would have sent a stolid Czech audience into gales of helpless laughter. He shouted. He wailed. He wept. He beat his breast. He used more, and more melodramatic, gestures than Hitler. And the Spaniards ate it up.

Of course, Vaclav understood not a word of the local language. As Benjamin Halévy had already shown, he could follow it after a fashion. "So what's he going on about?" Vaclav whispered.

"He's thanking us for not despairing of the Republic," Halévy whispered back.

"I should hope not!" Vaclav said. "It's the only country this side of Russia that doesn't want to shoot us on sight."

"It's a quotation. It goes back to ancient Rome," the Jew told him.

"If you say so." Vaclav had been on the vocational track in his school days. German . . . You couldn't escape German, not in a Czechoslovakia where one person in four was a Fritz. But only greasy grinds had anything to do with Latin.

German attitudes had rubbed off on Vaclav, or been drilled into him, in ways he didn't even notice. He'd often thought the French were less efficient than they might have been. They kept trying to muddle through and improvise instead of planning beforehand, the way anyone with a gram of sense would have. So it seemed to someone whose country had been ruled for centuries by Germans, anyhow (even if they were Germans from Vienna and not Prussians).

But the French had at least heard of planning, whether they bothered to do any or not. With Spaniards, there was nothing *but* muddling through and improvising. The Republic must have known ahead of time that the Czechs were on their way. Vaclav would have thought one official or another would have decided where the new force was to go and what it would do after it got there.

No matter what he would have thought, nothing like that had happened. Along with a bunch of his buddies, he got off the train in Sagunto—another town that Halévy said went back to Roman days—to take a leak. He'd already discovered that Spanish *pissoirs* were even nastier than French ones, but when you had to go, you damn well had to go. He tried not to breathe while tending to his business.

He came out blinking away ammonia fumes . . . and discovered, on the platform, a Spanish officer and a civilian official shouting and screaming and gesticulating as if their next step would be pistols at dawn tomorrow. Both of them pointed a lot at the train and at the Czech soldiers getting on and off.

Vaclav could no more follow them than if they were speaking Tibetan. He looked around to see if Halévy was anywhere close by. Sure as hell, the redheaded Jew (*just like Judas* ran through Jezek's mind) was just emerging from the odorous latrine. "What are they going on about?" Vaclav asked.

Halévy cocked his head to one side, listening. "Where the train's supposed to take us," he said.

"They don't know?" Vaclav said in dismay.

"They're Spaniards. What can you expect?" Halévy answered. So the men of the Republic looked sloppy even to someone used to French ways, did they? That was interesting—not reassuring, maybe, but interesting. And sure enough, Halévy went on, "It's a good thing the assholes on the other side are Spaniards, too, or this war would've been over a long time ago. God, I bet the Nationalists drive the fucking Nazis crazy. Serves the Germans right, you ask me."

"If the Germans went straight to hell and roasted for a million years on red-hot griddles with devils turning 'em every ten minutes with pitchforks, that might start to serve them right." Vaclav spoke with deep conviction. "A bunch of fucked-up Spaniards? Nah. They don't begin to cut it."

Halévy's smile reached his mouth but not his eyes. "When you put it that way, you're right."

The train ended up taking the Czechs through the heart of Spain to Madrid. Vaclav eyed the city with surprised respect. This side of China, it was one of the few places that had been bombed before Prague. All the others were in Spain, too. This was where the Nazis, and even the Italians, had learned their tricks. Mussolini hadn't done much with what he'd learned. Hitler, on the other hand . . .

An officer in a very plain uniform stood waiting for them on the platform. He wasn't a Spaniard—he was from the International

Brigades. "I am Brigadier Kossuth. I am sorry, but I do not speak Czech. Will you follow me if I use Russian?" he said in that language.

Vaclav could *almost* follow him, not least because he spoke slowly. Russian wasn't Kossuth's native tongue. The name he used and his accent both proclaimed him a Magyar. Vaclav had no use for Hungarians. They weren't as bad as Germans, but they weren't friendly neighbors, either. And so he wasn't sorry to shake his head and spread his hands. He wasn't about to oblige this fellow by stretching to try to understand Russian.

Most of his countrymen seemed to feel the same way. Brigadier Kossuth's stooped shoulders went up and down in a shrug. He switched languages as easily as he might change his cap: "All right. Do you understand me now?" he asked in German.

He still kept that fierce accent, but Vaclav had no trouble making out what he said. Neither did most of the other Czechs. The older men would have had German pounded into them when they went to school back in Austro-Hungarian days. Czechs Vaclav's age still learned it—it was their window on a wider world. The same evidently held true for Magyars.

"*Sehr gut,*" Kossuth said. No German had ever pronounced an *r* like that, but Vaclav knew what it was. The officer went on, "You will serve alongside the International Brigades. It was judged best to put you with men with whom you might be able to talk." He gave a thin smile: the only kind his weathered face seemed to have room for. "Sometimes this is an advantage."

Sometimes it wasn't, too, or so Vaclav had found in France. More than once, a blank stare and a mumble had probably kept him from getting killed—or from killing some half-smart French lieutenant.

Kossuth studied the Czechs with shrewd, experienced eyes. One eyebrow rose a millimeter or two when he noticed the antitank rifle slung on Jezek's back. He ambled up to Vaclav. "So, Corporal, do you use that against German panzers?"

"I have . . . *mein Herr.*" Vaclav wasn't surprised Kossuth could read Czech rank badges. He spoke the honorific grudgingly, but speak it he did. He added, "It is also an excellent sharpshooting piece."

"He's killed men out to two kilometers with it," Sergeant Halévy said helpfully.

The brigadier classified him with a single sharp glance. "*Wilkommen,*" he said, and then, "*Bienvenu.* You will find we already have a good many mouthy Jews among the Internationals." Then he said what was probably the same thing in French.

Vaclav wouldn't have been surprised if Halévy came back in Magyar; the French Jew was a man of parts. But if he knew any of Brigadier Kossuth's birthspeech, he didn't let on. He replied in Yiddish-tinged German so Vaclav could understand: "I wouldn't be a bit surprised, sir. I hope you don't hold it too much against us."

"Not . . . too much," Kossuth said slowly. If most Czechs didn't like Jews, most Hungarians *really* didn't like Jews. After a visible pause for thought, the brigadier went on, "The ones I resent are the ones who stayed home. Those who came here have shown they can fight. This is what the struggle demands."

"We agree there," Halévy said. By his tone, there would be plenty of other places where they didn't. Also by his tone, he wanted Kossuth to know that, even if he was just a sergeant and the other man a brigadier.

Something sparked in Kossuth's deep-set eyes. A beat slower than he might have, Vaclav recognized it as amusement. "You are another troublemaker," Kossuth said. "I might have known."

"Would I have come here if I weren't, sir?" Halévy said, and then, "Would you have come here if you weren't?" To Vaclav's amazement, Brigadier Kossuth proved he could laugh out loud.

Chapter 23

"This is the BBC news." Those plummy tones coming from the radio seemed out of place in a military hospital in Manila. Pete McGill was disgusted with the limeys for coming to terms with Hitler. He would have bet most of the British Marines he'd known and drunk with and sometimes brawled with in Peking and Shanghai were just as disgusted. But he was glad to listen to the BBC any which way. It gave more news and less bullshit than any American station.

He was also glad he wasn't the only one in the war who wanted to know what the Beeb had to say. Even Army files could figure out that what happened in the wider world had a lot to do with the way they did business. You didn't have to be a leatherneck to see that—but it probably helped.

"Sir Horace Wilson's government easily defeated a motion of no confidence in the House of Commons yesterday," the newsreader said. "Only a handful of Tories joined Labour and Liberal MPs in opposing the Prime Minister. Even abstentions were fewer than many had anticipated."

That meant England would go on doing what she had been doing:

kissing Germany's ass. Pete muttered something foul. He couldn't do anything about England's foreign policy, but he didn't have to like it. He also didn't like it when the newsreader went on about the triumphs the British Expeditionary Force in the East was winning. Less bullshit or not, the BBC man said nothing about the fact that the Tommies were fighting side by side with the *Wehrmacht* and the *Waffen*-SS. Maybe the radio network had a guilty conscience. If it didn't, it should have.

"In other news"—the broadcaster said *nyews,* where it would have been *nooz* in Pete's New York mouth—"the Empire of Japan has recalled its ambassador from Washington in protest over President Roosevelt's decision to stop sales of petroleum and scrap metal to the Japanese. No talks regarding this delicate issue have yet been scheduled." That came out *sheduled* instead of the American *skeduled,* but again Pete followed with no trouble.

"Aw, shit," said an Army corporal with a leg broken in a car crash. "Them Japs is gonna come after us next."

By *us,* Pete didn't know whether the Army guy meant the United States in general or the men in this military hospital in particular. Either way, the other two-striper was probably right. The Japs had signaled their intentions by making peace with Stalin. If they wanted to pick a fight with the US of A, they wouldn't have to worry about getting jumped from behind.

That much had been obvious ever since Japan and Russia started talking about peace. It gave the Russkis their free hand in the west, too. But if the Japanese ambassador was on his way home, things in these parts might start boiling over any day now.

And that wouldn't be good for American interests in the Far East. For one thing, the Philippines lay within easy range of the Japanese home islands and of Formosa, which had belonged to the Japs for most of the past fifty years. For another . . . "Just about all of my buddies are stationed in Peking or Shanghai, one," Pete said.

"Tough luck for them," the Army corporal replied. "But chances are they ain't a nickel's worth worse off'n we are right here, know what I mean?"

"Don't I wish I didn't?" Pete said glumly. "They're talking about letting me out of my cast pretty soon. Maybe they'll give me shipboard duty. At least then I'll be able to shoot back at the little slant-eyed pricks."

"That'd be good," the Army guy agreed. "You can make it to the bomb shelter, too, if they do. Me, I gotta lay here and hope the assholes miss me."

"Yeah, that's not a whole lot of fun," Pete said. "I've been thinking the same thing every time they hold an air-raid drill." He clicked his tongue between his teeth, considering. "If they're even halfway on the ball, they'll run a lot more of 'em from here on out."

That only drew a derisive snort from the other corporal. "If they're even halfway on the ball, they don't get assigned to the Philippines to begin with. Well, except maybe MacArthur, and everybody knows he's a fuckin' blowhard."

Pete didn't keep track of Army generals. It sure wasn't the first time he'd heard people bitch about Douglas MacArthur, though. A lot of guys still hated him for what he'd done breaking up the Bonus Army at the deepest part of the Depression; he'd heard that from other injured men here.

He did get the cast off his ankle the very next day. He was shocked to see how skinny his leg had got under it. "I want to go back to duty right away," he blurted.

"Yeah, and people in hell want mint juleps to drink," answered the medical technician who'd cut the cast off him. "Just 'cause you want it doesn't mean you can have it. Get yourself in shape again and see what the brass tells you then."

It was good, sensible advice, which didn't mean Pete liked it. How often does anybody ever like good, sensible advice? The world would be a different, and probably a better, place if more people took it.

But telling a Marine he needed to get fit was giving advice he was prepared to heed. Pete was already in the habit of exercising till everything screamed. He was used by now to screams from one part of him or another. He'd done the same kind of thing after his arm came out of its sling and cast. "You do heal well," a physical therapist told him. "Some people might have ended up in a wheelchair from what happened to you."

"Some people might have got killed," Pete growled.

The therapist blinked. "Well, yes." He didn't know about Vera.

She was another reason Pete pushed himself so hard. While he was working and sweating and hurting, he didn't think about her so much. He retreated into the gym the way another man might have retreated into the bottle. Sooner or later, though, a drunk sobered up. And, sooner or later, Pete had to quit working out and start listening again to the demons that lived inside his head.

There were lots of them. Some hated the Japs, not only as enemies of the United States but also as the people who made Chinese terrorists want to blow up places like movie houses. Some of his demons hated the Chinamen who'd blown up the theater and murdered the love of his life. (That they'd ruined him, too, was no more than an afterthought.)

And some of his demons hated his own superiors and the policies and regulations they had to uphold. If Vera hadn't been a stateless person, everything could have worked out. Pete thought so, anyhow. He and his lady love could have got married and gone back to the States together and done . . . something or other. Whatever happened afterwards (even if it was only Reno and a quickie divorce—not that Pete imagined any such thing), they wouldn't have been within thousands of miles of some sticks of dynamite attached to a ticking clock.

If he could kill lots of Japs, that would make him feel better. Because he understood as much, he pushed his ankle far past the point where a less determined man would have started gulping aspirins and cold beer. That fight wouldn't wait, and he was bound and determined to be ready for it when it came.

He couldn't get at the Chinamen, not any more. Even if he'd gone back to Shanghai, he wouldn't have known which of the goddamn Chinks to go after. They kept themselves secret from the Japs, which meant they also kept themselves secret from everybody else. So those demons would just have to stay unsated, their blood lust unslaked.

Consciously, Pete didn't want to go after Marine Corps higher-ups. But he didn't see the look on his own face when he eyed officers—especially officious, by-the-book officers, of whom the Corps had no fewer than any other outfit its size.

Those officers saw the black looks. Officious they might have been, but they weren't all stupid. Some of them recognized the scowls for . . . well, for some of what they were, anyhow. One man said to another, "We better get that guy out of here before he goes Asiatic and does something everybody'd be sorry about afterwards. Him, too, not that that would do anybody any good."

His friend nodded, but replied, "He's liable to do it wherever we send him."

"Yeah, sure. But it's not our lookout after that." The first officer was indeed an officious type.

He was also an officer with good personnel connections. And so, even though Pete McGill wasn't quite a hundred percent yet, he found himself released from the military hospital and assigned to the USS *Boise,* a light cruiser that was one of the heavier vessels of the Far East Fleet. He didn't complain. On the contrary. He thought somebody had done him a favor.

WILLI DERNEN THOUGHT he'd learned all about the *Wehrmacht* greatcoat's limits the winter before in France. He hadn't been in Russia long before he discovered his education in such matters was incomplete.

The biggest difference was, in France you could almost always find somewhere cozy to hole up. Villages clustered thickly. Even if you were stuck in a trench, the line didn't move much. You could fix up your hole till it was fit to live in. Yeah, it was cold outside. But if you had a fire and a wall to keep off the wind, you could put up with things pretty well.

It wasn't like that here. For one thing, the Germans and their allies were still advancing. You couldn't put down roots, the way *Landsers* had in France after the big push to sweep around behind Paris fell short. For another, there were far fewer places in which *to* put down roots. Russian villages were few and far between, and often seemed all but lost amidst the vastness of fields and forests. Willi had never imagined such a wide, wild country. The howls that came from the woods were wolves, not dogs. His skin had prickled up in gooseflesh when he realized that.

And finally, not to put too fine a point on it, the *Wehrmacht*-issue greatcoat wasn't up to the challenge a Russian winter gave it. If you wore one out in the open, with no fire to keep you warm, eventually you'd freeze to death. Or not so eventually, depending on how hard the wind howled down out of the north.

Willi stole a sheepskin vest from a Russian peasant's hut that—except for not running around on giant chicken legs—might have come straight out of fairy tales about Baba Yaga. The inside of the hut was filthy. The vest probably carried lice and fleas. Willi didn't care. He was already lousy and flea-bitten. A little more crawly company? So what? The damn thing was warm. And it fit snugly, and he could wear his greatcoat over it.

The find made his buddies jealous. "Only thing better would have been a jug of vodka," Adam Pfaff said. "That'd heat you up from the inside out—and you might even share it."

"In your dreams," Willi said sweetly. They both grinned. Pfaff might not have been with the unit very long, but he was a good guy. He was no combat virgin, either. He knew what needed doing, and he did it without fuss—and without freezing up in a tight spot. Willi was glad to have him at his back, and it worked both ways.

That vest also made Arno Baatz jealous, though Arno was no buddy of Willi's and never would be. The corporal kept hinting someone of higher rank—say, someone of corporal's rank—deserved the sheepskins better than a lowly *Gefreiter* did. As far as Willi was concerned, Awful Arno could hint till everything turned blue. He still wouldn't get his grubby mitts on the vest.

"Find your own," Willi told him. "If I can do it, anybody can. That's what you always say, right?"

Baatz came back with something else he said often, if not all the time. If taken literally, it would have swept Willi to a place too warm for him to need a sheepskin vest any more. Willi grinned at him, too, but more in mockery than in the comradeship he shared with Pfaff.

"He's got some nerve," the other *Gefreiter* said when Willi told the tale of the corporal's ponderous hints. "Who does he think he is?"

"God," Willi answered. "Or he thinks God would do a better job if only He listened more to Arno Baatz."

Pfaff laughed nervously. "You're kidding, aren't you?"

"Don't I wish!" Willi exclaimed. "That so-and-so's never been wrong once since the fucking war started. If you don't believe me, just ask him. Shit, we'd be in Paris if only the *Führer* listened to old Arno."

"I'd take him more seriously if you said we wouldn't be in Russia if only the *Führer* had listened to him," Pfaff said.

Willi glanced around. No, nobody else could hear them—and a good thing, too. "Nice to know you trust me," he said dryly.

"Hey, you've already had your fun and games with those blackshirt cocksuckers," Adam Pfaff answered. He threaded a bit of cloth through his gray rifle's barrel with a cleaning rod. "You're not gonna turn me in if I open my mouth and say what everybody can see."

"You're all right, you know that?" Willi lit a *papiros* looted from the same shack where he'd got the sheepskin vest. The tobacco wasn't the greatest, and there wasn't a whole lot of it at the end of the long paper holder. Why the hell *did* the Ivans make their smokes that way? Any cigarettes, though, were better than none.

Pfaff examined the cloth after finishing with the pull-through. He nodded to himself. "Yeah, that needed doing, all right," he muttered. Then he sounded more hopeful: "Let me have one of those, will you?"

"I'll let you have it, all right," Willi said in mock anger. A friend wasn't just somebody with whom you could speak your mind. A friend was somebody who could bum smokes off you, and who'd let you do the same when you were out. Willi handed Pfaff a *papiros.*

"Obliged," Pfaff said. And so he was. One of these days—probably one of these days soon—he'd pay Willi back.

Artillery rumbled, not too far behind them. Those were German 105s hitting the Russians up ahead. Before long, the Russians started shooting back. To Willi's relief, it was counterbattery fire. As long as the gunners went after one another, the infantry could breathe easy—well, easier. When the big guns started tearing up the front line, *Landsers* didn't enjoy it so much.

The Red Army had plenty of cannon, and used them as if they were going out of style. The Ivans also had an abundance of 81mm mortars. Willi particularly hated those. Every platoon of Russian infantry seemed to lug one along. They didn't have the range of ordinary cannon, but the Reds could drop a couple of bombs into your foxhole and shred you before you even knew they were around.

"Orders from the regiment!" Arno Baatz yelled, as if he were the one who'd issued them. "We advance under cover of the artillery barrage!"

"Oh, boy," Adam Pfaff said in hollow tones. "Into the meat grinder one more time." He managed a raspy chuckle. "Well, we aren't hamburger yet."

"Me, I'm from Breslau," Willi said, deadpan.

Pfaff sent him a reproachful look. "When you get your sorry ass shot off, chances are it'll be somebody from your own side."

"Nah, that's Awful Arno." Willi chambered a round and scrambled out of his shallow hole. "C'mon—let's go."

German soldiers loped across snow-streaked fields. Willi spotted Corporal Baatz trotting along with everybody else. And Baatz's eye was also on him, as it was all too often. Willi resisted the impulse to send an obscene gesture Awful Arno's way. It wasn't easy, but he did it. *Military discipline,* he told himself.

Occasional rifle shots came from the Ivans' lines a kilometer or so up ahead, but no more, not at first. Then the guys in those scrapes woke up and realized the Germans were serious about this business. A machine gun started spitting out death rattles: industrialized murder at its finest. Willi hit the snowy dirt. He wished he had a white camouflage cape and hood, so he'd be harder to spot.

He wasn't the only *Landser* going down. Shrieks said not everybody was taking cover. Some of the men had been hit. Medics and stretcher-bearers with Red Cross armbands and smocks rushed up to tend the wounded. The Russians shot at them the same way they shot at everybody else. Ivan didn't play by any of the rules. And if the Reds caught you, it was your hard luck. On the other side of the coin, captured Russians often got short shrift from the Germans who took them prisoner.

German MG-34s came forward with the assault troops. They spat their own curtain of death at the men ahead. Officers' whistles screeched. The soldiers got up and advanced once more. The Russians didn't have much barbed wire in front of their position: only a few half-hearted strands. Getting in among them was easier than it should have been. Some died. Some threw up their hands—most of those were actually allowed to surrender. And some fled to fight again somewhere else later on.

"Hot damn," Pfaff said, going through a dead Ivan's pockets. "We do this another couple thousand times, we win the fucking war."

Willi set a hand on his shoulder. "Anybody ever tell you you're beautiful?" Pfaff knocked the hand away. They both laughed. But it wasn't as if Willi didn't mean it. His friend understood how things worked altogether too well.

A SUNDAY-MORNING KNOCK on the door made Sarah Goldman flinch. Any knock on the door could make a Jew in the Third *Reich* flinch. This didn't sound fierce enough to be the *Gestapo,* but you never could tell.

"I'll get it." Father limped toward the door. He opened it. Whoever was outside spoke in a low voice. No, that wasn't any Nazi official. As soon as the people in uniform saw a Jew, they all started shouting at the top of their lungs. And Samuel Goldman turned around with an odd smile on his face. "We've got company," he announced. His voice sounded funny, too. Amused? Pleased? More knowing than it should have? All of those, and a couple of more besides—ones Sarah couldn't place so easily.

"Who is it?" she asked. Then her own voice rose to a surprised squeak: "Oh! Isidor!"

"Hello, Sarah." Isidor Bruck sounded nervous. She had no trouble figuring that out. He was wearing his best suit—possibly his only suit. The yellow Star of David on the left breast didn't disfigure the dark wool too much. Or maybe, by now, Sarah had just got used to the mark of shame. He gulped and had to try twice before he managed to go on: "I need to talk to you, and to your mother and father, too."

Somehow Sarah wasn't surprised to discover her mother standing right behind her at the back of the living room. Hanna Goldman said, "Well, come all the way in, Isidor. Whatever you've got to say, you don't need to say it standing in the front hall."

"Oh. Right. Sure." Isidor did take a couple of steps forward. That let Father close the door behind him. Now the neighbors wouldn't be able to see what was going on. Chances were they'd be disappointed. Well, too bad.

"Can I get you something to eat, Isidor? Something to drink?" Mother was automatically courteous. They had next to nothing in the house, but she would come up with whatever Isidor said he wanted. It would be tasty, too, whatever it was.

But he shook his head. "No, thank you, *Frau* Goldman." Asking was good form. So was declining. Everybody in the *Reich* knew how little everybody else had these days. And that little was bound to be even less if you were a Jew. Again, Isidor needed to gather himself before adding, "That's not what I came for."

"Well, what did you come for, then?" Father still sounded suspiciously genial, as if he already knew the answer.

"I came because—" Isidor paused to cough. To say he was nervous as a cat would have been unfair to every cat Sarah had ever met. He had to gather himself one more time before he could go on at all. Then he blurted, "Well, *Herr* Goldman, I came because I'm in love with your daughter and I want to marry her and I hope she wants to marry me. *That's* what I came for!"

"Oh," Father said, and not another word. Isidor looked as if he wanted to sink through the floor.

"What do you say, Sarah?" Mother asked.

Sarah knew what she would say, and she said it with as little hesitation as she could—she didn't want poor Isidor going any greener than he was already. "Of course I'll marry you, Isidor." The words came out as smoothly as if she'd rehearsed them. And so she had, to herself, many times. No, he wasn't taking her by surprise. She didn't think he surprised her folks, either.

Her answer at least half-surprised Isidor. "You will?" he exclaimed. "Wonderful!" He rushed up to squeeze her hands in his.

She squeezed back. But was it wonderful? She wasn't nearly so sure. Wasn't love, the kind of love you got married for, supposed to be a grand, consuming passion that swept away everything in its path like red-hot lava pouring down from Mount Vesuvius? (She might have accepted a baker's son, but she was a classical scholar's daughter.)

She didn't feel anything like that for Isidor. But she liked him well enough, and she couldn't very well say she felt nothing for him. His gently insistent hands were more clever than anything she'd ever imagined. And he certainly seemed happy when she returned the favor.

So what if it wasn't perfect? When it came to Jewish life in the Third *Reich,* the mere notion of perfection was a cruel joke. It was good enough. These days, good enough was more than good enough. Father would laugh at her if she said it like that, but he'd know exactly what she meant.

What he said now was "*Mazel tov!*"

"*Mazel tov!*" Mother echoed. Isidor awkwardly kissed Sarah on the cheek. She kissed him the same way. She had to dodge a little at the last second, because he'd nicked himself shaving.

"Well, well," Father said, and stumped back into the kitchen. A chair scraped across the floor. Creaking noises warned that he was climbing up onto it. Sarah shot Mother a look. What was he doing? Mother's microscopic shrug said she didn't know, either.

More creaking noises: Father descending. Then he pulled glasses out of a cabinet. He came out carrying a squat brown bottle Sarah didn't remember seeing before. "Where did you get *that*?" Mother said, so she didn't, either.

"I stashed it at the back of a high shelf seven years ago, for celebrations and other emergencies," Father answered, not without pride. Seven years ago: that would have been when the Nazis took over. Father had known what he was doing, all right. He carefully set the glasses on the table in front of the sofa. Then he poured fine French brandy into them, one by one. He raised his. "*L'chaim!*"

"*L'chaim!*" Sarah and Isidor and Mother echoed. They all drank together. The brandy was smooth as a kiss—smoother than some of Isidor's. It slid down Sarah's throat with hardly a snarl. Warmth spread from her middle.

"To life," Father said again, this time in German. He went on, "I don't know how hard or how complicated it is for two Jews to get married these days. It was a little simpler when Hanna and I did it—just a little. But where there's a will there's a lawyer, or maybe a raft of lawyers."

Isidor blinked. He wasn't used to Father putting a cynical spin on clichés. Not yet, he wasn't. But he was part of the family now, or becoming part of the family. He'd have to get used to it, and quick.

"Have *you* looked into it?" Sarah asked him.

"No. Sorry," he said. "I wasn't sure I'd be lucky enough to have you say yes, and I didn't want to talk to the Nazis when it might be for nothing, if you know what I mean."

Sarah nodded. Her knight in shining armor would have gone ahead, confident she would be his and confident he could overcome bureaucrats and Party flunkies. Well, she'd already figured out that Isidor wasn't a knight in shining armor. This wasn't a fairy tale, either. This was life. More often than not, keeping your head down was smart. If you stuck it up, something—something, say, wearing a black shirt and SS runes—was much too likely to knock it off.

"They'll probably give you the runaround," Father said. "As long as you don't let them get you angry, you're still ahead of the game."

"As long as I don't let them see they got me mad," Isidor said.

"That's right!" Father eyed him with more approval than he'd shown up till now. "That's just right! People like that have their fun getting other people's goats. Just do whatever they tell you, no matter how stupid you think it is."

"My father says the same thing," Isidor answered. "He has to deal with the morons who dole out the barley. He says they don't know enough to grab their *tukhus* with both hands, but he can't tell them so or they'd just come down on him even harder than they do already."

"He sounds like a sensible man," Father said: close to his highest praise. "Hanna and I have to meet your mother and father one of these days soon."

"That would be good," Isidor said. "They want to meet you, too."

"Something to look forward to. I haven't had anything—anything but *tsuris*—to look forward to for quite a while now," Father said.

Isidor looked as if he didn't know how to take that. Sensibly, he kept his mouth shut. Sarah also didn't know how to take it. And she didn't know how much to look forward to her own wedding. That also didn't strike her as the way things should have been. She knew what she could do about it: nothing, now. She could have said no. She wondered if she should have said no. But no, the way it looked to her, would have been even worse than yes. So what could you do but go on and see what happened next? Again, nothing, not so far as she could see.

LIEUTENANT COLONEL PONAMARENKO slammed his fist down on the rickety table that did duty as his desk. Papers and a bottle of ink jumped. Sergei Yaroslavsky wondered if the table would fall down. It never had yet. It didn't this time, either.

"We serve the Soviet Union!" Ponamarenko shouted.

"We serve the Soviet Union!" echoed the pilots and other flying officers assembled in front of him. Sergei brought out the phrase without conscious thought, as if he were responding to a priest's celebration of the holy liturgy in church. A pretty good atheist, he didn't think of it that way, which made the resemblance no less precise.

"We shall destroy the Fascists and imperialists!" the squadron commander yelled, as if working himself up into a frenzy.

"Destroy them!" Again, Sergei chorused along with everyone else.

Instead of falling down and rolling around on the ground and foaming at the mouth, Lieutenant Colonel Ponamarenko grew practical and cagey. "And this is how we're going to do it," he went on, pointing to a map. "The Nazis have gathered together a big supply dump west of Velikye Luki. Their forces are drawing on it, and so are the shameless French. If we can knock it out, we badly slow their movements in this sector. And so, *Tovarishchi,* that is what we shall do." But for his shaved chin, he might have been Moses bringing the tablets of the Law down from Mr. Sinai.

Moses, however, didn't have to worry about obsolescent, beat-up, unreliable SB-2s. Lieutenant Colonel Ponamarenko and his particular group of the children of the USSR damn well did. One of these days, the squadron would convert to Pe-2s and come back to fighting the war against the *Luftwaffe* on more or less even terms. In the meantime, they would do what night bombers could do.

How much that would be . . . Sergei had flown several night missions by now, before and after the *rasputitsa,* and he still wasn't sure. The advantage of night flying was that enemy interceptors had only the Devil's granny's chance of finding you up there in the big, black sky. The disadvantage went right along with that. You had a rough time finding your target and an even rougher time hitting it if you did find it. (As Sergei knew too well, the same could also apply at high noon on a cloudless summer's day.)

His breath smoked as he walked to his SB-2. Fur and leather flying togs kept him warm enough. Like most men lucky enough to have such gear, he also wore it a lot on the ground. Winter was just coming on, but in Russia you always had to treat it with respect.

Ivan Kuchkov waited for him and Vladimir Federov. "So—the motherfucking supply dump, is it?" the bombardier said.

"That's right," Sergei answered. The noncoms got briefings of their own, of course. But Sergei had the feeling Sergeant Kuchkov would know what was what even if nobody said a word to him. How? The same way a wolf tracked an elk through the forest. The wolf knew what supper smelled like, and Kuchkov . . . Kuchkov knew what trouble smelled like.

Groundcrew men started up the engines. The props blurred into invisibility. Sergei and Federov eyed the gauges and went through the checklist with uncommon care. The SB-2 was coming to the end of its useful life. Not to put too fine a point on it, the SB-2 had come to the end of its useful life quite a while ago. But there still weren't enough Pe-2s to go around, so the older machines kept flying.

Pilot and copilot nodded to each other and exchanged thumbs-ups. Everything looked all right. Fuel, oil pressure, hydraulics . . . As long as the airplane didn't fall apart five thousand meters off the ground, they were good for another mission.

Sergei taxied down the long runway, lit, at the moment, by a handful of electric torches. Red lanterns marked the end of the bumpy, frozen dirt strip. He yanked back hard on the stick. It felt as if he were hauling the SB-2 into the air by the scruff of its neck. He wasn't inclined to be fussy. As long as the beast got airborne, he wouldn't complain.

"All right, Comrade Navigator," he said to Federov. "Tell me how to get to this miserable Nazi supply dump."

"We fly a course of 260 degrees at 300 kilometers an hour for forty-seven minutes—and then we start groping around like blind men, the way we always do," replied the other man in the cockpit.

And that was about the size of it. You could make your course as precise as you pleased. You could measure your airspeed well. But you couldn't be sure how hard the wind was blowing, or from which direction at any given moment. Your dead reckoning would probably put you somewhere close to your target. Finding it on a moonless night like this was liable to be a different story.

"Shall I stick my head out the window for a better look?" Sergei asked when he thought they were about where they were supposed to be.

"If you think it will help," Federov answered.

The Nazis, or possibly the French imperialists, knew they were around. Antiaircraft fire started coming up from the ground. The tracers and bursts—scarlet and gold—were eerily beautiful. The old SB-2 shook in the air from a couple too close for comfort. But the gunners down below were firing more or less blind. The groundcrew men had painted the bomber's underside matte black, to make it as hard as possible to spot from below.

Ivan Kuchkov's voice floated forward through the speaking tube: "Where's this supply cunt at, anyway?"

"I'm still looking. They hide them, you know." Afterwards, Sergei felt silly for apologizing to a foul-mouthed supply sergeant. But that was afterwards. It seemed natural enough at the time.

Bombs started bursting down on the ground: red blooms of fire swallowed almost at once by smoke and dust. Were they landing on the dump, or were the aircrews dropping them at random so they could get the devil out of here? Sergei didn't know. And then, all of a sudden, he did. One of the Soviet bombs must have hit the Germans' ammunition store. Things down below started blowing up with great enthusiasm. The fireworks show, already spectacular, got ten times better. And, best of all, these pyrotechnics weren't trying to knock the SB-2 out of the sky.

"*That's* where we unload!" Sergei and Federov said together.

Sergei steered the bomber toward the continuing coruscations down below. Kuchkov would hardly need the order to let the bombs fall free. Sergei tried to look every which way at once, and wished for eyes in the back of his head. He wouldn't be the only pilot drawn by those blasts, and he didn't want to run into any of the others.

Ducking down into the plane's glazed nose, Federov peered through the bombsight. "Now, Ivan!" he shouted through the speaking tube.

"The bitches are fucking gone!" Kuchkov yelled back. Sergei felt the plane get lighter and friskier. He hauled the nose around and started back toward Soviet-held territory.

He hadn't got very far when an antiaircraft shell slammed into the SB-2's wing. Flame spewed forth and licked toward the fuselage. "Oh, fuck your mother!" he exclaimed, and then, his wits starting to work again, "Out! We've got to get out!" He yelled through the voice tube, too, to make sure Ivan knew.

And they had to hurry. The controls went from normal to mushy to nonexistent in nothing flat. The fire started invading the cockpit. He had to fight through flames to get out of his safety belt and down to the escape hole Federov had already used. He held his gloved hands and leather-covered arms in front of his face, trying to protect eyes and mouth. Maybe the flying suit was burning—or maybe that was his hide.

Then he was down and falling free. He hoped like hell the wind would put out the flames. He yanked the ripcord—and discovered his unfolding parachute was on fire above him. Only blackness below. Oh, it was a long way down!

Chapter 24

"Well, *that's* fucked up." Lieutenant Demange tried to speak with his usual savage satisfaction. In spite of himself, though, he sounded impressed.

"Oh, just a little," Luc Harcourt agreed. The Germans had been so sure nothing could happen to their massive supply dump. As far as Luc could see, the Germans were always sure. The trouble was, the damned *Boches* weren't always right.

A wan, watery sunrise through roiling clouds showed how very wrong they'd been here. Back before the shooting started, some expert or other had gravely warned, *The bomber will always get through.* Two years of fighting had proved that—surprise!—nothing would always do anything. But they also proved that almost anything would sometimes do something. And, this time, the Russian bombers *had* got through.

Smoke still rose from the devastated dump. Some of it stank of cordite—ammo of all sizes from small-arms to 155mm was still cooking off in there. The explosions—sometimes single spies, sometimes in battalions—made the dawn even more nervous than it would have been otherwise. And some of it smelled like the world's biggest and worst stew forgotten on top of a fire: probably on top of a forest fire. How many rations were burning up a couple of kilometers away? Enough to turn a quartermaster sergeant irrational.

The Nazis had assigned several French-speaking officers as liaisons with their enemies-turned-allies. Listening to the guttural rendition of his language coming out of one of their mouths did nothing to reassure Luc. Neither did the officer's arrogance, even if the German might have been more inclined to call it confidence.

"They got lucky," the fellow in *Feldgrau* insisted. "The advance will go on as if they had not."

"My left one," Lieutenant Demange muttered, which pretty much summed up what Luc thought of the German's declaration. Easier to advance when you had supplies than when you didn't. That should have been obvious even to a Nazi.

And also easier to advance when it wasn't so goddamn cold. At first, the Germans had been relieved when the ground froze. It let their tanks and halftracks and motorcycles and trucks move forward again instead of getting stuck in the mud every few meters.

But Russian cold didn't know when to quit. The winter before had been as cold as any Luc had ever known in France. Now he'd decided he was only a beginner when it came to frigid winters. He also feared he wouldn't be by the time he came home from Russia—if he ever did. Winters hereabouts were born knowing things their tamer cousins in Western Europe never learned.

If he ever came home from Russia . . . Neither he nor his countrymen had been thrilled about the idea of taking on the Red Army. A good many Frenchmen were Reds themselves, and not all of them had been weeded out of the expeditionary force, not by a long shot. Even the French soldiers who weren't Communists would have been happier to keep fighting Hitler's crew. The Germans, after all, had invaded them.

But their politicians had cut a deal, and this was what came of it. The Russians had dropped leaflets (written in better French than most Germans used) urging the French soldiers to go over to them, promising not just good treatment as prisoners but practically anything else their little hearts desired.

A few Frenchmen did desert. But the promises were so overblown, they roused Luc's ever-ready suspicions. Anything that sounded too good to be true probably was.

He and his comrades hadn't advanced against the Russians with any great enthusiasm. But the Russians, no matter how juicy the promises they packed into their leaflets, fought like wild animals. They weren't skilled military technicians, the way the Germans were. They had no quit in them, though. If you wanted to shift them, you had to kill them. They weren't about to run away.

And you needed to make sure you killed them all. They had the wild animal's gift for concealment. If you saw one, you could bet ten more were hiding close by. If you didn't see one, ten more were liable to be hiding close by anyhow. The Russians had the charming habit of digging foxholes camouflaged from the front and shooting troops who incautiously went past them in the back.

If you walked off into the bushes to take a crap, you were liable to get your throat cut. You were liable to have worse than that happen to you, too. One poor bastard in Luc's company had been found with a French flag—just the kind you might wave if you were lining the sidewalks at a Paris parade on Bastille Day—stuck up his ass. Luc wondered if that happened to the poor, sorry *poilus* who went over to the Russians with leaflets in hand. He hoped not, but he wouldn't have been surprised.

One thing the way the Red Army fought undoubtedly did: it made the French fight the same way. When the other bastards were sneaky and murderous and cruel, the international proletarian brotherhood looked a lot less persuasive all of a sudden. You wanted to do unto others as they were doing unto you. Wasn't that your best chance to stay alive?

The Germans sure thought so. They'd fought a pretty clean war in France: not perfect, but pretty clean. Luc, who'd seen *Landsers* shot while trying to give up, knew his own side hadn't fought a perfect war, either. Pretty clean, maybe, but not perfect. Here in Russia, the Germans didn't even pretend to try. They fought at least as foully as the Red Army did. Most of the time, they didn't bother taking prisoners. When they did, they often didn't bother feeding them.

They also often didn't bother feeding civilians in towns they captured. Whatever they got their hands on, they seized for themselves. In a way, that made military sense. In another way . . .

"They know how to make people love 'em, don't they?" Luc said after tramping through a village full of hollow-eyed peasants.

"Oh, maybe a little," Lieutenant Demange said. Somehow, he'd managed to keep himself in Gitanes. Luc, these days, was smoking anything he could find. Russian tobacco was bad; German, worse.

"Tell you one more thing?" Luc went on. Demange nodded and raised an eyebrow, waiting for whatever the one thing was. Luc said, "I've always been glad I'm not a Jew, you know? I mean, who isn't? But what with the way the *Boches* and the Poles treat 'em here, now I'm *really* fucking glad I'm not a Jew."

"I dunno. If you'd got your cock clipped right after you were born, you wouldn't've had to come here. For some reason or other, the brass doesn't think Jews and Nazis mix so well," Demange said.

"Wonder why that is," Luc said. "Maybe they aren't as dumb as they look."

"Couldn't prove it by me," the older man answered. "But the other funny thing is, the Germans aren't doing anything to the kikes in Poland. They can't stand 'em, and neither can most of the Poles, like you said. But the government there doesn't want the Nazis fucking with 'em, on account of they're *Poland's* kikes. Politics can spin your head around faster'n absinthe."

"You ever drink that shit?" Luc asked. It had been illegal about as long as he'd been alive, but Demange was old enough to have tried it before it was outlawed . . . and afterwards, if he respected the laws against it the same way he respected everything else.

"Oh, sure," the veteran said casually. "Take some mighty strong brandy and smoke some hashish while you're pouring it down. That'll give you the idea."

"Got you." Luc had no more smoked hashish than he'd drunk absinthe, but he wasn't about to let on. Demange would have been as ready to scorn lower-middle-class respectability as he was with anything else that drew his notice. Strong brandy Luc did know. He'd heard about the kinds of things hashish did, so he could make what he thought was a halfway decent guess about absinthe.

If Demange saw through him, the veteran didn't let on. He didn't have much time *to* let on: the Russians started shelling the French positions. They might have most of Europe in arms against them, but they showed no signs of giving up. Holland and Belgium, Luxembourg and Denmark had fallen down on their backs with their legs in the air and their bellies showing when the Germans invaded them. Czechoslovakia and Norway hadn't lasted much longer. Now that they were conquered, they weren't giving the Nazis much trouble any more.

Only France had fought back hard (with, Luc grudgingly admitted to himself, some help from England). France . . . and now Russia. France hadn't—just barely hadn't, but hadn't—let the *Wehrmacht* nip in behind Paris. Moscow was a hell of a lot farther from the German, or even the Polish, border than Paris was from the Rhine. The same held for St. Petersburg—no, it was Leningrad these days—and Kiev. The Russians could trade much more space for time than France had been able to.

Luc wished he hadn't had such thoughts with Red Army 105s crashing down all around him. He wanted to hope he'd go home one day, not to know he'd be stuck in this goddamn Russian icebox forever and a day. What he wanted and what he was likely to get no doubt weren't even related to each other.

CHAIM WEINBERG HAD seen Czechs in Spain before. There were more than a few of them in the International Brigades, along with men from just about every other country in Central Europe. *That's why they call 'em Internationals, smart guy,* he jeered at himself. He admired what he'd seen of them, too. They had the same solid virtues as most Germans, without being such assholes about it. Almost all of them spoke German, and they could make out his Yiddish, so he could talk with them. He approved of talking. Plenty of people said he did it too fucking much.

He'd never seen so many Czech soldiers all at once, though. And he'd never seen so many who weren't all solidly Marxist-Leninist, either. But the Popular Front was alive and well in Republican Spain. These Czechs might not be Communists, but nobody could say they weren't anti-Fascist. They'd hated the Nazis enough to keep shooting at them even after their own country went under.

Chaim rapidly discovered they were damn fine soldiers, too. Nothing they saw outside of Madrid fazed them, not even a little bit. On the contrary: they'd learned their trade in a harder classroom than any Spain offered. One guy used an antitank rifle as a sniper's piece. That struck Chaim as swatting flies with an anvil, but the Czech was a damn maestro with the brute. Anything that moved, out to a mile away from him, maybe farther, was liable to stop moving very suddenly.

His name was Votslav, or something like that. He looked down his rather blunt nose at Marshal Sanjurjo's men. "They don't know much about taking cover, do they?" he said in slow, deliberate *Deutsch*.

"They're brave. They're Fascist *pishers*, but they're brave." Chaim admired the courage of the Spaniards on both sides. As far as he was concerned, they carried it to, and sometimes past, the point of insanity.

But Votslav, a military pragmatist, only shrugged. "A fat lot of good it does them. They wouldn't be so easy to kill if they didn't parade around like a bunch of dumbheads left over from Napoleon's time."

It wasn't the first time Chaim had heard a European talking about Napoleonic tactics when he meant something old and outdated. The guys from the Abe Lincoln Battalion who thought about history (some cared no more about it than Henry Ford did) spoke of the Civil War the same way.

The other *Civil War,* Chaim reminded himself. A redheaded guy in a new-looking tunic with Czech's sergeant's pips came up to them in the trench. He spoke to Votslav in Czech, but Chaim needed no more than the blink of an eye to realize what he was. "*Vos macht a Yid?*" Chaim said.

And the other fellow needed only a moment to size Chaim up. "You'd know the *mamaloshen,* all right," he said. "Who are you? Where are you from?"

"I'm Chaim Weinberg, out of New York City. You?"

"Benjamin Halévy. Paris. My folks came from Prague, so I grew up with a bunch of different languages. I was liaison for the free Czechs till Daladier decided to turn into Hitler's *tukhus-lekher.* Now I'm here." His wave didn't get higher than the parapet—the Nationalists would have snipers, too. "The *verkakte* Garden of Eden, right?"

"*Verkakte* is right, anyway." Chaim didn't need to look around to know how abused the landscape was.

"Go slow," Votslav said. "I have trouble keeping up when you guys jabber like that. It's not the German I learned in school."

"Bet your *putz* it's not, buddy," Chaim said, not without pride. Benjamin Halévy chuckled. The real Czech only sighed and scratched his head. Both he and Halévy wore Adrian helmets. They covered less of the head than the ones the Spanish army issued. Chaim liked them better even so. Spanish helmets looked too much like the German *Stahlhelms* they were modeled on. He didn't like looking like a Nazi storm trooper—no way, nohow. He sometimes did it; he'd seen too many men dead from a piddly little fragment that happened to pierce their skull to want to avoid that if he had any chance at all. Nothing could make him happy about it.

Halévy waved again, this time toward Sanjurjo's lines. "Jezek's right—those guys aren't such hot stuff. We ought to advance and clean 'em out."

Was I that eager when I first got here? Chaim supposed he had been. He was still willing. He wouldn't have stood in this chilly trench if he weren't. But he doubted he'd ever be eager again. He said, "The French must have been feeding you a lot of raw meat."

Benjamin Halévy's crooked smile was all Jew. "Because we're new here, we think everything's easy, you mean?"

"Yup." That was English—of a sort. Halévy and—Jezek, was it?—understood anyhow.

"Maybe this is true. And maybe we have reason for it." The Czech soldier's German could be awkward, but it worked. It was a hell of a lot better than Chaim's Spanish. Jezek explained, "Now that we cannot shoot Nazis any more, we have to make do with people who get into bed with Nazis."

"People who dance the mattress polka with Nazis," Halévy amended. Chaim grinned. The Yiddish phrase had more bounce than the polite German, both literally and figuratively.

Thinking about dancing the mattress polka naturally made him think about La Martellita. He'd got what he wanted from her, all right. And he'd also got much more than he'd bargained for when he first jumped on her *shikker* bones. She didn't want to see an abortionist. Even under the Republic's liberal laws, they were illegal, which didn't mean business ever went bad for them, here or anywhere else.

That she didn't want to find one had surprised Chaim. La Martellita seemed such a perfect Red, somebody who wouldn't think twice about something like that. Maybe taking the girl out of the Catholic Church was easier than taking the Catholic Church out of the girl. Heaven knew that was true about plenty of Jews who converted to Christianity.

So now things were official. The civil ceremony took a minute and a half—two minutes, tops. He didn't feel particularly married afterwards. Married or not, he hadn't been anywhere close to sure his brand-new bride would let him touch her again. That, in fact, was an understatement. He'd wondered if she would plug him as soon as the "I do"s were over. A widow could give a baby a legitimate last name, too.

But no. He really must have pleased her the second time they made love together, when she'd let him touch her after he tenderly battled her hangover. And so he got one night's worth of honeymoon back at her cramped flat. It would have been just his luck to have a Nationalist air raid interrupt things at some critical moment. But, again, no.

And, again, he worked hard to please her. Despite that second time, when they started as man and wife she looked ready to spit in his eye and tell him he was the lousiest fuck in the history of fucking. Had she kept that attitude after they turned out the lights, he would have begun with three, maybe four, strikes against him.

One more time, though, no. She seemed to decide that, as long as she was going to do this, she might as well do it right. When she did it right, she did it up brown. She was no blushing virgin bride—anything but. Some of the things she did without being asked might have surprised a pro. They sure surprised Chaim, not that he complained.

Afterwards, his heart still thundering, he blurted, "When I can see again, I'll try to tell you how marvelous that was."

"You are . . . as good as I remember," La Martellita answered—tepid praise compared to his, but better than he'd hoped for. She added, "Get off me now. You're squashing me flat."

"Lo siento." And Chaim *had been* sorry. He hadn't wanted to do anything to ruin this. And, some time in the not very indefinite future, he'd looked forward to another round, and then, with luck, one more after that.

Dancing the mattress polka . . . He smiled, there in the trench. One of these days before too long, he'd get another furlough. And then he'd hurry back to Madrid, hurry back to his new wife. If he had only not quite nine months of marriage ahead of him here, he aimed to make the most of them.

JULIUS LEMP HATED winter patrols. A U-boat would roll in a spilled glass of water. When the seas were high and the wind howled down from the north, he feared the U-30 would capsize. That wasn't likely; U-boats were designed for these conditions. But the sour stink of puke never left the boat when she tossed and capered like a badly spooked pony.

He'd hoped things would be better in the Baltic's close confines than in the North Sea or the wide, wild winter waters of the North Atlantic west of the British Isles. And things were . . . better. That only illuminated the vast gap between better and good.

Some of the waves the harsh winds stirred up here were big enough to send deluges of frigid seawater down the hatch at the top of the conning tower and into the U-30. Besides drenching the sailors, the water shorted out electrical equipment, gave the pumps a workout, and even threatened the massive batteries that powered the U-boat's electric motors while she was submerged.

"If we stayed at *Schnorkel* depth, skipper, we wouldn't have to put up with this," Gerhard Beilharz said up on the conning tower, water dripping from his oilskin cape and headgear.

"Maybe," Lemp answered. "But maybe not, too. When we're running seas like this, what are the odds a big wave—or a bunch of big waves, one after another—would make the *Schnorkel*'s safety valve shut? And then how long would the diesels take to suck all the fresh air out of the pressure hull? Or, if the valve didn't work, water would come down the pipe and flood the engines, and then we'd really be screwed."

A little stiffly, Beilharz said, "That safety valve is plenty reliable."

"All right," Lemp said in magnanimous tones. "We wouldn't get flooded. We'd just have to learn to breathe diesel fumes instead."

"That . . . can happen," the engineering officer admitted. A good thing for him, too: Lemp might have pitched him off the conning tower and down into the pale gray sea had he tried to deny it. Still sounding like a maiden aunt talking about the facts of life, Beilharz went on, "That's only possible with waves like these. When the water's calmer, the snort behaves just fine."

"I know. I know." Lemp also knew the *Schnorkel* wasn't the only thing with a slightly unreliable safety valve. Gerhart Beilharz had one, too. Since Lemp didn't want it to stick and Beilharz to explode, he kept on soothing the tall junior engineering officer: "It's very valuable most of the time. But you don't want to use it when the seas run this high."

That *you* was deliberate. Beilharz had made it plain he *did* want to use the snort now. Lemp made him think twice. At least he *could* think twice, which put him one up on a lot of people Lemp knew . . . and two up on some. With a sigh, Beilharz said, "When you put it that way, I guess you're right."

"Happens to everyone now and again." If Lemp laughed at himself, he beat other people to the punch.

As usual, the ratings atop the conning tower swept sky and sea with their field glasses. The sky was cloudy, with a low ceiling. The sea's mountains and chasms changed places without cease. The Ivans were unlikely to come across them till things moderated . . . which might be tomorrow and might be next spring. But *unlikely* didn't mean *impossible.* The ratings stayed alert. They were solid men. Lemp didn't have to get on them to make sure they stayed that way.

Having escaped one Russian plane, he didn't want another one to run across him. He might not stay lucky twice. The Baltic wasn't very deep or very wide, not when you set it alongside the Atlantic, but it had plenty of room to let a U-boat's crushed hull disappear forever.

And if a Russian destroyer suddenly appeared out of seaspray and mist . . . In that case, Lemp would take the U-30 down as fast as she could go, and pray the Ivans' depth charges didn't peel her open like the key to a tin of sardines.

But the heavens stayed good and gloomy. That made enemy shipping harder to spot at any distance, but it also meant no Red Air Force planes were likely to swoop down on the U-boat. Given the choice, Lemp preferred the low, scudding clouds.

Gerhart Beilharz eyed the sky, too. His thoughts ran down a different track. "How bad will it get in the middle of winter if it's already like this? Will we be able to operate at all? Or will the whole sea freeze solid?"

"Not the whole sea," Lemp answered. "That doesn't even happen up around Murmansk and Archangelsk, and they face on the Arctic Ocean, for heaven's sake."

The younger officer nodded, but he didn't let go. "Oh, sure, Skipper. But they have the Gulf Stream going for them, so warm water flows up to them from the southwest. Without it, they'd probably be icebound all year around, not just in winter."

"I wish they were. It would make our lives easier." Lemp gave Beilharz a grudging nod. "Well, fair enough—you've got a point. But the Baltic doesn't freeze all the way across. There will be ice on it some way out from shore, but the Ivans have icebreakers to clear the way for their U-boats when it's at its worst. We can't be rid of them so easily, however much I wish we could."

"Too bad." Beilharz grinned crookedly.

"Isn't it just!" Lemp agreed. "Everything would be a lot easier if the enemy acted like a *Dummkopf* all the time." *Or if the people on our own side weren't* Dummkopfs *themselves, more often than they ought to be.* He sighed, wondering whether the *Reich* had been wise to get entangled with the Soviet Union. Most of Russia might be undeveloped, but that colossal sweep of red on the map remained intimidating.

Again, Beilharz's thoughts ran in a different direction: "Now that we've patched things up with England, will the Royal Navy come into the Baltic and give us a hand against Ivan? Battleships, aircraft carriers, more U-boats . . . We sure could use 'em."

"I know," Lemp said. Germany's only carrier, the *Graf Zeppelin*, remained incomplete and unlaunched. He wondered whether it would ever be finished and go into action, or if the powers that be would find better uses for all those thousands of tonnes of steel and order it broken up. That wasn't for him to say. Hell's bells—he couldn't even give the *Schnorkel* man a straight answer. "If the limeys *are* coming this way, nobody's told me about it. And now you know as much as I do."

"It'd be nice if we found out ahead of time," Beilharz said plaintively. "We shoot an eel at an English dreadnought by mistake, that won't make 'em want to stay friendly with us."

"No. It won't." Were the Baltic as cold as Julius Lemp's voice, it would have frozen solid from surface to bottom on the instant, and never thawed out again afterwards. Lemp had already sunk one important ship by mistake. He didn't even want to imagine another screwup so monumental.

Beilharz hadn't joined the crew when the *Athenia* went down. The *Schnorkel* man had joined the crew, in no small measure, *because* the *Athenia* went down. And what they'd seen since! The failed *putsch* against the *Führer,* with history playing out before their eyes to the accompaniment of machine-gun chords. And then the great reversal, so that machine guns stopped firing in the west and started up against the Reds.

Hitler had a lot to be proud of . . . if he could beat the Russians and make it stick. The last people who'd managed that were the Mongols. They'd done it a devil of a long time ago now. They'd stormed out of the east, too. Coming from the west, Germans, Austrians, Poles, Swedes, Turks, English and French together . . . everyone had failed.

Which didn't mean the *Reich* and its shiny new Anglo-French alliance *couldn't* succeed where everybody else had had to toss in the sponge. Of course it didn't. *Of course it doesn't,* Lemp told himself, thinking louder than he might have. The previous track record sure didn't improve the odds, though.

Track record? On land these days, the track was muddy where it wasn't frozen. The *Wehrmacht* and its allies kept gaining ground all the same. They just had to go on doing it, that was all. And the U-boats and the rest of the *Kriegsmarine* had to help.

THEO HOSSBACH WONDERED why he seemed to play football only when it was bloody cold. Here he was, standing in goal on another snow-streaked, bumpy pitch, watching his buddies and—this time—a bunch of Tommies pound up and down. They got warm. Running the way they did, they would have stayed warm at the South Pole.

He, by contrast, was freezing his ass off. A goalkeeper was often as much a spectator as the Germans and Englishmen watching—and betting on—the action from the sidelines. Well, he always had been more a detached observer than a participant in life. If you were going to play football at all, goalkeeper was about the best you could do along those lines, as radioman was if you happened to be part of a panzer division.

Sometimes the world came after you whether you wanted it to or not. A shell from an enemy panzer or antipanzer gun could smash through your armor unless you were good, or at least lucky (or was that *lucky, or at least good*?—no one seemed to know).

And sometimes a grinning Tommy in khaki dribbled past what were supposed to be your rear four defenders and drew back his leg to drive the ball into the net—they had proper goals this time, loot from a Russian school. Unlike an antipanzer round, he couldn't blow you to smithereens. But he could humiliate you, which hurt almost as much and was far more public.

Make yourself big. That was what they told goalkeepers in trouble. Theo duly did it, running out at the Englishman to cut off the angle, waving his arms over his head, spreading his legs, and for good measure yelling at the top of his lungs. The Tommy shot. The ball banged off Theo's left foot and slithered out of bounds for a corner kick.

"Fucking 'ell," the thwarted footballer snarled. Theo didn't speak English, but he recognized an endearment when he heard one. He smiled sweetly.

As the two sides jostled each other before the kick, his own teammates thumped him on the back. "That's the way to play it," Adi Stoss said. "You couldn't have done any better."

"Thanks," Theo muttered. Praise on the pitch from Adi was praise indeed. As usual, the panzer driver seemed to be in his own world here. He far outshone his countrymen. He far outshone his opponents, too, and the English had invented the game. He'd already scored once, and only a leaping, sprawling save by the other 'keeper kept him from claiming another goal.

The Tommies did the same thing other German sides did: they tried to knock him off his game by knocking him around. Nasty tackles sent him sprawling a couple of times. In a professional match, they would have got the guilty parties sent off. If nobody needed an ambulance here, you just kept playing.

Adi was no fool. He could tell which way the wind blew. He'd probably known it would blow his way long before it did. And he took care of things on his own. One of his tormentors went down in a heap and didn't get up again for a long time. At last, when Theo was starting to wonder if they *would* need an ambulance, the Englishman staggered to his feet and play went on. A few minutes later, another Tommy skidded a long way on his face. He rose with blood running from his nose, looking for a fight. Adi stood right there. If the fellow in khaki wanted one, he could have it. He decided he didn't want it. The match resumed once more.

At last, the English lieutenant serving as timekeeper and referee blew his officer's whistle. Play ground to a stop. The *Landsers* had beaten the Tommies, 5–3. A few of the Englishmen seemed amazed they could lose at their own game, even in a pickup match like this. A couple of others seemed furious. Most, though, were as winded as their German counterparts. They and the Germans clapped one another on the back, clasped hands, and tried to talk, using fragments—often foul fragments—of their opponents' language.

On the sidelines, cash and chattels personal—especially tobacco and liquor—changed hands as bettors settled up. One of the Germans who seemed to have done well for himself went up to Adi. Whatever he said didn't sit well with Theo's crewmate. Stoss turned away, obviously angry.

The other German said something else. Adi snarled something in return. Theo trotted over to them, ready for anything. You didn't let your buddies down, on the battlefield or on the pitch.

But the fellow who'd infuriated Adi didn't want to bang heads. He just looked bewildered at what he'd started. "You can clear off, pal," he said to Theo. "I didn't mean to get him mad at me."

"Oh, yeah?" Theo only half-believed that. On the one hand, nobody in his right mind would want Adi Stoss mad at him. The Englishman with the bloody nose had seen that. He'd backed off, too. On the other hand, Adi wasn't a guy with a short fuse. He didn't go looking for trouble or start it. He didn't get sore for no reason at all, either.

Or did he? The other German said, "Yeah. Honest to God. All I said was, he played as well as the last time I saw him on the pitch."

"Liar," Adi said, and if that wasn't murder in his voice, Theo had never heard it.

"I don't think so." Theo might have heard the danger in his voice, but the other fellow plainly didn't. He went on, "I was selling stuff in Münster three, four years ago, and Bayern München was playing a friendly against some town side—the Foresters, that's who they were. I'm from Munich, so I went. I remember you 'cause you were the only good thing on the pitch for your club."

Adi shook his head. "I don't know who you're talking about, but that wasn't me."

"Right." The man from Munich didn't believe it for a second. "Then it was either your twin or your ghost—that's all I've got to tell you."

"Could have been either one," Adi said. "All I've got to tell *you* is, it wasn't me."

"Huh!" No, the stranger wasn't convinced. But what could he do in the face of such stubborn, stony denial? Walk off shaking his head, was the only thing that occurred to Theo. And that was just what the fellow from Munich did.

Adi Stoss swore, loudly and foully. He kicked at the half-frozen ground under his feet. "Now I can't even play fucking football any more," he muttered.

"Don't worry about it." Words never came easily for Theo. He found a few more anyway: "He's from Munich, not Münster. Whatever you're running from, he doesn't know anything about it."

Sudden hard suspicion filled Adi's voice: "Why do you think I'm running from anything?"

He'd been ready to kill the guy from Munich. *He's liable to want to murder me, too,* Theo realized. *And, all things considered, how can you blame him?* He picked his next words with even more care and reluctance than he usually used: "It's not like half the guys in the company don't already know."

"Know what?" Stoss demanded.

This time, Theo didn't say a word. He glanced toward the crotch of Adi's black coveralls, held his eyes there long enough to make sure the driver noticed him doing it, and then looked away.

Adi was swarthier than most Germans. That didn't keep him from going white now. "You . . . know?" he whispered.

"'Fraid so," Theo answered.

"And you didn't turn me in to the *Gestapo* or the SD or the rest of those pigdogs?"

"Oh, sure I did. Six months ago. The rest of the panzer guys have done it dozens of times," Theo said, deadpan.

Stoss stared. For a second, maybe a second and a half, he believed Theo. He didn't know whether to clout him with a rock, look around frantically for blackshirts, or just start running. Then he realized he'd tripped over irony. "You son of a bitch!" he said, and he couldn't have sounded more relieved if the Panzer II's armor had just held out a burst of machine-gun fire. "You *son* of a bitch! Maybe the whole world's not out to ruin us after all." He didn't say which *us* the world was after, but Theo hadn't, either. They both knew, all right.

Chapter 25

Things weren't going well for the Soviet Union. The news broadcasts from Moscow did their best to disguise that, and their best was surprisingly good. Had Anastas Mouradian not been a frontline fighter, he never would have realized how rotten things looked.

But he was, and he did. It wasn't even that the front kept moving east. The USSR was an enormous place. Trading space for time was an old Russian strategy, and now a new Soviet one. The way the Red Army and Red Air Force were making the trade, though . . .

Stas heard much more about all the Devil's relations than he wanted to. Bad language about them filled the military frequencies. Among Russians, that was a sure-fire sign things were badly buggered up. And generals and colonels kept getting replaced, one after another. Nobody said anything about what happened to the men who were relieved. Mouradian could draw his own pictures. They weren't pretty, which didn't mean they weren't true.

The replacements came in and gave enthusiastic orders. The Germans and the allies they'd seduced into campaigning against Socialism kept gaining ground regardless. In weeks or days or sometimes hours, the enthusiastic replacements got replaced themselves. Some of them probably didn't even know why they went into the gulags, which didn't stop them from going.

There were times—there were quite a few times, in fact—when Mouradian was glad to be only a lowly lieutenant. All he had to do was follow orders from above. As long as he did that, he was safe—well, as safe as any Soviet frontline fighter. He just had to worry about the Nazis and their allies. He didn't have to worry that the NKVD would blame him for the next unauthorized retreat.

Josef Stalin spoke on the radio, something he seldom did. "Workers and peasants of the Soviet Union, you must not take one step farther back," he declared. His Georgian accent was thicker than Mouradian's Armenian intonations. Russians threw everybody from the Caucasus into the same pile. People from the Caucasus knew better. Georgia and Armenia bordered each other, but so what? Their peoples were as different as Magyars and Czechs. To them, it was obvious. To Russians . . . But what did Russians know? Georgians and Armenians were both dark, and both used peculiar alphabets nobody else could read. If that didn't make them brothers . . . you weren't a Russian.

"We must hold the enemy in place. The country is in danger," Stalin went on. "Every wrecker and traitor we capture must and shall face the most severe punishment."

Around Mouradian, heads in the squadron ready room solemnly bobbed up and down. Stas made himself nod, too, so as not to seem out of place. Anyone who paid attention to what he read and heard followed more than the mere words blaring out of the radio speaker. *The most severe punishment* was a government euphemism for execution, commonly by bullet in the back of the neck. And, by *every wrecker and traitor,* Stalin meant everyone who disagreed with him, even in the slightest or most trivial way. The show trials and purges before the war proved that.

"We shall fight for the *Rodina*! We shall fight for holy mother Russia!" Stalin declared. "Alexander beat Napoleon! Peter the Great beat the Swedes! We beat the Teutonic Knights—filthy, plundering Germans—when *they* invaded us! And our cause, the Russian cause, is just again! We will win again!"

Several of the flyers in the ready room banged their hands together and burst into cheers. The ones who did were Russians to a man.

As for Mouradian, he had to fight the impulse to dig a finger into his ear and see if the canal was clogged with wax. Stalin had mentioned the workers and peasants of the Soviet Union in his speech. He'd mentioned them, yes—and then he'd proceeded to forget all about them. Instead, he'd used as many symbols from Russian history as he could find. Not Soviet history—Russian. Stas had never dreamt he would hear a Soviet leader talk about holy mother Russia.

That Stalin himself was no more Russian than a Kazakh or an Uzbek obviously bothered the General Secretary of the Communist Party of the USSR not at all. Holy mother Russia didn't mean much to Stas Mouradian. That wouldn't bother Stalin, either. Armenia was only a little place, jammed into the bottom left-hand corner of most maps. The vast expanse of Russia *was* the map.

Martial music thundered out of the radio. It wasn't martial music Stas had heard before, which meant exactly nothing. Stalin had factories from here to Khabarovsk cranking out planes and tanks and guns and uniforms as fast as they could. He had swarms of collective farms cranking out food as fast as they could (and if he had to starve millions of people to force more millions to labor on those farms, he'd proved he would do that without batting an eye). Of course he would have conservatories full of composers cranking out martial music as fast as they could. If the composers didn't feel like serving the Soviet Union that way, what would they do then? They'd start *de*composing, that was what.

And the crazy thing was, the martial music worked. By the time the piece finished, Mouradian wanted to belt somebody in the chops—by choice, somebody in a field-gray uniform and a coal-scuttle helmet. He understood that he was being manipulated. Understanding it and being able to stop it were as different as tea and tobacco.

The squadron CO was, not surprisingly, a Russian. The Soviet Union held as many Russians as all its other peoples put together. And the USSR had sprung up like a flower fertilized by the Russian Empire's corpse (some would say, like a vulture feeding on the Russian Empire's corpse, but not—usually—Mouradian). It was no surprise that Russians still ran so much of the USSR. Depressing, sometimes, but no surprise.

Lieutenant Colonel Tomashevsky waited till the last strains of the brand-new martial composition had faded away. Then he stood up and said, "You all heard Comrade Stalin's brilliant speech. He promised the Soviet people victory. We are going to deliver that victory, Comrades. We are going to use our wonderful new airplanes—the finest products of Soviet science and engineering—to show the Fascist hyenas and their plutocratic lackeys hell on earth. Less than the sons of bitches deserve, too."

As the flyers had nodded for Stalin, so they nodded for the squadron leader. Anastas Mouradian made sure he wasn't behindhand there. All the same, he got the feeling Tomashevsky hadn't listened to the General Secretary so closely as he might have. Tomashevsky talked about the Soviet people, about Soviet science and engineering. That had been the Party line for a long time. By the way Stalin talked today, though, the line was changing. Stalin talked about Tsar Alexander and Peter the Great, about *Russian* victories over invaders from the west.

Stas had heard rumors that people in the northwestern Ukraine were welcoming the Germans and their allies as liberators. He didn't know if the whispers were true. But anyone who repeated a story like that took his life in his hands. Stas did know the Ukrainians had little reason to love Stalin or the Soviet government, not after the way they were starved by hecatombs during collectivization. After that, even the Nazis might look good by comparison.

"Today, we fly against Velikye Luki," the squadron commander continued. "The Poles and the French are staging through there, building up for an attack farther east. Our mission is to strike the train station and the railroad yards." He paused, then asked, "Questions?"

"What are the German defenses like, Comrade Colonel?" Mouradian said. Even if the Poles and French were coming through Velikye Luki, the fighters above the place and the antiaircraft guns inside would be operated by Germans. He was as sure of that as made no difference.

Tomashevsky only shrugged. "It does not matter. We are to strike the city regardless."

"I serve the Soviet Union!" Mouradian replied. Maybe the squadron commander had no idea what was waiting for them. Or maybe the Germans were loaded for bear. Before long, everybody would find out which.

Even if the *Luftwaffe* had Bf-109s patrolling over Velikye Luki, Stas knew he might get away anyhow in a Pe-2. He wondered how Sergei Yaroslavsky and the Chimp were doing in that ancient SB-2. Pretty soon, with any luck at all, they'd start flying the more modern bomber, too.

After his bold question, the mission turned out to be . . . a mission. Bf-109s did fly above occupied Velikye Luki, but not in swarms. There was a lot of ground fire, but there wasn't a *lot* of ground fire. He watched in dismay as one bomber in the formation fell out of the sky and cometed groundward trailing flame and smoke. A couple of shell fragments clanged against his plane's aluminum skin, but they did no damage he could find.

At Ivan Kulkaanen's command, Sergeant Mechnikov let the bombs fall free. Stas could only hope they landed on the target or close to it. Bombing from 6,000 meters was not an exact science. You aimed them as best you could, you dropped them, and you got the hell out of there. Stas had sat in Kulkaanen's seat. He knew how hard the job was. Once you landed, you made the after-action report sound good. That was also part of the job. Yes, another mission, all right. And how many more still to come?

HARBIN HELD ENOUGH Japanese settlers to keep a daily newspaper in business. Copies came down to Pingfan, sometimes on the day they were printed, sometimes the day after. The local rag would never run the *Yomiuri Shinbun* out of business, but Hideki Fujita read it avidly just the same. Along with the radio, it helped remind him that there was a world beyond Shiro Ishii's bacteriological-warfare camp.

He needed the reminder, too. When you dealt with *maruta* every day, when you sent them into the secret center compound and they never came out again, you really did start thinking of them as logs. The other choice was remembering that they were human beings, even if they were Russians or Chinese. Considering the kinds of things that happened to them in there (Fujita neither knew nor wanted to know the details: the broad outlines were more than bad enough), they would have been better off if they were made of wood.

The local paper was full of a rising tide of abuse aimed at the United

States. Whoever wrote the stories roared out hatred against the country across the Pacific for refusing to sell Japan any more of the raw materials she needed. *Roosevelt thinks he can bring us to our knees through economic warfare,* an editorial declared. *He has yet to learn that the Empire of Japan goes to its knees before no man and no nation. He has yet to learn this important fact, but we Japanese stand ready to teach him the lesson.*

Shinjiro Hayashi read the newspaper, too. He was less enthusiastic about what he found in it than Fujita was. "Are you ready to fight another war so soon, Sergeant-*san*?" he asked. "We just patched up a peace with Russia, and the war with China goes on and on."

"War with the United States isn't our worry," Fujita answered. "The sailors will carry the load on that one."

"Some of it, sure, but not all of it," Hayashi said. "The Philippines sit just south of the Home Islands, and who runs them? The Americans, that's who. If war breaks out, we'll have to take them away from the USA. Otherwise, they're a perfect base for enemy ships and planes. And it won't be the sailors who do most of the fighting down there. It'll be bowlegged bastards like us."

Fujita laughed. Neither he nor Hayashi was bowlegged, but he knew what the senior private meant. The Navy was the aristocratic service. The Army took peasants and turned them into men. It had done just that with Fujita. It had turned Hayashi into a man, too, even if he'd put on more airs than peasants before conscription—and some sergeants' hard hands—knocked them out of him.

"All right. Fine. That's the Philippines," Fujita said. "But it will still mostly be the Navy's war."

"I suppose so, Sergeant-*san*," Hayashi said, by which he meant he supposed no such thing but wasn't stupid enough to come right out and tell Fujita he was wrong. "But if a fight like that starts, it won't be a halfway affair. French Indochina, Singapore, the Dutch East Indies with oil and rubber and tin . . . When you grab, you should grab with both hands."

"If you grab too much, your hands fill up and you trip over your own feet," Fujita responded. "There's such a thing as getting greedy, you know."

"I suppose so," Hayashi said again. "But sometimes you only get the one chance. If you don't take hold of it while it's there, you may never see it again. It's like a chance with a pretty girl, *neh*?"

"You always grab with both hands then!" Fujita made as if to cup breasts in his callused palms. Both soldiers barked harsh male laughter.

A couple of days later, Lieutenant Ozawa summoned Fujita to his tent. He had a little coal stove in there for warmth, but it was fighting out of its weight against winter in Manchukuo. "I need your squad to take care of something for me," the officer said.

"Yes, sir!" Fujita said, and saluted. He had no idea what Ozawa would tell him to do. That hardly mattered. Whatever it was, he and his men would take a whack at it. If the lieutenant wanted him to bring back a piece of rock from the moon, he wouldn't fail through lack of effort.

But Ozawa had nothing so ridiculous in mind. "Take as many Russian and Chinese *maruta* as you need," he said. "Build a new prisoner compound. Site it at least fifty meters away from any others. Make it of a size to hold, oh, about a thousand men."

"Yes, sir!" Fujita repeated. For good measure, he saluted again, too. This was something he knew how to handle. "How soon do you need it ready?"

"Three weeks should be plenty of time," the lieutenant answered.

Fujita considered. "That'll be a little tight, sir, for running up all the barracks halls and everything. The weather won't help us any." If he didn't get the job done on time, he wanted his excuses lined up in advance.

"You take care of it," Ozawa said. "You don't want me to assign the work to someone else, do you?"

Part of Fujita wanted just that. But if he admitted it, he wouldn't get any other interesting work as long as he stayed at Pingfan. Not interesting in the good sense of the word, anyhow. They might give him things no one else wanted to do or was able to do, and then blame him when he had trouble. That wouldn't be good. And so, with no hesitation the officer would notice, he replied, "No, sir."

"All right, then. Three weeks. See to it," Ozawa said. "Dismissed."

Fujita didn't even mutter under his breath till he left the tent and the lieutenant couldn't hear him any more. You didn't want to give the jerks who ordered you around any kind of handle to let them screw you even harder. They already had enough advantage on account of their rank.

He told Senior Private Hayashi about the new assignment and directed him to gather up the labor they'd need to construct a new compound. Hayashi might have had his own opinion about people whose rank let them give orders. If he did, he also had the sense not to put it on display.

Laying out the barbed-wire perimeter around the new compound was easy. Any *maruta* could handle it, because it needed no skill. But the barracks required people who could use hammer and saw, chisel and plane. The prisoners clamored for the work, because they knew they'd get fed a little better while they were doing it. They also wouldn't have to go into the secret inner facility while they were working. Hayashi efficiently weeded out the ones who were only pretending to be carpenters. He and the other Japanese soldiers beat up some of them to teach them not to play stupid games with their betters.

Chinese and Russians, forced to work together, screamed and gestured at one another, trying to communicate without a common language. Hayashi knew a little Chinese; no one in Fujita's squad spoke Russian. He had drawings to show what he required. Those pictures were worth an untold number of words. The barracks rose on schedule.

The next interesting question was, who would live in the new compound? When new shipments of Chinese came to Pingfan, they got dumped in with their countrymen. Those barracks grew insanely crowded? So what? The same had been true of the Russians, though no new Red Army men were coming in now that peace with the Soviet Union had been arranged.

Didn't a new compound argue for a new kind of prisoner? So it seemed to Fujita. Lieutenant Ozawa either didn't know or didn't want to talk about it. You couldn't properly grill officers, however much you wanted to: one more proof that they weren't good for much.

PETE McGILL GOT something he never expected in a million years: a combination Christmas and get-well card from the leathernecks of the Shanghai garrison. Almost everybody signed it, even guys he couldn't stand and who he knew couldn't stand him. Herman Szulc wrote, *You don't know how lucky you are to get away.* Max Weinstein said, *Power to the proletariat!* If he'd told that to Pete face-to-face, Pete would've wanted to punch him in the snoot. Seeing the cramped scrawl on the card only made Pete miss the stubborn pinko.

More air-raid alarms sounded in Manila these days. At first, they'd panicked the Filipinos. Now the locals ignored them. So did Pete. He was up and about, but not exactly swift. Even though the *Boise* had accepted him aboard, he remained on light duty. There were times when he wondered if somebody'd pulled strings to get him out of the military hospital, but he didn't worry about it.

He still wished he were back in Shanghai with the men he'd known for so long. If the Japs did jump, the leathernecks in China would get it in the neck. They couldn't very well do anything else except run—and running wasn't Marine Corps style. They'd make the best fight they could, but when there were hundreds of them and zillions of little yellow monkeys. . . . Even the hero of a bad Western shoot-'em-up couldn't blast that many redskins before they got him.

Pete remembered the bet he'd won from his buddies by barging into a line of Jap soldiers and watching a movie with them. The samurai warriors in their movie wore funny clothes and had funnier haircuts. They used swords instead of six-shooters. They spoke a language he didn't begin to understand. Such minor details aside, the flick might have been a grade-C Hollywood oater.

Whenever Pete heard airplane engines over Manila, he got nervous. The Japs bombed the crap out of Chinese cities every chance they got. If they decided to mix it up with the USA, of course they'd do the same thing here. They'd have to be nuts not to.

For a wonder, the American government seemed to realize as much. Some of the engines Pete heard belonged to P-40 fighters. People said those would blast the Japs' scrap-metal planes out of the sky. Others came in pairs on fat-bellied B-18 Digby bombers. If the Japanese did come, flying to their bases and blowing them sky-high looked like a pretty decent plan.

The American government also waved its magic wand and turned Philippine Field Marshal Douglas MacArthur back into American General Douglas MacArthur. Some of the guys Pete drank with off duty applauded that. Others just jeered. The longer soldiers had served under MacArthur, the more skeptical they seemed. Pete leaned toward the doubters. MacArthur belonged to the Army, didn't he? Of course that meant he was likely to screw things up.

Christmas came. So did New Year's. Pete got a wire from his folks in the Bronx. That was nice, but it might as well have come from another world. The card from the fellows he'd served with meant more to him.

Foreign news didn't get any better. No one would confuse 1941 with the Millennium, not any time soon. The Nazis and their little friends kept bashing heads with the Reds. The Japanese kept banging away in China. Their foreign minister said, "No power can accept the dictates of another without becoming a slave." That was the translation, anyhow. Maybe it sounded friendlier in Japanese, but, again, Pete leaned toward the doubters. Then the foreign minister clammed up altogether. Nobody at all took that for a good sign.

Manila went right on having air-raid drills. The day after New Year's, a nervous antiaircraft-gun crew opened up on a Digby. They shot it down. That was good news as far as gunnery went. Pete didn't suppose the other Digbys' flyers thought so. If a bunch of jumpy, half-trained American soldiers could knock a B-18 out of the sky, what would Jap veterans do to them? What would Jap fighters do to them? Those were . . . interesting questions, weren't they?

The second Sunday of January was the twelfth. The night before, Pete had gone out and got crocked. He couldn't remember how many times he'd got crocked on Saturday nights in the Far East. He couldn't remember what all had happened on some of those nights, either. That was the point, for him and a swarm of guys just like him. If getting crocked on Saturday night wasn't a great American military tradition, he didn't know what would be.

Maybe waking up on Sunday morning feeling like death. Pete lived up to that one, in spades. "The fuck?" he muttered, trying to figure out exactly what kind of ungodly racket had ripped him untimely from the womb of sleep—and from the oblivion of all the cheap whiskey he'd poured down the night before.

He didn't need long to figure out what the racket was: all the air-raid sirens in town were going off at once. "Jesus H. Christ!" groaned the guy in the bunk above his. "Has to be that cocksucking MacArthur. He's the only asshole big enough to boot us out of the sack at sunup on a fucking Sunday morning!"

If MacArthur was that big an asshole, Pete was all for stringing him up by the balls. He was also all for gallons of hot coffee, a handful of aspirins to finish corroding his stomach lining but quiet his pounding head, and some more ZZZs after the sirens quit screeching.

If they ever did. A moment later, antiaircraft guns added a bass note to the cacophony. *More Digbys?* Pete wondered vaguely. Some of the guys at the guns would catch hell.

Or would they? If those were Digbys overhead, they were fighting back. Bombs crumped down. They didn't land that close to the cruiser—but they weren't that far away, either.

"Holy motherfucking shit! I think we're under attack!" exclaimed the Marine in the upper.

"Nothing gets by you, does it, Sherlock?" Pete said.

"Huh?" the other guy said. It wasn't a brilliant comeback, but Pete didn't gig him for it. Instead, he scrambled out of the bunk, trying to find out what the hell was going on. He didn't forget his hangover—he would have had to be dead for real to do that—but he did shove it aside. For once, he had more important things to worry about.

Klaxons hooted. "All hands! Battle stations! All hands! Battle stations!" boomed from the loudspeakers.

On light duty, Pete didn't *have* a battle station. He got topside as fast as he could anyway. The sky was full of planes and puffs of antiaircraft fire. Shrapnel started pattering down. He suddenly wished for a tin hat. Some of those chunks of shell casing could put your lights out for good if they came down on top of your head.

Most of the planes overhead had unfamiliar lines—but not *that* unfamiliar, not to him. He'd seen them every now and then in China. He'd seen the big red meatballs on their wings and fuselages, too. Sure as hell, they were Japs. He didn't know why he should be so surprised and outraged, but he was. The Philippines belonged to the US of A, God damn it to hell! Those enemy warplanes had no business coming here, no business at all.

Overhead, a brightly painted Peashooter dueled a Japanese fighter. Americans laughed at the shit the Japs manufactured, but the plane with the meatballs was far faster and more maneuverable than the (admittedly obsolescent) American machine. The Peashooter spun toward the ground, trailing a plume of fire and smoke. No parachute blossomed in the muggy air. *Scratch one American flyer,* Pete thought.

Then the Japanese fighter's pilot spotted him and the other Marines and sailors on the *Boise*'s deck. He dove on them, machine guns blazing. Pete couldn't move fast no matter how much he wanted to—and he wanted to one hell of a lot. Bullets spanged off steel. Wounded men screeched. The fighter roared away at not much over stack height.

Something not nearly far enough away blew up with a rending crash. Of course the Japs were coming after the Far East Fleet. Small as it was, they were bound to have carriers offshore. They'd want to make damn sure nobody could go after those precious ships.

They knew how to get what they wanted, too. A bigger explosion followed the first one. An enormous cloud of black smoke toadstooled up into the sky.

"Rifles!" yelled another Marine coming up from below. "I've got rifles, so we can shoot back at the lousy yellow bastards!"

Pete gratefully grabbed a Springfield. You could shoot down a plane with a rifle. (You had to be mighty goddamn lucky—*mighty* goddamn lucky—but you could.) And even if you didn't shoot anything down, you were trying to. You were in the fight. No—you were in the war. It had taken almost two and a half years, but the United States was finally in the war.

WAR! THE HEADLINE on the *Philadelphia Inquirer* took up most of the space above the fold. Peggy Druce had to turn the newspaper over to learn that Japan had launched attacks on the Philippines and Hawaii, and was also moving into French Indonesia and British Malaya.

It wasn't that she didn't already know some of that—she and Herb had been glued to the radio ever since news of what was going on halfway around the world broke here in the States. But the paper had more details than the hasty radio bulletins she'd heard before, many of them delivered by men who sounded as if they could hardly believe the copy they were reading.

She brought the *Inquirer* in to her husband, who was eating fried eggs and buttered toast and getting down a second cup of coffee heavy with sugar and almost white with cream. She remembered some of the rationed breakfasts she'd had in Europe, and what passed for coffee in Germany. Americans didn't always understand how lucky they were.

She handed Herb the front page without a pang. She'd glanced at the headlines, and he'd fill her in on anything important she might have missed. He took the *Inquirer* with a word of thanks. As soon as he had it in front of him, he lit a cigarette. Breathing out smoke, he said, "Lord, what a mess!"

Peggy nodded but didn't answer. She'd been in the middle of such an exploding mess. Herb, of course, had seen and done even worse things when he went Over There a generation earlier. That wasn't quite the same, though. The mess then had already exploded by the time he got to it. He knew what he was supposed to do and how to go about it. Things now were up in the air, as they had been when Peggy found herself too close to the German border as Hitler marched into Czechoslovakia. Some of those things had been machine-gun bullets and 105mm shells and 500kg bombs. They'd come down, much too close to her head.

"Looks like Manila got caught napping," Herb remarked, exhaling more smoke. "Hawaii's not so bad. We were ready for 'em there—but why didn't we spot 'em while they were on the way, darn it?"

"Maybe they came from a funny direction," Peggy said.

"Maybe they did—but we ought to be looking every which way at once when there's liable to be a war on, don't you think?" Herb opened the *Inquirer* to get a look at the inside pages. He shook his head. "We were ready in Hawaii, and we still lost a carrier and a battlewagon and some of the fuel store we've got there." He held up a page with a photo for Peggy. She supposed it was smoke from burning fuel oil or whatever the hell. It looked more like a volcano going off.

"What about Manila?" she asked.

"It's a lot closer to the Japs, and it got hit a lot harder," Herb answered. "They'll probably try invading the Philippines if they haven't already." He went to another inside page. "MacArthur says, 'We shall prevail.' That sounds pretty, doesn't it?"

"It sure does," Peggy said. "I wonder how he expects to do it, though."

"Ha!" Her husband finished the toast and stubbed out his cigarette. "There's the sixty-four-dollar question, all right."

"What does FDR have to say about it?" Peggy asked, adding, "There wasn't anything on the front page."

Herb nodded, acknowledging that she'd looked as she brought in the paper. He settled his bifocals more firmly on his nose as he looked for an answer. He grunted, not much liking what he found. "A White House aide says, 'Obviously, we are at war. Obviously, we didn't want to be.' "

"Our goldfish could tell us that much, and we haven't got a goldfish," Peggy said.

"Yeah, I know." Herb nodded. Then he let out a different grunt, one that said *Now we're getting somewhere.* "The President's going to address Congress at noon. Emergency session. It'll go by radio all over the country."

Peggy wondered how many people would miss church to hear him. It was still Sunday morning here—still very early Sunday morning on the Pacific Coast. It had been Sunday morning for quite a while in Manila, though. Hawaii had got hit at midday Saturday, their time.

When Peggy remarked on that, Herb grunted one more time, now as if to convey *Well, what do you expect?* "Some of the guys there were still sober, I bet," he said. "Odds are that's why they did better."

"Why does everybody get smashed on Saturday night?" she wondered.

His look told her she could have asked a better question. She thought he'd grunt yet again, but he fooled her: he only rolled his eyes. "You're in the service, what else is there to do?" he said. Then, slowly and deliberately, he lit another cigarette. His cheeks hollowed as he took a deep drag. When he let it out in twin streams through his nose, he looked like a locomotive venting steam. Peering down at the paper rather than at Peggy, he went on, "If they'll have me, hon, I'm going to put the uniform on again."

"Oh, no!" But that was dismay, not surprise. Peggy knew him too well for such a thing to surprise her. She did take her best shot at changing his mind: "You did your bit the last time around—your bit and then some."

Herb chuckled sourly. "If they have to stick a Springfield in my paws, the USA's in deep water, all right," he admitted. "But I know some stuff I didn't back in 1918. All kinds of things'll run smoother if somebody like me who knows the ropes is there to keep an eye on 'em."

She imagined swarms of canny, successful middle-aged men with gimlet eyes and skeptical stares descending on war plants all over the country and telling Army regulars how to do their jobs better. "If you think the regulars will thank you for it, you're nuts," she predicted.

She squeezed another chuckle out of him. This one might in fact have been amused. "They may hate us, but they'll need us."

Maybe he was right, maybe wrong. Maybe the Army wouldn't take him back. Peggy hoped it wouldn't and feared it would. She said, "I don't remember the last time I wanted a drink so bad first thing in the morning."

To her amazement, Herb built her a strong one and himself one stronger yet. "What the dickens?" he said. "We don't go to war every day, thank God. And if we get sleepy later on, so what? It's Sunday." Ice cubes clinked as he raised his glass. "Here's to the USA!"

"To the USA!" Peggy echoed. The bourbon hit her hard in spite of her morning coffee. But Herb couldn't have put it any better. *What the dickens? So what?* They both had another hefty knock after the first one. The newspaper stopped being interesting. Reading felt like too much effort. And, on the morning the United States found itself at war, the funnies weren't very funny.

Peggy turned on the radio. She and Herb took turns spinning the dial. Music and prayers—many of them hastily and badly written to take account of suddenly changed circumstances—and confused war news came from one station after another. Peggy didn't worry about any of it. She was paying attention to the state of the nation, which was what the times called for.

A little before noon, Herb turned the dial to 610 for WIP, the Mutual Broadcasting System's local affiliate. No doubt most stations would carry FDR, but you could count on that one. Right on the hour, an announcer spoke in hushed tones: "Ladies and gentlemen, the President of the United States addressing a joint session of Congress . . . Here is the President."

"Mr. Vice President, Mr. Speaker, members of the Senate and the House of Representatives, yesterday the Empire of Japan attacked American possessions without warning or provocation," Roosevelt said, his voice raspy with anger. "The Empire's despicable action shows that its leaders think us weak and irresolute. Like it or not—and no sane man can relish war—we are at war with the Japanese. They have started this fight. We will finish it, and we will win it."

A great cheer rose from the members of Congress. FDR went on to ask them to make a formal declaration of war against Japan. That cheer told Peggy he'd get exactly what he asked for.

Chapter 26

The Ivans were getting frisky. Somewhere a long way ahead lay Smolensk. The orders for Willi Dernen's regiment said it was one part of a giant pincer that would help encircle the Russian city. But to encircle a place, you first had to nip round behind it. The orders came out of Berlin, and Berlin didn't get what was going on all these kilometers to the east.

Willi hadn't shaved since . . . he couldn't remember quite when. His face fungus helped a little when it came to keeping his cheeks and chin warm. It would have done more if it weren't full of rime from his breath. And he was better off than many. He had his greatcoat and the sheepskin vest underneath. And he had a pair of fine felt boots some Russian didn't need any more. His feet wouldn't freeze . . . too soon.

Compared to those of his buddies still stuck with *Wehrmacht*-issue gear, he was well off. Compared to the French and English, whose cold-weather clothing was nowhere near so good as what the Germans made, he was incredibly lucky.

But the Poles didn't have to scrounge to get their hands on stuff like this. They knew ahead of time what these winters were like. Seeing German troops collect pitying stares from a bunch of damn Poles was galling, to say the least.

Red Army men had clothes made for this hideous weather, too. They also had gun oil that didn't freeze up when it got really cold, unlike the fancy shit the Germans used. Willi carried a little tube of that, taken from the dead Russian who'd supplied him with *valenki.* The action on his Mauser still worked just fine.

He shared the gun oil with his friends. He even shared it with Awful Arno, more from expediency than affection. Baatz might be the world's biggest pain in the ass, but he was almost as dangerous to the bastards on the other side as he was to his own men.

Fighting went back and forth, back and forth. German panzer lubricants didn't like the bitter weather any better than German gun oil did. Sometimes you could get panzer support, sometimes not. Russian panzers didn't seem bothered. They had wider tracks than German machines, too. They could go through or over mud and snowdrifts that made German panzers bog down.

Squatting by a fire in a hut in a wrecked village, Willi said, "If the Ivans even halfway knew what the fuck they were doing, they could run us back into Poland in about a week and a half."

"Nah." Adam Pfaff shook his head. He was as grimy and shaggy as Willi. "We'd hang on for two weeks, easy."

Arno Baatz crouched by that crackling blaze, too. He didn't growl at Pfaff for defeatism. He just bummed a *papiros* off of him. There might not be much tobacco in the damn things, but what there was was a lot stronger than German-issue smokes. Willi also had some *papirosi* in a greatcoat pocket. It wasn't as if there weren't plenty of dead Russians to frisk.

"Poor brave stupid shitheads," he went on. "Their officers tell 'em to do something, they keep on trying to do it, no matter how dumb it is."

"You mean, like charging off to surround Smolensk?" Adam Pfaff inquired. Awful Arno stirred at that, but for a wonder he didn't say anything. Maybe he was taking mental notes. If he was—well, fuck him.

And Willi shook his head. "No, not like that. We're trying all kinds of ways to do it."

"None of 'em's come close to working yet," Pfaff said. Arno Baatz stirred again.

Willi ignored him. "But they're all different," he said. "The Russians keep doing the same goddamn thing over and over, no matter how many of 'em get killed. It's like they don't care, or they don't dare get any ideas for themselves."

"Always more Russians to throw in," Baatz said. For once in his life, he wasn't even close to wrong. Soviet generals spent men the way a sailor on leave spent money on girls. *More where those came from* seemed to be their guiding principle. The Germans always killed more enemies than they lost themselves. But the Ivans kept on coming.

The thought had hardly crossed Willi's mind before a sentry out at the edge of the village yelled, "Halt! Who goes there?" Only a burst from a Russian submachine gun answered him. The burst must have missed, because the German fired back and an MG-34—not too frozen to operate—chattered to irate life.

"Fuck!" Awful Arno grabbed his rifle. Like Willi, he'd slapped whitewash on the stock and barrel so the piece wouldn't stand out against the snow. Adam Pfaff's remained gray—not perfect camouflage, but not bad, either. Since whitewashing his own Mauser, Baatz had quit riding Pfaff about it.

"*Urra! Urra!*" The Russian battle shout dinned through the village. The Red Army soldiers were probably liquored up—their daily ration was a hundred grams of vodka, and their officers upped it when they went into action. Booze drove fear into the background.

Willi wished for a hundred grams of potent spirits himself. He burst out of the hut, Pfaff and Baatz at his heels. Bullets cracked past them. They ran toward the heaviest fighting at the eastern edge of the village.

Most of the Ivans wore white snow smocks, on the same principle as the whitewashed Mausers. The Poles had them, too. German quartermasters kept promising to produce some, and kept breaking promises. Some *Landsers* improvised their own from captured bedsheets, but there weren't nearly enough of those to go around. Willi wished he had one. His *Feldgrau* greatcoat turned him into a big blot against the snowy background.

He flopped down behind the burnt and mashed wreckage of another hut and snapped off a shot at the oncoming Russians. One of the snowsuited figures went down. Was he hit or just taking cover himself? No way to tell, not from where Willi sprawled.

Adam Pfaff lay on his belly ten or fifteen meters away, also firing at the Ivans. "After we capture Smolensk . . ." he said, slapping a fresh five-round magazine onto his rifle.

"Fuck that shit," Willi answered. "All I want to do is get out of this lousy place in one piece."

"That's on account of you've got your head on straight," Pfaff said. "Now if the clowns in Berlin did, too . . ."

"Wish for the moon while you're at it." Willi fired at another Russian.

Enemy fire eased off. None of the Germans in the little village relaxed. The Russians loved to play games like this, to lull their foes into a false sense of security and then jump on them again from a new direction.

Sure as hell, the next attack came in from the south. Mortar bombs burst here and there. Then it was another wave of drunken Ivans bawling "*Urra!*" at the top of their lungs.

This time, the Russians broke into the village. No matter how frigid the weather was, the work got very warm for a while. The MG-34 worked fearful execution among the Ivans. They couldn't bring their heavier, clumsier machine guns up for close combat, but raked the village with them at long range.

Willi's head might have been on a swivel. He tried to look every which way at once. "Adam!" he screamed. "Behind you!"

Pfaff heard. And the gray Mauser knocked over a Russian who would have rammed a bayonet through his kidney in another few seconds. Pfaff shot the Russian again, deliberately this time, to make sure he wasn't shamming. He wouldn't pull a Lazarus now, not with the top of his head blown off. His blood steamed in the snow.

"Obliged," Pfaff said. "This is a whole bunch of fun, isn't it?"

"If you say so," Willi answered. The other *Gefreiter* chuckled.

Sullenly, the Russians pulled back. Bodies littered the ground, some in snow smocks over khaki, others wearing *Feldgrau.* Wounded men wailed. Injured Russians and Germans sounded pretty much alike. The *Landsers* kept a few wounded Ivans for questioning and disposed of the rest. It wasn't as if the Red Army men wouldn't have done the same to them.

Willi went back to that hut, hoping the fire was still burning. As a matter of fact, the hut was on fire—it had taken a direct hit from a mortar. Anything but fussy, Willi got as close to the flames as he could stand. Warmth meant more than anything else he could think of.

Adam Pfaff came up beside him, also soaking in heat like a lizard in the sun. "Smolensk . . . Moscow . . . All easy, right?" Pfaff said.

"Well, sure," Willi drawled in a way that left no doubt about what he really thought. They both grinned. It wasn't as if they could do anything about where fate—and the *Wehrmacht*—had stuck them. A Russian machine gun fired a burst from the woods beyond the fields that surrounded the village. Willi flopped down in the snow again, but no quicker than his friend.

"REDS BOMB SCAPA FLOW! Read all about it!" a newsboy shouted, waving a paper on a London street corner. Alistair Walsh handed him a broad copper penny and got a *Times* in exchange.

Sure as the devil, the Russians had hit the great British naval base in the Orkneys. Walsh couldn't imagine how they'd done it. The story told him. They evidently had some huge, lumbering four-engined bombers to which no one in the Royal Navy had given a second thought . . . till they lumbered southwest from Murmansk, struck the great anchorage, and droned away homeward before the RAF could give chase.

Radio Moscow's claims as to the damage inflicted on our ships are grossly exaggerated, a Royal Navy spokesman has stated, the *Times* story said primly. Once upon a time not so long ago—before he resigned from the Army—Walsh would have been sure that was true. Trust the Russians ahead of his own government? Not a chance!

But there was a chance, and maybe a good chance. If a Bentley could run down a prominent critic of the government's policy, what was safe after that? Not a thing, not so far as Walsh could see.

Not for the first time, he wondered if he was safe himself. He supposed so—he was too small a fish to worry the likes of Sir Horace Wilson. The same didn't hold, though, for his newfound friends. That he should be friends with MPs still amazed him. If the wind had blown Rudolf Hess' parachute a few fields over, odds were he'd still be a senior noncom today.

"Odds were I'd be happier, too," he muttered. That, however, was easier to say than to prove. He might be fighting the Russians right this minute, and wondering how the hell his country came to make the big switch.

As things had worked out, he bloody well knew how. Whether he was better off knowing was a different question. Somebody'd once said you didn't want to look too closely at what went into making sausages or politics. Walsh was damned if he could remember who the bright bastard was. Any which way, he'd hit it spot on.

Walsh walked down the street, soaking up more war news from the *Times.* Japanese troops had landed in the Philippines. The Yanks were fighting now, whether they liked it or not. And more Japanese troops had invaded French Indochina. More still were in Malaya, and others in the Dutch East Indies. He scanned the paper for reports that they'd landed in Madagascar, or possibly Peru. He didn't see any. He supposed that was good news. Other good news about Japan seemed harder to find. None of the stories said anything of Japanese troops retreating. Wherever they'd landed, they were moving forward.

If the same were true of English troops in Russia . . . Walsh knew he still would have been disgusted at allying with Hitler's Germany. But it wasn't true. Winter had frozen the front line solid, except where the Red Army prodded at it. Berlin, Warsaw, Paris, and London denied any serious Soviet penetrations. They might all have been telling the truth. If they were, it would have been a world's first for Radio Berlin.

With a grimace, Walsh chucked the paper into a rubbish bin. The Nazis had a particularly nasty radio traitor, an Irishman named William Joyce, who was usually called Lord Haw-Haw because of the posh, affected accent he could put on. Lots of people listened to him, though few took him seriously. Ever since the big switch, he'd been broadcasting variations on the theme of *I told you so.* It made Walsh want to chuck a rock or a pint mug at the wireless set every time the louse's voice came out of it.

He'd just turned away from the bin when he noticed the skinny fellow with the fawn fedora and the big ears. He'd seen the man a couple of times before as he walked through London. He hadn't paid much attention to him; London was the biggest city of the world, and full of people. Now he wondered if he was being followed.

Well, he could find out. He walked rapidly down the street and turned a corner. Then he stood in front of a shop window, pretending to admire a display of Wellingtons. Sure as hell, here came the little pitcher with the big ears. He jammed on the brakes when he saw Walsh going nowhere fast.

Walsh turned away from the Wellies and ambled on as if he hadn't a care in the world. He rounded another corner. This next block had exactly what he was looking for: a deep doorway in which he could stand and wait.

He didn't have to wait long. The little man walked past him, then stopped in dismay when he realized he no longer had his target in his sights. He turned around—and there stood Walsh, right behind him. "Hello, chum," Walsh said, almost pleasantly. "Do we know each other?"

"Not to my knowledge," the little man answered, sounding nearly as affected as Lord Haw-Haw. But his ears betrayed him: they flamed red.

Seeing that told Walsh he wasn't imagining things. "Then why are you following me?" he demanded.

Even though the stranger's ears went redder yet, he said, "I'm sure I don't know what you're talking about."

"And I'm bloody sure you do." If Walsh clouted the bugger right here, a bobby would bring him up on charges, and that wouldn't be so good. He deliberately kept his hands in the pockets of his civilian topcoat. "Go tell whoever's paying you that I'm wise to him, and he'd damn well better leave me alone from here on out."

The little man licked his lips. "You don't know who you're messing with, mate," he said, trying for bravado.

"Hell I don't. You can tell that to Sir Horace himself, by Jesus," Walsh said.

This time, the little man's ears went white, as if he'd rubbed them with crushed ice. He wasted no more time trading words with Alistair Walsh. Instead, he ran off like a fox pursued by a prime pack of hounds.

"Cor!" a Cockney voice said from in back of Walsh. "Yer didn't 'arf put the fear o' God in 'im, did yer?"

"Whatever I gave him, he deserves worse," Walsh said.

Later that day, he met Ronald Cartland and some of the other insurgent MPs at a pub not far from the Palace of Westminster. When he described his shadow, Cartland whistled thoughtfully. "I do believe I've made the acquaintance of that particular gentleman," he said, knocking back the whiskey in his glass. "He gets his pay from Scotland Yard."

"Bleeding hell!" Walsh burst out. "They're making it into the *Gestapo,* then! He had no warrant from a judge, to give him the right to follow."

"The government has no warrant for worse things than that," Cartland said.

"Ah, well. They spy on us, we spy on them. They diddle us, we diddle them. The game's not all one-sided, not by a long chalk." One of Cartland's comrades in insurgency did his best to wax philosophical.

Philosophy didn't appeal to Alistair Walsh. "They tell people what to do. They tell the blasted *country* what to do, and the blasted country damned well does it. And we . . . We sit around in pubs and complain."

"Oh, we do rather more than that," Cartland said. "We do a good deal more than that, as a matter of fact. I'd tell you more, but the walls have ears."

If Scotland Yard tapped telephones, if it used operatives to follow the likes of ex-Sergeant Walsh, no doubt it could and would plant microphones in the public houses the insurgents frequented. "God help the poor blighter who's got to wade through all the other drivel—" another MP began.

"Before he wades through our drivel." Cartland's interruption neatly capped him.

"Talk is cheap," Walsh said. "We've got to take the country back from them, is what we've got to do."

By the way they eyed him, he might have been something escaped from a zoo. Or, then again, he might not. "There's been no successful *coup d'état* here since 1688," Cartland said in musing tones. "Maybe it's high time for another one."

"Maybe it's past time," Walsh said, and he might not have been such a strange beast after all.

EVEN BEFORE THE NAZIS took over, German bureaucracy had been among the most formidable in Europe. German functionaries didn't invent pseudo-rational reasons for denying requests: that was a French game. They didn't casually lose or forget about papers, the way their Italian counterparts were known to do. Once a paper landed in a German file, it was there forevermore, and ready to be retrieved at a moment's notice.

Efficiency.

Before the Nazis took over, Sarah Goldman's father had taught her to admire Germanic efficiency. He hadn't altogether changed his mind even when that efficiency began to be aimed at him.

Sarah, now, Sarah had a different opinion. The downside to German bureaucracy was that everything had to be perfectly aligned before anything moved. If a signature was missing, if a permission was not in place, if a rubber stamp was applied so that a few millimeters of colored ink came down outside the box officially designated for them, whatever you were trying to achieve ground to a halt until the defect could be remedied.

When you were trying to get married, that wore on the nerves even more than it did any other time. Sarah was convinced it did, anyhow.

The real trouble was, the Nazis didn't want Jews getting married to begin with. They wanted fewer Jews in Germany, not more of them. But, damn them, they weren't altogether stupid. They recognized that Jews denied the right to marry would cohabit without benefit of ceremony and registration, and would then produce more little Jews in spite of everything. And so they didn't deny them the right to marry. They just made it as hard as they possibly could.

After yet another infuriating and fruitless afternoon wandering the corridors of Münster's city hall, Sarah trudged home ready—eager—to bite nails in half. "Those rotten, filthy pigdogs!" she snarled to anyone who would listen: which meant her mother and father.

"That crazy Kafka, in Austria, saw all of this foolishness coming right after the last war," her father said. "He couldn't get his stories published. People thought they were impossible nonsense. Everybody laughed at him. But he'd have the last laugh now, if he were still alive."

"Was he a Jew? Did they kill him for being a Jew?" Sarah asked.

"He was a Jew, all right, but that's not what killed him," Father answered. "He had consumption, and he died of it. He died young, poor devil. Or maybe he wouldn't have wanted to live to see that he knew what he was talking about after all."

Sarah had no way to guess about that. She said, "For all the trouble they're putting me through, you'd think I was marrying an Aryan."

"You wouldn't have any trouble with them then," Mother said.

"Huh?" Sarah replied.

"They'd tell you no, and that would be that."

Father nodded. "New marriages between Jews and Aryans are as *verboten* as Jews' serving in the *Wehrmacht.* We can't pollute the state with our blood, and we can't shed our blood for the state, either." He still sounded bitter about that.

"One of the clerks asked me for a certificate showing my Aryan bloodlines," Sarah said. "He got mad when I couldn't give him one, even though I had the Jewish star right where I was supposed to." She patted the front of her ratty coat. Even brown coal was in short supply for Jews, and the inside of the house got almost as cold as the outside. All the Goldmans wore plenty of clothes all the time.

"Too bad you couldn't," Father said. "I've heard there are some Jews who've bought themselves an Aryan pedigree. I'm only sorry I don't have the connections to do it myself."

"Or the money," Mother put in.

"Or that," he agreed.

"I don't want to be an Aryan. I just want to be what I am and not have people hate me on account of it," Sarah said. "Is that too much to ask for?"

"I didn't used to think so. I was a grown man before I had to wonder. These days, though, the answer seems to be yes—it is too much to ask for," Samuel Goldman said.

"They took over not long before my thirteenth birthday," Sarah said. No need to wonder who *they* were. "I don't even know what it's like, being a grown-up without laws against me."

"Neither did my great-grandfathers, but the laws against them weren't as bad as these, and they came off one by one instead of getting piled on again and again." Father sighed. "I used to believe in progress. I really did. Now? Now I wonder. How can you help wondering?"

"You think it's progress that a professor of ancient history and classics at the university should become one of Münster's finest pavement repairers?" Mother said.

Sarah stared at her. Father was usually the one who came out with those sardonic gibes. Mother was sunnier—except, all of a sudden, she wasn't anymore.

Father chuckled self-consciously. "You give me too much credit, sweetheart. If you don't believe me, ask my gang boss. If I'm anything more than one of Münster's slightly below average pavement repairers, I'd be amazed." He turned back to Sarah. "So what did the clerk say when you couldn't give him the piece of paper that would have made his heart go pitter-pat?"

"I told him I was a Jew. Like I said, he could already see I was, but I told him anyhow."

"Good. Never underestimate the power of human stupidity. And then?"

"Then he told me he'd have to talk with—to consult with, he said—his superior, so he could get orders about what to do. And he slammed down the brass bars in front of his window thing, and he went away, and he didn't come back."

"He'll be there tomorrow," Mother said.

"I know." Sarah was anything but delighted. "That means I have to go back there again, too. Just what I want!"

"Is Isidor having as much trouble getting his permission?" Father asked.

"He was the last time I talked to him, a couple of days ago." Sarah still wondered whether she'd done the right thing when she said yes. Even though she and Isidor pleased each other in bed or wherever else they could find a little privacy, she couldn't make herself believe they had a grand passion. And wasn't that what marriage was supposed to be about? She made herself finish answering: "He makes it sound as though he's having more *tsuris* than I am."

"Well, you're prettier than he is," Father said. "If you think that doesn't make a difference, you're crazy."

"It shouldn't," Hanna Goldman said.

"Which wasn't what I said," her husband replied, and so it wasn't.

"The Nazis *are* harder on Jewish men than they are on women," Sarah said. "They haven't thrown Mother and me into a labor gang, for instance."

"They're soft on women any way you look at it," Father said. "From bits and pieces I've heard, the other countries that are fighting have put a lot more women into war plants than the *Reich* has."

"*Kinder, Kuche, Kirche,*" Mother said, with no irony a microphone was likely to pick up. That was what the Nazis wanted out of women, all right: children, cooking, and going to church. Anything else, anything more, was modern and degenerate—two words that often marched side by side in National Socialist propaganda.

"It will be interesting to see how long they can keep that up if the war against the Russians drags on and on." Father might have been talking about a bacteriologist's experiment, with cultures of germs growing on agar-agar in Petri dishes. But he wasn't. The Nazis experimented with human beings, with whole countries, with whole continents.

So did the Communists. Maybe the war would show that one bunch of those gangsters or the other was wrong. Maybe it would end up showing that both bunches of gangsters were wrong. It looked that way to Sarah.

Which proved . . . what, exactly? She could almost hear her father's dry voice asking the question. They might be wrong, but they were running things. And the past eight years she'd seen, without any room for doubt, that who had the whip hand carried more weight than who happened to be right.

NOBODY'D COME LOOKING for Adalbert Stoss. Nobody'd come looking for anyone using another name, either. As far as Theo Hossbach was concerned, sometimes—hell, often—the very best thing that could happen was nothing at all.

He'd considered telling Adi it would be smart not to play football any more, for fear of giving himself away. But Adi had thought of that for himself. Besides, telling him not to play didn't have a prayer of working. Whenever a match was on, the panzer men clamored for him because he played so well. How was he supposed to say no to them when they did?

So Theo did what Theo did best: he kept his mouth shut. He didn't see the Munich man who'd recognized Adi from a Münster football pitch again. Maybe the fellow'd stopped a mortar bomb with his face. Maybe his unit had got shipped hundreds of kilometers away, to shore up the line against Russian counterattacks from the south. Maybe . . . Maybe a million things.

But that *Landser* wouldn't be the only one. Sooner or later, somebody else would work out who—and, more to the point, what—Adi was. It might not matter. Despite the Nazis' best efforts, not everybody cared. Theo certainly didn't. Too many people did, though.

It also might not matter another way. Adi might end up slightly dead, or more than slightly, before any snoopy Germans cared about who he was. If he did, Theo had much too good a chance of ending up dead with him. The Russians didn't really know how to fight with panzers. All the same, they had a lot of them, and they kept on trying. Not only that, but almost all of their machines mounted better guns and armor than a Panzer II.

And if the Ivans didn't do for the aging machine's crew, the Russian winter was liable to take care of it. Theo had never dreamt he would have to build a fire under the engine compartment to thaw out the lubricants before the panzer's engine would turn over. You risked setting the panzer on fire and wrecking it. You also risked drawing Ivans with the flames. But if you didn't build that fire, there you were, stuck in the snow without a prayer of starting. And so, morning after freezing morning, Theo helped get the beast going any way he could.

So did Adi. Like any soldier worth his boots, he pissed and moaned about it, too. "I bet the Russians don't have to put up with this shit," he grumbled, chopping wood almost as fine as kindling. The less gasoline they had to pour over the fuel to get it burning, the better.

Sergeant Witt threw a match on the fire. Such were the privileges of a panzer commander—not that there weren't plenty of days when he'd done his own share of chopping wood and then some. Flames leaped up: fortunately, not too high. All three panzer men huddled close to the fire, soaking up as much warmth as they could. After a bit, the gasoline heated the wood so it dried out and caught, too.

"Now if we had some sausages to roast for breakfast . . ." Witt said.

"Then we'd be going from bed to wurst," Adi put in.

Witt groaned. Theo winced. He'd loathe himself forever if he turned in a man for being a Jew. For a pun like that, though . . . Who could blame him? The panzer commander said, "Don't be more ridiculous than you can help. When's the last time you slept in a bed?"

"That brothel they set up for us . . . Only I wasn't sleeping," Adi said.

"I should hope not!" Witt studied the fire. "Why don't you climb in and see if you can get her running?"

That sounded like a polite request, which was the way a good panzer crew worked together. It was in fact an order. Adi took it as such. That he said "Right, Sergeant!" instead of "*Zu befehl!*" changed things not a bit. He scrambled up and into the driver's position. Theo hoped the self-starter would fire up the engine. If not, they'd have to crank it—hard labor even in frigid weather, and labor that could break your arm if you weren't careful when the engine did catch.

Grinding noises came from the starter, as they would have from a car with a low battery. Witt rolled his eyes. Theo swallowed a sigh. Holding a charge when your battery cells froze up was no fun, either.

Adi tried again. The grinding noise was louder this time, and went on longer. A cough, a bang, and the Maybach engine burst into full-throated life. The exhaust blatting out of the tailpipes was the sweetest thing Theo'd smelled this morning—though he did still yearn for sausages.

He paused for a moment atop the Panzer II before sliding down into the radioman's seat. The morning might be cold, but it was clear. Sunrise would come soon. The eastern sky near the horizon held no color at all—not gray, not white, not blue. It was as if God had left the windowshade up a little bit and let a mere man get a glimpse of the Nothing that lay beyond the edge of the universe. Given Russian vastness, that didn't seem so absurd as it would have back in Germany. Theo took his place and closed the hatch behind him with more relief than usual.

With the engine growling right behind him, Theo soon stopped freezing. Before long, he started sweating instead. A panzer man had only two temperatures: too cold and too hot. So it often seemed, anyhow.

The panzer company picked up a battalion of infantry half a kilometer to the north and advanced on a large village or small town that was supposed to hold a Red Army garrison. The place did, too. Mortar bombs started falling near the panzers as they approached. Fragments of red-hot metal clattered off the Panzer II's sides. Witt hastily ducked down into the turret and slammed the hatch shut.

What were those bombs doing to the *Landsers* who loped between the panzers? The poor bastards had no armored shelters into which they could retreat. Then again, they also didn't have to worry about antipanzer guns. Theo supposed it evened out. If you were at the front, you got the shitty end of the stick no matter how you fought.

As usual, once the Ivans dug in somewhere, they didn't feel like leaving. Sergeant Witt fired the Panzer II's main armament several times, and squeezed off burst after burst from the coaxial machine gun. That, and the panzer commander's occasional obscenities, were as much as Theo knew about the details of the fighting.

Enemy bullets and more fragments rang from the panzer's armored hide. Nothing big enough to get through hit the machine. Theo's missing finger twinged even though it wasn't there. Phantom pain, the docs called it. He knew what happened when a panzer brewed up. If you were lucky—and he had been—you bailed out. Then the enemy shot at you as if you were a *Landser.* That was how Theo had got hurt. He hadn't had anything with which to shoot back. A submachine gun hung on brackets near the radio set now, yes. If he was bailing out again with the panzer on fire, though, he doubted he'd worry about taking the Schmeisser along.

Regiment kept relaying orders to the panzer company. Theo dutifully passed them on to Hermann Witt. The panzer commander laughed at some, swore at others, and ignored almost all of them. "If those shitheads were up here with us, they'd know better than to sound like a bunch of jackasses," he said.

"You hope," Theo answered.

Adi let out a sudden warning shout: "Left! Fast! Bastard with a Molotov cocktail!"

Witt had no time to traverse the turret. He popped up through the top hatch like a jack-in-the-box. He didn't forget *his* Schmeisser. A long burst from it sent cartridge cases of yet another caliber clanking down onto the fighting compartment's floor. "*Got* the mother," he said as he ducked down again. Theo's heart descended from his throat. Burning gasoline dripping in through vision ports and under hatches? No, that wasn't his idea of a good time.

Firing eased off. Theo knew what the quiet meant: no live Ivans left to fight. One more village taken. A few more hectares now belonged to the *Reich* . . . except for the Red Army soldiers still wandering across those snowy hectares with rifles in their hands and anger in their hearts.

Russia went on and on and on. *Could* you ever come to the end of it? Germany and her allies seemed determined to try. Theo didn't know whether they could or not. He didn't much care, either. He was alive. He'd probably stay that way a while longer. He wouldn't get any more maimed than he was already. For now, that would do just fine.

Read on for an excerpt from

THE WAR THAT CAME EARLY

Coup d'Etat

HARRY TURTLEDOVE

PUBLISHED BY DEL REY BOOKS

Manila harbor was a mess. Pete McGill hadn't expected it to be anything else. And the fierce Philippine sun beat down on him even though it was January. The past few years, he'd served in Peking and Shanghai. He was used to winter blowing straight down from Siberia. This muggy tropical heat, by contrast, seemed like too much of a good thing.

He still wasn't as steady on his pins as he wished he were, either. The bomb in Shanghai that killed his ladylove came much too close to finishing him, too. The docs here did as good a job of patching him up as they could, and he'd had time to heal. All the same, an ankle ached and a shoulder twinged every time he took a step. His face was set in a permanent grimace, not least so nobody would notice him wincing and try to send him back to the hospital.

Or maybe no one would bother any which way. It looked to Pete as if they'd take anybody with a pulse right now. A fireboat played streams of water on a burning barge. Whatever was going up didn't seem to care. Black, greasy, stinking smoke rose high into the sky.

That wasn't the only fire burning around here, either—nowhere close. Pete coughed harder than he usually did after his first morning cigarette. Jap bombing raids had hit the airports and the harbor hard. Now the only question was when the slant-eyed little monkeys would try to land an invasion force. Pete was sure it wouldn't be long.

Maybe all the smoke here would keep them from bombing accurately. Maybe . . .

"Out of the fucking way, Corporal, goddammit!" somebody bellowed behind Pete.

"Sorry." He sidestepped as fast as he could, which wasn't very. A petty officer went back to yelling at the Filipino gun crew manhandling an antiaircraft gun into place. The swab jockey must have served here for a while, because he was as fluently profane in Tagalog as he was in English.

Pete picked his way through the chaos toward the light cruiser *Boise.* The U.S. Asiatic Fleet wasn't very big. This part of the world was too close to Japanese waters for the USA to risk much around here. Chances were that meant the Philippines would fall, something the Marine tried hard not to think about.

Bomb fragments scarred and dented the *Boise*'s metalwork, but she hadn't taken any direct hits. If—no, when—Japanese planes came back . . . with luck, she wouldn't be here. Exhaust from her funnels meant she could get going in a hurry. She could, and she probably would.

But she hadn't yet. Mooring lines and a gangplank still tethered her to the wharf. Ignoring the pain in his leg, Pete strode up the gangplank and saluted the fresh-faced ensign standing at the far end of it. "Permission to come aboard, sir?" he asked the officer of the deck.

After returning the salute, the kid asked, "And you are . . . ?"

"Corporal Peter McGill, sir, reporting as ordered."

The ensign checked the papers in the clipboard he carried in his left hand. "McGill . . . Yes, here you are." He made a check mark with a mechanical pencil he pulled from his breast pocket. The United States might be at war, but that didn't mean you didn't have to dot every *i* and cross every *t.* Not yet it didn't, anyhow. Once the sacred check mark went into place, the youngster unbent enough to add, "Permission granted."

"Thank you, sir." As soon as Pete set foot on the ship, he turned and saluted the Stars and Stripes at the stern. The flag fluttered in the warm, moist breeze.

"Dalrymple!" the ensign called. As if by magic, a tall, redheaded able seaman appeared beside him. "Take Corporal, uh, McGill to the Marines' quarters. We'll let them decide how best to use him." As if catching himself at that, he asked Pete, "You *can* serve a five-inch gun, can't you?"

"Oh, yes, sir," Pete answered at once. Marines aboard battleships and cruisers often manned the big ships' secondary armament. The *Boise* fought other ships with half a dozen long six-inch guns mounted in three turrets. The stubbier five-inchers and a variety of smaller, quick-firing weapons tried to keep planes off her.

When they weren't serving the secondary armament, shipboard Marines also did duty as constables. Pete didn't look forward to that. He wanted to fight Japs, not his own countrymen. Along with everything Hirohito's bastards had done to him, he had Vera to pay them back for, too. A million slanties might be enough for that. Two would definitely be better, though.

"Come on with me, Corporal. I'll show you where you can stow your duffel and all," Dalrymple said.

"I'm coming," Pete said. The sailor took long, quick steps. Keeping up with him made Pete's ankle whimper, but he took no notice of it.

He knew about where he'd be going, but not exactly. He'd served aboard two destroyers and a battleship before going to Peking, but never a cruiser. Steps between decks might almost have been ladders: the treads were that narrow and steep. He managed to stay close to Dalrymple, anyhow.

Two corporals and two sergeants were playing pinochle in the cramped bunkroom to which the able seaman led him. They glanced up with no particular interest or liking. But one of the two-stripers looked vaguely familiar. "You're Joe Orsatti, aren't you?" Pete said.

"Yeah." The other guy's swarthy face scrunched up as he eyed Pete in a new way. "We were in the *Brooks* together, weren't we? Sorry, Mac, but screw me if I remember your handle." His New York City accent might have been even more clotted than Pete's.

"McGill," Pete said, and stuck out his hand. Orsatti reached for it. Their trial of strength was a push, or near enough. Pete chucked his duffel onto a top bunk. He wasn't surprised to run into somebody with whom he'd served before. The Marines were a small club, and noncoms in the Corps a smaller one.

Orsatti introduced Pete to the other card players. They switched from pinochle to poker. Pete lost a little, won a little, lost a little more. He was down five bucks when the general-quarters klaxon hooted. He hadn't heard that noise in years, but it still raised his hackles.

"What do I do? Where do I go?" he asked as they all sprang to their feet. "You guys are the only ones I've seen."

"C'mon with me," Orsatti said. "Our shell jerker's got a bad back. I bet you can feed us ammo faster'n him."

Pete hadn't said anything about his own injuries. He didn't say anything now, either. Instead, he followed Orsatti to a portside five-inch gun.

"Step aside, Jonesy," Orsatti snapped to the private standing next to the ammunition hoist. "We got a new guy here who ain't gonna keel over on us."

"I'm okay, goddammit," Jonesy said.

"Move," Orsatti told him, and the other Marine moved. Such was the power of two stripes.

Pete grabbed a shell and handed it to the loader. How much did it weigh? Fifty pounds? Seventy-five? He wasn't in anything like good hard shape. He'd have to do the best he could—that was all. He could hear planes overhead. The more they could knock down or scare off, the better.

The gun roared. The smaller antiaircraft guns were already stuttering out destruction. He seized the next shell and passed it on. Sweat was already springing out. Only dead men didn't sweat like pigs in the Philippines.

A plane with big red meatballs on the wings and fuselage plummeted into the harbor, trailing smoke and fire. The blast as its bombs exploded staggered Pete; water they kicked up drenched him. And a glistening metal fragment tore out Jonesy's throat. His cheers turned to horrible gobbling noises. He clutched at his neck with both hands, but blood sprayed and gushed all the same. His hands relaxed. He slumped to the deck. He couldn't hope to live, not with his head half cut off.

More bombs whistled down. In spite of blast and whining, screeching fragments—in spite of almost literally being scared shitless—Pete went on feeding the five-inch gun. Maybe the intense antiaircraft fire from the *Boise* did scare off some Japs. Maybe the light cruiser was just lucky. Any which way, she picked up a few new dents and dings, but no more. Some of the other gun crews also had men down, wounded or as dead as Jonesy. All the same, she remained a going concern.

Her skipper decided it was time for her to *get* going, too. As soon as the Japanese bombers droned off to the west—back toward Jap-owned Formosa, Pete supposed—he ordered the lines cast off and the gangplank raised. Then he took her out of the harbor as fast as she would go. Nobody aboard had a bad word or, Pete was sure, a bad thought about that. If she stayed where she was, odds were she wouldn't stay lucky a third time. All the old boring jokes about sitting ducks applied.

And Pete had more new buddies than Joe Orsatti. Go through a fight with a gun crew and you were all pals if you survived it. Jonesy—his first name was Elijah—went into the Pacific shrouded in cloth and weighed down by shell casings, along with half a dozen other dead men. The *Boise* raced south at upwards of thirty knots, looking for . . . Pete didn't exactly know what. Whatever it proved to be, he hoped he'd come out the other side again.

January 20, 1941, was a miserable, frigid day in Philadelphia. Sleet made the roads anywhere from dangerous to impossible. Ice clung to power lines, too, and its weight brought some of them down. Peggy Druce wouldn't have wanted to be without electricity in this weather. If you didn't use coal, if you had an oil-fired furnace that depended on a pump, losing power meant that before long you'd start chopping up your furniture and burning it so you didn't freeze to death.

Washington lay less than a hundred miles south, but it was conveniently on the other side of the cold front. Lowell Thomas assured his nationwide radio audience that it was in the forties, with clouds moving in front of the sun every now and then but no rain and certainly no sleet. Peggy, who hadn't seen the sun since last Friday, was bright green with envy.

"We are here on this historic occasion to observe the third inauguration of President Roosevelt," Thomas said in his ringing, sonorous tones. "This is, of course, the first time in the history of the United States that a President will be inaugurated for a third term. And, with the nation plunged into war little more than a week ago through the Empire of Japan's unprovoked attacks on Hawaii and the Philippines, the President surely has a lot on his mind."

Peggy wished Herb were sitting there beside her listening to the ceremony, too. Things weren't so easy between them as they had been before she got back from Europe. She wished like hell some of what had happened there hadn't happened. Those wishes did as much, or as little, good as ever. Still, she would have enjoyed what were sure to be his sarcastic comments about the ceremony farther south.

But her husband had taken the Packard in to his law office regardless of the slick, icy roads. He hadn't called with tales of accidents, and neither had the police or a hospital, so Peggy supposed he'd made it downtown in one piece.

He was bound to have the radio on if he wasn't with a client, and maybe if he was. Herb was always somebody who kept up with the news. Till Peggy got stuck in war-torn Europe, she'd wondered whether that had any point. She didn't anymore.

Lowell Thomas dropped his voice a little: "Ladies and gentlemen, Chief Justice Hughes will administer the oath of office to President Roosevelt. With his robes and his white beard, the Chief Justice looks most distinguished, most distinguished indeed. He also gave the President the oath at his two previous inaugurations."

Only a few old men wore beards in these modern times. Well, Charles Evans Hughes was pushing eighty. He'd probably grown his before the turn of the century, decided he liked it, and kept it ever since. He'd come as close as a bad Republican turnout in California to unseating Woodrow Wilson in 1916. The world would be a different place if he had. Peggy wasn't sure how, but she was sure it would be.

"Are you ready to take the oath, Mr. President?" Hughes sounded younger than he was, even if rumor said he would step down from the Court before too long.

"I am, Mr. Chief Justice." No one who'd ever heard FDR's jaunty voice could mistake it.

"Repeat after me, then," Hughes said.

And the President—the third-term President—did: "I, Franklin Delano Roosevelt, do solemnly swear that I will faithfully execute the Office of President of the United States, and will to the best of my Ability, preserve, protect and defend the Constitution of the United States."

"Congratulations, Mr. President," the Chief Justice said.

"They are shaking hands," Lowell Thomas said quietly.

In the background, applause rose like the sound of surging surf. "Thank you very much," Roosevelt said, and then again, a moment later, "Thank you."

"He is holding up his hands to still the clapping," Thomas noted. But the clapping didn't want to still. Back in 1933, FDR'd said we had nothing to fear but fear itself. Well, we had other things to fear now, starting with Japanese planes and carriers and battleships and soldiers.

"Thank you," Roosevelt said once more. Slowly, the applause ebbed. Very slowly: it was as if people didn't want the President to go on, because if he did they would have to look out across the sea at the big, dangerous world. Into something approaching quiet, FDR continued, "Believe me, I do thank you, from the bottom of my heart. What greater honor can any man claim than the continued confidence of the American people?"

That drew more applause and cheers. Now, though, they quickly died away. "I am going to tell you the plain truth," Roosevelt said, "and the plain truth is, things could be better. When I ran for reelection promising not to send American boys off to fight in a foreign war, I meant every word of it."

Peggy coughed as she inhaled cigarette smoke. Nobody in the United States played a deeper political game than FDR. When he started going on about what a plain, simple fellow he was, that was the time to hold on to your wallet.

"But we have had war delivered to us no matter how little we want it." The President let anger rise in his voice. "And our freedom is threatened not only in the Far East. Whoever wins the great European struggle, liberty will be the loser."

He was bound to be right about that. Whether Hitler beat Stalin or the other way around, the winner would be big trouble for the rest of the world. Right now, with France and England trailing along in his wake because he'd pulled German troops out of France, the Nazi seemed to have the edge on the Red. But there could be more big switches after the one Daladier and Chamberlain had pulled. Nobody would know under which shell the pea lurked till all the sliding around stopped.

Some people suspected Roosevelt's intentions, too. "No European war!" a man yelled, loud enough for Lowell Thomas' microphone to pick it up.

Hitler hadn't declared war on the United States. If he did, it would hurt his palsy-walsy relationship with the last two surviving Western European democracies. It wouldn't do the Third *Reich* any good, either. Peggy'd spent much more time in Nazi Germany than she ever wanted. The Germans didn't understand how strong the USA could be. But even the *Führer* seemed to want to take things one step at a time.

"I do not intend to get us involved in a European war," Roosevelt said firmly—so firmly, in fact, that Peggy got that wallet-clutching urge again. Did that yell come from a shill? Then the President proceeded to hedge: "I did not intend to get us involved in war against Japan, either. The only things I know for certain now are that the road ahead will be long and hard and dangerous, and that the United States of America will emerge triumphant at the end of that road."

He got another hand then. Peggy remembered that, back in the days of ancient Rome, people used to keep track of how many times the Senate applauded the Emperor when he addressed it. She didn't know how she knew that, but she did. Maybe Herb told her once upon a time—they'd rammed a big dose of Latin down his throat in high school and college. Somebody needed to keep track of the ovations in Washington today.

"We are going to become the arsenal of democracy, as I said in my Fireside Chat not long ago," the President continued. "We must be strong enough to defeat the enemy in the Far East and to ensure that no enemy anywhere in the world can possibly defeat us."

Yet again, people clapped and cheered. How many of those people had the faintest idea what war was like? Oh, some of the men would have gone Over There a generation before. They'd seen the elephant, as their grandfathers would have said in Civil War days. Most of FDR's audience, though, didn't really have any idea of what he was talking about.

Peggy did. She'd watched the Nazis storm into Czechoslovakia and promptly start tormenting Jews. She'd watched them march off freighters and into Copenhagen, ruining her chances to get back to the States for a while. She'd huddled against their bombs—and, while she was stuck in Germany, against English bombs, too, and maybe even against French and Russian bombs as well.

So she knew as much about what war was like these days as anyone who hadn't carried a rifle could. Some people cheering Roosevelt would find out just that way. And others would learn when young men they loved came back maimed or didn't come back at all. Would they still be cheering then?

The truly scary thing was, all the anguish and agony Roosevelt wouldn't talk about in an inaugural address were going to be needed. The horror Peggy had seen and gone through in Europe made her much too sure of that.

Sarah Goldman eyed the clerk behind the barred window in the Münster *Rathaus* with nothing but dismay. She'd never faced this fellow before. It wasn't that he was gray-haired and had a hook where his left hand should have been. No one young and healthy would have sat behind that window. Young, healthy German men wore *Feldgrau* these days, not a baggy brown suit that reeked of mothballs.

But a button gleamed on the clerk's left lapel. It wasn't the ordinary swastika button that proved somebody belonged to the Nazi party. No: the gold rim on this button showed that the clerk was one of the first

100,000 Party members. He'd been a Nazi long before Hitler came to power, in other words. He'd like Jews even less than most National Socialists.

"You wish?" he said as Sarah came to the head of the queue. He sounded polite enough for the moment. Well, why not? She was a pretty girl—not beautiful, but pretty. And, with her light brown hair, hazel eyes, and fair skin, she didn't look especially Jewish.

"I need . . ." She had to nerve herself to speak louder than a whisper. "I need to arrange the paperwork for my wedding." There. She'd said it, and loud enough for him to hear it, too.

"You should be happy when you do that, dear." The clerk might be graying and mutilated, but he noticed a pretty girl, all right. Behind the reading glasses that magnified them, his own pale eyes seemed enormous as he studied her. He held out his good hand. "Let me have your identity booklet, and we'll begin."

"All right," Sarah said as she took the indispensable document out of her purse. It wasn't all right, and it wasn't going to be.

He held the document down with the hook and opened it with the fingers of his meat hand. He was no slower or clumsier than someone who hadn't got hurt. How many years of practice and repetition lay behind him?

"Oh," he said in a voice suddenly colder than the nasty weather outside. Of course the booklet bore the big stamp that said *Jude.* The Nazis had made all German Jews take the first names Moses or Sarah. Since Sarah already owned the one required for women, she'd briefly confused the bureaucracy. She didn't confuse the clerk now. She just irritated him, or more likely disgusted him. He shook his head. "*You* wish to . . . marry?"

"Yes, sir," she said. Staying polite wouldn't hurt, though it might not help, either. "It's not against the law for two Jews to marry each other, sir."

That was true—after a fashion. Law for Jews in Germany these days was whatever the Nazis said it was. Jews weren't even German citizens anymore. They were only residents, forced to become strangers in what most of them still though of as their *Vaterland.*

"Well . . ." the clerk said ominously. He pushed back his chair and stood up. He was shorter than Sarah expected; the chair let him look down on the people he was supposed to serve. Shaking his head, he went on, "I must consult with my supervisor."

The stout middle-aged woman behind Sarah in line groaned. "What's eating him?" she said.

Sarah only shrugged. She knew, all right, but she didn't think telling would do her any good. She waited as patiently as she could for the clerk to return. The woman and the people in the queue behind *her* grumbled louder and louder. Anything that made him leave his post obviously sprang from a plot to throw sand in the system's gear train.

He came back after three or four minutes that seemed like an hour. With him came another functionary, this one a little older, who also wore an *alter Kämpfer*'s gold-rimmed Party button on his lapel. The newcomer eyed Sarah as if he'd have to clean her off the bottom of his shoe.

"*You* want to get married?" he said, his voice full of even more revolted disbelief than his subordinate's had held.

"Yes, sir," Sarah repeated. Whatever she thought of him, she carefully didn't show.

"And your intended is also of Hebraic blood?"

"That's right." Sarah supposed her family had some Aryans in the woodpile. Isidor Bruck looked like what everybody's idea of looking Jewish looked like. He came by it honestly—so did his father and mother and younger brother.

"What is his name?" the senior bureaucrat asked. She gave it. The senior man sneered. "No, that is not correct. He is Moses Isidor Bruck, and will be so listed in our records."

"Sorry," said Sarah, who was anything but. She was mad at herself. She'd just been thinking about the forced name change, but she'd forgotten to use it. Nobody remembered . . . except people like the ones on the other side of the window.

"I see by your documents that you are twenty years old," the senior man said. "And what is the age of the other Hebrew?" It was as if he couldn't even bear to say the word *Jew*.

"He's, uh, twenty-two," Sarah answered.

"Why is he not here to speak for himself?" the bureaucrat demanded.

"He's working, sir. He's a baker, like his father." Bakers never starved.

When rations for most German Jews were so miserable, that wasn't the smallest consideration in the world.

"Mrmp." The functionary was anything but impressed. He scribbled a note on a form, then glared out through the bars that made him look like a caged animal. But he and his kind were the ones who kept Jews in the enormous cage they'd made of the Third *Reich.* "And what is your father's occupation?"

"He's a laborer," Sarah said, as steadily as she could. "He used to be a university professor when Jews could still do that." Both Nazi bureaucrats scowled. To wipe those nasty expressions off their faces, Sarah added, "He's a wounded war veteran, too. Wounded and decorated."

Benjamin Goldman's Iron Cross Second Class and his limp did matter. Nazi laws mandated better treatment for Jews who'd fought at the front and their families. Not good treatment—nowhere near good treatment—but better.

Sarah almost told the clerk and his boss that her father and brother tried to volunteer for the *Wehrmacht* this time around. But she didn't want to remind them she was related to Saul Goldman, who was wanted for smashing in a labor gang boss' head after the other fellow hit him and rode him for being a Jew once too often. On the lam, Saul had stolen papers or got his hands on a forged set, so he was in the army now even though the Nazis didn't know it. The less they thought about him these days, the better Sarah liked it.

Both men with gold-rimmed Party badges went right on looking unhappy. No matter what Nazi laws said about Jewish front-line veterans, a Jew with a medal and a wound was plainly just another kike to them. "Laborer," the senior fellow said, and he wrote that down, too.

"When will Isidor—uh, Moses Isidor—and I hear about getting official permission to marry, sir?" Sarah asked. This wasn't her first trip to the *Rathaus.* Official policy made everything as difficult as possible for Jews. Marriage was definitely included. The Nazis wished there were no more Jews in Germany (or anywhere else, come to that). No wonder they weren't enthusiastic about anything that threatened to produce more people they hated.

"When?" the functionary echoed. "When we decide you will, that's when."

"All right." Sarah fought down a sigh. She didn't want to give the Nazis the satisfaction of knowing they'd annoyed her. They might be pretty sure, but she didn't aim to show them. She was her father's daughter—no doubt about it. She even managed a smile of sorts as she said "Thank you very much" and left the window.

"Well! About time!" said the stout gal who'd waited behind her. The woman started pouring out her tale of woe to the bureaucrats. Sarah didn't hang around to find out how she fared. Any Jew in Germany had plenty of worries of her own.

PHOTO: © M. C. VALADA

Harry Turtledove is the award-winning author of the alternate-history works *The Man with the Iron Heart; Guns of the South; How Few Remain* (winner of the Sidewise Award for Best Novel); the Worldwar saga: *In the Balance, Tilting the Balance, Upsetting the Balance,* and *Striking the Balance;* the Colonization books: *Second Contact, Down to Earth,* and *Aftershocks;* the Great War epics: *American Front, Walk in Hell,* and *Breakthroughs;* the American Empire novels: *Blood & Iron, The Center Cannot Hold,* and *Victorious Opposition;* and the Settling Accounts series: *Return Engagement, Drive to the East, The Grapple,* and *In at the Death.* Turtledove is married to fellow novelist Laura Frankos. They have three daughters: Alison, Rachel, and Rebecca.